# TRIANGLE OF BLOOD

Bob Richards

Ukiyoto Publishing

All global publishing rights are held by

**Ukiyoto Publishing**

Published in 2024

Content Copyright © Bob Richards

**ISBN 9789361727887**

All rights reserved.
No part of this publication may be reproduced, transmitted, or stored in a retrieval system, in any form by any means, electronic, mechanical, photocopying, recording or otherwise, without the prior permission of the publisher.

The moral rights of the author have been asserted.

This is a work of fiction. Names, characters, businesses, places, events, locales, and incidents are either the products of the author's imagination or used in a fictitious manner. Any resemblance to actual persons, living or dead, or actual events is purely coincidental.

This book is sold subject to the condition that it shall not by way of trade or otherwise, be lent, resold, hired out or otherwise circulated, without the publisher's prior consent, in any form of binding or cover other than that in which it is published.

www.ukiyoto.com

# ACKNOWLEDGEMENTS

This book is dedicated to the men and women from Bermuda, the USA and other NATO nations who served the cause of freedom in the four SOFAR facilities in Bermuda during the Cold War.

Many thanks to Bruce Hallett and all the contributors to the *Sofarbda.org* website, without whom this book could not have been written.

Also, I would like to thank the Bermuda National Museum and the Bermuda Public Library for their resources and assistance.

A special thanks to my mentor, and little sister, Dr. Angela Barry, who has patiently guided me along this path of creative writing.

And last, but not least, special thanks to my wife, Pauline, and the rest of my family for their enthusiastic and unwavering support for all my endeavors.

# Contents

| | |
|---|---|
| Prologue | 1 |
| The Athenaeum-1943 | 3 |
| Nathan Philips | 6 |
| Evelyn | 12 |
| Columbia (Summer, 1945) | 16 |
| Early Warning (1949) | 20 |
| Captain Crunch | 23 |
| The Royal Barge | 28 |
| The Inquiry | 40 |
| Nato | 46 |
| La Pescadora Langosta | 56 |
| Blackjack | 60 |
| The Consulate | 64 |
| Jenny Tucker | 74 |
| The Drop | 77 |
| Evacuation | 79 |
| Gracie | 83 |
| Visitors From London | 888 |
| Sharks! | 93 |
| T-Boat | 98 |
| Tour Of Sofar | 1088 |
| Barr's Bay Park | 115 |
| Court Street | 125 |
| Drinks | 136 |
| The Governor | 145 |
| Longtails | 148 |
| Dinner At Chelston | 159 |
| Celebrity Fishing | 168 |

| | |
|---|---:|
| K137 | 176 |
| Ria | 1812 |
| Ocean Research | 188 |
| New Assignment | 195 |
| SSN 591 | 200 |
| Close Call | 202 |
| December 1962 | 206 |
| Speedbird | 214 |
| The Aftermath | 227 |
| The Voice | 231 |
| The Bankers | 233 |
| Question Time | 236 |
| 'Fess-Up | 244 |
| Celebration | 251 |
| Fact and Fiction | 258 |

# Prologue

The charter fishing boat skipper guided her out past Cathedral Rocks, around Wreck Hill, out into the channel, then gunned her past the Tripod Marker, out toward Challenger Bank, 14 miles Southwest of Bermuda. When they reached Challenger, he stopped the engines and dropped anchor. The weather was fine with a soft southerly breeze. The clients aboard were two Greek shipping executives. One of them was talkative but the other said little to nothing, his eyes scanning this way and that, in a manner that caused the skipper to think, *This guy has the reptilian, cold eyes of a cobra that's about to strike.*

He started chumming the waters of Challenger Bank for sharks, ladling the foul-smelling concoction overboard. He had some small fish on board that he would intermittently cut up for the chum with a curved, thin bladed knife that he also used for scaling. After several minutes, the skipper pointed and exclaimed, "Hey, here they come! Look!" To the untrained eye, at first, there was nothing, then the dorsal fin of one of the sharks broke the surface.

"Oh yes. Look!" exclaimed the talkative executive. The other one didn't move. There were many sharks around the boat now.

"Those are White Tipped, reef sharks. Look, that one's a Bull shark, they're dangerous," the skipper explained. The sharks were all swirling around the boat and the skipper busied himself preparing the baited hooks.

Then there was a shout, "Skipper! What's that?" A large shape emerged from the deep, much bigger than the others, over 15 feet long. It moved slowly, with ultimate assurance, it had a blunt nose with striped markings on its grey body.

"Jingas, bye, that there's a Tiger shark!" The skipper declared.

Suddenly the reptilian executive came alive. "Oh, let me see!" As he neared the transom, nobody noticed that he was holding the skipper's scaling knife, and as the skipper leaned over to get a better look at the Tiger shark, he struck. His arm and hand were a blur as the blade traced out an arc in the air, an arc that intersected with the skipper's neck. He clutched at his throat and looked astonished to see bright red blood pulsating over his hands. He then gave the reptilian executive a confused, questioning look, as if to say, "Why?" His carotid artery had been severed and his racing heart was squirting his vital fluid everywhere. Blood dripped into the water and the sharks became even more excited. The skipper was losing consciousness, due to lack of blood to the brain. The executive coolly bundled him overboard.

Within seconds the sharks had him, in a feeding frenzy. A Reef shark bit off his hand, but in the frenzy that ensued, the Bull shark bit clean through the Reef shark, cutting it in two. The big Tiger shark took command of the situation and grabbed the skipper's torso and violently shook it from side to side, banging it against the boat's hull. The sea turned red as the other sharks tore the body apart.

"Nice work," the other said, "But what do we do now? You know how to get us back to shore?"

"No, but there are other boats out here. Let's try the radio."

He picked up the ship-to-shore radio handpiece, pressed the button and shouted, "Mayday, mayday, mayday! This is *Captain Crunch*. We have an emergency here. Can anybody hear me?"

After a minute or so the radio crackled, "This is the SOFAR *T-Boat*. I have a visual on you. What is your emergency?"

"What's a SOFAR *T-Boat*?" he asked his reptilian partner, who shrugged his shoulders.

Depressing the button on the handpiece, he spoke into it, "The skipper's gone over the side and the sharks have him. We need help."

"Ok, *Captain Crunch*, hold on, we're coming to you."

# The Athenaeum-1943

John (Jack) Henry Bessemer was enjoying the Pasadena, California sunshine, lounging on a park bench outside the famous Athenaeum Club, his long lanky, six-foot four-inch frame having difficulty finding a comfortable position on the hard, rough lumber. Covering his pale skin was an unkempt reddish beard that was matched by rust coloured, Albert Einstein styled hair. With his horn-rimmed reading glasses perched on his sharp nose, he was studying an electronics textbook, voraciously absorbing the complex formulae and technical material it contained. His concentration was broken by a brief wafting of the sweet scent of perfume. Jack looked up to discover its source, just in time to see a female student taking her seat at a nearby bench. She was strikingly beautiful: long, silky jet-black hair, high cheekbones, flawless complexion and full lips – incredibly exotic looking. Jack stared and caught her eye. She smiled. He forgot all about the electronics textbook, put away his glasses, picked up his books, took a chance and approached the girl.

"Hi," he said. "Are you a student here?"

"Why yes, I am. Why do you ask? This is a university, isn't it?" Jack detected a foreign accent. He had no idea where it was from.

"Well, I don't mean to be rude, but this isn't just any old college, this is Caltech and, you know, there aren't many girls here."

"Yeah, I noticed."

"What's your major?" Jack inquired.

"Oh, I'm a physics major, third year. Did you know that three Nobel Laureates for science, Einstein, Millikan, and Michelson were here at this club all at the same time, not that long ago? I come to this place from time to time to see if some of that genius will rub off on me. It hasn't worked so far, but we can live in hope, right?" She grinned – a megawatt smile. Jack was smitten. "Oh, by the way, I'm Anna." She extended her hand. He shook it.

"I'm Jack, Jack Bessemer. I'm a PhD student here – electrical engineering."

"PhD, wow! Bessemer, Bessemer, that's a pretty famous name in science. Are you related to the famous Henry Bessemer, the inventor of a process to make steel, by any chance?"

"Well, my dad claims him as a distant relative. But actually, we're from the poor side of the Bessemer clan. My folks had a corn farm out in Kansas but got wiped out during the depression and the dustbowl in the 30's. I've been fortunate to get through school on scholarships."

"A lot of people compete to get those scholarships, so, I guess that makes you pretty smart, huh?" she said, studying his face. Jack felt embarrassed, looked away and blushed. She noticed and said, "No need to be self-conscious about it. I like smart guys." He felt much better. "It's hard for a girl who is majoring in physics to find someone interesting to talk to.

"So, what's a young able-bodied man like yourself doing here and not out there fighting against tyranny?"

Jack was surprised at her directness. "Well, there's more than one way to fight for your country, you know. This war demands new scientific and engineering innovations to help us defeat our enemies. Look, the Germans have invented a new rocket that can deliver a large bomb from France or Holland clear over to London, and it doesn't even have any wings! You think the soldiers invented that?" His voice was starting to rise. "No! It's the scientists and engineers! Our navy can target and strike Japanese ships in the dark of night, without turning on one single searchlight – using radar. You think the admirals developed that? No, it was us engineers! We're in a technology race with the Krauts and Japs to develop the next new weapon. If we lose that race, we lose the war!"

He had become quite worked up by now and she realized that she'd touched a nerve. "Alright, alright, calm down," she said in a soothing tone. "So, what are you working on now?"

"Well, we're working on an improved sonar system for the Navy, but it's classified, and if I tell you, I vill have to kill you," he said with a fake German accent and a sideways smile. "Anna, forgive me, but you're not from around here, are you. Where are you from and what are you doing all the way out here, out west?"

"Well, it's a bit complicated. My family name is Sokratis, my father was a Greek scientist, mother was Turkish, they emigrated to the UK so my brother, Dino, and I grew up in London. My parents don't have any money either. I'm like you, here on scholarship."

"I guess that makes you pretty smart, huh?" Jack said, smirking.

She laughed out loud. "OK, that's one for you! So, now we're Marie Curie versus Isaac Newton."

"Love the hyperbole, but I would rather, Curie and Newton. I never want it to be 'versus'".

"OK, me too."

"So, why come all the way out here?"

"My Dad encouraged me to come to the States to study because he said all the groundbreaking stuff is taking place over here now, not in England. For instance, there's supposed to be really leading-edge stuff going on in Los Alamos. Top secret and all that. What's that about?"

Jack shrugged his shoulders, "I've no clue."

She looked at her watch. "Yikes, I've got a class in 10 minutes and its clear on the other side of campus."

"Can I walk with you?"

"Sure!" And off they went.

# Nathan Philips

Jack was a nerd. He generally felt awkward and self-conscious around girls, except Anna. The problem was that, while she appeared to like Jack very much, Anna was totally focused on academics, and although they spent a lot of time together, it appeared that she regarded Jack as a good friend, nothing more. Jack, on the other hand, found Anna to be incredibly sexy, often becoming totally aroused by just being near her. Sometimes, from her body language, he thought she was attracted to him too, but then he noticed her catching herself and refocusing herself on her studies. And indeed, she worked very hard on achieving her goal, which was one of excellence. Jack, on the other hand, perhaps being more naturally gifted, didn't have to work that hard to achieve the high level of excellence he expected from himself. Therefore, he had time to play, but she didn't.

Jack's only other close friend at Caltech was Nathan Philips. Nate was also in the PhD electrical engineering program. Like Jack, Nate was highly gifted, particularly in math. But unlike Jack, Nate's family was wealthy, and he was at Caltech partly in rebellion against his father, who wanted him to continue the family tradition and study law, and partly because he just loved science and engineering. Nate was Jack's regular drinking partner at the university watering hole, the Domino House, universally known as the "DH". Anna would join them occasionally, but generally she was focused on more serious priorities.

One night, at the bar, Nate said, "Hey Jack, there's a party at Scripps College tomorrow night. I got a date with a girl over there. Look man, I can hook you up."

"Awe man, I don't know. I'm too old for this blind date stuff."

"Man, what you got to lose? I know you're still hot on Anna, and believe me she's a hot gal, but you don't stand a chance against those books. Man, you're getting nowhere with that."

"Guess you're right. But a blind date. I don't know."

"Look, man, let me hook you up. My girl, Shirley, is real cool, and classy too. She wouldn't hook you up with some dog. Come on, man, leave it to me."

"Ok, Ok. But if your girlfriend's best friend is 'Uglisha', I promise you I will electrocute you in the lab when you least expect it."

"Alright, alright. I'll get back to you later on tonight."

At about 10:30, the hallway phone in Jack's dorm rang. "It's Nate, we're on. Meet me at 5 o'clock tomorrow afternoon. It'll take us a few hours to drive there to be in good time. See you then."

Jack met Nate outside his dorm. Nate's vehicle more than made up for the fact that Jack had no car of his own. Nate's car was the essence of cool: the 1938 Packard 6-40 Deluxe Eight Roadster – a two-seater convertible that could be transformed into a four-seater with the rumble seat. Nate fired up the big, straight-eight engine, put the top down and off they roared for the 150-mile, 3-hour drive to Claremont, where Scripps College was located.

They arrived in good time, as Nate had paid scant attention to the speed limits posted along the route. Scripps was a small, exclusive, women-only college, and both men knew that they had to be on their best behaviour, particularly while on campus. They wore jackets with elbow patches and thin dark-coloured ties. Jack even made a faint effort to trim his scraggly red beard. They found the building where the party was being hosted and Shirley spotted them as soon as they appeared in the doorway. She hurried over and was visibly bubbling with excitement. She was petite, well-proportioned with blonde hair and sparkling blue eyes, one of those girls that exuded so much charisma and charm that all bystanders were obscured by her radiance and energy. She gave Nate a big hug.

"Shirley, this is my friend I told you about, Jack Bessemer. Jack this is Shirley Sterling."

"Oh, Jack. Nate's told me so much about you. My, you're even more handsome than he said you were!" Jack shot a quizzical glance at his friend who shrugged his shoulders.

Then Jack, determined to conceal his nerdiness, put on his best smile and said, "It's nice to finally meet you, Shirley."

Then she exclaimed, "Oh my gosh, I almost forgot about Evelyn!" With that, she hooked one arm around Nate's, the other around Jack's and waded them through the crowd. It was a big party with all the young women in evening gowns, dressed to the nines.

Jack was overcome with a sense of foreboding. *Shirley seems to be the 'Queen Bee' amongst all these honeybees,* he thought. *I'm sure my date is not likely to compare favourably to her. In fact, I give it an 95% probability that my blind date is two standard deviations below the average in this room.* His quantitative brain summed up the situation.

They finally reached the other side of the room and stopped – face to face with a girl who was looking and smiling straight at Jack. She was tall and willowy, exquisitely dressed, accented by what looked like real diamond earrings, a gold neckless with a large diamond pendant and gold bracelets. Her brunette hair was shoulder length, her large jet-black eyes were accented by long, black, curling eyelashes. Her brilliant smile showed perfect, white teeth.

"Jack, this is Evelyn Benadetti. Evelyn, this is Jack Bessemer from Caltech," Shirley said, completing the introductions.

"A pleasure to meet you, Jack." Evelyn said.

"Believe me, the pleasure's all mine, Evelyn." *So much for probabilities!*

The men went off to get some drinks and Nate said, "Told you I'd hook you up!"

"Unbelievable! I owe you, man!"

"You bet your sweet ass you do!" Nate said. "Look, I know a place here in Claremont that's open late. It's somewhere we can take these chicks after this affair closes down."

"OK."

The on-campus evening progressed under the watchful gaze of college chaperones. When the time to wrap it up was approaching, Nate said to Shirley, "I know a place, called The Underground, that we can go to take in some cool jazz and have a few laughs. You game?"

Shirley glanced over to Evelyn and she nodded. Then she said, "We have a curfew here on campus, but we can take care of that, leave it to me." She and Evelyn went over and conferred with two other girls, then they returned. "OK, we'll leave this party now and you guys can walk us back to the dorm. Then go and get your car and meet us in the parking lot behind the Administration Building."

When they dropped off the girls at the dorm, Evelyn gave Jack a gentle peck on the cheek and she and Shirley went through the dorm main doors.

Jack could see eyes looking at them from within the building. The men turned and headed for the Packard. Nate wasn't very familiar with the Scripps campus and had some trouble finding the parking lot in question. Jack, of course, having never been there before, was of no assistance whatsoever. When eventually they turned the final corner to enter the parking lot, the girls were already there waiting for them. Not only that, but they had also changed outfits as well. Gone were the precious jewels and the evening gowns, replaced by outfits more suitable for clubbing. They both still looked ravishing. *These chicks are miles ahead of us,* Jack thought.

"So, how do you girls get around the curfew?" Jack asked.

"Well, some of the girls that aren't going out after the party cover for us. You know, when the dorm monitor comes around, counting heads, they may say we're in the shower or they'll put pillows under the covers to make it look like we're already in bed. Depends on the monitor. Some of them understand that we need to have some freedom and fun and look the other way. Others are a bit more hard-nosed, so we try to get dirt on them to use as leverage when the time comes." They both chuckled. "Some others require a bit of palm-grease for us to make our escape. That's not a problem either." Evelyn said. They all cackled with laughter as the Packard roared into the night.

Nate slowed down and turned the corner into a narrow street. Halfway down, there was a red neon sign that said, The Underground. Nate pulled the Packard alongside the curb, and they all went in. The place, as expected, was thick with cigarette smoke. The clientele was markedly different from the soiree they had just left. Half the patrons were black, the other half a mixture of Latinos and college kids like themselves. Once they were seated, the girls struck up Marlboros and the men Chesterfields.

Evelyn, who had been somewhat reserved at the party, had now become quite loquacious. Jack asked her why she was studying political science at Scripps. "I really don't know." She replied. "When I finished high school, I only had one thing on my mind, and that was to get out of the house. My father had emigrated from Italy to the States with only the clothes on his back. He had worked at a vineyard in Italy, but he moved out to the Napa Valley and started his own winery. And now it's huge! Have you heard of Roberto Benadetti Wines?" Jack shook his head. "My mother is Italian too, but she met my father in New York when he first arrived and was broke. She married him to get out of her father's house too. My father is still traditional and wanted to marry me off at 18. But I wasn't having that, so I convinced him that Scripps was the next best thing to a convent." They both laughed.

Jack was curious. "So, Evelyn, hope you don't take this the wrong way, but how is it that a girl, as beautiful as you are, is without a date at a big school function like this? I mean, look at you, I'd have thought you would be swatting men away like flies."

"Well, thanks for the compliment," she said. "I had a steady boyfriend, but he turned out to be a cad, a real shit. He lied all the time and had other women on the side. I couldn't take it anymore, so we broke up. That's why I didn't have a date for tonight. If it's one thing I can't stand, it's deceitful men!"

Jack put one hand on his heart and raised the other and said in mock solemnity, "I promise never to be a cad to Evelyn, or a shit for that matter." She giggled.

*I like this girl!*

The music was hot. They got up and danced the jitterbug on the crowded dance floor. As the night wore on, the music got slower and Jack slow-danced with Evelyn. In heels she was almost as tall as he was, but that made slow dancing even more sensual. He felt the warmth and suppleness of her lithe body as it pressed against his. He placed a few kisses on the nape of her neck, then she leaned back, and their lips met, passionately, devouring each other on the dancefloor.

When they eventually returned to their table, he noticed that Nate, who had not done much dancing, had a glazed look in his eyes and his speech was slurred. Shirley had lost much of her prior radiance and looked disgusted. Jack realized it was time to call it a night.

"Come on buddy, time to go home. Nate, I'm driving – you're in no condition. Come on, get up." Everybody seemed to agree with those sentiments. On the drive back to Scripps they switched places, with Jack and Evelyn up front and Shirley and Nate in the rumble seat. Evelyn gave Jack directions. When they got there, it didn't take Nate and Shirley long to say goodnight. But the goodnighting between Evelyn and Jack was very long and very passionate. By the time Jack returned to the Packard, Nate had passed out on the rumble seat. Jack used his memory and sense of direction to negotiate the long drive back to Caltech. By the time they arrived it was 8 o'clock the next morning.

Nate woke up bleary-eyed but alert enough to say, "Jack, man, you owe me big-time!"

# Evelyn

After the Scripps adventure, nothing was the same for Jack Bessemer at Caltech. He had finally found something that interested him as much as electrical engineering. That something, or more accurately, someone, was Evelyn Benadetti. It was not that his magnetic attraction to Anna had disappeared. He still found her intoxicatingly sexy, but the road to Anna was a string of red lights that didn't ever seem to turn green.

The lab's research for the Navy often took him to San Diego, home to the largest naval base on the Pacific coast. They were carrying out tests for the lab's latest sonar upgrade package for the Navy. He found the voyages onboard the research naval vessel very exhilarating. They were putting the new sonar through the ringer, simulating all kinds of combat scenarios to see how the gizmo performed. It was meeting or exceeding the Navy's criteria.

Caltech would provide him with a car to drive to San Diego, but he would always leave a day early and take the route through Claremont and visit Evelyn. Even when there was no trip to San Diego as an excuse, he would borrow Nate's Packard and blast over to Claremont to see his girl. There they shared many idyllic days and nights, including occasional visits to the smokey club, The Underground.

It was there, late one evening, as they were slow dancing, locked in each other's arms, that he felt the pressure was building to such a great level that, if he didn't say something, he would explode. He leaned back and gazed into her big, dark eyes and said, "Evelyn, I love you. Love you with all my heart. I'll be graduating in a few months; will you marry me? Will you be my wife?"

"Oh, Jack, seems like I've been waiting forever for you to ask me that. I love you too, darling, and yes, I'd love to be your wife." They sealed it with a long, delicious kiss.

Returning to their table, he said, "I'm sorry, I haven't prepared for this moment. I don't have a ring or anything and I haven't even met your father yet, much less received his permission. But I've applied for a job back East to work for Columbia University and I'm pretty sure I'll get it."

"Don't worry about Daddy. I'll take care of him," she laughed.

Then an idea flashed into his mind. On his right pinkie he wore the "Iron Ring," the symbol of a professional engineer, bestowed on every recipient of a bachelor's degree in engineering. "Here," he said, taking it off his pinky finger. "Let this be the symbol of our engagement." She reached behind her neck, released the clasp of her gold necklace and slipped it through the iron ring, then secured the clasp behind her neck once more.

"Now we're truly engaged," she said beaming broadly.

Spring break, 1945, was approaching, and Evelyn decided it was time to take Jack home to meet her parents. They took the train from Los Angeles to San Francisco. They were met by the family chauffeur who collected their luggage, and the limousine conveyed them to the Roberto Benadetti Winery in the Napa Valley. When they arrived through the arched gate of the property, they were surrounded by acre after acre of cultivated grape vines, row after neat row of them, as far as the eye could see. They drove for almost 10 minutes before they arrived at the main house.

"THIS is where you live?" he asked, half rhetorically, half incredulously. "This looks more like a hotel!"

"There's Daddy! Come on!" Evelyn cried.

She ran to him and threw her arms around a large, somewhat rotund, casually dressed gentleman who exclaimed, "Welcome home Sugar!"

"Daddy, this is Jack Bessemer, soon to be Doctor Jack Bessemer."

Benadetti extended a meaty hand which enveloped Jack's. "Nice to meet you, Jack. Any man that can make my Sugar this happy is a good man in my book. Come on in and meet the Missus." They entered through a set of large, panelled, oak, double doors. The cavernous vestibule of the mansion was clearly modelled after a Tuscan aristocrat's villa, either from Roberto's childhood memory, or his imagination. The walls were decorated with paintings of famous Tuscan bridges: Ponte Vecchio, Ponte della Maddalena, and Ponte Amerigo Vespucci, coupled with several scenes from Firenze. Also, there were a number of paintings featuring red-roofed Tuscan villas, nestled between rolling hills, cultivated with straight rows of grapevines, just like he had seen upon entering the estate. The vestibule also featured a wide array of ornate, old-world, fixtures attached to gold-leaf framed polished oak panels. There was a large crystal chandelier hanging in the middle of the room. He shouted, "Lisa, Sugar's home!"

Lisa Benadetti emerged from another section of the vast building and embraced her daughter. She was effervescing with excitement. "So, this is Jack. We've heard so much about you. Welcome to our home Jack."

"Thank you, Mrs. Benadetti. I didn't expect to see anything like this." He said waving his arm to indicate his surroundings!

"America has been good to us," she said. "Now, come in and make yourself comfortable. Charles!" she said to the chauffeur, "Take the kids' bags up to their rooms, please." Jack noted the plural – they would not be sleeping together in Lisa's house. "Why don't we go out to the sunroom and have some wine?"

"Ottima idea, my dear," said Benadetti, leading the way.

*I think I'm gonna like being part of this family,* Jack thought.

The research Jack had been doing for the Navy for the past two years formed the basis for his PhD dissertation. A few months after his joyous welcome at the Napa Valley estate, the time came for his graduation from Caltech. Naturally, Evelyn came up from Scripps to witness the convocation. After the ceremony Jack, Evelyn and Nate were celebrating at the DH when Anna, who had also graduated with a bachelor's degree in physics, came in and congratulated Jack with a hug and a kiss on the cheek. She looked ravishing – without even trying.

Jack said, "Thanks, congrats yourself. By the way I want you to meet Evelyn, my fiancé. Honey, this is Anna Sokratis."

"Oh, so she's the reason you've been out of town so much. Nice to finally meet you, Evelyn. You've got a good man here." She stuck out her hand.

Even though she replied with a pleasant, "Hi, Anna, nice to meet you," for Evelyn, it was instant enemy recognition. Jack saw it in her eyes and her body language. And for the rest of the evening, he went out of his way to make a fuss over Evelyn, to the virtual exclusion of Anna.

Anna said, "Well Jack, now that you've finished with Caltech, what's next for you?"

"Well, I'm taking a job back east with Columbia University. They're doing all the latest research on sonar over there, and I want to be a part of it."

"Sounds very exciting," Anna replied.

"But we're getting married before we go," interjected Evelyn.

Anna just smiled.

"Anna, what are you gonna do?" Jack inquired.

"I'm going back to England. That's where my family is. Britain has been decimated by the War, and now that Germany's surrendered, they'll need people with my qualifications to help rebuild. So, I'm going home."

Nate stood up and raised his glass. "So, let's everybody raise their glasses, here's to Caltech and the exciting new lives we're embarking on, in far flung places!"

"Cheers!!"

After the celebration was over and Jack and Evelyn were alone at his place, she said, "That Anna's a very beautiful girl, was she a close friend of yours?" She looked piercingly in his eyes.

"Not to worry, it was never anything like that," he said evenly.

"Like what?"

"Like romance. We had a common interest in science, that's all. She didn't have time for any kind of romantic entanglements because her head was always in the books. Never seen anybody so studious."

"Oh, really?" She said impishly, cuddling up to him.

"Yeah, really."

She reached down inside his trousers, found what she was looking for and whispered, "Jack, remember, from now on, this belongs to me."

Jack shuddered with excitement.

# Columbia (Summer, 1945)

The June wedding was a very lavish affair, situated in the picturesque gardens surrounding the Benadetti mansion. The happy couple honeymooned on the shores of Lake Louise, surrounded by the majestic Canadian Rockies. After that, they took the long train ride to New York by way of Calgary, Edmonton, Winnipeg, Toronto and the Hudson River valley. As a wedding present, Roberto had bought the couple a mini-mansion in Greenwich, Connecticut, fully furnished and stocked with an ample supply of Benadetti wines, of course.

Three weeks after the wedding, Jack took the Metro-North commuter train from Greenwich to New York's 116th Street Station for his first day at work at Columbia University. Thankfully, his job was as a research fellow, avoiding having to give lectures to dim witted undergrads.

He was met by the head of the Acoustic Sciences Department, Dr. Henry Armstrong, originally from New Orleans, but no relation to Louis. Armstrong drawled, "Welcome to Columbia, Jack. We're very happy to have someone with your extensive background in sonar development working with us."

"I'm honoured to be chosen, Dr. Armstrong."

"Please, call me Hank. We're very informal around here. Let me introduce you to Doug Jones. Doug's going to be your assistant here and his first day is today too."

"Nice to meet you, Doug. I guess we'll be feeling our way around here together."

"Pleasure to meet you Dr. Bessemer."

"You can call me Jack."

Hank said, "Doug, this is mainly for your benefit, as I'm sure Jack is quite familiar with this subject. The two of you will be working with our unit that's on contract with the Navy on the propagation of sound through the deep ocean. This stuff is still classified but since you're on the team now, you should know that early in the War, some of our guys at Woods Hole tested a theory that low-frequency sound can travel long distances in the deep ocean. They anchored a boat off Woods Hole and dropped a hydrophone over the side. Another ship lowered an explosive device to a specific depth below the ocean surface, some 900 miles away, and detonated it. That sound was clearly heard 900 miles away by that hydrophone. 900 miles! So, the sonar you boys developed out there in San Diego is really just scratching the surface in terms of us being able to hear things in the ocean."

"900 miles! So far away, that's amazing!" Doug exclaimed.

"SOFAR – Exactly!" Hank replied.

"Huh?" Doug queried.

"There seems to be a channel in the ocean where sound can travel a very long way. We call it the SOFAR channel."

"SOFAR?"

"Yeah, SOFAR – it stands for SOund Fixing And Ranging. Well, I tell yuh, we got a bunch of Einsteins working on this project, but most of them are theoretical guys, you know. We need guys like you, Jack, who can create devices and instruments to be able to better measure this oceanic phenomenon and use it to enhance our national security."

"National security? Does anybody else know about the SOFAR channel, and the possible military uses it could be put to?" Jack asked.

"Well, I reckon that, currently, the only people that really know how to use it aren't actually people."

"Come again?"

"Well, I don't know this for sure, but I have a hunch that the only individuals who know how to use the SOFAR channel are marine mammals – whales."

"Whales?"

"Yeah, whales. How do you think that a guy whale and a gal whale can find each other in the vastness of the ocean? You know, birds and animals have mating calls, right? But those sounds travel only for a few miles, at best. How could you attract a member of the opposite sex if she were, say, 900 miles away?"

"Telephone?" Jack suggested with a chuckle.

"Not under water you wouldn't. I got no proof, but I'll bet you them whales know a hell of a lot more about the SOFAR channel than we do.

So, here's some of our research on the subject that you can study," he said handing Jack a thick folder.

"Errr, Hank, I don't get the urgency of interest on the Navy's part. What are we doing, planning for a confrontation with the global whale population?"

"Actually, the international whaling industry has already defeated the whales. But the War's been good for whales."

"Huh? How's that?"

"We humans have been so keen on killing each other over the last 4 years, we've left them alone. But in all seriousness, if we could figure out a way to send signals through these SOFAR channels, we could better communicate with our submarines, even while they're submerged. Or we might even be able to detect enemy subs hundreds of miles away using some new form of sonar."

"Look, Hank, the War's almost over. The Krauts are done, and the Japs are on the run. We're creaming them over there in the Pacific. What enemy are we talking about?"

"You know, I asked the Navy guy the exact same question. You know what he said? He asked me, 'After the war is over who will be left standing?' I said, 'Us!' And he said, 'No, us and the Russians.' And he said, 'You think them Commies are just going to let us take over the whole world?' I replied, 'They're our allies!' You know what he said then?" Jack shook his head. "He said, 'For now.'"

"Jees! I never thought about it like that," said Jack.

"Anyway, your group is on the 3rd floor, I'll take you up to meet the rest of the team." And they set off up the stairs.

A few days later, Jack was in Hank's office. Hank said, "Jack, with your knowledge of sonar, you can help us build a jumbo sonar system that can take advantage of the SOFAR channel in the open ocean."

Jack replied, "That's an interesting concept. If sound can travel as far as you say it does, we could send a ping, like we do from a warship, through the ocean and wait for the reflected signal to come back, measure the time lag and track the object. Except the ping will have to be sent from inside the SOFAR channel, not the surface.

"But there still will be a bunch of challenges in making the system practical. One, we don't know what the optimum frequency for this will be. We'll have to use trial and error to find out. Two, we don't know how much power to use to get a signal powerful enough so that we will be able to measure its echo, but I suspect it might have to be very big. Three, we have to set up the active device in the right place so that land masses, or other obstructions, don't get in the way. We probably will have to set it up on a ship of some kind. Four, we don't know what depth to set the pinger. Five, where will we set up the listening stations? I doubt if only listening posts along the East Coast will be adequate. Six, how do we know the difference between a Soviet submarine and a large biologic, like a blue or fin whale, both of whom are likely very active in the SOFAR channel. So, we've got to be able to develop devices to better analyze what we hear."

"I see you've been thinking about this, Jack," Hank replied.

"Yeah, Hank. Here, I've written up some more detailed thoughts on this subject." Jack handed Hank a folder. "We're going to need a big team of scientists and engineers, and a really big budget to turn this thing from an idea into a working system. Can we get those kinds of resources?"

"I'll do my best, Jack."

# Early Warning (1949)

Jack loved his work, being on the "bleeding" edge of the study and advancements in underwater Sonar technology. His intercom buzzed. It was Hank. "Jack, can you come to my office for a moment. I need you to hear this."

"Sure-thing Hank."

When he entered the room, he saw a familiar face, Commander Barney Henson, their naval attaché and liaison.

Hank said, "Barney, perhaps you can give Dr. Bessemer the latest summary of the geopolitical situation in relation to what we're trying to accomplish here."

"No problem, Hank. As you know, the result of the War is that there have emerged two dominant powers: the USA and the Soviet Union.

"While the Russians suffered major devastation from the War, it has emerged as a major military power, thanks mainly to our assistance, a military power with a political ideology that is diametrically opposed to ours. They are intent on expanding their own empire to replace Hitler's. So former allies are now adversaries. That's the geopolitical picture.

"The strategic situation has deteriorated significantly too. Not only do the Russians now have The Bomb, they also have ballistic missiles, as do we. The Krauts were world leaders in rocket technology. We spirited away a bunch of the top German rocket men for our purposes, but the Russians got a good number of them as well. Our nuclear tipped missiles can reach them because they're based in Europe and in Turkey, but their missiles can't reach us, at least not yet, except for Alaska, of course. But that's changing because we know there is a crash program over there to place nuclear missiles on submarines which will be deployed in the Atlantic within range of our major East Coast cities.

"They also have a crash program under way to increase the number and capability of these submarines. So, if you gents with the PhD's don't come up with something soon, the Russians will soon be able to park nuclear tipped missiles off of New York, Washington DC, Boston and Philadelphia without anybody knowing where they are. That's over 12 million people gentlemen.

"We already have the ability to destroy them, if we can find them. So, it is imperative that we have an early warning system to detect and track these missile subs."

"Whew!" Jack said. "We've got a lot of work to do."

"Look at this." Hank took out a large map of the North Atlantic and laid it out on a table in his office. Look how far these subs have to come to get within range. We've got to find a way of detecting them once they leave European waters and get in the open ocean. Now, if we could get a listening post here, in Bermuda, there would be no barrier between the island and the Scandinavian North Cape close to where those missile boats launch from."

"Naw, Hank. That's not right!" the naval officer said. "This map uses a Mercator Projection – it makes a round world flat, and in doing so, distorts things and makes countries close to the poles look bigger than they really are. So, on this map a straight line has to be drawn as a curved one. Navigators call these the "Greater Circle" routes. If we do that, the route from Bermuda to the North Cape in Russia is interrupted by Greenland. Having said all that, Bermuda still looks like the best place to set up a receiving station for early warning."

"We have two US bases there already, one Navy, the other Airforce – legacy of the War," Hank said rubbing his chin.

"Well, for this new stand-off with the Russians, looks like Bermuda is going to be vitally important, once again. We're gonna need something there, Hank, something substantial," Henson replied.

"What about our budget?" Jack asked, recalling the issues he'd had with the bean counters in San Diego.

"Dr. Bessemer, what budget? Just build it and make it work," Henson flatly declared.

"Alright!" Jack gushed.

"Thank you for your perspective, Commander," Hank said. "We can solve the budget issue by dividing things up into different budgets. There is a budget for us here in New York, for the new SOFAR Station in Bermuda, for the Navy and for Bell Labs who are working with us on this project. We should be able to get the funding we need."

"Yeah, I'll start working on it immediately." Henson took his leave.

"Jack, we've got Carl Cardigan as director of the SOFAR Station in Bermuda. I need you to go to Bermuda. I want you to work in both the Tudor Hill facility with the Navy and the Bell Labs guys, as well as the scientists at SOFAR. Sort of one foot in each camp. That way we can have the Navy using the latest and greatest of technology to find those Soviet subs before they can menace our cities."

"Uh… Hank?"

"Yeah, Jack."

"Doesn't that require me to have three feet?" Jack asked with a wry smile.

"Oh, yeah, right. You'll figure it out."

# Captain Crunch

Crenshaw Ulysses Nelson DeSilva was born in Warwick, Bermuda, to a black West Indian mother and an Azorean Portuguese father. His father was a hard-working fisherman, scraping a living in his open rowboat in Bermuda's near shore waters. Perhaps, due to his occupation, but no one knows for sure, he was called Scaley. His mother worked as a cook and housekeeper for one of the wealthy families that resided in the Warwick area. Young Crenshaw was always the shortest and slightest boy in his class, and he felt he was obliged to overcompensate for his diminutive stature by displaying an excessive degree of swagger and confidence.

While his mother called him Crenshaw, sometimes "Cren" for short, he hated his name, considering it to be a name suitable for a bookworm or somebody who was "soft". It certainly didn't comport with the swaggering, tough guy image he wanted for himself. One day, in school, Miss Prince, his teacher, read the class a story about the adventures of a charter fishing boat duo named Crunch and Des. He was captivated by the story, and since his three names could be abbreviated to CRUN, he decided, on his own, that he wanted to be called "Crunch", and he threatened to crunch any boy's head that refused to call him by this nickname – even though he was smaller than all of them! It didn't work. His incredible swagger didn't cow any of his mates, to his dismay, and everybody started to call him by his father's nickname – Scaley DeSilva. He eventually had to accept it.

Scaley loved the sea, and as he grew up, he learned how to navigate Bermuda's waters from his father. But he didn't want to be a rowboat fisherman. He wanted to be like Crunch, as in Crunch and Des. He wanted to be a charter fishing boat skipper. By the time he was in his teens he would skip school to be a mate on the established sport fishing boats. He gained tremendous experience at these jobs, particularly the art of entertaining the client-fishermen aboard. But always he burned inside to have his own boat. But where would he get the money for such an enterprise?

He pondered long and hard on this problem, then eventually hit upon a bold plan that involved asking Mr. Bayard Smith, who employed his mother, to invest in a charter fishing enterprise. He asked his mother first.

"I don't know, Cren, it's taking a risk." She still called him Cren. "Just make sure you don't act brattish if he says no. You should always be polite, even in the face of rejection, is that clear?"

"OK, Mum."

"I'll let him know that you want to talk to him."

The next day Scaley appeared before Mr. Smith. "Mr. Smith, I've heard that you have a good eye for a profitable investment."

"You have, have you? What can I do for you young man?"

"Mr. Smith, I'm sure you've noticed the growing number of visitors to the island. One of the most exciting things our visitors can do in Bermuda is to go deep sea fishing. Most of these people have never seen anything bigger than a trout or a bass or some other small freshwater fish. They've never, ever, seen anything the size of a wahoo, a big tuna, a sailfish, not to mention a marlin; or anything as beautiful as a dolphin fish. As you know, it takes a good boat and an expert skipper to take these byes out there and show them where they can fight a big fish. With our growing number of tourists, there's money to be made in deep sea charter fishing."

"So, what are you proposing, young man."

"Mr. Smith, I need money to buy a charter fishing boat. I hear you can buy'em cheap in the States. If you provide the money for the boat and gear, I'll split the profit 50:50 with you, plus give you 25% extra until the cost of the boat and gear is repaid to you. Then it's a straight 50:50 after that. How 'bout it, sir?"

"Bye you've got some Moxy coming up to me with such a proposal, I'll give you that. I'll think about it. Come back here tomorrow and we'll talk about it some more."

"Yessir, Mr. Smith." Scaley was elated that he had not been just turned down flat.

He returned the next day.

"Look, young fella, I like your style, but how're you going to just buy a boat in the States?"

"Somebody's going to have to go out there and look 'em over, sir."

"You? ... I don't think so, you're not old enough. You know, I come from a long line of sea farers myself. One of my forebears was a privateer! I'm going to go to buy this craft, and you can come with me."

"Yessir, that would be best," his heart almost bursting out of his chest.

"Here, I've prepared a demand promissory note for you to sign." Bayard slid over a demand note and Scaley signed it. "There! Seeing that we're going to be partners you can call me Bayard."

"Yessir, Mr. Smith."

About a month later, Smith and DeSilva flew to New York, then caught another flight to Miami where there was a major sport fishing industry and lots of used boats for sale. There were so many it was hard to choose. Then they came upon a boat with "Thresher" across her transom. She was a beauty: 54 feet long, twin diesels, outriggers, twin fighting chairs, all the heavy gear required for catching heavy fish, and a flybridge from which to conn the boat.

Scaley said, "There's nothing like this back home. This boat would be the top boat on the island for deep sea fishing."

"I agree," said Smith.

Scaley closely inspected the interior and engine spaces while Smith haggled with the owner over the price. They finally agreed on terms.

"Scaley, you stay behind and make all the arrangements to transport her back home. It's bound to take you a few days because you've got to find a flat-bed truck to transport it to New York, then a ship to bring it home. I'm going straight back home. By the way, you want to change the name?"

"Ya."

"What do you want to call her?"

Scaley laughed, "*Captain Crunch*!"

Smith burst out laughing, "*Captain Crunch* it is."

When *Captain Crunch* finally arrived in Bermuda and started to operate as a charter fishing boat, it caused a sensation in the local boating and fishing community. Locals had never seen a fishing vessel so large, fast and well equipped as the *Crunch*. And people that knew Scaley DeSilva couldn't figure out how this young man could pull off this coup. Nevertheless, *Captain Crunch* was a huge hit with tourists.

A typical conversation skipper DeSilva would have with his customers would go like this. "Skipper, where do we go to find the big fish?"

Scaley would answer, "Well the best fishing grounds are in the region of the two banks: Challenger Bank, 14 miles Southwest, and Argus Bank, 25 miles Southwest."

"What are these 'banks'?"

"They're seamounts. Bermuda sits on top of a massive seamount formed from an ancient volcano whose crater is much bigger than the island. The island sits on only about 10% of the volcano's crater. There are two smaller seamounts that don't break the surface: Challenger and Argus. The ocean is about 190 feet deep there, shallow enough for coral to grow on them. The coral attracts the small fish, the small fish attract the bigger fish and they attract the really big fish. Those are the guys we're after."

"So how long will it take to get out there?"

"Well, you're on *Captain Crunch*, the fastest fishing boat in Bermuda. We'll be at Challenger before you know it and do some trollin' out there. If we don't catch anything in quick time, we'll head out to Argus. See them other byes?" He said indicating some other charter boats. We goin' leave them byes in our smoke. Let's get crackin'!" Whereupon he would gun the powerful engines and leave the competition behind.

Scaley DeSilva found he could charge higher rates than his competitors and still be fully booked. He had plenty of money to spend, even after meeting his obligations to Bayard Smith. He liked to frequent some of the local bars and clubs where he would often have one or two too many and occasionally engage in games of poker and blackjack in the bars' backrooms. Sometime the stakes got pretty high, but even if he lost, he could make it back from the next charter or two. In one such club, called Aces High, there was a waitress named Maria Almeida. Everyone called her Ria. She was exquisitely beautiful, and all the male patrons continuously hit on her. Scaley reckoned she must have come from a very poor Portuguese family to continue with this job in the face of such harassment. But for him, it was love at first sight. With the absence of even one shy bone in his body, he decided he would be her, "Knight in Shining Armour," and habitually came to her defence when she was harassed.

She was most grateful, but when he asked to take her out on a date, she told him that her family was very strict with her and that he had to meet with her father first. Scaley, confident he could overcome any challenge, agreed and appeared at the Almeida's humble home on a Sunday afternoon. Ria's father, Manuel, was not at all pleased when the young man who wanted to take out his daughter turned out to be coloured. He spoke very little English but enough to dismiss the young man by saying, "You no good, you no good!" However, Scaley, the son of a Portuguese fisherman, was well versed in Azorean Portuguese, and was able, through his linguistic abilities and sheer bravado, to blunt, then eventually overcome, the old man's prejudices. After making his case that his intentions were strictly honourable and that he had a successful charter fishing business, Manuel relented and gave permission for him to "see" his baby girl, Maria.

It wasn't long before Scaley and Ria were engaged. He wanted to impress the Almeidas with his business success, so he decided to buy a home for his bride to be. He found a modest cottage just off South Road in Warwick and purchased it with a mortgage provided by his friendly backer, Bayard Smith. Within a year, Ria gave birth to a nine-pound baby boy whom they called Nelson Manuel.

# The Royal Barge

At the apex of the Bermuda Triangle, the warm waters of the Gulf Stream, flowing straight through the Triangle between Bermuda and the US East Coast, mysteriously spin off a large eddy each spring. It surrounds the island of Bermuda, embracing it with its warmth, enabling the flourishment of the world's northern most living coral island eco-system. By mid-November, the eddy was retreating as inexplicably as it began, cooling the air above the island. In November of 1955, the weather was still fine, but cool, from a fresh northwest breeze, due to a retreating dome of high-pressure over the western Atlantic.

Joshua Jones was called Josh by his family, but boys often got called by their fathers' nicknames during the usual schoolyard shenanigans. At first, he became known as "Little Hooks." This was never going to stick – too complicated. The fishy theme was carried forward and somehow morphed into "Snapper." This nickname stuck.

Snapper and Scaley were schoolmates and shared a strong attraction to everything nautical. Unlike Scaley's, Snapper's family was very strict. As teenagers, Scaley used to skip school to crew on charter fishing boats, but there was no way Snapper was ever going to get away with that in the Jones' household. Both Edith and Hooks placed a very high premium on education and not only was Snapper required to stay in school, he also was expected to perform well, his end of term report card coming under close scrutiny from both his parents.

Instead of playing football or cricket, Snapper spent most of his spare time with his dad, either in the wheelhouse of the ferry *Frances* or fishing aboard *Jezebel*. It was during these hours spent together, that Hooks' encyclopaedic knowledge of Bermuda's waters, channels and reefs was passed on from father to son. Hooks didn't do much lecturing; he would put Snapper behind the wheel of the ferry and give cryptic tips and instructions as his son attempted to accomplish whatever nautical task he had been set. Unsuspecting passengers had no idea how many times they were in the hands of a youngster. Hooks was always close at hand in case the boy was going too far off course.

Snapper's favourite subject at school was geography. He was so good at it that he won a 5-year subscription to National Geographic Magazine. He devoured each monthly edition that arrived at his Somerset Bridge home and was keenly interested in the frequent articles featuring oceanic explorer, Jacques Cousteau, whose research vessel, *Calypso* was an occasional visitor to Bermuda. The wonderfully colourful, large maps in National Geographic sparked Snapper's interest in formal navigation, as opposed to the type that Hooks Jones practised. But that would have to wait.

Edith, Snapper's mother, buried her fears about her men folk's night fishing trips. Despite her discouragement, her son was destined to follow his father's path and become a Bermuda pilot. Tragically, one evening Hooks took *Jezebel* out for some night fishing alone, and never returned. Shortly after that, Snapper joined the Bermuda Ferry Service.

Snapper Jones became the youngest man ever to be skipper in the Bermuda ferry fleet. As the son of the legendary Hooks Jones, the ferry pilot who, during the War, exposed a Nazi spy and assisted in his demise along with a U-boat off Bermuda's North Rock, great things were expected from Snapper, in terms of his skill as a mariner and navigator of Bermuda's treacherous waters. And he didn't disappoint them. He quickly rose through the ranks and was given the privilege and responsibility of commanding the ferryboat *Wilhelmina*, pride of the Bermuda ferry fleet.

*Wilhelmina* was indeed a beauty. She was purchased in America in 1943 for £12,000 by the Bermuda Transportation Company. Built in 1927 in Canada as a luxury pleasure yacht, she was 110 feet in length with a 19.5 foot beam. Some of her former owners were whispered to have had mob ties, but nothing was confirmed. But such reputational blemishes were consigned to the dustbin of history, as she was chosen to convey the newly coronated Her Majesty, Queen Elizabeth II and the Duke of Edinburgh from Hamilton to Somerset on Her Majesty's first visit to the Island in 1953, thus becoming a "Royal Barge." Her skipper on that occasion was Snapper's predecessor, Norman Smith. He was senior pilot of the service and highly experienced, but subsequently drank himself into an early grave, providing Snapper with this opportunity to skipper the "Queen of the Fleet."

*Wilhelmina* shared responsibility for commuter service to the west end of the island with the venerable *Corona*, the coal burning, former Hudson River ferry. On Saturday, November 12th, 1955, *Wilhelmina* departed Hamilton on her last run of the day, at 6:00pm, with 64 souls aboard: 58 passengers and 6 crew. The spectacular daily atmospheric display of reds and oranges of the Bermuda autumn sunset was rapidly giving way to the gathering gloom, as the vermillion orb sank beneath the hills of Somerset Island. No one knew that the fiery sunset would be the harbinger of things to come.

Unlike the smaller or older ferries in the fleet, the *Wilhelmina* had real ships' engine telegraphs, instead of the old fashion bell system. These telegraphs flanked the large oak steering wheel in the wheelhouse. Snapper, like his father before him, kept his vessel in ship-shape, the telegraphs being highly polished, enabling anyone to see his/her reflection in the burnished brass surfaces.

Pilot Snapper Jones stood outside the port side door of *Wilhelmina's* wheelhouse, his smooth, dark brown, clean-shaven face exhibiting no wrinkles, despite many years of sea and sun. His athletically built frame, standing six feet tall, was smartly attired in his navy-blue uniform, pilot's cap cocked smartly to one side. He surveyed the situation. It was time to depart.

"Bully!"

"Yeah, Snap."

"Let go that stern line!" James "Bully" Simons, the burly stern deckhand, let go the stern line. "Noel, wrap up that forward post." Noel Smith, the forward deckhand, obeyed the command and wrapped a dock line around the post. Snapper rang up slow ahead on the starboard engine telegraph. *Wilhelmina's* stern swung away from the dock. "OK, Noel, let go." Snapper rang up slow astern on both engines and the ferry backed out of her slot at Albuoy's Point. When she had moved well away from the dock, he rang up full ahead and *Wilhelmina* came to cruising speed. All systems were functioning normally.

As their services would not be required until later on in the voyage, the crew went forward, below decks, to relax until the ferry neared her first destination, Watford Bridge. Edward Stone, chief engineer, went to his quarters just forward of the auxiliary engine room, itself located just forward of the main engine room. His assistant, Wilbert MacDonald, known to everyone as Mackey, went forward, with three other crew members, to the crews' quarters which were in the ferry's bow. Stone could see diagonally through the auxiliary engine room into a section of the main engine room from his door. It was empty, despite regulations requiring it to be manned by at least one person while the boat was underway. In any case, Stone could hear the telegraph ring from his quarters over the pulsating din of the diesels and generator, if the skipper wanted a change in propulsion.

Most of the passengers were Somerset residents on their way home from a long day at work or from shopping. In those days, Saturday was a working day, Thursday afternoon being the half day off from the standard five-and one-half day work week. Of course, there was no school on Saturdays, so there were several school aged youngsters aboard. The social structure on board ship was a world apart from the Bermudian society of the day, as people from all walks of life, of all racial and ethnic groups, mingled freely while on board, a situation starkly different from segregationist strictures back on land.

With a refreshing breeze out of the Northwest, *Wilhelmina* headed through Two Rock Passage, and it was a straight shot to Watford Bridge from there. About a mile from Watford Bridge one of the crew up forward exclaimed, "Hey, there's smoke in the engine room!" Mackey relayed the message to the Chief. The two men went to investigate. The diesel generator was running but there was no smoke in there. They entered the main engine room and saw a haze of smoke aft of the starboard engine. In that section of the engine room was a workbench on the outside of the starboard engine, five oil cans and a five gallon can of kerosene. But they could see no fire on the workbench, just smoke.

Then Stone's eye caught the dazzle of a flame. "There!" He cried, pointing just forward of the starboard engine around the sump switch. "What's burnin'? There ain't nutt'n there to burn!"

Stone started up the steps contemplating his next course of action. "Maybe I should use the pyrene." The Pyrene fire extinguisher, that used chemicals to suppress fires, was strapped to the forward bulkhead of the engine room nearest him. But it was best for small fires. "Maybe I should use the foam fire extinguisher." But it was located further forward in the auxiliary room. As he momentarily pondered these options, the fire, having spread to some unseen highly flammable fuel, suddenly flared up in front of him. The pyrene was out of the question now. Stone was shocked into action. "Hey Mackey! Go tell Snapper we got a fire down here and that he shouldn't try to dock at Watford Bridge 'cause we won't be able to control the engines." Mackey beetled off to the wheelhouse.

As Stone climbed to the top of the stairs where the release handles for the $CO_2$ bottles could be reached, he felt a wave of heat waft past his left cheek. He turned and saw that the fire had flared into a blaze. "My God!"

A still unseen fuel on the deck alongside the engines was ablaze, wickedly hissing and flashing as though it were a living, breathing, evil demon. "What the hell is burning down there? Can't be fuel oil, it don't burn that easy! Well, at least the wooden superstructure isn't burning." As he reached the top of the stairs, he could see that there were flames licking around the main fuel tanks. "Got to use the CO2!"

*Wilhelmina's* primary firefighting weapon was an array of pressurized carbon dioxide bottles, connected to nozzles placed around the engine room. By now fire was licking around the CO2 release handles and it was difficult to reach them without getting roasted. Stone sidled around, avoiding the flames, and pulled down the handles as hard as he could. He fired off three 450-pound bottles of CO2 into the engine room. There was a loud whooshing sound from the release of high-pressure gas.

Stone gaped in horror. Instead of smothering the fire, the force from the compressed CO2 bottles, or whatever was actually in those bottles, drove the flames and flaming fuel up into the wooden superstructure and set it alight! Throughout all these pyrotechnics, the big reliable diesels kept right on pulsating, driving *Wilhelmina* forward.

*Wilhelmina*, like most of the Bermuda Transportation Company ferries, had her engine room modified that provided a vertical space that ran from the engines right up to the top of the vessel. This helped to ventilate the engine spaces, replacing expensive ventilation ducts and fans. On the main deck, passengers could look through internal windows right down to the engines. Even under normal circumstances the heat and noise coming through those windows was enormous.

Meanwhile up on the passenger deck, Mrs. A. Rowland was knitting with her daughter, Audrey. She saw some smoke. "Audrey, look, there's some smoke," she said.

Audrey said, "Mummy, I'm going to be nosey," and off she went to investigate. She returned and reported, "Mummy, the engine room is full of smoke!" Mrs. Rowland just kept on knitting; that is, until she saw flames.

Mr. John Joseph Card, of Sandys Parish, was sitting aft and decided to take a stroll forward. He saw a glow and when he reached the engine room it was ablaze! He turned around to a coloured woman nearby and said, "Do you see that?"

"Ya, it's been like that for a little while," she said, quite nonchalantly. Card went forward to the wheelhouse to inform Captain Jones of fire aboard ship. He arrived just after Mackey who had been dispatched by the Chief Engineer a mere two minutes ago.

Elsewhere, Mr. Ernest William Hart, of Boaz Island, had been sitting on the port side, aft, with his wife. He noticed what smelled like a man smoking, except, there was no man. He didn't take much notice of it until, a few minutes later, he smelled it again. Then he saw, a tongue of flame come out of an engine room window about the length of a man's arm. He rose and approached another passenger, a Canadian Naval officer, and calmly said, "This ship's on fire, sir." Before the two could investigate, people from the aft cabin started to come further aft amid more smoke and sparks. *Dear Lord, please let these engines keep running!* Hart prayed.

Upon hearing that his ship was on fire, the skipper's reaction was immediate and decisive. The ship was at full cruising speed, and he knew that if there was a fire in the engine room the biggest immediate problem, next to the possibility of explosion, was that he couldn't stop the vessel. While the ships' telegraph system aboard *Wilhelmina* was more sophisticated than onboard the other ferries, it was still a manual system. Once he gave a signal from the wheelhouse, say, to stop engines, somebody in the engine room would have to manually stop the engines. If there was a fire down there, he knew his orders probably could not be executed and, therefore, he couldn't stop the boat, unless of course the engines stopped on their own.

Snapper heard the $CO_2$ extinguisher bottles go off, so he rushed out on the bridge wing and looked aft. Instead of suppressing the inferno, he observed that it had caused the superstructure to become fully ablaze.

He instantly spun the big, oak helm of the ferry to starboard and headed for Boaz Island. *I've got to get the passengers off! As quickly as possible – and in as shallow water as possible.* Having played this and other disaster scenarios over in his mind many times before, he headed straight for the narrow, shallow bay between Watford Island and the southern tip of Boaz Island where there was a small beach.

"Mackey!! Get these passengers that are already forward of the fire as far forward as possible, and for those trapped aft, see if you, or another one of the guys, can get them as far aft as possible. And make sure everybody puts on their lifebelts. Remember they're under the seats!"

"Um…Um." Mackey was struggling with the stress of the moment.

"Mackey! You hear me bye!!" Snapper bellowed.

"Yeah, yeah, Snapper. I got it. I got it." He turned around and started shouting orders to passengers.

*Wilhelmina* approached the entrance of the bay. There was no way Snapper could have ever practised approaching or entering this bay in a vessel the size of *Wilhelmina*. Having been tutored by his father, Hooks Jones, Snapper knew every rock and shoal around the island. He remembered that there were a few invisible shoals on the port side of the entrance to this bay that made the entrance very tight. He was going to have to squeeze a big vessel through a small, shallow gap, traveling at full speed – in the dark.

Meanwhile, below decks, with chief Stone still near his post in the auxiliary engine room, the main engine room was engulfed in flame. In spite of the fire around them, both the diesel generator and the diesel engines were still running; both ahead full. Stone stuck his head out of one of the portholes on the starboard side, and saw the southern tip of Boaz Island, protecting the bay. "Looks like we're going 'round to Little Watford. It's now or never!!" He reached into the engine room, again risking getting roasted, and sidled along the bulkhead. The searing heat from the flames was burning his arm, chest and face. Stretching as far as he could, his left hand finally found the valves controlling the fuel supply to both engines. They were made of bronze and were very hot to the touch. Gritting his teeth, he continued.

"Ah…….!!!," Stone roared from the pain burning his hand and arm as he closed one valve then the other. He quickly withdrew holding his trembling, burnt left hand, his clothes drenched in sweat.

The starboard engine stopped at a critical moment – as they were entering the narrow entrance to the bay. In the wheelhouse, Snapper felt the ferry sheer to the right because thrust was now coming solely from the port engine. He adjusted his helm to keep her on course. The port engine stopped just before *Wilhelmina* touched the sandy bottom of the bay. Her forward momentum causing her to plough further up on the sandy beach.

"Abandon ship! Abandon ship!" Snapper shouted. "Everybody off, everybody off, now!" Even though *Wilhelmina* was beached, there was still plenty of water there for people to drown in. While it was just a foot or so close to the bow, off her stern the depth could still have been up to 10 feet of black water.

There were 58 passengers and six crew aboard *Wilhelmina* that fateful night. Many were women and children. The ferry was burning furiously amidships now, her wooden superstructure perfect fuel for the demonic flames.

People who had moved forward of the engine room were the most fortunate. Most of them merely jumped off the bow and landed in water in which they could stand. However, folks who had assembled aft of the engine room were trapped there by the blaze amidships. They would have to jump overboard in deep water. Snapper helped passengers over the side up forward but couldn't do anything about those near the stern, except to shout orders to his crew. Albert Henry Dawson, known as Bert, was standing alongside Snapper.

"Bert, get over the side and see if you can help those passengers who are stuck at the stern."

"Sure, skipper." And over the side he leapt.

There were other heroes of November 12th, 1955. One of them was Vernon Fubler, a passenger who stayed on board, braving the smoke and flames to help many of the passengers to get overboard and into small boats that had come to the rescue. From a distance, many people on land had witnessed the flaming ferry sheering away in the middle of the dark Great Sound. Some nearby had jumped into small boats to help. Leslie Ryder was one of them and he arrived with his boat in time to rescue several stricken passengers. The furious flames provided fierce, orange lighting to make for excellent visibility for everything, except objects under water.

Another hero was deckhand, Bert Dawson, who had been dispatched overboard to help ashore passengers already in the water. He observed Fubler, at the stern of the burning ferry, helping four women get off. After the women went over the side, Dawson shouted, "Come on Vernon, get off. Time for you to get off, bye!"

The smoke was causing Fubler to have spasmodic, violent, coughing spells. "Albert, I ... I ... I can't swim, bye!"

"Come on, bye, this boat's goin' explode any minute now. You got to get off! Come on, now. Dun worry, bye, um here to help you! Jump, bye!

Jump!" So, he jumped and flopped into the dark water. His head popped to the surface close to Dawson.

"You alright?" Dawson asked, noticing that Fubler was doing a sort of dog paddle.

"Ya, ya, I'm alright," still coughing.

On hearing that, Dawson turned to assist some women who were still in the water. After helping a few other passengers to get into Leslie Ryder's boat, Dawson returned to Fubler. He was about eight or nine feet from him when he saw him go under. Dawson dived under the black surface, groping around until he touched something. Then he grabbed him and brought him up. "Vernon, Vernon, you alright?"

Fubler said, "Amen, brother, you got me?"

"Ya, bye, take it easy, I got you." He turned him on his back and started towing him to Ryder's boat. Then Fubler started to violently gag and choke again and foam at the mouth. He was unconscious by the time they reached Ryder's boat.

Dawson yelled, "Hey, Ryder! Look here! Help me, bye, Vernon's in trouble! Quick!" They pulled him aboard.

Ryder said, "We got to do mouth to mouth on him. Bert, take over this here wheel and get us to shore." Then he started to perform the emergency procedure on Fubler.

On shore, Dr. The Hon. Eugene "Muddy" Cannfield, a Somerset resident, had come to the scene to assist. When they brought Fubler to him, he tried all he could, but could not revive him, his lungs being too damaged. Vernon Fubler was the only fatality of the *Wilhelmina* disaster. Later, the coroner's jury determined that had Fubler not stayed behind to help fellow passengers to safety, his lungs would not have been so damaged by the smoke and fumes. He gave his life for his fellow passengers.

Snapper called out, "Hey Bert, any more people onboard?"

"No, Skipper, I dun see no more. Vernon Fubler was the last one."

"OK, I'm getting off." Captain Joshua (Snapper) Jones abandoned his charge. Shortly after he went ashore all heads turned with the sound of a loud bang. *Wilhelmina* exploded, throwing burning debris, sparks and flames high into the air. Two high pressure air tanks had suddenly surrendered to the excess pressure caused by expanding superheated air.

Meanwhile, Edith Jones, widow of Hooks Jones who had been lost at sea, and Snapper's mother, was serving Maisie, one of her friends, and long-term customers in her shop, when the phone rang. She picked it up on the third ring, cradling the receiver between her neck and her shoulder while ringing up her customer's purchase on the manual cash register. "Hello, Bridge Variety. What! The *Wilhelmina*! On fire! Oh my God!" She dropped the receiver on the counter. Her face contorted in terror. "Dear God, not again. Please God, not again!" she cried, tears streaming down. Memories of all the anguish, pain, sorrow and anger after Hooks was lost at sea exploded back into her consciousness, from a place that she had laboriously imprisoned years ago, in order to get on with her life. She knew that, as a Christian woman, it was wrong to be angry with God, and it had been so difficult to shutter that anger genie away, locking it away in the remotest corner of her mind. She had thought that she had been successful in banishing it forever. But the mere thought of Snapper being snatched away by a mishap at sea, essentially an "act of God," was more than she could bear, the anger genie bursting out of the mental prison she had constructed, coming roaring back. It petrified her.

"Edith, what on earth is wrong!" Her friend inquired.

"The *Wilhelmina's* on fire. Josh is her skipper," she said quietly, her voice trembling, as if in a trance.

"Edith! … Edith! Where? Where is the *Wilhelmina* now?" Maisie shouted, trying to break through to her entranced friend.

"Um … um, Boaz Island, I think." Edith replied, still in shock.

"Come, girl. My husband is outside in the taxi. We'll take you up there. Come now, you can't just assume that something terrible has happened to Snapper. We've got to learn the facts. Come, close down this-here shop and let's get crackin'!"

"OK, ok, I'm coming."

She hurriedly shut up the shop and they jumped into the surrey-with-the-fringe-on-top taxi, heading across Somerset Bridge toward Boaz Island. As they passed through Somerset Village everything appeared quiet, perhaps too quiet. When they approached Watford Bridge the stench of smoke assailed their nostrils. Edith began trembling and her friend put her arm around her in support. Drawing closer, they could see, against the surrounding darkness, the eerie flickering orange glow reflected on the adjacent trees. Many people were running toward the scene. As they approached Little Watford, the short wooden bridge connecting Watford Island with Boaz Island, the burning wreck of *Wilhelmina* came into full view.

"Oh my God!" Edith gasped. She jumped out of the car, even though it was still moving, looking for her son. The area was clogged with neighbours, gawkers, survivors and those there to help. She spied someone she knew: Dr. Eugene "Muddy" Cannfield. "Doctor, doctor!"

"Edith! What are you doing here?"

"Josh, um ... um, Snapper, have you seen him?"

"Snapper? No, I haven't seen him. There's one man dead here and several others with minor injuries." Looking over to the burning hulk, he said, "A bleddy mess, init?" Then they felt the concussion and heard the boom of a powerful explosion onboard the ferry, followed by a mushrooming fireball erupting from the midsection of the wreck.

"Oh my God!" Edith broke off from Muddy Cannfield and pushed her way through the crowd toward the burning ferry.

"Edith, come back! You shouldn't go down there, it's dangerous!" Cannfield shouted. But to no avail, she completely ignored him. Then she saw a small group of men at the waterside, one was shouting something at the other three, then they dispersed, clearly doing the shouter's bidding. She recognized him as her son.

"Josh! Josh!" She cried, running to him. She grabbed him, clinging to him, sobbing loudly with relief. "Lord, Jesus, thank you. Thank you, Jesus!"

Snapper said, "Mum, what're you doing here?"

"I heard about the fire. I was afraid you ... you...," she started to tremble.

Realizing what was going through his mother's mind, Snapper adopted a more empathetic tone. "I'm alright, Mum. Really, I'm alright." He bent down and looked directly in her eyes. "Look at me, Mum. I'm alright." She managed a faint smile. "Now, you need to move away from this fire, there could be more explosions. He put his arm around his mother and led her off the beach. He asked Maisie to take her home.

He remained on the scene until after midnight making sure all passengers and crew were accounted for. Firefighting elements from the US Naval Operating Base (NOB) attended the blaze and eventually doused the flames, but the once elegant lady known as the *Wilhelmina*, "Queen of the Fleet," was a total loss.

Snapper was required to answer many questions from police and newspaper reporters. After they were done and he was on his way home, he reflected on the evening's events, particularly details regarding any aspect of his own actions, and if he could have done anything differently to bring about a better outcome. After considering this matter for some time, he concluded that, as the ferry's pilot, there was nothing he could have done differently to have saved Vernon Fubler and the elegant lady under his charge.

# The Inquiry

Snapper Jones was hailed as a hero by the establishment daily newspaper *The Royal Gazette* as well as the semi-weekly, black owned paper, *The Bermuda Recorder*, but the Official verdict was another matter. First there was a report provided by the Marine Inspector, Mr. James Barker, who was also responsible for maintenance of the ferry fleet. Second there was a Court of Inquiry whose remit was to determine the cause of the fire and to attribute blame.

Matters came to a head when the findings of the Court of Inquiry were debated in Bermuda's Parliament.

As it often happened, if a business owned by the local oligarchs became unprofitable, it was merely sold to the government. As they controlled the government, the same people were on both sides of such a transaction. It went without saying that the taxpayers received the short end of that stick. As a government operation, losses were borne by all taxpayers, not just the oligarchs. Such was the fate of the ferry fleet of the Bermuda Transportation Company. By the early 1950's, the ferry service had been sold to the Bermuda Government and run by a department known as the Board of Trade.

The first speaker on the disaster was Mr. William Hempworth, Member of Colonial Parliament (MCP). "Mr. Speaker, in relation to the *Wilhelmina* disaster, the Court of Inquiry, of which I am the Chairman, has found that regulations were not followed by the crew and that the failure to abide by said regulations was the major factor in the ferry fire. Specifically, Mr. Speaker, the regulations require that at least one crewman be present in the engine room at all times the vessel is under way. The Chief Engineer has admitted that no one was in the engine room when the fire started.

"Mr. Speaker, in addition, the Court of Inquiry found that the pilot of the vessel failed to adequately control his crew and ensure that the engine room was manned and ready at all times, and that he, therefore was also at fault.

"Therefore, Mr. Speaker, the Board of Trade has, under its authority, reprimanded the Chief Engineer, Mr. Stone, and suspended his engineer's license for six months. The pilot, Mr. Joshua Jones, has also been reprimanded but he has been allowed to retain his pilot's license.

"The precise cause of the blaze has not been determined but the Marine Inspector, Mr. Barker, has postulated the possibility that a spark from a smoking passenger may have entered a porthole of the engine room and fallen on flammable material therein. Thank you, Mr. Speaker."

Mr. Collingwood Birchfield, MCP, from St. George's, one of the black members of parliament, rose to speak on the matter. "Mr. Speaker, I rise today to speak on the findings of the Court of Inquiry and the statement by the Honourable Member who just took his seat, speaking on behalf of the Board of Trade, the operators of the ferry system. First of all, any report on a disaster where human life was lost, that is prepared by a body containing the very same people who are responsible for operating the system in which the loss of life occurred, must be viewed with extreme caution. Mr. Speaker, I would venture to say, with strong suspicion."

MCP Hempworth jumped up, "Point of order! Mr. Speaker."

"Yes, Honourable Member Hempworth. What is your point of order?" The Speaker asked.

"The Honourable Member is impugning improper motives! This is against standing orders of this Honourable House."

Birchfield continued, "Mr. Speaker, I am not impugning improper motives, I am merely pointing out that the Marine Inspector, Mr. Barker, who is responsible for the safe maintenance of the ferries, including the *Wilhelmina*, and their fire protection systems, and the Marine Board which is responsible for the safe operation of all ferries, just might have a SLIGHT CONFLICT OF INTEREST in this matter."

"Proceed Honourable Member," the Speaker ruled.

"Thank you, Mr. Speaker. Let us look at the facts, shall we. The *Wilhelmina*, while beautiful, was an ageing vessel, her original engines being 27 years old. The Chief Engineer testified that her fuel lines leaked. Where would that fuel end up? In the bilges, Mr. Speaker. The Marine Inspector testified that *Wilhelmina*, 'Didn't make much water,' meaning that there was not much water leaking into the bilges through the openings for the propeller shafts, the so-called 'stuffing boxes.' That means that the bilge pump, that automatically pumps out the bilges when it reaches a certain level, sort of like the float system in a toilet, doesn't have to kick in very often. So, Mr. Speaker, with a leaky fuel line and infrequent bilge pump-outs, there would likely be considerable diesel fuel floating on top of the bilge water.

"Mr. Speaker, the Chief Engineer also testified that the first flames he saw were close to the bilge pump on the starboard side. We all know that electric motors can sometimes spark when they kick in. It seems highly likely that this was the source of the fire. We'll get back to why this obvious conclusion wasn't reached by the official report a little later.

"Mr. Speaker, that's not all. Chief Stone testified that he saw flames on the deck next to the engines but couldn't see what fuel the fire was burning. Diesel fuel is dark, and it doesn't catch fire that easily. If it was diesel fuel the Chief would have seen it. Could there have been another flammable liquid present? Well, Mr. Speaker, yes there could have been. There was a can of kerosene present in the engine room as well as a large can of gasoline. Both of these are highly flammable, much more so than diesel. If either of these liquids were also in the bilges, they could have easily been set alight by the sparking bilge pump and in turn set the diesel fuel alight.

"Mr. Speaker, the question begs, what were those two highly flammable liquids doing in the engine room? One of the main reasons for using diesel engines is their safety, diesel fuel being difficult to set alight. We aren't told what the kerosene was doing in there, but presumably as a cleaner or solvent. But it clearly represented a fire hazard. Worse still was the presence of gasoline. *Wilhelmina* had a diesel generator but had a gasoline back-up generator. Gasoline is so volatile, and its fumes even more so, there is no way it should have been kept beneath decks on a passenger ferry. While the gasoline tank miraculously didn't explode during the fire, any leaks from it would have found their way to the bilges."

"Point of order! Mr Speaker." MCP Hempworth exclaimed, jumping to his feet again. "The Honourable Member is speaking as though he is an expert in marine engineering. He is misleading the House!"

"Honourable Member Birchfield?" the Speaker queried.

"Mr. Speaker, I am from St George's, the end of the island with a maritime tradition that dates back 300 years. In St. George's we know boats."

"I too know something about boats, Honourable Member Hempworth, and the member is making sense. Proceed, Honourable Member."

"Mr. Speaker, what we have here is a ferry that had systemic fire hazards built into her. This was the responsibility of the owners and operators of the vessel, not Chief Stone. And who put the fuel tanks in the same room as the engines? No safe vessel would have that design feature. *Wilhelmina* was a big boat, there were lots of other places below decks that they could have placed the fuel tanks, other than close to the engines.

"Mr. Speaker, there's something else."

"Something else?"

"Yes. Mr. Speaker."

"Proceed Honourable Member."

"The other strange thing about this disaster was the effect the $CO_2$ bottles had on the fire. Instead of putting the fire out, as you would expect $CO_2$ to do, it spread it. How could that happen?

"Mr. Speaker, nowhere in this report does it say that the Board of Trade recovered any one of those bottles and tested it to see exactly what indeed was in those bottles – $CO_2$ or compressed air."

"Is that so Honourable Member Hempworth?"

"No, Mr. Speaker, they were not checked."

"Proceed Honourable Member Birchfield."

"Mr. Speaker, the effect of the released gas from those bottles had on the fire was more like compressed air, than $CO_2$. Who was responsible for the maintenance of those $CO_2$ bottles? The Board of Trade."

"So, Mr. Speaker, it is clear that heaping blame on the crew by the Board of Trade is using them as convenient scapegoats for the real situation which was that *Wilhelmina* had major systemic fire safety risks built into her, risks that were the responsibility of the Marine Inspector and the Board of Trade, not the pilot and the Chief. This is why they couldn't conclude the obvious, which was that the genesis of the fire was a spark from the bilge pump. If they had done that, it would have pointed the finger of blame at some of their own. And we can't have that!"

There was uproar in the Chamber.

"Point of order, Mr Speaker! The Honourable Member is definitely impugning improper motives now!" Hempworth protested.

The Speaker banged his gavel many times, "Order! Order! Honourable Member, I've given you a great deal of latitude, don't press it."

"Thank you, Mr. Speaker. I'm almost done. It was by Almighty God's providence and the heroic action of Skipper Jones and Chief Stone, who suffered severe burns to his hand and arms, that more lives weren't lost that fateful evening. This report is a whitewash! A complete whitewash! "Thank you, Mr. Speaker."

There was more uproar in the Chamber. The Speaker banged his gavel again and again. "Order! I will have order in this Chamber!" After members calmed down somewhat, the Speaker continued, "I now recognize the Honourable Member, Mr. J. Fred Tucklington. Honourable Member, you have the floor." Mr. Tucklington was a very portly gentleman with a bushy toothbrush type moustache, an architect by profession, and another of the black MCP's. He rose to speak.

"Thank you, Mr. Speaker. I have read the official report and all the reports from the newspapers. It is clear that the conduct of pilot Joshua Jones was exemplary, for his quick thinking, skill and cool head under what must have been a highly stressful situation. To blame him and reprimand him for not ensuring that there was always someone in the engine room is an insult to common sense and a travesty. He was up in the wheelhouse, steering the vessel. How was he to ensure that the engine room, which was on the lowest deck beneath his feet, was always manned? He had no physical way of seeing into the engine room from the wheelhouse through the deck. It was impossible. To blame him is just plain nonsensical! He is a pilot and a hero, but he is not God. He could not see through a teak deck!

"Mr. Speaker, I am reluctant to point this out, but the fire safety record of the Bermuda ferry service has been anything but exemplary. Why, it was just two years ago that the ferry *Dragon* blew up right off Albuoy's Point in a most spectacular fashion. She is now being rebuilt. We also know that the former ferries *Moondyne* and *Neptune* also met fiery ends. And the venerable ferry *Corona* has burned down twice, only to be rebuilt both times. Luckily, none of these incidents resulted in loss of life, but their existence speaks to a systemic problem, rather than the dereliction of duty by a particular member of the crew. Fire safety is clearly not a priority of the Bermuda Ferry Service.

"Mr. Speaker, I agree with the Honourable Member that just took his seat. The pilot and crew have been made scapegoats for deficiencies that were the responsibility of The Board of Trade and the Marine Inspector. The Board of Trade was unable, or unwilling, to find itself guilty. Thank you, Mr. Speaker."

As no vote was required, the House took note of the report of the Court of Inquiry into the *Wilhelmina* disaster.

Meanwhile, back at the Board of Trade office, Snapper Jones was given his official reprimand, in writing, from the management. He was furious and disgusted. "You guys ain't going to use me as no scapegoat. I'm outa here. Get some other fool to drive your boats. I quit!"

## Nato

Even though Evelyn had graduated from Scripps College with a bachelor's degree in political science, she was more pleased with the acquisition of her MRS. degree, that is, becoming Mrs. Jack Bessemer. She had no intention of using her tertiary education in any kind of professional or occupational capacity. Roberto and Lisa Benedetti had pampered their little princess from birth and there was no way she would be working somewhere from 9 to 5. Despite being a home maker, she, nevertheless, read the New York Times from cover to cover every day. Evelyn had become quite the hostess, relishing the frequent social functions she and Jack had either at their mini-mansion in Greenwich, or attended elsewhere with his academic colleagues. She delighted in engaging them on current affairs and politics and watching their astonishment when she articulated her insightful knowledge of world affairs and seeing their surprise at the realization that she was not just a pretty face, or some vacuous rich bimbo. She even was able to throw in some occasional scientific jargon she'd picked up from Jack.

But that social scene came to a screeching halt when Jack informed her that they were moving to Bermuda. "What! Bermuda? What's in Bermuda? Where the hell is that anyway. Some primitive backwater in the Caribbean?"

"No, darling, it's in the Atlantic, not that far from here. They've given me a very important job there, all leading-edge stuff. Stuff that'll be vital to our national security."

"National security. Really? what's it all about?"

"Vell, my dear, if I tell you I vill have to kill you," he said raising one eyebrow with a smirk.

"That important huh? Really?" He nodded.

"But what about my condition?"

"Not a problem, we'll get there long before your delivery date. The hospital there is very modern, I checked it out already. You and the baby will be fine."

"Oh, all right then," she said. Then pausing for a moment before her eyes lit up with a big grin on her face, she flew into his arms exclaiming, "It's going to be so exciting!"

And so it was, the Bessemers moved from Greenwich, Connecticut to Bermuda, but not without some hiccups. First of all, Evelyn was in her third trimester and was, "As big as a house," according to her own description. Notwithstanding this hyperbole, her condition did somewhat inhibit, but only somewhat, her natural inclination to organize, supervise and prioritize all aspects of their relocation to their new home. They boarded the Pan Am, Super Constellation at New York's Idlewild Airport, destined for Bermuda. After almost 3 hours, the announcement was made that they had started their descent to Bermuda. Shortly thereafter, Evelyn, who was seated by the window, exclaimed, "Jack, look! Look at that!" He leaned over and looked down at the ocean. It had transformed from a deep, marine-blue to a crystalline aqua colour, the likes of which the two of them had never seen before.

"Wow!" was all Jack could say. Then, as they glided over the outer northwest coral reefs, he exclaimed, "Look at that – coral reefs! I didn't think you'd be able to see them so clearly. Over there, the Island's over there," he said pointing to Commissioner's Point. That must be the Royal Navy Dockyard."

"That sailboat over there, floating over the reefs, looks like nothing's supporting it, nothing at all," Evelyn said in wonderment. The Constellation was in its final approach. It glided lower and lower, yet still they were over water. "Jack, where's the runway?"

"I guess we're making a water landing today," Jack said – face in a deadpan expression." She had seen this deadpan trick of his before and jabbed him in the ribs with her elbow. As they sank lower, looking very much like they were making a water landing, they suddenly skimmed over the top of some white roofed houses, over some more water, then, three years after starting work at Columbia, they touched down at Kindley Field Airforce Base, the home of Bermuda's only terrestrial airport.

It took the couple over an hour just to exit from the airport because they had so much luggage. Evelyn had brought everything that was not nailed down in the mansion in Greenwich. They had to hire three extra taxis to convey their belongings to the home they had rented in Fairylands in Pembroke Parish. "The cars here are so small," Evelyn observed.

A few weeks after arriving, Evelyn gave birth to a healthy baby boy whom they named Dwight, after the all-conquering President Dwight D. Eisenhower. Jack launched himself at his new duties and found himself spread between the SOFAR research facility in St. David's and Tudor Hill at the other end of Bermuda where there were two facilities: there was the Lab building where he worked with electronics and telecommunications experts and right next door was the actual US Navy listening post known as the NAVFAC. While the distance from SOFAR to Tudor Hill was not very far, from an American or British perspective, from the Bermudian perspective it was indeed far because it took over an hour to drive from one facility to the other, at the island's speed limit of 20 mph. The Navy had provided him with a small, ugly, grey, rattletrap Morris Minor. Evelyn grew to love the island and seamlessly slotted into wealthy Bermudian society.

Two years passed by very quickly while pushing the outside of the technology envelope in the field of underwater acoustics and analysis. One day the phone rang, and the receptionist quickly picked up, then buzzed Jack. "Dr. Bessemer, it's Dr. Armstrong on the line." Jack rustled through the chaos on his desk to find the telephone.

"Hank, how are you? If you're calling long distance, I know it must be pretty important."

"Hi Jack, how's it going out there in paradise?"

"Freakin' awful! You know, the same old grind: sunny warm days, perfect pink beaches with gorgeous girls in skimpy bikinis and all that sort of stuff. Man, this is a real hardship post you've lumbered me with – where's my hardship pay?"

"Alright, Alright. Don't rub it in! You know I'd switch places with you in a heartbeat."

"Now, Hank, I know you didn't call me all this way to talk about broads in bikinis. So, what's up?"

"You're right Jack. I've got a favour to ask."

"Sure, you name it. Anything, except coming back to New York to work."

"No, nothing like that. You know the threat posed by Soviet submarine launched missiles is not just to America, it's to all members of NATO. Our friends in Western Europe are even more threatened than we are. There's a technical conference taking place in London next week that I'm supposed to attend to update some of our NATO allies about Artemis. Now, I've got some fires that I need to put out in Washington – some senators have got some crazy ideas about what we're doing down there on the Island – ideas that need to be stamped out. So, I can't go. I'd like you to make the update in my stead. Can you do that for me?"

"Sure, why not, Hank. Exactly when is it?" Jack scribbled down the details on a yellow memo pad.

"I can arrange for the Navy to provide a transport, if you like."

"Oh, hell no! No thanks. I've already been on those flying rattletraps. I prefer an airliner, thank you very much. BOAC runs to London several times per week."

"Whatever you like. Thanks, old buddy." Then he hung up.

After Jack parked the SOFAR Morris Minor in the yard of his mansion in Fairylands, he was met by Evelyn, dressed casually, but very elegantly, as always, and little two-year-old Dwight ran out to greet him, crying, "Daddy, Daddy!" Jack picked him up and kissed Evelyn.

"Darling, I've got some news."

"What news?"

"Hank has asked me to brief our friends in London about Artemis. I'm booked to leave next Friday on BOAC."

"Can we come?" She asked.

"I'm afraid not, honey. This is strictly business and security is tight. You know, the usual cloak and dagger stuff. Anyway, I'm only going to be in London for three days, then I'll be back."

"Yeah, I know. We'll still miss you."

"Anyway, you'd be bored out of your wits. The repartee between engineers doesn't really make for an enjoyable evening, unless you speak technobabble."

"Uh-huh. I guess you're right."

The next Friday, Jack, Evelyn and Dwight were in the lounge waiting for the boarding of the BOAC flight to London. They were in the civilian part of Kindley Field, named after Captain Field Eugene Kindley, an American aviator ace who served with the Royal Airforce during World War I. The aircraft parked on the apron being refuelled was the fat, ungainly, four engine, double-decker, Boeing 377 Stratocruiser, the world's largest airliner. The only thing streamlined about the plane was the airline's "Speedbird" logo on the tail. *How does this thing even fly?* Jack thought. Their route to Europe would take them north to Gander, Newfoundland, for refuelling, then east to Shannon, Ireland, for further refuelling, then southeast to London's Heathrow airport.

The boarding announcement blared over the PA system and the assembled travellers started their walk across the tarmac to the plane. They were, as was the custom, dressed to the nines: men in business suits, including obligatory fedora hats and women similarly dressed in suits, their heads adorned with the latest in stylish headgear. Jack was attired more like an academic. He wore dark wool trousers, a tweed jacket with elbow pads, white shirt and dark striped tie, with an overall dishevelled appearance.

He kissed Dwight, then Evelyn saying, "Bye, darling, I'll be back before you know it."

The Stratocruiser was the last word in luxury. The best part was the lounge on the lower deck where passengers could socialize and stretch their legs, even though there was plenty of leg room in the seats on the main deck. The downside was the constant loud roar of the four 28-cylinder Pratt & Whitney Wasp engines and the fact that they had to endure two additional take-offs and landings before they reached their destination. Gander, Newfoundland, was particularly rough because of foul weather. Nevertheless, they safely arrived at Heathrow after a 12-hour journey. He now knew why they called it a "Red Eye" flight because after the overnight journey his body clock was totally askew.

Despite the travel fatigue, he had to report to the conference that afternoon for a briefing. After being required to show his ID documents several times, he was finally ushered into a large waiting room. There were many military officers from various NATO nations present as well as scientists like himself. There were also a few political figures present with their obligatory retinues of advisors. Jack was thankful that the actual meaty stuff on the agenda would not be until the next day, when he would be presenting his paper. Today was about the agenda itself and security clearances etc.

Just as these matters were winding down, Jack became aware of a sweet scent, a scent that was hauntingly familiar. He turned around and there, standing in front of him, was Anna Sokratis, smiling her megawatt smile.

Jack was stunned into silence, he just gaped. "Hello Jack," she said. "Are you just going to ignore an old friend?"

"Anna, what're you... how did you, I mean, you're the last person... Anna... I, I," he stammered.

She flew into his arms giving him a warm, tight, long hug. He felt the softness and voluptuousness of her body which sparked a cascade of memories of longing from years ago. Finally collecting himself, he said, "Anna, it's wonderful to see you, but...but, what are you doing here?"

"I'm part of the Ministry of Defence's science team! He really doesn't have much of a technical background, so my colleagues and I sift through all the jargon and prepare briefs for him that are understandable in plain English. But we weren't expecting you here either, we were expecting some other bloke from New York."

"He couldn't come, so he asked me to stand in for him."

"That's lucky for me," she said, shooting him a stare and another megawatt smile.

Jack's head was spinning. This was like all his fantasies from six years ago were coming true.

"Look," she said, "Now that we're virtually finished here, I'm meeting my brother Dino at the pub, why don't you come along? It would be great fun!"

"Sure, why not."

After the meeting was over, they took the Tube and got off at the fifth stop, walked across the street and got a table in the pub, The Spartac Arms. A few minutes after they received the first round, a tall athletically built man entered the room, smiled and came over giving Anna a kiss on the cheek. "Jack, this is my brother Dino. Dino, Jack, from Caltech, nowadays, from Bermuda."

"Oh right. Jack from Caltech. Heard a lot about you. Nice to meet you." Dino was quite pleasant but shortly after their first round he said, "Sorry but I've got to go. Got to take care of a few things."

"So soon?" Anna, said.

"You two have got a lot of catching up to do, you won't miss me. Jack a pleasure to meet you. See you again sometime." He shook Jack's hand and departed.

Jack was thinking, "This is how I'd wished it was when we were at Caltech, but I'm a married man now. Bad timing!"

After the third round she said, "We haven't had anything to eat yet. Why don't you come over to my place and I can whip us up something? It's just a short walk from here."

*Uh oh*, Jack thought. "We could eat here and save you the trouble."

"The food's awful here, come on." She got up, Jack settled the tab and they went outside. It was raining a London drizzle. Jack hoisted his brolly and she hooked her arm around his as they walked along the cobblestone sidewalks.

They reached her flat which was small but reasonably well appointed. She turned her focus on preparing a quick meal. "This is the Anna I know, focused on the task at hand." In very little time they were enjoying a tasty repast complete with generous portions of red wine.

Jack said, "Anna, you're so different now."

"Really, how's that."

"Well, you were so studious. Those books were like a castle, shielding you from all admirers. Now you seem so much more relaxed, more ... free, in fact. What happened to you?"

"Well, at Caltech, I had to work hard. There weren't many women in science in those days, and I was determined that nothing was going to get in my way, not even that sexy PhD engineering student that I met there." Jack grinned. "I had to prove myself."

"And did you?"

"Yes, things are working out brilliantly!" She exclaimed triumphantly.

"So, what's with the rest of your life? No husband, boyfriend, or kids? I mean, no offence."

"None taken. I had a boyfriend, but it didn't work out."

"Sorry."

"Don't be sorry. My life is my work, anyway."

After dessert Jack said, "I'd better be going, I've got a presentation to make tomorrow." She looked disappointed – even pouted a bit.

She helped him into his coat and handed him his hat. "Anna, it's been wonderful seeing you again. Thanks for dinner." Whereupon he bent over to give her a peck on each cheek, but after the second peck he found her big dark eyes looking up, imploringly, into his, and his lips were just one inch from her ruby, slightly open and puckered lips. Then she whispered, "Jack Bessemer, you and I have unfinished business."

*"Good lord, a goddess and a mind reader too?"* he thought. "Unfinished business?" He mumbled. She nodded.

His lips met hers and a torrent of pent-up passion was instantly unleashed.

His coat which had just been put on, came straight off. Their breathing became heavy as desire further engulfed them. They left a trail of items of discarded clothing leading to the bedroom, like the trail of crumbs through a dark forest. The bedroom, which was barely large enough to contain the queen size bed, contained a small vanity in one corner, featuring a large, decorative mirror. There was another large, ornately framed mirror on the wall behind the bed head.

He slipped off her blouse and bra. Her skin was so soft, so smooth, like warm satin, and he caressed her all over. The nipples of her perky breasts were erect, further inflaming his passion. He devoured them. She moaned with pleasure. Removing the rest of her clothing, he planted kisses in every conceivable part of her body. She then grabbed his belt, unbuckled it, unzipped the zipper and pulled down his trousers and boxers, giving a little playful exclamation at what then popped up. Then she returned the favour, moving her lips all over his body, especially the part that she had just unleashed.

Their amorous encounter lasted most of the night. Jack didn't get back to his hotel room until early morning, just enough time to shower, shave, change his clothes, gather up his papers and head for the conference. Fortunately, he had already fully written out his remarks before hand. After the business of the conference finished each day, Jack and Anna spent the night together.

The morning after his last sexual encounter with Anna before returning home, Jack reflected on his visit to London. He thought about Anna and smiled to himself, but almost immediately, the image of Evelyn popped into his head, and he was overcome with guilt. The conflict within him was, on the one hand, there was a sense of satisfaction of having realized a fantasy he had carried with him ever since he first met Anna outside the

Atheneum at Caltech, and on the other hand, shame in betraying his vows to the love of his life. He didn't know what to think. The more these thoughts rummaged around in his mind, the more upset he became with himself. He had always considered himself, "One of the good guys," but now he wasn't so sure. He eventually determined that this brief London interlude was a momentary aberration and that he needed to get back to his real life – a life that was good, with Evelyn at the centre of it.

While packing for his return trip, he heard a quiet knock on the door of his hotel suite. When he opened it, he was surprised to see Anna's brother, Dino, in the doorway. "Hi, Dino. This is a surprise. To what do I owe this pleasure."

Dino looked serious. "It's about Anna. May I come in?"

"Anna? Of course, come on in."

Dino entered the room and took a seat next to the coffee table with Jack sitting on the opposite side. "Now, what's happened to Anna?" He asked with great concern.

"Well Jack," Dino said in an even tone, "I regret to tell you things are not quite as they seem."

"Oh? How so?"

"Jack, the woman you know as Anna Sokratis is not who she says she is. Her real name is Anna Petrova and she doesn't work for the British Defence Ministry, she works for the KGB."

"The KGB! That's preposterous! I've known her since she was a student at Caltech!"

"When she was at Caltech, she was already a KGB agent, on assignment to find out about what was going on with the Manhattan Project in Los Alamos." A recollection of Anna asking him about Los Alamos back at Caltech flashed into Jack's mind, and he began to feel lightheaded. "You should also know that my name is not Dino Sokratis, it is Dimitri Tovovich. I am also employed by the KGB and am not her brother." Blood drained from Jack's face. "We have in our possession a treasure trove of film footage of you and Anna during the past three nights." He reached into his valise and showed a small reel of 8mm film.

"Jack, we know all about you and the lofty lifestyle that your wife and her family keep you in – way higher than your salary justifies. I wonder what she would think if she were to have a look at some of this film. I wonder what her Daddy would say if he found out. I wonder what the US Navy would think if they discovered that you were sleeping with a Russian agent?"

Jack went as white as a sheet, as he slumped in his chair. "Oh my God." He whispered. "Why me? I'm not important, I'm just a lowly engineer in Bermuda. What do you want from me?"

"We want to know about Project Artemis."

"Oh my God!"

Dino paused, allowing the importance of what he wanted to sink in.

"Don't worry, nothing's going to happen to you or your family. You can return to your Island and resume your normal life, as long as you remember you work for us now. With your superior intellect, you will figure out a way to tell us how Artemis works. I, or my designate, will be in touch with you when the time comes. Have a nice flight back home." Dino got up and left the room. Jack jumped up, rushed to the toilet and puked violently in the commode.

## La Pescadora Langosta

Yuri Kashenko's straight blonde hair was sticking to his head underneath his seaman's cap. Rivulets of sweat ran down the sides of his face, some of it getting in his eyes and burning them. He cursed loudly in Russian and extracted a grimy handkerchief from his pocket to wipe is face. He hated this assignment, hated his bosses, hated the system that put him under their control and, above all, hated Havana. As a seafaring man, his idea of an ideal assignment would have been cruising the Baltic off Leningrad, trawling in the cool crisp air for some big Baltic salmon while listening and observing what the Finns, Danes and Swedes were up to. But instead, he was stuck in the oppressive humidity of Havana, awaiting orders for a voyage to some unknown destination.

Furthermore, he didn't speak much Spanish, so it was going to be difficult communicating with his crew when the time came. While training to become a KGB agent, they made sure his English was passable, but this didn't help him for this assignment in Latin America. He was convinced he was ill equipped to serve Mother Russia in Cuba, and he plainly declared this to his superiors. But they refused to hear it, and he was posted here anyway.

The only upside to being posted in Havana was the senoritas. The Havana women came in such a wide variety of delectable colours and flavours, it made Yuri's head spin. Furthermore, the Castro revolution had impoverished the whole island, and so many of them were in such dire financial straits, the money he had in his pocket made him a magnet. All he had to do was to go into a bar and the girls would flock around looking to rent themselves to him for the evening. Each night he had a different one. While he enjoyed these distractions, he was a serious man and was impatient to commence his mission.

Yuri had inspected his command for this assignment. It was an old, small, rust-bucket that looked barely seaworthy. She had *La Pescadora Langosta* printed across her stern. The winch and other fishing gear were ancient, and the engine looked like an antique. Down below decks, the bilges sloshed around with mysterious things dissolved in them and floating on them. The bilge pump was going to have to run almost continuously to keep the bilges from overwhelming the vessel. The only thing that was modern on *La Pescadora* was her wireless and radar equipment, subject to the reliability of the old generator onboard. It was state of the (Russian) art, circa 1959. She had an extra high mast and a powerful transmitter. Moreover, her eavesdropping capabilities were excellent across a wide band of frequencies. Yuri had the crew working hard to improve the ship's seaworthiness in preparation for departure, whenever that was, and wherever their assignment was going to be.

Dawn peeked over the Sierra Maestra mountains. Yuri dismissed his consort from the previous evening with a sharp smack on the bottom. The girl yelped and shouted something at him in Spanish that he couldn't translate but understood. She grabbed her things and departed, making sure she took the money she had earned with her. Yuri took a cold-water shower that felt delightfully warm to him, dressed quickly and walked the short distance to the office of the Havana Import Company, a front for Russian activities in the island. He strode without stopping, past reception and secretaries' offices, through to the manager inside. He had already mentally prepared a strongly worded speech and was about to deliver it when the manager smiled and placed a large manila envelope in his hand.

"New orders, comrade." He said curtly in Russian.

Yuri hesitated. He didn't expect this development. He took the envelope and opened it. It contained detailed instructions, but before he could read them the manager said, "Bermuda. The Americans are up to something strange up there and we need to know what it is and how it's going to affect us, particularly our missile boats."

"When do I leave?"

"When will you be ready?"

"We've been ready for weeks!"

"Then you should sail before sunset."

"Da." He turned on his heels and headed for the door, turning to say, "Dasvidaniya."

Yuri went back to his apartment and collected the belongings he would need for this voyage. He had already packed them in a large sack which he slung over his back as he headed for the rust-bucket trawler. Most of his crew were already on board. They spent the rest of the day making final preparations and slipped their lines at 5:00pm. *La Pescadora Langosta* headed out of Havana harbour at full speed, a stately 10 knots.

Yuri checked the map from his spartan cabin. At best speed it would take his boat a little over a week to reach Bermuda waters, some 1,660 miles away. "Wait a minute, if I follow the Gulf Stream, my speed can be increased by 4-5 knots. I can cut days off my travel time, and fuel too." He set the appropriate course. With the absence of significant twilight in the tropics, before long, *La Pescadora Langosta* was chugging alone in the dark, underneath the vault of a starry sky, in the waters of the Bermuda Triangle.

The next morning Yuri noticed that the ocean was darker than the waters around Havana and a little rougher, even though the trades were of the same strength as the day before. He checked his plot and realized that they were transiting the Florida Straits where the Gulf Stream was squeezed between the Florida peninsula and the Bahamas and the ocean current was at its strongest. He intended to ride this baby all the way to Bermuda.

Even though *La Pescadora* appeared to be an old rust bucket, she had very powerful radar, thanks to Mother Russia, and after a few days of totally uneventful sailing, onboard radar picked up a blip bearing 040 degrees. It wasn't a ship because it was not moving, but it was very small.

"Alfredo, let's see what this blip is. Change course to 040," Yuri ordered.

"Si, Capitan, 040," the helmsman replied. Alfredo was a typical Cuban fisherman. He was descended from a combination of enslaved Africans, indigenous Amerindians and Spanish colonists. He was stockily built, with a prominent broad nose on his dark, brown-skinned face. His straight black hair was pulled back into a short pigtail and his scraggly beard was turning grey. He handled the helm with huge hands, gnarly from a lifetime of fishing in the waters of the Caribbean basin.

After a few hours, Yuri was able to get a visual on the object through his binoculars. At first, he couldn't make it out through the haze of humid ocean air. But as they drew nearer, he could see that it was some sort of offshore oil platform, the kind that could be found off the coast of oil rich Venezuela.

"Alfredo, you seen anything like that before?" He gave the binoculars to the helmsman to have a look. Alfredo had decades of experience at sea, particularly around the Caribbean basin. He peered through the glasses and studied the object.

"Looks like an oil platform to me. Maybe they've discovered oil off Bermuda, eh?" Yuri said.

"No, Capitan. I seen mucho oil platforms down in Venezuela, this no look like that. It too small. And no oil in these waters, Capitan."

"Then, what the hell is it?"

"Dunno, Capitan."

"Let's investigate."

"Si, Capitan."

They kept the trawler's bow directly on the object. As it drew nearer Yuri realized his helmsman was right, it was too small and spindly for a drilling platform. While there was a crane, oil platforms typically had a large tower on them which facilitated the assembly of the drilling pipes etc. The tower on this platform appeared to be a radio tower. As they approached, he could make out large lettering on the platform that said, "Argus Island." Then he saw an American Flag painted on one of the panels.

"Ah, Alfredo," he declared, "This is what we've come to investigate. I wonder what the Americans are up to?" He checked his plot. "This platform is seated on one of the two seamounts southwest of Bermuda. Let's cut our speed to 7 knots, make one slow circle around it, then we'll head towards the island to get a good look around."

"Si, Capitan."

He switched on the radio and sent a terse message to Havana – *La Pescadora Langosta* on station.

# Blackjack

When the Cuban fishing trawler appeared, then lingered around the Argus Tower, everybody concluded that it was the Russians trying to figure out what was going on out there. Jack knew that if he had any chance of saving his own bacon, he would have to devise a plan to get some intel to that ship. He knew he was committing treason and hated himself for it, but the KGB had him by the balls. He didn't know very much about the KGB, but he knew enough to be fearful for himself and his family. He would have to play along with them until he could figure out some way to extricate himself from their steel grip. He wanted to see this Cuban trawler for himself, so, he decided to conduct an "instrument inspection" out at the Tower.

His transport to the Tower was via *T-Boat,* skippered by Snapper Jones, and about 20 minutes after they sighted the Tower, initially low on the horizon, he caught sight of *La Pescadora Langosta,* slowly cruising about 5 miles beyond the Tower. Upon closer inspection, through his binoculars, he observed that the crew were executing their charade of deep ocean fishing.

"Hey, Snapper, that trawler, is that her usual proximity to the Tower?"

"Ya, Doc. I've never seen it get much closer than that. Never gets much farther away than that either. She's definitely a spy boat."

"Yeah, right."

As they drew closer to the Tower, he noticed there were a few other boats in the area. One of them was the *Captain Crunch,* Bayard Smith's boat. He knew Smith socially and knew he was a drinker and a gambler. As he watched the charter fishing boat slowly zigzag back and forth with its outriggers splayed, a crazy idea started to crystalize in his mind. "Is the *Captain Crunch* out here often?"

"Ya, Scaley likes the Argus Bank a lot," Snapper replied.

*That's never going to work,* he thought. But the more he thought about it, the more he realized it could actually work – under the right circumstances. After inspecting the electronic gear on the Tower, he spent a long time observing the *Captain Crunch* and *La Pescadora Langosta* through his binoculars on his way back to the mainland. By the time he disembarked

*T-Boat* at Albuoy's Point he had a fully developed plan of action in his mind.

The next day, at the Yacht Club, he spied Bayard Smith quietly having a drink by himself at a corner table. Jack invited himself to the table, much to Bayard's delight. After a few rounds Bayard said, "Jack, I often have a few of my mates over to the house on Friday nights to have a few drinks and play cards. You want to join us?"

"Sure, Bayard. Why not."

When Jack arrived at the Smith home there were a few guys who also frequented the Yacht Club there. He made sure he brought plenty of money with him. They had the card table all set up. They played a variety of card games, but Jack noticed that Bayard loved to play Blackjack. After four hours of drinking and gambling, Jack called a taxi which drove him home. He had, deliberately, lost almost all the money he had brought with him.

The next Friday, Jack took even more money with him. He had been sandbagging Smith last week because he had not revealed his ability to mentally calculate the probabilities of the types of cards turning up as the game progressed. His opponents had clearly forgotten that he had a PhD in electrical engineering – a quantitative science that could be adapted to "counting cards." Jack also used his first session to observe the players as they became more and more intoxicated as the evening wore on. His observation of Bayard was that the more alcohol he consumed the more risks he took.

This evening started as before, but this time Jack didn't intentionally lose. He slowly but steadily increased his stash, ensuring that the other players had sufficient time to become thoroughly inebriated. He nursed the same drink the whole evening. Eventually, the moment arrived. Jack had calculated the odds of Bayard having a hand that could beat his as extremely remote. He took all the money that he had, that which he brought with him plus all that he had won during the evening. "I'm all in," he declared, "Five thousand pounds."

Bayard peeked at the card that was face-down, then said, laughing heartily, "Jack, I don't have that much cash here, but I'm not caving! Will you take an IOU?"

"Come on Bayard, why don't you just cave?" one of the other players said.

"Oh, no. He's bluffin', I know it! He's bluffin'!" slurring his speech. "Well, Jack, will you take an IOU?"

"OK, here's an idea, why don't you put up your stake in the *Captain Crunch*? That ought to cover it." Jack countered.

"You Yanks drive a hard bargain, but OK, what I got here on the table plus my stake in the *Crunch*." Jack nodded. "I got you now, bye!" Smith declared.

He turned over his cards, the four of them added up to 20. "Beat that!" he bellowed.

Jack turned over his four cards – they added up to 21. Bayard's bloodshot eyes bulged. "Shit! Yuh one bleddy, lucky son-of-a-bitch. I can't believe it!" He reached for a half empty glass of rum and coke and drained it. "Let's go again. I want to get my money back! Let's go again, all or nothin'!"

Realizing this was getting serious, one of the other players said, "Come off it, Bayard! You've got nothing to bet with. You're already cleaned out! Just pack it in!"

Bayard started dealing cards to Jack and himself using the remaining cards in the deck. Jack put his hand on the cards, "Hold on, Bayard. What are you putting in the pot now?"

Bayard glowered at Jack, he was genuinely angry now. "Seeing that you've already got the note on the boat that bye Desilva owes me, I'll throw in the mortgage he owes me on the house. That will more than enough cover what you've got."

Jack said, "You sure you want to do this? Why don't we call it quits right now and call it a night, huh?" Jack already had what he came for – the note on the *Crunch*.

The other players chimed in, "Yeah, let's call it a night – now!"

"No, no, no! One last hand!" Bayard bellowed.

"Ok, ok," Jack said reluctantly, knowing full well what cards were left in the deck. One of the other players took what was left in the pack, shuffled them and dealt them to each player. Each peeked at the card facing down. Jack said, "Hit me." It was the Ace of Clubs. Bayard said, "Hit me. Hit me again." His face fell, the two cards showing were the queen of spades and the king of hearts. The only way for him to win was if the downward card was an ace. He was "busted." Jack turned over his card, it was the queen of hearts – blackjack!

"Well, gentlemen, I guess that's it. We'll settle up tomorrow, Bayard. Goodnight." He gathered up his winnings and departed, totally unconcerned that Bayard might renege on his bet. The bets were done in front of his peers and there was only one thing worse than losing money, and that was losing face.

# The Consulate

Upon arrival at the civilian airport, Bob Carpenter was greeted by his driver, Tony Fox, who was giving him a guided tour of places of note on the drive from the airport. One thing he did notice was that his was the only American car anywhere to be seen. All the other vehicles were of the British variety with the steering wheel appropriately on the right-hand side. His car was a left-hand drive vehicle, even though they still had to drive on the left-hand side of the road. It was somewhat disorientating. The consulate car also had little flags of Stars and Stripes fluttering from the front fenders.

"Tony, who are all these folks on those motor bikes?" Carpenter asked.

"They're your folks, sir, Americans – tourists. They're everywhere this time of year."

"My folks, huh."

"Ya, you can easily tell them from their rental mopeds."

"So, what's the difference between a motorbike and a moped?"

"A moped is a motorcycle that also had pedals that the rider can use to help out its very small engine either to get started or climb hills. It's a combination of a motorbike and a pedal bicycle. As you can see, most of these folks are quite unsure of themselves on our roads because virtually none of them have any experience riding mopeds. Added to that, Bermuda roads are very narrow, hilly and winding. And most importantly, being from the States, they are unaccustomed to driving on the left-hand side of the road."

"Right."

Due to the narrow, winding roads, there were few opportunities for Tony Fox to overtake, so most of their drive was behind these slow, wobbling riders whom Carpenter found quite comical. Occasionally, a local rider would overtake both the consulate car and the wobblies at what seemed like, by comparison, death defying speeds.

On those occasions Tony Fox would mutter, "Them bleddy diddlybops!"

"Er... Tony, what was that, a diddy .... what?

"A diddlybop, sir."

"Tony, what the heck is a diddlybop?" Carpenter inquired.

"I'm sorry, Mr. Carpenter, I'm afraid I was thinking out loud. Not a good idea."

"No problem, but I'm curious as to what a diddlybop is. Never heard that word before."

"Well, sir, it's what we-byes call those youngsters with those souped-up bikes that zigzag in and out of traffic. They're a menace to other drivers."

"Diddlybops, huh. Well, I guess that's part of my first day's education in Bermudian lingo."

"I guess so, sir," Fox replied with a chuckle.

Carpenter remembered driving in official cars in the Caribbean and Latin America and being accompanied by a phalanx of outriders that cleared the way for official cars. He noted that, by contrast, in Bermuda everything was low-key, no outriders, no fuss, no bother. They slowly drove along, stuck behind wobbling tourists like everybody else, except, of course, the diddlybops. *I think I'm going to like it here,* Carpenter thought.

They drove through a pair of pillars with the name Chelston written on them. Upon arrival at the front door, they were greeted by Chelston's butler, Milton Lawrence, who was a slim dark-skinned Bermudian, greying at the temples, with a big smile. "Welcome to your new home Mr. Consul General. My staff and I are at your service, at all times. Nothing is too small or too trivial for us not to consider it a priority."

When Carpenter emerged from the white consulate car, Milton was slightly taken aback by the imposing physical presence of the new Consul General. He was a tall man with broad shoulders, looking like he could have been a line-backer for an American football team in his younger days. His hairline was now slightly receding, with a touch of grey at the temples. However, his manner was very easy going, meeting Milton with a warm, firm handshake and a disarming smile, one almost as big as Milton's.

Milton thought, *This is going to be alright.*

In an island paradise that had, since the War's end, become the playground for the wealthy international elite, it was difficult for any luxurious estate to stand out. Despite this plethora of lavish residences, Chelston was unique. When Milton showed him around his new home, Bob was astounded by the new digs and the estate that Uncle Sam had provided him with.

"Milton, I've been to a number of US embassies around the world, but I've not seen anything quite like this before. It's almost like something out of a Hollywood movie. How did the US Government come to own an estate of this size and splendour? Do you know the history of this place?"

"Why yes, Mr. Carpenter, I do. This property goes back over one hundred years and has been owned by several prominent Bermuda families, families for whom some Bermuda streets and roads are named up to today. However, in 1937 it was purchased by a certain Mr. C.P. Dubbs, from Texas. Believe it or not, the "C" stood for Carbon and the "P" stood for Petroleum. Guess what business he was in?"

"Shipbuilding? Hotels?" Carpenter asked in a phony puzzled, inquiring tone.

"Mr. Carpenter, surely you jest." Milton wasn't yet accustomed to his boss's sense of humour.

"Of course, Milton. The oil business."

"Not just the oil business, sir, but he was a Texas oil man. 'CP', as he was known, was a chemical engineer who invented and patented an improved process for cracking crude oil into its more commercially useful, refined constituents, most importantly gasoline. Even though his process was soon rendered obsolete, these patents were widely used and earned CP a great deal of money. So much so that he decided to move to Bermuda where there is no income tax. He bought Chelston, completely demolished the house and stables, then built much of what you see here today."

"Well, how'd it become the property of the US State Department?"

"Well, Mr. Carpenter, while CP moved to Bermuda, he didn't just disappear. He travelled to the States a great deal, and shot off his Texan mouth an awful lot, particularly about how he was stiffing Uncle Sam. He ended up in court and the legal battles between him and Uncle Sam went on and on and on. Well, it wore old CP right out and he died. To settle his estate, and his tax problems, his heirs transferred the ownership of Chelston to the US Government, and that's how it became the residence of the US Consul General."

"That's a very interesting story, Milton. I guess CP's loss is my gain, at least while I'm here on this assignment."

"Well, sir, I hope you enjoy your stay at Chelston.

"Thanks Milton."

The Consulate office was in Hamilton, in an office building called the Vallis Building. After settling in, Bob Carpenter called in his secretary, Janice Morrison. Janice was originally from England, first coming to the Island as part of the 1,500 strong army of censors that the Imperial Department of Censors His Majesty's Government used to read all transatlantic mail during the War. She fell in love with one of the SeeBees who came to the Island to build the two US bases, one for the Navy, the other for the Air Force. They were married and stayed on after the War was over. She had taken US citizenship. Her considerable language skills were a great asset to the Consulate.

Waiting to see him was the head of security, Major Eugene Lewis Vindham, United States Marine Corps. He was the officer in charge of security at both the Tudor Hill facilities: the top-secret NAVFAC buildings and the Tudor Hill Lab, as well as the Argus Tower, also known as Argus Island. Vindham was a professional soldier. He was a World War II veteran, having stormed ashore under heavy Japanese fire in various, now forgotten, dots on the map of the Pacific Ocean. He also served in combat in Korea, thus acting in and witnessing the opening act of the Cold War, even though the only thing cold about the Korea conflict was the weather, the military activity was anything but cold. His posting in Bermuda was supposed to be an easy one, a reward for a long and faithful combat career for his country. He had tried marriage twice but neither worked out. His official line was that his only spouse was the USMC – because the Corps was, if nothing else, totally predictable. After the usual introductory pleasantries, the Major suggested that Carpenter tour the US facilities on the island.

The next day Carpenter's white consulate car was waiting for him outside Chelston. While the item on his agenda for the day was a tour of Tudor Hill, the tour of the western parishes of the Island started the moment Tony Fox left the driveway. They drove slowly and Tony pointed out places of interest along the route. Carpenter was amazed how beautiful the island was, with its pastel-coloured houses, white roofs and its incredible state of cleanliness. The ocean was never far away, and he couldn't believe that so many shades of blue were possible. Part of Carpenter wished that he was not on business and that he had time to stop and linger at some of the more interesting places. He decided that he would have to make time for that later. They came upon one of the few straightaways to be found on the island's roads. Just beyond its halfway point, a colourful sign in the shape of a fish came into view, with its nose pointing into a side road. On it was written "Pompano Beach Club." Fox turned left into the narrow road which was flanked on both sides by cultivated farmland. Looking up the road, Carpenter saw that it disappeared over a hill that was thickly wooded with casuarinas. Nothing else was visible from the main road. Carpenter asked, "Uh… Tony, are we detouring for a drink at this hotel's bar?"

"No sir. We'll be at Tudor Hill momentarily." There was a fork in the narrow side road as it approached the hill and Tony veered right. It wound through a thicket of casuarinas. When they rounded the last turn, instead of finding themselves at the entrance of the Pompano Beach Club, they were confronted with a high chain-link barricade, and a pair of turnstile security gates that were guarded by US marines, carrying rifles.

"This is the Tudor Hill Facility, Mr. Carpenter," Tony declared.

"Right!" Carpenter replied. "Quite tucked away, isn't it!"

After showing their credentials to the marine in charge, they headed for the building on the right – the Lab. There they were met by Major Vindham. He started the tour in the communications room of the lab providing Carpenter with an opening briefing.

"Welcome Mr. Consul General." He knew that the new Consul General was well connected in Washington DC and therefore needed to be handled respectfully and carefully.

"Mr. Carpenter, I'm not certain how fully you have been briefed on the Navy's operations on the island, so please forgive me if I cover ground that you are already aware of. While our operations here are critically important and classified, we are painfully aware that it is impossible to hide the actual presence of the Argus Tower from the public. It's there for any fisherman to see, but we have endeavoured to mask its real purpose, to the greatest extent possible. Moreover, it is imperative that our operations at this facility at Tudor Hill be kept top secret. We are on the island's most sparsely populated sector where there is a straight line to the Argus Tower, 25 miles southwest. It has all the security features one would expect for a facility of this nature, barbed wire fencing and warning signs, high security access gates that are guarded by US Marines 24 hours a day, 7 days a week. The location of the facility on the west coast lends itself to security.

"The Tower and these two facilities are critical elements in a network of listening posts scattered across the Atlantic, designed to protect the homeland against the threat of submarine missile attack from the Soviet Union."

"Hmm, yes. I can see now why this place must be secure." Carpenter interjected. "Sorry to interrupt Major, please proceed with your briefing."

"Thank you, sir. Taken together, the entire system is called SOSUS, which stands for Sound Surveillance System. It is vital that the existence of the leading-edge technologies being developed here are not revealed to the Russians, and it is my job to ensure that will never happen."

"Yes, I see," repeated the Consul General, gravely.

"But there is a problem sir."

"Oh, what's that, Major?"

"The problem is that the people developing these technologies are scientists and engineers – not soldiers or sailors, or diplomats like yourself. And, as brilliant as they are, I do not think they are 100 percent trustworthy."

"Is that right? Do you have evidence of treasonous activity?" Carpenter queried.

"No sir, not at this time. However, you will remember that it was the scientists, like Karl Fuchs and the Rosenbergs, who gave the Soviets America's A-Bomb secrets, allowing them to develop their own bombs so very quickly. To make matters worse, Fuchs, who was part of the team that developed the Bomb in Los Alamos was a British citizen. Therefore, my conclusion is that British security services, like MI5, are totally inadequate and that the whole of the British scientific community, is riddled with communists or their sympathizers."

"That's quite a sweeping indictment, Major, isn't it?"

Ignoring Carpenter's question, Vindham continued, "Therefore, it logically follows that, as a British colony, Bermuda is similarly riddled with Russian agents. "To make matters worse, most of the scientists and engineers at SOFAR here in Bermuda, aren't actually Navy personnel at all, instead they work for US electronics companies under contract to the Navy. This loose arrangement makes my life even more complicated."

"Yes, I can see that, Major. I'll keep my eyes and ears open on my end," he said with a wry smile that infuriated the paranoiac Major.

Vindham swallowed his irritation from this smarmy, slimy diplomat and said, "Shall we continue with the tour sir?" And he gestured forward gallantly.

"By all means, Major."

Nevertheless, the Major had developed detailed files on every staff member, military or civilian, and tried to keep tabs on their movements both on and off base.

"One more thing, Mr. Carpenter, I regularly visit and spent time at the Argus Tower and carefully observe procedures out there. There is a Cuban registered trawler, *La Pescadora Langosta* that prowls around the Tower like a giant shark circling its prey, at about a 5-10 mile radius, waiting for an opening to strike. Of course, striking isn't her mission, is it? Her mission is eavesdropping and visual observation. The Argus Tower is well beyond Bermuda's territorial waters, so there is nobody, neither the British nor the Americans, that can do anything about it. I'll bet you a million bucks there's at least one member of that crew that speaks Russian."

"I'm not taking that bet," Carpenter laughed.

They passed by endless electronic devices, some with dancing oscilloscopes, some with flashing tiny LED's, some with regular analogue dials and some that looked like oversized tape recorders, none of whose purposes was explained, primarily because Vindham had no clue what they were for.

He continued, "Of course, the official purpose of the Argus Tower is to conduct 'marine research.' Most people in Bermuda interpret that to mean the Navy is interested in the marine life in the area, or the exploration of the deep ocean – something like a naval version of Jacques Cousteau. The local fishermen use the Tower as a navigational aide. It helps them find the Argus Bank more easily. Also, the structure does actually attract fish."

They crossed over to the next building.

The Major continued, "You are now entering the NAVFAC building. This, sir, is the most secret building in Bermuda." They entered into a very large room with a high ceiling. At one end was a huge map of the Atlantic Ocean with icons on it.

"Those icons are the Russian submarines that we are currently tracking and their positions in the Atlantic." There were about 40 naval technicians stationed at an equal number of consoles. "These units are what we call LOFAR desks, which stands for Low Frequency Analog Receiver. You see, Mr. Carpenter it is the low frequencies that travel best under water."

"Oh, I see."

"These units are connected to arrays of hydrophones that fan out on the ocean floor out over 100 miles. These units analyze the signals from the hydrophones to tell us what kind of boat we're tracking, and also what it's doing. Amazingly, each boat has its own particular acoustic pattern, something we call an acoustic signature. So, we can actually tell what boat it is. The difficulty is that the ocean is a noisy place, so it is the job of these units to filter out the noise so that we can analyze the important sub sounds. These units are manned 24 hours a day, seven days a week."

"Bermuda was the first of these facilities to be set up by the Navy, as we are perfectly positioned as a listening post here. The data gathered here are routed to CINCLANT, then to our surface and submarine fleet commanders in the Atlantic."

"CINCLANT? Speak English Major."

"'CINC' stands for Commander in Chief. 'LANT' stands for Atlantic. There's also a 'CINCPAC'," Vindham said patiently. "The information we provide is so secret that our fleet doesn't even know where the information comes from."

Another man joined them.

"Ah, Jack, meet the new US Consul General, Mr. Robert Carpenter. Sir, this is Dr. Jack Bessemer, one of the leading scientists at this station. He knows a hell-of-a-lot more about the workings of this station than I ever will."

"Pleasure to make your acquaintance Mr. Carpenter."

"Please call me Bob."

The Major didn't approve of such informalities.

"OK. Bob," Jack continued. "The Tower and the Tudor Hill Lab were built to facilitate research and the deployment for Project Artemis. The concept of Artemis is to construct a giant Sonar machine. The initial sonic pulse, or more precisely a blast, is emitted from a powerful array of transducers connected to a specially designed ship out there in the ocean. The pulse travels thousands of miles through the ocean, via the SOFAR Channel, bounces off any submerged submarines in the area, and the echoes from them are picked up by hydrophone arrays laid off Argus bank. These hydrophones are connected to the Tower, then rerouted via another submarine cable to Tudor Hill for processing and analysis.

"How do you know if they are Russian subs or not?"

"Well, we know where ours are, so if they're in a different location we assume they're Russian. Bob, here we've had to become inventors, fabricators and testers of all this stuff. Much of it doesn't really exist anywhere else in the world. My specialty is hydrophones. We've actually had to invent devices and instruments to build these new listening devices in NAVFAC and invent others to measure the meaning of their output, and yet more instruments to interpret whether the devices were functioning properly. It is a very busy place and heaven for scientists and engineers in the field."

"We have developed third and fourth generation hydrophones right here at the Tudor Hill Lab, plus a lot of the signal analyzers as well."

"So, the Lab does the research, and the NAVFAC puts it to use," Carpenter observed.

"Yeah, through the SOFAR channel we can actually hear them a thousand miles away. We've discovered that Russian subs are quite noisy, even when submerged, and each sub has its own acoustic signature. Any one of these guys here can identify a Russian sub just from listening to it, and we're in the process of developing devices that can automatically I.D. enemy subs without human intervention."

"Incredible!" Carpenter was truly impressed.

Listening to Dr. Bessemer, the Major thought, *This guy is quite interesting. Most of the personnel at the Tower and Tudor Hill socialize with other American base personnel from the nearby Naval Operating Base or other GI's from the Air Force Base at Kindley Field. Jack Bessemer, on the other hand, lives in one of the most upscale neighbourhoods in the Island, known as Fairylands, and regularly socializes with the local muckty-mucks. Scuttlebutt has it that his wife is loaded.*

After an hour of looking at dials and consoles and squiggly lines on long strips of paper, whose purpose he did not understand, and talking to scientists who appeared to be from planet Xenon, Carpenter had become quite weary, and was glad when the tour was over.

On the drive home Carpenter mused, *Vindham doesn't like me – thinks I'm just another Washington insider who has been given a plumb assignment in the sun, sea and sand for having raised huge piles of money for somebody's election campaign. He has no way of knowing of my previous activities with the OSS, during the War, now the CIA. The principal reason I'm here is the security of the critically important Naval facilities in Bermuda. But that info is on a 'need to know' basis and clearly Vindham, or anybody else, doesn't need to know, do they?*

# Jenny Tucker

Major Eugene Vindham told everybody that, after two failed marriages, he was now, "Married to the USMC." Although there was some truth to this, in terms of his dedication, the USMC did not satisfy the full spectrum of his physical needs. He therefore became a regular customer of the Grenadian Hotel, an establishment where a customer could obtain a drink and compliant female companionship at a reasonable price. The hotel premises had lost some of the splendour that it once possessed during the war, but there were enough US servicemen stationed on island to provide an inexhaustible supply of willing customers.

Whenever Eugene Vindham climbed up the stairway into the main bar, he would be warmly greeted by the hulking, jocular figure of Dick Grenadian, aka "Papa Dick," the hotel's proprietor. "Welcome, Major. It is wonderful to see you again." As an astute businessman, Dick would, without prompting, steer him over to his favourite table in the corner and give the bartender the signal to bring him his usual libation. Then, as if by magic, a Grenadian Hotel "Hostess" would appear and take her place at the Major's table.

Papa Dick knew that this particular client had very particular tastes. It could not be just any of his hostesses, it had to be Jenny Tucker. As with most military men, they were not just creatures of habit, you could set your watch by their habits. So, each Tuesday and Friday at 20:00 the Major would appear at the Hotel bar. Therefore, Jenny would always be ready for him.

Like all Papa Dick's hostesses, Jenny Tucker originated from a very disadvantaged background. She never knew her father. The only thing she knew about him was that he was a British sailor on shore leave in Bermuda. Jenny's black Bermudian mother had been one of Papa Dick's girls from before the War, but she had died from an unknown affliction shortly after Jenny was born. She was raised by her mother's relatives in the poorest area of Hamilton, known as "Back a Town."

Jenny was poor but not without resources. Her most potent resource was her looks. Her long, naturally curly, rust-coloured hair framed a light brown face that featured prominent dimples and a few freckles on either side of full lips. Her large, medium-brown eyes were captivating. Dick had noticed her as a teenager. He told her if she needed money, she could be a waitress at the hotel. Indeed, it was in that capacity that she served while she was still underage. Jenny was a true diamond in the rough, having grown up Back a Town, and had no airs, graces or social affectations that were part of the bag of tricks typical of Papa Dick's hostesses. Dick knew that she had the potential to be good for his business and assigned one of his senior girls to train and help her refine her craft and explain to her the financial benefits of becoming a hostess at the Grenadian Hotel. Jenny Tucker learned her lessons well, and, as she matured, she became one of Papa Dick's most exotic and sought-after hostesses.

Vindham was completely bewitched by Jenny. The spell she cast on him was all encompassing. He would often give her personal gifts on top of the standard remuneration for her time and favours. Jenny, having become a master of psychological manipulation, continuously pressed him for more favours.

She had her own pet-name for the Major — Vinny. When they were in bed she told him, "Vinny, I want to get out from under Papa Dick's grip and be your lady — alone. Only then can you be my only man." He kept giving her personal gifts, but she merely used them as leverage to up the ante and pressure him to take her from under Papa Dick's control. She said, "Vinny, I love you and really want to be your woman, just yours, but you need to show me how much you love me."

"Jenny, you know I love you. How can I prove it to you?" Vindham asked.

"I want my own house, a house we can share. Vinny, can you buy me a house? Can you do that for me?"

"I don't know, Jenny. Houses cost a lot of money. Where am I going to get that kind of money on a Marine Corps salary?"

"You want to make me happy, don't you? You want us to be together, don't you?" her big eyes gazing straight into his.

"You know I'll do anything to make you happy, but this ain't easy, you know. I don't know how I can do that."

She started to pout, her brown eyes welling up, morphing into soft sobbing.

The tough old Major, veteran of two wars, struck his colours and surrendered.

"Ok, ok, I'll see what I can do," he said.

"Really?" she cried. He nodded. "Oh, Vinny, you make me so happy!" The tears instantly evaporated, and she kissed him passionately, then rolled on top of him and gave him a bonus, "On the house!"

In the subsequent weeks, Vindham quietly took Jenny to see several houses to decide which one she preferred. Eventually, she found one to her liking – the biggest of the lot. He quietly settled with the seller, no mortgage involved. Unfortunately for him, this was not the end, in fact, it was just the beginning. He ended up paying for all her living expenses, a car, clothes, furs, jewellery and trips abroad. Jenny Tucker had struck the motherload! Also, she wasn't exactly discreet about her newfound affluence. She believed in the adage "If you've got it – flaunt it!"

Papa Dick was not at all pleased with Jenny's departure. "I invested a lot of time and money in that girl, you know," he grumbled, "And now she just walks out on me. Just like that – with one of my best clients, at that! Whatever happened to gratitude and loyalty?" Despite all his intimidating bulk and confident swagger, Dick was not a vindictive man. He had suspected that Jenny was playing the Major but was surprised at the extent of it. But, as a seasoned businessman, he knew that it really didn't matter to his business in the long run. He would merely adjust.

# The Drop

Surveillance could be an extremely boring affair. *La Pescadora Langosta* spent virtually all its time slowly cruising in the vicinity of the Argus Tower. Most of the time within visual range, but always within radio range. Most of the communications between the Tower and Tudor Hill were, in fact, audio signals and unencrypted. That was because most of them were routine housekeeping messages. Sometimes encrypted signals were sent via Morse Code that Yuri couldn't decipher at all. Other times the audio transmissions used code words that were meant to fool unauthorized listeners, like him, but by continuously listening he was able to guess what some of these code words meant and therefore was able to infer at least some of their meaning. Yuri was also convinced, "There must be a hard line between the Tower and the onshore base as well."

It became clear to him that the Argus Tower was some kind of listening post, perhaps part of an American effort to detect Russian submarines. Yuri could plainly see what looked like heavily armoured submarine cables connected to the platform going down to the ocean depths. And, despite appearing to the naked eye to be in the middle of an empty ocean, the Argus Bank was a fairly busy place. Utility boats called regularly from Bermuda, as well as many charter fishing vessels that came daily to try to catch "Big ones" out here on the Bank.

Early one morning, just as dawn was breaking, such a craft appeared at the Bank, trolling for game fish. He had his outriggers splayed and was following a zig zag course at about 8 knots. But the fishing boat was getting closer to *La Pescadora* with each zig. Yuri could occasionally read the name on the boat's stern – the *Captain Crunch*. *Strange name*, he thought. The boat changed its course once again and plainly was heading right for them. Yuri was watching the boat intently because of its behavior. They'd been on station for months, and, except for being overflown by the occasional naval patrol plane, no one had ever approached them – until now.

There appeared to be only one person aboard the *Crunch*, as it approached. It passed them by only about 10 meters, and as it did so, her skipper tossed a glass bottle in the water between them. The boat continued on its course, zig zagging from time to time at 8 knots.

"Alfredo, have one of your men pick up that bottle and bring it to me," Yuri ordered. Alfredo went himself, fetched a net on a long pole, retrieved the bottle and brought it to his skipper. He opened it and the message was simple and direct, "Be here tomorrow morning – same time." Yuri returned to his cabin and checked his plot. He returned to the deck and took a bearing on the Tower. The crew were all looking at him. He glared at them and shouted, "Volver al trabajo!" (Get back to work!) He returned to studying the *Captain Crunch* as it receded.

Next morning, just after dawn, Yuri spied the charter boat, in trolling mode, zig zagging, as before. Eventually the *Captain Crunch* approached to about 10 meters and the skipper tossed a bottle overboard and proceeded on his way. Yuri opened the bottle with great anticipation. He spread the paper on the cabin table, his breath caught in his throat. The paper contained a schematic diagram of an American hydrophone fully labelled and documented. He took the paper, folded it carefully and locked it in the cabin safe. He turned to the plot and plotted his course back to Havana.

"Alfredo, secure fishing gear. Set course to 230 degrees, we're going home."

The helmsman smiled, "Si, Capitan." He was pleased to be returning to Havana.

# Evacuation

It was September 1959, and Snapper Jones, stood at the SOFAR Station on top of St. David's Island. After quitting his job driving ferries for the Bermuda Government, he had become a utility pilot for SOFAR, being licensed to drive all their vessels, from the largest to the smallest. He surveyed the entire expanse of the Kindley Field Air Force Base. The 59th Weather Reconnaissance Squadron was stationed there. Among the usual jam of aircraft on the Base, he could easily distinguish the Hurricane Hunters – WB40's, converted World War II B-29 long range bombers. They stood out, due to their bright orange and yellow tails. They were quite busy because of Hurricane Gracie. She was a large and powerful hurricane whose meanderings around the Western Atlantic had created quite a stir in Bermuda's military and nautical circles. This was what the 59th lived for. Consequently, the lumbering Hurricane Hunters were launching and landing from the base around the clock. Gracie was one of the most unpredictable hurricanes ever, first coming through the Greater Antilles, approaching the US mainland, turning out to sea, then backtracking.

The 59th were having a challenging time keeping track of Gracie, as little was known of the underlying factors causing the motion, direction and intensity of hurricanes. Thus, the Hurricane Hunters had to continuously fly into these storms and endure being constantly bashed about, to monitor their location, measure wind speed, barometric pressure, humidity, size and overall intensity.

Bermudians, on the other hand, had developed methods over the centuries of oceanic island living to help forecast these big weather events. While Snapper respected the scientific methods used by the Hurricane Hunters, he also was skilled in the more traditional tools of weather forecasting, passed down from his ancestors to his father and then to him. There was one primary tool – shark oil. Shark oil, when properly prepared, was a reliable predictor of stormy weather. It acted somewhat like a barometer. Kept in a glass jar hung outside, the oil naturally contained sediment. When the weather was going to be fair, the sediment settled to the bottom leaving a clear liquid on top. However, a fall in the barometric pressure caused the clear oil to become turbid – a warning of impending foul weather.

Experienced Bermudian mariners also always kept an eye on cloud patterns and the sea itself. All Bermudian mariners knew hurricanes announced themselves days in advance with the nature and size of the waves on the island's south coast. Snapper's small apartment overlooked the south shore, and he could tell, even without seeing the activity of the 59th, that something was brewing out there. When he arrived at SOFAR that morning, he entered the Director, Carl Cardigan's, office and said, "Carl, we need to get them byes off the Argus Tower and back to the island."

"Why, what's going on?"

"We might have a blow comin'."

"Well, I've seen the Hurricane Hunters getting really active, but I thought we were supposed to be in the clear."

"Carl, look at yuh barometer." He went over to a large mercury barometer on the wall. "Pressure's fallin', init?"

"Yeah, but that doesn't necessarily mean ..."

"My shark oil's cloudy and look at them waves."

"Waves?"

"Ya, come outside."

They went outside and looked out towards the south.

"Feel that?"

"Feel what?"

"Ya, exactly. There ain't no wind, init?"

"No, hardly any."

"Right! Now, take these-here binoculars and look at those swells along the coast."

Carl peered through the binoculars. "Yeah, I see 'em. So what?"

"See how those swells are coming in, all in line-like; something like soldiers all lined up, marching in formation. There's no wind, right? What's pushing those swells, huh?"

"Well ..."

"Some disturbance over the horizon, a long way away. Something big, big enough to drive ocean swells hundreds of miles."

"Like a hurricane."

"Right, waves driven by local wind don't look like that. They tend to be less organized, more disjointed. Those are hurricane swells, mate. They weren't there yesterday. That's tellin' me Gracie is getting closer. If that thing gets much closer, them byes at the Tower need to get the hell outa there. The swells are naturally big out there anyway, so Gracie don't have to actually hit us to take them byes right out, init?"

"Right. You better take *T-Boat* out there and evacuate them. I'll send them a message and advise them you're coming. Is *T-Boat* fuelled and ready?" Just then, their attention was distracted by a loud roar. They looked over toward the Base and saw a silver, four-engine plane with an orange and yellow tail rising off the runway on its way to rendezvous with Gracie.

"Ya, she's ready. If I leave now, we should be able to get back by nightfall," Snapper said. "I'll get crackin'." He left Cardigan's office, went directly down to the dock and after some final checks, slipped *T-Boat's* moorings and chugged out of St. George's Harbour, turned to starboard, proceeded around St. David's Head, past Gurnet Rock, along the South coast toward the Argus Tower. *T-Boat* was constantly rolling from the hurricane swells on her port beam. They passed over Challenger Bank, and 11 miles further they arrived at Argus.

Manoeuvring to embark passengers required all of Snapper's skills, as the swell was very large. "This is going to be tricky guys," Snapper said to his crew. "I want everybody to put on life jackets."

"What? You kiddin'?" one of the crew said.

"No, I'm not kidding. Every single one of you!" Snapper ordered.

"Ok Skipper."

He told each of the Navy personnel on the tower to do the same. "I'm not about to lose a man out here." Each man had to time his jump onto the deck to perfection and Snapper had to get close enough to the ladder without colliding with it. From top to bottom each swell was almost 10 feet. It was a harrowing 20 minutes, particularly for Snapper. *T-Boat* was single screw, making close quarter manoeuvring even more difficult.

The last man off was the senior officer responsible for the Tower, Captain Russell. He entered the *T-Boat's* cockpit and shook Snapper's hand heartily. "Skipper, mighty grateful for your help to get us off this tower.

The swell out here is getting pretty hairy. Even though we're all sailors, my crew and I were starting to worry about the approach of Gracie."

"Not to worry Cap'n, we wouldn't leave you byes out here to get busted up by no hurricane." When the embarkation was complete, he was exhausted and said, "Hey, Malcolm, take us back home, bye, I'm busted. And take us around Dockyard to avoid some of this swell."

"OK, Skipper." Snapper went below and brewed himself a hot cup of coffee and allowed himself to relax.

That night he slept like a log. The next morning, he was awakened by the thunder of pounding surf. With blurry eyes he gazed toward the shoreline. The ocean had changed her mood overnight. Just yesterday the view from his window was translucent blue waves marching shoreward, glistening in the morning sunshine, their symmetry being early signs of hurricane swells. They would curl up close to shore and form a natural concave lens that would enable you to actually look underneath the surface, momentarily. Sometimes you could actually see fish in there, visually magnified by the lens effect. Then the wave would smash itself on the pink sand and run onto the beach for a few yards in a pink and white slurry, before returning back to itself and start the process all over again.

Today the ocean had turned from docile to menacing, even though there was still no wind. The colour had changed to whitish/green formations of ominous swells, marching in lock step, one long line after the other towards the shore. When they reached the reef line they would tumble over the reefs and themselves, turning into a furious white froth, roaring loudly. But such was their power, they carried on, diminished but not defeated, marching towards the shore. In the shallows, each one mounted up sharply to a peak, then fell over itself, thunderously striking the shore, after which its remaining momentum carried it further, rushing far up on the beach. When its energy was finally spent, the opaque whitish suspension of froth and sand was strongly sucked back into the ocean, so that a child could easily have been sucked into the ocean with it. *Looks like we got them byes off the Tower just in time,* Snapper thought. "I sure as hell wouldn't want to be out on the Argus Tower in these conditions."

Gracie, being a fickle girl, changed her mind about Bermuda and never got any closer than that day.

# Gracie

24 hours from Bermuda waters, aboard *La Pescadora Langosta*, Yuri was monitoring US radio stations and heard reports of a hurricane that the National Hurricane Service was calling Gracie. She had already caused heavy damage to Haiti, the Dominican Republic and some of the islands of the Bahamas. After tracking towards the US mainland, the latest reports indicated the storm was curving east, back out into the Atlantic. He would chart his course to avoid Gracie by going through the Gulf Stream and hugging the coastline, just outside US territorial waters, of course.

For the next 40 hours his strategy appeared to be working. Then he started to worry when he observed that the barometer in his cabin was falling fast. The breeze freshened out of the southeast and the sea started to build. He gathered his crew and said to them, "Batten the hatches, amigos. I thought we could manoeuvre around this hurricane Gracie, but it looks like we're going to be in for a blow."

The crew, all seasoned mariners, went about their duties without comment. They had seen off storms before. Yuri went back to his cabin and monitored the radio again. He groaned when he heard the weather bulletin, "The latest reports from the hurricane hunters from Bermuda indicate that hurricane Gracie has intensified, and she has abruptly turned almost 180 degrees and is once again headed for the US coast – South Carolina specifically."

"Oh, no!"

*La Pescadora Langosta*, a Cuban/Russian spy ship, was trapped between this monster storm and the US coast. They would have to ride it out.

He called for the chief engineer, Enrique.

"Eh, Enrique, how's the engine?"

"Well, Capitan, she an old, tired engine, but I keep her runnin'."

"Look, Enrique, we're in for some really bad weather, and no matter what, you have got to keep that engine running. Do whatever it is you need to do, get as much help from the crew as you need, but we have got to have power or else we're going to be in real trouble. Comprendé?"

"Si, Capitan," Enrique left the cabin and Yuri could hear him commandeer another member of the crew to assist him with something below decks.

Soon it was blowing a full gale and the waters of the Gulf Stream were being kicked up into large frothy waves. The little, ancient *La Pescadora* bravely rode the roller-coaster, the bow booming each time her nose struck an oncoming swell. Yuri was still trying to keep her southerly course but as the wind was in the southeast, she was rolling wildly. She couldn't take any more.

Yuri was inside the wheelhouse with the helmsman, and shouted over the shrieking wind, "Alfredo, keep her hove-to into the wind!"

"Si, Capitan." He brought her a few degrees to port, putting her directly into the waves. The rolling diminished but didn't stop. Realizing Yuri was not all that familiar with these waters, Alfredo added, "Capitan, when high winds meet the flow of the Gulf Stream, they cause steeper than usual waves." Yuri nodded. It was getting dark now and the winds had increased dramatically to hurricane force, in excess of 75 miles per hour. You could no longer see the waves coming. They could only feel the sudden lifting of the whole ship, then momentarily being suspended, trembling from the propeller being out of the water, then plunging down the backside of the wave, only to have her slam her nose into the next mountain of water with a boom, a shudder and blinding spray crashing against the wheelhouse.

*We're in Gracie's grip now*, Yuri thought. He checked his wind gauge: the wind increased further, sustained winds of 100 miles per hour, gusting to over 120 miles per hour. The wind was whipping the sea into a frothy soup. The sound alternated between a violent, howling-shrieking creature to a terrifyingly deep-throated roaring beast. Visibility – nil. Hour after hour, the assault was relentless.

Keeping one's nerve under nature's most extreme onslaught was totally exhausting for Yuri and his crew, and they thought it would never end. Beneath decks, where most of the crew were, was unbearable. Without being able to see outside, the motion of the ship – pitching, rolling and yawing, was completely disorienting. Even though all of them were veteran sailors, several were violently seasick. Moreover, the thundering of the bow against oncoming waves, reverberating throughout the hull, was deafening and terrifying. The ship's twisting and turning caused seams to loosen on old, riveted plates, letting in more water. Two men were assigned to operating a manual pump to assist the overworked, electric bilge pump. When they were exhausted two others took their places. The hot humid air, putrid with the stench of diesel oil and vomit, made the men reluctant to inhale, but nature had its demands.

Enrique busied himself by constantly checking the engine and its components. In between shifts on the hand pump, Manolo, the cook, took out his battered wallet with the picture of his wife and daughter in it and looked at them wondering if he would ever see them again. He was out here at sea to provide for them. Esteban, the youngest crew member, had been weakened from being violently ill. When he was not on the pump, he just sat there, trying not to puke anymore. His thoughts turned to his girlfriend, Laura. In visualizing her, he was able to shut out the din, stench, motion and terror around him. He could see her smile, hear her laughter, and feel the silky smoothness of her cocoa butter skin. At the moment he was completely absorbed in his fantasy, he was nudged by Manolo, their shift on the hand pump had returned.

Just when Yuri thought the brave, little old ship could take no more, the wind suddenly died, and visibility was restored. The sea was still highly agitated but at least, now, there was only a breath of wind. The air was warm and oppressively heavy with moisture.

"Well, Alfredo, looks like we've seen off the worst of it," Yuri said with a weak smile. He looked up to the heavens and could see a few fleeting stars through the thick, grimy atmosphere.

But Alfredo was a Caribbean mariner. He was not smiling. "No, Capitan, we're in the eye of the hurricane. The worst is yet to come."

"Oh, blyad! I'll check with the engine room." He ducked through a hatch and went below. He could feel the reassuring pulse of the old diesel engine through the deck. "Enrique! How's she holding up?"

"She's OK Capitan. The bilge pumps can't quite keep up with the leaks, so I've got some of the men on the hand pump. But so long as we don't push her too hard, we'll be OK."

"Well, we need just enough headway to keep her nose into the wind. We're not going anywhere until this blow is past." And as those words passed his lips, he felt the ship start to awkwardly roll again. "I'm going back up now."

Upon entering the wheelhouse again, he said to Alfredo, "What's happening?"

"The eye is about to finish passing over us, we have to come about because the wind is starting to swing around to the northwest." Alfredo, without waiting for the order from Yuri, spun the spoked wheel to starboard and the little rust-bucket came about.

Within what seemed like a few moments, the watery, black mountains were back, and so was the shrieking-growling monster. Sheets of rain mixed with salt spray hammered the windshield threatening to shatter it, but it held fast. Alfredo was right, the mountains were steeper in the backside of the hurricane, as the wind was blowing against the flow of the Gulf Stream. After plunging down the back of each huge wave, her bow would bury itself into a wall of black water and after momentarily being submerged beneath it, she would emerge, streaming with sea water, as if readying herself for the next one. Lightning was flashing through the opaque atmosphere all around them. The dazzling light show would have been awe inspiring if it weren't so terrifying. The booming sound of the electric discharges was almost drowned out by that of the wind and the bow striking the waves. The noise was enough to drive one insane. Then a bolt of lightning struck the ship's main mast, where the radar unit was housed. Despite the rain, an explosion of sparks ensued. They were instantly swept into oblivion by the howling winds. Another bolt of lightning, then another, then another – like the climax of a great fireworks show. The last one hit the deck with a resounding boom. All the lights aboard ship flickered then went out.

Then Yuri felt the ship's pulse skip a beat, then stop. Without forward momentum it only took a few seconds for *La Pescadora* to start to sheer to port. Alfredo spun the helm hard-a-starboard with all his might to pull her back with the rudder, but it was to no avail, he had no propulsion. The ship breeched with her broadside to the wind, and, as if a giant, invisible hand was pushing them, over she went, 40, 50, 60 degrees! There was nothing to stop her. Everyone grabbed something and was hanging on for dear life. Those who could not find anything that was firmly attached were thrown head over heels. Her leeside gunwales were awash now, and seawater came rushing into the wheelhouse, even though all the doors were shut tight. Yuri looked over at Alfredo. His eyes were closed but his lips were moving, inaudibly – praying. Yuri, being a true communist, didn't believe in God, but was nevertheless overcome by terror and black desolation.

Another huge mountain of water rolled under and lifted *La Pescadora Langosta* and she capsized, carrying all hands, plus a schematic diagram of an American hydrophone, down with her to Davy Jones' Locker. She became an undocumented victim of hurricane Gracie, lost in the Bermuda Triangle.

# Visitors From London

Dino (Dimitri Tovovich) and Anna Sokratis (Petrova) sat sipping Guinness in a small pub across from the Woods Green tube station, in the Greek neighbourhood of London. The conversation, albeit in semi-whispered tones, was very intense.

"We've not heard from your 'friend' in Bermuda. He was supposed to deliver those designs to our people months ago." Dimitri said.

"You need to give him more time," she responded.

"Time is one thing we don't have! Our people need to know if our missile boats can be detected in the deep ocean. They need to know that now!"

"I'm sure he's trying his best to get the information we need. He's deadly afraid of being exposed to his wife and risking that good life that she provides."

"Anna, I'm beginning to think you have a soft spot for this American!"

"Don't be stupid!" She snapped, glaringly. "Are you questioning my loyalty? You've become totally paranoid!"

"Getting a bit touchy, aren't we?" He paused. "I think Dr. Jack Bessemer needs a little motivation."

"Really? What do you have in mind?"

"He needs a visit. You can't go because his wife might see you, so I'll go."

"Alright."

"I'm going to have Ivan tag along."

"Ivan! No, not him! This is taking things too far!"

"Orders from Control."

"Oh my God! That awful creature always leaves a grisly trail of corpses wherever he goes."

"Don't worry, we're not going to hurt your 'boyfriend.'" She shot a glare that, if looks could kill, Dimitri would have been a pillar of salt. "We're leaving at the weekend," he added. He finished off his Guinness and took his leave. She sat there stewing.

Ivan Bassler was an East German, Stasi operative, an assassin they had the occasion to work with from time to time. She loathed him. He was a born killer who took gratuitous pleasure in his gruesome work. He had a thousand different ways to take human life and another thousand ways to make them suffer great pain before he administered the final Coup de Grâce. To her he was reptilian, the lowest form of predator, in human form. *Snakes kill to eat or when threatened, but Ivan kills for sport. Well, at least Dimitri said they weren't going to harm Jack. In any case, we need Jack to get the info we want.*

The two men, dressed in business suits, traveling under British passports in the names of Dino Sokratis and Ivan Kairis, checked in, with BOAC at London's Heathrow Airport. The bulbous Boeing Stratocruiser would have to stop twice for refuelling before reaching its final destination of Bermuda, 13 hours later.

Upon arrival, they checked in at a small hotel in Somerset called The Ledgelets. It was quiet there and was conveniently close to the Somerset Bridge ferry stop. In half an hour, they could be in Hamilton by ferry. Aware of Bessemer's desire to hobnob with the rich and powerful, there was one place that they knew their quarry would eventually appear, the Royal Bermuda Yacht Club (RBYC). Dino was posing as a wealthy Greek shipping magnate, owner of Sokratis Shipping Ltd. His club in London had a reciprocal arrangement with the RBYC. Thus, after a few quick arrangements, he was offered the use of the Yacht Club's facilities. He and Ivan would spend time at the club, until Jack Bessemer showed up.

Jack eventually entered the bar area, greeting Derrick, the bar tender, and other members, smiling with familiar ease. Derrick got him his drink without him asking what he wanted. He turned his back on the bar to survey the room which was profusely decorated with nautical artwork, ships models and yachting memorabilia. His expression suddenly changed to a mixture of shock and fear as he recognized one of the two men sitting in a booth in a corner. Dino rose from his seat, strode over to the bar greeting Jack with a grin and a slap on the back, "Jack, old boy! What a coincidence seeing you here. Wonderful to see you again." He grasped Jack's listless hand and squeezed it. "Jack and I are old friends," he said to the bar tender. "Come over and have a drink with us." Dino steered Jack toward the corner booth.

"Jack, meet Ivan Kairis,"

"How do you do," mumbled Jack.

"Ivan's with Sokratis Shipping. He is in charge of the breaking and disposal of ships that are no longer profitable to the company." Dino went silent and stared unwaveringly into Jack's eyes. It took Jack a moment to get Dino's meaning, but when he did, he felt lightheaded, and a green wave of nausea swept over him. Fortunately, none of the other members in the room took any notice of Jack's reaction. Derrick, on the other hand, like many bar tenders, was a student of human behavior, and he took note of how Dr. Bessemer's face and behavior had changed with the encounter of these two gentlemen from London. Being virtually invisible, except when required to serve, he had the opportunity to observe many a strange thing while quietly wiping the Yacht Club's bar and polishing its glasses.

"Jack, where's the package?" Dino said in a low voice.

"What? You didn't get it? Look, we can't talk here. Let's go outside." Jack got up and the others followed. They strolled out of the Club's front door out to the waterside of Albuoy's Point where there were a few park benches. There were plenty of people milling around, mostly American tourists. Jack decided that they should hide in plain sight.

"You didn't get it?"

"We wouldn't be here if we did, now, would we?"

"Look, like I told the last guy you sent here. What was his name? Uh… Steiner. I 'played' this local charter fisherman into being indebted to me for everything he owned. Now I have him by the balls, right? I tell him if he doesn't play ball with me, I'm going to call his mortgage and loan, and he'll be homeless and ruined. Surprise, surprise, he decides to play ball.

"So, one day I charter his boat for deep sea fishing and give him the specs for the hydrophone sealed in a glass bottle. In two days, he takes his boat out to Argus Bank alone, pretending he's trolling for game fish. He comes close to your spy trawler *La Pescadora Langosta* and makes the drop in broad daylight. She'd been snooping around the Argus Tower for months, but after that drop, she took off and we never saw her again. So that's what happened, I swear it!"

"Well, Jack, old boy, that's all well and good, but we haven't heard from *La Pescadora Langosta* either! Dino replied. "And we're no further ahead. Maybe your fisherman friend betrayed you, or maybe you're trying to 'play' us. Maybe my associate here should take you to the shipyard for breaking and disposal, to be sold for scrap!"

Jack turned bright red. "No, No! I'm sure Scaley made the drop. He's terrified of me now! I don't know what happened after the drop, but I'm certain the drop was made. Look, Dino, I've done as you asked!"

"Keep your voice down!" Dino snapped. After a moment he got up, "We'll be in touch, Doctor." They turned and left Jack alone with his thoughts and fears.

When they returned to The Ledgelets, Dino asked the front desk about the possibility of chartering a deep-sea fishing boat and was told the best such boat was *Captain Crunch*, and that she was moored next door to the hotel at Somerset Bridge. They booked her for two days hence. That evening Ivan ambled out to where the boats came in after a day on the water. He observed *Captain Crunch* returning with a good catch of wahoo and tuna. The skipper and the mate, Rusty Roberts, moored nearby and after cleaning the boat they skulled back to shore. They split up, Desilva taking his "KK" motorcycle home and Rusty picked up a pedal bike, making his way home in the opposite direction, into Somerset.

Ivan had rented a bicycle and casually followed Rusty to his residence. Ivan observed that Rusty lived with an older woman, probably his mother. He found a discreet place to observe Roberts who, after supper, sat outside on his porch drinking a beverage which Ivan assumed was rum. After several hours of surveillance, Ivan returned to The Ledgelets. The next morning, he told Dino his plan. "Now Ivan, I don't want any blood bath. You must refrain from unleashing your innermost demons. I just want people to think this guy had too much to drink and was too hung over to get up. We want to give our friend Doctor Bessemer a moment of clarity, we don't want a local uproar. This island's a quiet, peaceful place, and we want it to stay that way. Am I clear?"

"It's your mission Dimitri. We do it your way," Ivan grouched.

The next evening Ivan followed Rusty Roberts home, jimmied open the screen of the bedroom window and hid in the closet while Rusty drank himself into a stupor. He eventually staggered into the bedroom and collapsed in his bed. Ivan waited until his victim's breathing became heavy and regular. He then slowly emerged from the closet and, as silent as a shadow, approached the bed. He firmly gripped the pillow under Rusty's head with his left hand without disturbing it. Then, with his right hand, he delivered a sharp karate chop directly on the victim's larynx, instantly crushing it into his trachea. He quickly whipped the pillow from under Roberts' head and smothered the hapless victim's futile efforts to get air into his lungs. After a few seconds of fighting, Roberts succumbed to asphyxiation and lay still. Ivan replaced the pillow under his head and silently exited the house via the window.

Captain Scaley DeSilva would be without the services of his mate, Rusty Roberts, on tomorrow's fishing excursion on the *Captain Crunch*.

# Sharks!

As dawn was breaking, Dino Sokratis and Ivan Kairis boarded the *Captain Crunch* at the Somerset Bridge dock. Scaley DeSilva, her skipper, delayed shoving off, waiting for his mate, Rusty Roberts. Eventually, he decided to leave without him, cursing under his breath. However, he turned to his customers and said brightly, "Well gentlemen, although I'm without my mate today, I can assure you you're gonna see and catch some big fish. What kind of fish do you fancy fishing for today?"

"Sharks," said Dino immediately. "I've always wanted to catch a big shark. Got any big sharks in Bermuda waters?"

"Sure, bye! Lots of sharks out there! Fortunately, they don't come on our beaches but out on the banks there's lots of them. You gotto chum for them though."

"Chum, what's that?" Dino asked.

"It's this-here, bye!" Scaley said, and he opened a container next to the transom containing a slushy and disgusting smelling mixture of blood, pieces of fish and fry. "We're goin' out to Challenger and ladle this stuff in the water to attract the sharks. This stuff is like catnip for sharks. Then we'll lower our hooks and see if we can catch a few."

Scaley guided the boat out past Cathedral Rocks, around Wreck Hill out into the channel, then he gunned *Captain Crunch*, passing several other slower boats on their way past the Tripod Marker, out toward Challenger Bank, 14 miles Southwest of Bermuda. When they reached Challenger, Scaley stopped the engines and dropped anchor. The weather was fine with a soft southerly breeze. He noticed that the other man, called Ivan, said little to nothing, but his eyes scanned this way and that in a manner that was disconcerting. Scaley thought, *This guy has the reptilian, cold eyes of a cobra that's about to strike.*

He started chumming the waters of Challenger Bank. He had some small fish on board that he would intermittently cut up with a curved, thin bladed knife, that he also used for scaling, and put the pieces in the bucket of chum. After several minutes Scaley pointed and exclaimed, "Hey, here they come! Look!" To the untrained eye at first, they saw nothing, then the dorsal fin of one of the sharks broke the surface.

"Oh yes. Look Ivan!" Ivan didn't move. There were many sharks around the boat now.

"Those are white tipped, Reef sharks. Look, that one's a Bull shark, they're dangerous," Scaley explained. The sharks were all swirling around the boat and Scaley busied himself preparing the baited hooks. Normally this would be the job of the mate, but he was a mate once and he knew exactly what to do. It was just a little less efficient.

Then Dino shouted, "Skipper! What's that?" A large shape emerged from the deep, much bigger than the others, over 15 feet long. It moved slowly, with ultimate assurance, it had a blunt nose with striped markings on its grey body.

"Jingas, bye, that-there's a Tiger shark!"

Suddenly Ivan came alive. "Oh, let me see!" As he neared the transom, nobody noticed that he was holding Scaley's scaling knife, and as the skipper leaned over to get a better look at the Tiger shark, Ivan struck. His arm and hand were a blur as the blade traced out an arc in the air, an arc that intersected with Scaley's neck. Scaley grabbed at his throat and looked astonished to see bright red blood spurting over his hands. He then gave Ivan a confused, questioning look, as if to say, "Why?" His carotid artery had been severed and his racing heart was squirting his vital fluid everywhere. Blood spilled in the water and the sharks became even more excited. Scaley was losing consciousness now due to lack of blood to the brain. Ivan coolly bundled him overboard.

Within seconds the sharks had him in a feeding frenzy. A Reef shark bit off Scaley's hand, but in the frenzy that ensued, the Bull shark bit clean through a Reef shark, cutting it in two. The big Tiger shark took command of the situation and grabbed Scaley's torso, violently shaking it from side to side, banging it against the boat's hull. The sea turned red as the other sharks tore Scaley's body apart.

"Nice work," Dino said, "But what do we do now? You know how to get us back to shore?"

"No, but there are other boats out here. Let's try the radio."

Dino pressed the button on the handpiece of the ship-to-shore radio, and shouted, "Mayday, mayday, mayday! This is *Captain Crunch*, we have an emergency here. Can anybody hear me?"

After a minute or so the radio crackled, "This is the SOFAR *T-Boat*, I have a visual on you. What is your emergency? Where's Scaley?"

"What's a SOFAR *T-Boat*?" Dino asked Ivan, who shrugged his shoulders.

Depressing the button on the handpiece, he spoke into it, "The skipper's gone over the side and the sharks have him. We need help."

"Ok, *Captain Crunch*, hold on, we're coming to you."

"Where are you?"

"On your starboard bow, about 7 miles away. We'll be there shortly."

Dino and Ivan looked around. They spied an unusual looking craft with a high mast and a large steel bracket protruding from her bow. It was coming their way. When the vessel finally got close up, they could see it was some kind of work boat, the name on her bow was, *T-426*. They could see about 5 crew aboard, including the skipper who guided his craft alongside with expert ease. A crew member jumped aboard the *Crunch* with a rope in his hand and lashed the two boats together, making sure that fenders were used so that there was no damage to either vessel.

*T-Boat's* master hopped onboard the *Crunch* and greeted the two tourists, "Good morning, I'm Snapper Jones, what happened here? And where's Scaley DeSilva?"

Dino spoke, "Well Mr. Jones, we were fishing for sharks and our captain had been chumming the water to attract the sharks and a bunch of them came around the boat, including one big Tiger shark. He was standing on the transom here setting the hooks when he slipped because, you can see that it's really slippery with all that chum on it. Anyway, he slipped and fell overboard, and the sharks got him."

"He slipped?" Snapper asked with more than a little incredulity.

"Yeah, he slipped."

"Where is his mate?"

"He didn't make it. We waited for him, but he never showed."

Snapper surveyed the condition of the *Crunch*. The sharks were now gone. There was chum all over the deck and the transom as well. Growing up with Scaley, he knew he ran a tight ship and wouldn't normally tolerate this kind of mess on the deck of his precious *Captain Crunch*. He also observed these tourists, both with British accents; one seemed pretty normal, but there was something quite repugnant about the other one. He was wiry and pale, with sallow, gaunt cheeks, and those eyes – the eyes of a cobra, or indeed, a shark. Snapper also noticed that, in spite of all the chum, the hooks on the rods in the fighting chair were not set, neither were the lines on the other rods.

He decided to say no more and take these folks back to port and let the authorities handle it. The *Crunch* was in perfect working order, so he let one of his crew drive *T-Boat*, while he took over the *Crunch*. He called the authorities on *Crunch's* ship-to-shore radio, and the two-boat flotilla made its way back to Hamilton where they were met by police.

While on the radio, Snapper gave some of the details of his encounter on Challenger Bank to the authotities. Police Commissioner Radcliff was informed by one of his officers that there had been a misadventure on a charter fishing boat, and as this was such an unusual occurrence on the island, he decided to meet the *Captain Crunch* himself when she put into port. He personally interviewed the witnesses and was completely satisfied that this was an unfortunate boating accident.

The next morning Dr. Jack Bessemer picked up the morning *Royal Gazette* outside his front door. He glanced at the headline on his way to the kitchen table. It read, "Local Fisherman Killed by Sharks!" When he read the words "Scaley DeSilva," a wave of nausea swept over him, and he spent the next hour with his head in the toilet.

Evelyn was worried. "Jack, shall I call the doctor?"

"No, honey, it must be something I ate at the club."

"You should stay in bed today, or at least until you feel better. I can slide in bed with you, if you like."

"Just the thought of that makes me feel better. Darling, I've got to clean myself up and get to work."

That same afternoon, after a brief telephone conversation with Jack Bessemer, the two Sokratis Shipping Ltd. executives took a leisurely ride in a surrey-with-a-fringe-on-top taxi to the airport and boarded the Stratocruiser for the long flight back to London, satisfied that their business in Bermuda had been successfully executed – they had delivered the appropriate message to Jack Bessemer.

The KGB agents and Jack agreed to use a more direct means of communication, one not involving third parties that could disappear in the Bermuda Triangle. The Russians would set up a fake UK based organization called the "Imperial Institute of Oceanographic Research," complete with post office box number and street address. They were confident that anything that Jack would mail there would appear to be merely routine scientific correspondence. The new plan worked smoothly, with one exception, that being that Jack continued to send them out of date, or technically flawed information. He knew he was taking a risk that one day they would discover what he was up to, and he would be finished. He didn't know what else to do.

## T-Boat

The next day at the Consulate office, Carpenter buzzed his secretary. "Janice, can you get Major Vindham at Tudor Hill on the phone please?"

"Certainly, Mr. Carpenter."

In a few moments she poked her head around the door, "Major Vindham for you, sir."

He picked up. "Major, Carpenter here. I was wondering if you could arrange for me to have a tour of the Argus Tower?"

"Certainly, sir. I'll get right on it. You should know, sir, you'll have to put aside an entire day for this jaunt, due to the long transit time there and back. There's also the issue of the weather. But I'll get back to you." With that he hung up.

*Strange bird,* Carpenter thought.

Later on that afternoon, Janice poked her head in his office again and said, "Major Vindham for you sir."

He picked up. "Major, what do you have for me?"

"Sir, the weather looks good for tomorrow. The *T-Boat* will pick you up at 05:30 tomorrow at Albuoy's Point."

"*T-Boat*, what's that?"

"Oh, it's just the name of one of the utility boats that the SOFAR station in St. David's uses to run provisions and equipment out to the Tower. It's nothing fancy, sir, so you should dress informally. I'll accompany you, sir."

"Major, that's not necessary, you know. I don't want to put you out."

"Not at all, Mr. Carpenter, I periodically inspect their operations, for security purposes. I'm overdue for a visit."

"Ok, see you tomorrow." He rung off.

"Janice, clear my calendar tomorrow, I'm off to the Argus Tower."

Tony Fox pulled the white US Consul General's car onto the dock at Albuoy's Point. There alongside, waiting for him, was a white vessel with black trim. She had T-426 written on her bow. Major Vindham, in uniform, was also waiting for him on the dock.

"Good morning, sir. Nice morning for a boat ride."

Carpenter had plenty of experience with small boats, as a former OSS case officer. However, he never really felt fully comfortable aboard them, although he had a strong stomach and never became seasick.

"It's only morning in theory, Major. As far as I can see, it's still in the middle of the night."

"Come aboard, sir. I'd like you to meet the master of this fine vessel, Joshua Jones."

Carpenter clambered aboard and extended his hand. "Hi, I'm Bob Carpenter."

"Mornin' Mr. Carpenter. Most people call me Snapper. Snapper Jones. Only my mother calls me Joshua. Pleasure to meet you, sir, and welcome aboard. We'd better get under way, this here *T-Boat* ain't no speed boat. It's gonna take us over three hours to get to the Tower."

The skipper snapped a few quick commands to his two crew members. He spun the wheel and reversed away from the dock, then shifted to full ahead and *T-Boat* came up to her full speed, a stately 12 knots.

Carpenter took note of his surroundings. He was standing next to Snapper, looking forward through the open windshield. Even though it was before the crack of dawn, he noticed that Snapper Jones was neatly attired in what looked like a pilot's uniform. He was tall and athletically built with his white pilot's cap, with the black peak, cocked perfectly to one side.

The cockpit around him was quite spartan with three chairs, one for the helmsman and two others, bolted firmly to the steel deck. He decided to take one for himself. The Major remained standing. The two other crew members disappeared below deck. After a few minutes, one reappeared with a tray with three piping hot cups of coffee on it. After he performed this duty, he disappeared below again.

"Snapper, what is the story behind this boat? Where'd she come from?"

"Well, sir, she's old US Army surplus." Snapper had to raise his voice because, as a steel boat, the sound of the single engine was magnified by sympathetic vibration. "They made a number of these workboats to perform a wide variety of tasks. The truth is, most of them were never used very much by the US military. The SOFAR station got this one cheap. They have a bigger one called the Sir Horace Lamb which was built during the War as a mine sweeper.

"Sir Horace Lamb? How'd a US run operation like SOFAR come up with an ultra-English name like that?"

"Sir Horace Lamb was a British scientist who founded the science of how sound travels through water, so they named the ship after him. Well, she goes out on deep ocean operations. On *T-Boat* we do much shorter local runs and runs out to the Tower for replenishment and equipment transfers, and stuff like that.

"*T-Boat's* sturdy, with a 65 foot steel hull. And look at the construction of the cabin and cockpit here, all steel, built to take hard work and heavy weather. We helped lay those hydrophone arrays out there at Argus. Hell of a job that was! The sea out there ain't like it is in here. The swells are large, and it was difficult to keep this thing straight long enough so that the cables could be laid straight. Anyway, we got it done. How long you been in Bermuda, Mr. Carpenter?"

"Not long."

"Well, it's still pretty dark out here now, but let me point out a few things out here." They proceeded out through "Two Rock Passage," the gateway to Hamilton Harbour and headed for the Royal Navy Dockyard. *T-Boat* had a very tall foremast with a radar unit on top of it. The mast, along with a boom and a winch, was used as a crane for a variety of functions. This meant that she could not transit under Watford Bridge, so they had to steer around Commissioner's Point – the tip of the Bermuda "giant fishhook." They followed the channel around the outside of Somerset Island, around Daniel's Head along the west coast of the island.

"That's Tudor Hill over there on our port side," Snapper said. By this time, dawn had broken, and it was to be another lovely day in Bermuda. They approached the Tripod channel marker, then turned past it and headed southwest. "It's a straight shot to the Tower from here," Snapper said. Carpenter looked out over the bow and saw nothing.

To pass the time Snapper Jones regaled the Consul General with local stories, including his own involving the *Wilhelmina* fire. Carpenter found himself spellbound, as Snapper was quite a good raconteur.

Carpenter said, "And they wanted to blame you for that?"

"Ya."

"They should have pinned you with a medal, a written commendation, or something."

"But, you know, Mr. Carpenter, those '40 Thieves' stick together."

"40 Thieves? Who're they?"

"That's what we-byes call the white establishment, you know, the old byes that own and control everything in Bermuda. No offence, Mr. Carpenter, but you ain't one of them. They knew they were to blame, but there was no way they were going to take the blame. They had to find some coloured byes to take the rap: me and Stone. I would'a taken the blame if it had been my fault. But it wasn't. That's why I quit. I quit the job I loved."

"That must have been very difficult for you."

"It wasn't easy, cause I needed the money, but my Deddy taught me a long time ago to stand up for what is right. And that wasn't right, it just wasn't right."

Carpenter thought, *It's always nice to meet a man prepared to stand up for principle. This is a man I can trust.*

After two- and one-half hours, Snapper said, "Look, Mr. Carpenter, you can see the Tower now." He looked but could see nothing. Snapper opened a cabinet and took out a pair of binoculars and gave them to him. After adjusting the focus, there it was, dead ahead. It was partially shrouded by the salt and humid air, and it also looked low in the water, much lower than Carpenter had expected. But as they approached it, its actual scale became more apparent. It was by no means small, but not nearly as massive as the offshore platforms in the Gulf of Mexico. He noticed that there were already a few fishing boats in the area.

"Major, are these boats allowed in close proximity to the tower?"

"Yessir. If you will recall, our cover here is that we're conducting oceanographic research, so if we treated it like it was some top-secret Naval facility it would only attract more interest. None of these boats around here are a problem. But several months back there was a Cuban fishing trawler called, *La Pescadora Langosta*, that prowled around here incessantly. One day she just took off, never to be seen again.

"See the steps on the Tower? They have been damaged from big waves," Snapper said, pointing out the twisted steel stairs below the Tower. "By the way, those stairs are the only way up."

*You asked for it, you dumb shmuck!* Carpenter thought.

He really hadn't noticed it while they were under way, but as they drew close to the tower's massive legs, he noticed the ocean swells and how *T-Boat* rose, fell and rolled with them.

*How am I going to get onto that ladder with this boat imitating a roller-coaster!*

As if he had heard him thinking, Snapper said, "Don't worry, Mr. Carpenter, my byes will help you out."

*T-Boat* approached the stairs very slowly. One of the crew lashed the bow to one of the pipe-like legs and the stern to another. Then they maneuvered the boat close to the stairs. But as part of the stairs was missing due to storm swells, there was no ideal solution. When they got as close as they could to the stairs, Vindham athletically leapt forward and grasped the step when the boat was on the crest of the swell.

"Come sir, I'll help you. You have to time your jump at the top of the swell, or you'll miss it and fall into the drink. I'll grip your arm."

*Right, that's just great!*

Snapper said, "Mr. Carpenter, put on this life vest, just in case."

*Swell!* Carpenter thought as he slipped it on. Snapper was holding him steady on *T-Boat's* gunwale.

The boat rose with the swell. Carpenter hesitated; it was too late. It fell again and the ladder was out of reach. He waited for this to happen a few times – to get the rhythm.

Snapper said, "The next one, sir." Carpenter nodded. *T-Boat* rose.

"Now!" Snapper shouted. Carpenter leaped up and forward. He desperately reached for the steel step and grasped it with both hands. He felt Major Vindham's steely grip under his right arm, pulling him up.

"You're OK, sir," he said. They climbed up the rusting steel ladder, up into the belly of the Argus Tower. It was a two-storey structure with one level for equipment, electronic consoles and other technical gear, while the other storey was for accommodations, the galley, the head and other requirements for the human occupants. On the top of the tower was a large crane that loaded and unloaded provisions and equipment. There were also various antennae protruding from the structure to communicate with the headquarters at Tudor Hill.

Carpenter collected himself and met all the Navy personnel at the Tower. They tried to explain to him exactly what was going on there, but it all made his eyes glaze over.

After that, things improved. They had lunch, washed down by a cool lager. "So, gentlemen, what about this supposed Cuban spy ship?"

"Well, sir, I think nobody here can explain that trawler's actions any other way except for it to be a surveillance ship."

"Can they actually get any intel from visual observation?" Everybody shook their heads. "What about radio intercepts?"

"Well, we use a code for radio transmissions, and if they're competent spies, they could decipher some of it. But for anything important we use the undersea cable between here and Tudor Hill," Vindham volunteered.

"Where is the Cuban ship now?"

"It disappeared around the time Gracie was in the area."

One of the technicians volunteered, "One thing I want to say to you, Mr. Carpenter. This tower is not adequately designed for the conditions out here. It's not high enough. If a hurricane hit the island, this Tower would be history, and anybody on it." Carpenter nodded and took note.

Vindham said, "Mr. Carpenter, it's approaching 15:00, it's time we were heading back."

After bidding the personnel on the Tower farewell, Carpenter shuddered thinking about his re-boarding *T-boat*. However, his fears were largely unfounded, as it was much easier jumping down than up. After having been under way for about an hour, Snapper Jones said, "Mr. Carpenter, we're passing over Challenger Bank."

"How do you know that?"

"Look." He pointed to the display of the depth sounder. "See, the depth has decreased dramatically."

"Oh yeah!"

"A little while back, I was on my way to the Tower and received a distress call from a charter fishing boat out here over Challenger. I knew the boat, it was the *Captain Crunch*, but I didn't recognize the voice. So, we responded to their distress call. When we arrived, they were anchored on the Bank and had been chumming for sharks."

"Chumming?"

"Yeah, chumming is when you dump a lot of blood and pieces of fish overboard to attract the sharks. It's horrible stuff, slimy and it stinks. But it works! Anyhow, when we came along side there was no sign of the skipper. He's a well-known charter captain, called Scaley."

"Scaley?" Carpenter laughed.

"Yeah, Scaley was nowhere to be seen and when I asked, 'Where's Scaley?' One of the customers aboard claimed that Scaley was standing on the transom, slipped on the slimy chum and fell in the drink. Of course, at that time the boat was surrounded by sharks, especially a large Tiger shark and they made quick work of Scaley."

"Wow! What did you do?"

"I gave one of my guys the helm of *T-Boat*, and I took over the *Captain Crunch* and brought her back to port. Bye, that is one sweet boat. Would give my eye-teeth for somethin' like that. But anyway, it was very strange."

"Why?"

"There was bloody chum all over her deck. Scaley loved that boat to death, and it was always spotless. He would never have allowed that to happen. Another thing that was unbelievable was that Scaley slipped on chum and fell overboard in the middle of a bunch of feeding sharks. Really? Scaley was a real pro! That ain't goin' to happen. And finally, the hooks didn't even have bait on them, and they weren't overboard. How were they going to catch any sharks?"

"Did you tell this to the police?" Carpenter asked.

"Yeah, I did. But they didn't take much notice of me. They were more interested in what the British customers had to say. And one more thing, one of them was a very weird looking guy."

"What do you mean, 'weird'?"

"Well, the other guy talked a lot, and he was the one that told the story. But the weird guy hardly said anything, but he was the most evil looking man I have ever seen. He had eyes of a predator – dead eyes, like a shark's. I have seen a lot of things out here on the ocean, but I've never seen anything as scary as that guy. He gave me the creeps."

"What was his name?"

"Ivan somethin' or the other. The cops took both their statements, but I'm sure they've gone back to England by now. Anyway, the whole thing was a crying shame. Scaley had a wife and child and without him they won't have any income ..." His voice trailed off.

Soon they were within sight of the Tripod channel marker. "Won't be long now, Mr. Carpenter, we'll soon have you at Albuoy's Point."

"You can call me Bob, you know."

"Ok, Bob."

When *T-Boat* docked, the white US Consul General's car was waiting for them. "Thanks Skipper," Carpenter said. "I enjoyed the ride and the conversation."

It was 6:30 when the white American car pulled away from the curb. As it did, Snapper spied his friend Derrick coming off his shift tending bar at the Royal Bermuda Yacht Club. Derrick waved and thought, *He's Come a long way since he was just Hooks' little bye, init.*

Snapper said, "Hey bye, let's go get a drink. I've spent the whole day on the water and could use a little taste."

So, they went to a bar on Queen Street that was frequented by local blacks, called "Papa's Place." This bar was owned by one of the islands most successful black entrepreneurs, Dick Grenadian, AKA, "Papa Dick." He also owned the notorious hotel called, "The Grenadian Hotel," an establishment where a patron could get good liquor but also very compliant female companionship, after the appropriate financial terms were met, of course.

They pushed through the swinging doors and there in front of them was the tall, black, hulking figure of Papa Dick. His white teeth formed a broad grin beneath his large, bushy, greying, moustache. "Hey, Derrick! I see yuh got yuh mate, young Snapper in tow. How're you guys doin', anyway?" He slapped each man on the back – hard.

"Doin' OK, Dick" Derrick said.

"Have a drink on me. Yuh know, you-byes should come over to the Hotel and hang out with some of my girls. They'll show you a real good time."

"Thanks, mate, but I'm not sure my wife would approve," Derrick replied with a laugh.

"What about you, Snapper. Young buck like you could take on a few of my fillies at the same time."

Snapper gave a sly smile, "'Preciate the offer, Papa, but I'm chasing longtails these days."

"Longtails! Look here! My business is the provision of pleasure, right? At the appropriate price, of course. But these days, I'm getting competition from all over the place. How can a man make an honest living when longtails are giving away what I'm selling for free!

"And then I have clients stealing my investments. You know I had a guy steal one of my girls, took her away and set her up in a house. He's a real fool! That girl's going to take him to the cleaners. Even bought the house for her! Can you believe that? A house! You know him, Snapper. You work with him."

"I do? Who you talkin' 'bout?"

"Um … um, Vindham, Major Vindham."

"What? Major Vindham! Couldn't be. He lives on base like a monk!"

"No monk on earth is getting what he's getting', believe me. That girl used to work for me, now he has set her up with a house, in her name, no less, plus he's paying all her expenses, plus a new car, fur coats and trips to the States. And her sugar-daddy is Vindham. Heard he paid for the house in cash, wrote out a cheque, no mortgage. She's been blabbing her mouth all over town."

Snapper was shocked. "I dun know anything 'bout that!"

Dick continued, "Anyway, as it relates to longtails, you'll soon get tired of that. Don't know what's wrong with you young byes of today. Longtails? Huh! Anyway, look, it's a standing invitation."

"Thanks a lot mate."

Papa Dick headed through the bar's swinging doors and Derrick and Snapper looked at each other and burst out laughing.

After a few shots of Black Rum, Snapper said, "You know, Derrick, that new US Consul General, um…um, Carpenter, is a pretty OK guy: not stuck up like some of them English byes or a loud know-all like some of them GI's. He was real interested in what happened to Scaley out there on Challenger Bank."

"Yeah, bye, that was a cryin' shame. Nobody would want to go out like that," Derrick mumbled.

"I told him I couldn't imagine that Scaley would be so careless as to slip and fall into a pack of frenzied sharks. And the boat was filthy – with chum all over the deck. You know how fussy he was about *Captain Crunch*."

"Yup, you could eat off that deck!"

"And one of those English customers looked so evil. He had dead eyes, just like a shark."

Derrick perked up, "I seen a guy that looked like that at the Club. He and another Englishman came in every day for a few days. On the last day they met that American guy from up there at Tudor Hill, um… um, Dr. Bessemer. He knew 'em and I'll never forget the look on his face when he saw 'em. He turned white as a sheet. He was scared shitless! They went outside to talk, but you could tell he didn't want to be with 'em."

"Then in two days' time Scaley ends up eaten by sharks with those same two guys onboard his boat."

"That guy with the dead eyes was like a shark on two legs."

"Ya. Got that right!"

"I wonder what's the connection between Bessemer and those two?"

"Donno, bye. Anyway, I got to go. Thanks for the drink. Check you later." Snapper finished his drink and went into the street where his Zundapp moped was parked.

## Tour Of Sofar

Three days later, Carpenter decided he should continue his tour of US facilities on the Island.

Janice made the arrangements for his tour of the SOFAR Station in St. David's. When they pulled up in front of the modest facility, Carpenter alighted from the car and exclaimed, "Wow! What a view!" SOFAR enjoyed spectacular views over the Eastern ramparts of the Island. Situated in the shadow of the St. David's Lighthouse, on the highest hill in St. David's, it overlooked an uninterrupted arc of the Atlantic from South Southwest, leftward to North Northwest.

It also overlooked the eastern end of the main runway of the Kindley Field Airforce Base which was congested with a wide variety of aircraft, including: F-100 supersonic Super Saber fighter jets; heavy transports – C124 Globemasters with "MATS" emblazoned on their fuselages, bombers, including the sleek B47 Stratojet, B29 Hurricane Hunters and blimps.

Carpenter was greeted by the director of the facility, Dr. Carl Cardigan, who personally showed the Consul General around. Carpenter gestured toward the base, "A whole lotta planes down there."

Cardigan replied, "Yes, Kindley Field serves as a major refueling station for transporting military materiel to Europe via those big MATS Globemasters. There are always lots of them at Kindley. Also, the base is a refueling station for SAC, the Strategic Air Command, and its 24/7 US airborne nuclear strike force. Those B47 bombers as well as their aerial refuelling planes the KC 97 Stratofreighters are common sights around here.

"If you look at the far western end of the base, you'll see where you came in at the Civil Air Terminal, connecting Bermuda with the world.

"Aren't those water colours of Castle Harbour and Ferry Reach amazing? Never get tired looking at it."

"Yes. Amazing!"

"Now, let me show you around our facility here, right this way."

SOFAR consisted of several buildings, vessels and a tall communications tower. Unlike the NAVFAC at Tudor Hill, the staff of SOFAR were civilians: a hodgepodge of local Bermudian staff and American scientists. However, as Cardigan explained, "While we are officially under the auspices of Columbia University, the majority of our work is under contract for the US Navy. Like our friends up at Tudor Hill, we have a few cables that run out into the deep from here that have hydrophones which we monitor from up here.

"Mr. Carpenter, I know the guys up at Tudor Hill have told you how great they are, but you should know that the science of sound through the ocean is a relatively new discipline and we're studying it down here and using the results up there, almost simultaneously. We've made some important discoveries down here at SOFAR."

"Oh, really. Do tell."

"Well, a few months ago the Australian navy detonated a 300 pound bomb underwater in the SOFAR Channel off Perth, and we clearly heard it on our hydrophones here in Bermuda, 3 hours 43 minutes later, that's a distance of about 12,000 miles."

"What! Perth? That's SOFAR away!" Carpenter paused, with a smirk.

The play on words initially wrong-footed Carl, but when the penny finally dropped, he couldn't help rolling his eyes.

"Seriously Carl, how is that possible?" Carpenter said.

Cardigan spread out a map on a table. "Look, according to this map, sound waves can't get to Bermuda from Perth because they are blocked by Southern Africa. But this is a Mercator projection map that shows the earth as flat, and, as we all know, the Earth is round, not flat."

"So, sound would travel on a Greater Circle route, just like ships and aircraft do," Carpenter interjected.

"Exactly! Mr. Carpenter, I see you know your navigation." Carpenter smiled. "On a Greater Circle route, sound waves bypassed Africa and travelled over 12,000 miles to the other side of the world in the SOFAR Channel, to Bermuda. This so-called Perth/Bermuda experiment proved that the theory of the SOFAR Channel and its ability to carry sound incredible distances is actually fact. All the latest work for the US Navy here, at Tudor Hill and Argus Island, as it relates to submarine detection, is based on what we discovered here at SOFAR."

"Wow! I'm impressed!"

"Mr. Carpenter, would you like to see some of our fleet?"

"Certainly. I want to see the vessel with that most British name."

"Oh, *Sir Horace Lamb!*"

"Yes, she's in port today."

They toured rooms crammed with electronic gear, like Tudor Hill, but also the swelteringly hot machine/carpenter shop, where they fashioned much of the equipment they used for underwater acoustic research. Carpenter talked to a number of the staff there and discovered that many of them were local Bermudians who, in spite of not being American citizens, appeared just as enthusiastic and dedicated to SOFAR's mission as were the American staff. The two men hopped into the official white car and drove down the hill to the public dock in St. David's. They boarded a small launch and motored across St. George's Harbour to the *Sir Horace Lamb*. She was alongside McCallan's Wharf which was next to the main St. George's deep-water dock, Penno's Wharf. There they met her skipper, Clem McCann and some more scientists and crew. Carpenter then saw a familiar face, Snapper Jones.

"Hello, Snapper. Good to see you again. What are you doing here?"

"Hello, Bob, I serve as first officer and alternate skipper here from time to time."

Cardigan raised an eyebrow at the familiarity of greeting between the two men.

"Snapper, please don't take this the wrong way, but you can drive this thing too?"

Cardigan interjected, "Mr. Carpenter, you should know that Snapper here is fully qualified in all aspects of oceanic navigation. He essentially taught himself all the math and science required for him to sit the US exams for a ship's captain, and he now holds a US ship's captain license."

"Wow! Extraordinary!"

Snapper asked with a smirk, "Mr. Consul General, have you recovered from the swells at the Argus Tower yet?"

Both men laughed out loud. Carpenter turned to Cardigan and said with a conspiratorial smirk, "You see, Director, Snapper, here, was part of a fiendish plot to assassinate the new US Consul General and make it look like an accident, when that inept official failed to properly grasp the ladder while boarding the Argus Tower."

"Who foiled the plot?" Cardigan asked, playing along.

"Why, it was Major Vindham. He grabbed me just in time!"

When the tour of the *Sir Horace* was finished and Carpenter was bidding the ship farewell, Snapper said, "Bob, may I have a word please?"

"Sure, Snapper, what's this about." They stepped aside outside the earshot of the others.

"Well, I heard something that bothers me. After we dropped you off at Albuoy's Point the other evening, I had a drink with one of my mates. He's the bar tender at the Yacht Club. Remember I told you about the two guys who we rescued out at Challenger Bank after the skipper, Scaley, got eaten by sharks?"

"Uh-huh."

"Derrick, the bartender, said he saw these same two guys meet Dr. Bessemer at the Club and that he looked, pardon the expression, scared shitless when he saw them. Then two days later Scaley was dead. And I just heard that Rusty Roberts, the mate on the *Captain Crunch*, died in his sleep that same day. That's why Scaley was on the boat with those two byes by himself! I don't know how to connect the dots, but it sounds fishy to me."

"You say the mate died in his sleep the same day that they went out on the *Captain Crunch*?"

"Well, the night before actually. Scaley left Somerset late that mornin' waiting for Rusty. But when he didn't show, he went out without him. The Brits told the cops that."

"Hmmm. Thanks for telling me, Snapper. Leave it with me." They shook hands and Carpenter disembarked the *SHL* and got into the big white car which had driven from St. David's around Mullet Bay to the dock while they were on board.

On his return to the office, he called out to Janice. "Get me Commissioner Radcliff on the phone please." He had met the Commissioner during his round of official introductions. He wasn't quite sure what to make of Radcliff.

In a few minutes she said, "I have the Commissioner on the line sir."

"Thanks." He picked up. "Commissioner, how are you?"

"Excellent, Consul General. To what do I owe this honour?"

"I hear you had a rather unspeakable maritime tragedy recently where one of your charter boat skippers fell overboard and was savaged by sharks. I'm curious. Is this a common occurrence in these islands? I was thinking about going out there for some fishing myself, but if it's going to be that dangerous, I may give it a wide berth."

"Well, Mr. Carpenter, I can say with great confidence, that this was quite an unusual occurrence. The fact is, as far as I'm aware, it's never happened before. The thing is that DeSilva was one of our top skippers. For a ghastly thing like this to happen to a skipper of his experience is quite a tragedy, but, you know, there are sharks out there."

"I hear the customers were two landlubbers. Could barely call for help on the radio. Is that right?"

"Yes, quite so. They had to get help from a passing vessel because they didn't know how to operate the boat themselves, much less bring her back to port."

"Were they two of mine – Americans?"

"No, they were Brits. Their names were Dino Sokratis and Ivan Kairis – shipping executives." Carpenter scribbled down the names on a yellow memo pad. "I took statements from them myself. Seemed credible to me, although one of them was quite, how should I say it, unusual."

"How so? Which one?"

"One of them had strange eyes. Dead, you know, somewhat like a snake. He was Ivan Kairis. They left on BOAC a few days ago. Anyway, the case has been closed, as a tragic accident."

"*Captain Crunch* must have been a very unlucky boat – losing its skipper and mate the same day."

"Mate, what mate?" Radcliff asked.

"Rusty Roberts! I'm sure you knew he was the mate on the *Captain Crunch*."

"Oh yes, of course! Of course!" Radcliff lied. "I guess you're right, Consul General, a very unlucky boat indeed."

"Thank you very much, Commissioner, for indulging my morbid curiosity. Goodbye."

Radcliff mused, "What the devil was that all about? Why would he have any interest in a local fisherman getting eaten by sharks? Hope this new Yank isn't going to be the interfering type."

Back in the Vallis Building, Bob Carpenter scowled. There was something itching him in the inside of the back of his head, a place where he couldn't scratch. Having been an OSS case officer for so long, he didn't believe in coincidences. "The fact that these two Brits know Bessemer but are clearly not his friends, is a flashing red light. Bessemer is the key scientist up at Tudor Hill. He is one of the few, perhaps the only civilian to have access to both the Tudor Hill Lab and the top-secret NAVFAC facility. The guy who not only knows all its secrets, but the guy who invented most of them."

He searched in the inside pocket of his jacket and finally extracted a small black book containing names and telephone numbers. After flipping through its dog-eared pages for a few minutes he found the name he was seeking – Stanley Ross. "Janice! I want you to place a long-distance call to this man please." She beetled off to place the call. After about a half an hour she told him that Ross was on the line. He closed his door to the outer office.

"Stan, you, old son-of-a-bitch! Hasn't the Director shot you for treason yet, or at the very least shot you for sleeping with his wife? I can't believe the fate of the Western World is in the hands of an old hound dog like you. How you doin' man?"

Carpenter could hear, through the hiss of the short-wave radio connection, that Ross was choking himself laughing. Overseas calls from Bermuda were dicey at best – heavily dependent on atmospheric conditions, particularly during the day. After a few ribald jokes, the two men got down to business.

"Stan, I'd like you to run down two names for me, both British passport holders: Dino Sokratis and Ivan Kairis. They're posing as Greek British shipping executives, but I have a hunch they may be in our business, or should I say, your business, myself having been put out to pasture."

"Man, you're like an old racehorse having been put out to stud-farm, surrounded by fillies, in bikinis no less!"

"Well, so far I haven't seen many eligible fillies."

"OK, I'll get back to you if I get a hit."

"Thanks Pal. Appreciate it." He killed the connection.

Janice poked her head around the door, "Mr. Carpenter, don't forget you have a dinner party at Government House this evening – seven o'clock."

"Thanks, Janice." *Let's see if there are any fillies at this function.*

# Barr's Bay Park

The day after having met Bermuda's "polite society" at Government House, the Governor's mansion, Carpenter sifted through the usual consular paperwork. Reflecting on the previous evening's events, *Government House is impressive, particularly the vistas from the various impeccably manicured terraces that formed the gardens. But, the building's somewhat of an ancient relic from a distant past. It certainly doesn't compare favourably to Chelston. But it was an opportunity to meet the local elite and their spouses. Ha! They were very interested in the fact that I'm an unattached bachelor. Didn't meet any unattached ladies, so the search for "fillies" was a total bust. In fact, virtually all the ladies were somewhat matronly appendages to their bumptious husbands who were eager to impress me with their prominence or importance in either local society or the business community.*

As with every rule, there was always the exception. This exception was neither matronly nor a mere appendage. She was Commissioner Radcliff's wife, Christine. *Can't figure out how a man like Radcliff, someone of somewhat less than average intellect, and short on charm and facially rodential, could capture a woman of such striking beauty and self-assured intelligence as Christine. She must be about 40, but based on her face and figure she could easily be in her mid to late 20's. Was fascinated by her recounting of her days, like Janice, as a censorette during the war, and subsequent settling down here. To top it off she speaks French! Nice to be able to have a brief conversation, "en Français!" She totally eclipses the Commissioner when the two of them are together. I guess it's a case of, "Opposites attracting."*

Early that afternoon, Janice announced that he had a long-distance call from the States. It was Stan Ross. So soon? He immediately picked up. "Stan, what've you got?"

"Look, Bob, can't say much over this line. You know what I mean?"

"Uh huh." Long distance calls to and from Bermuda could be monitored by anyone with a short-wave radio.

"I'm putting something in the diplomatic pouch now. You should get it by tomorrow."

"Ok. Thanks Stan."

"I must have stumbled onto something, or else Stan wouldn't be so serious and taking such strict security measures."

Late the next morning Janice brought the contents of the regular diplomatic communication into his office. "This one is for your eyes only," she said, raising one eyebrow and handing him a large, sealed envelope.

He took it and reached into the top drawer in his desk and pulled out a letter opener with a very ornately carved handle made of coral. As though this simple device held some telekinetic powers, his mind was instantly transported back to the island of Trinidad and the exotic woman who gave it to him. In an island renowned for its beautiful women, she was still outstanding. Her name was Maya, and she was, what Trinidadians called, a "Dougla" – Afro-Indian, the daughter of a lawyer employed by one of the oil companies on the island.

Officially, Carpenter was an oil consultant to the local Texaco office, but in reality, he was an OSS agent, stationed there to keep tabs on the geopolitical developments in the region. As part of the famous Destroyers for Bases deal between President Roosevelt and Prime Minister Churchill, both the navy and the army had a base on the Trinidadian peninsular called Chaguaramas. These bases were strategically important, as Trinidad guarded U-boat access to the Panama Canal and the Venezuela oilfields. Of additional concern was the fact that the colony of French Guiana, which was nearby, had been taken over by a government that had pledged loyalty to the Vichy Regime in France, a puppet regime of Nazi Germany. Furthermore, Suriname, formerly known as Dutch Guiana, had become politically unstable with the fall of the Netherlands to the Nazis in Europe.

Carpenter's job was to travel extensively in the region, to Venezuela, Panama, and French Guiana, to gather intelligence that was helpful to Uncle Sam's strategic objectives in the region. Having studied French and Spanish at Princeton he was considered the perfect choice for this mission. He found he had a knack for this type of work and had exposed a number of Nazi informants during his time there.

He met Maya at a social function put on by Texaco. They immediately hit it off and the relationship flowered into a passionate love affair. However, he couldn't, and didn't, reveal his real job to her. He was from an all-white small town in rural Pennsylvania, and even after attending Princeton, his contact with black people was minimal at best. However, his relationship with Maya exposed him, for the first time, to the complexities and difficulties of multiracial society, and how differently people of another race and culture could perceive situations he had previously taken for granted. Moreover, while the "Trini's" welcomed the Yankee Dollar in their country, there was noticeable tension between the locals and the Americans in their midst.

He had fallen in love with Maya, in spite of his better judgement, which told him that their relationship was based on a lie, and that, in the end he was going to break her heart. As the war in the Atlantic wound down, he knew his reassignment was inevitable. Whether it was woman's intuition, or her ability to see into his soul, he didn't know which, but she too eventually sensed that they would soon part. Perhaps, it was her recognition that his world in the States was not likely to accept her as Mrs. Carpenter. So, she bravely took the initiative and tearfully broke it off with him, giving him this ornate letter opener as a memento.

Carpenter breathed a long sigh of regret, then refocused his mind on the present and opened the envelope. It contained a folder stamped, "Classified – Top Secret" in red. He flicked it open. His eyes beheld a photo of a remarkably malevolent looking man. Just as Snapper had said, eyes of a cobra or a shark – killers' eyes! There was a notation below.

Ivan Bassler. Also known as Ivan Kairis or Ivan Immonovic. Stasi agent, often on loan to KGB. One of KGB's top assassins. Has no particular M/O as his expertise includes blades, sniper, explosives and martial arts. His record indicates he enjoys his work. Known by his colleagues as "Ivan the Terrible."

The file then listed a number of murders associated with Ivan.

There was a hand-written note stapled to the file, in Ross' handwriting.

"Bob, we don't know who the other guy is, but if there were any untimely deaths on your island during the time Ivan was there, you can bet Ivan caused them. You need to find out what's behind his visit, buddy."

Carpenter took his letter opener and carefully slipped it under Ivan's photo and slowly jimmied it off the page. He slid it in his pocket, then opened the safe behind his desk and locked the file in it. He called out, "Janice!"

She poked her head in the office, "Something I can do for you, sir?"

"Yes, how do I get a membership of the Royal Bermuda Yacht Club?"

"You already have one, sir."

"Really, how's that?"

"Well, sir, the US Consul General, whomever he may be, automatically and immediately gains membership. So, you're already a member."

"Well, that's quite convenient! Do I need a reservation to have lunch there?"

"No sir."

"Well, it's almost lunchtime, I think I'll go over there and have a drink, then lunch," he said, grabbing his jacket from behind his chair. He wanted to confront Bessemer, but not at Tudor Hill. Vindham was certain to be sticking to him like glue up there, so if he could catch Bessemer at the Club, it would be best.

He strolled leisurely down Par-La-Ville Road and crossed Front Street in front of the Bank of Bermuda. The Club was behind the bank, adjacent to Albuoy's Point. Despite his leisurely pace it took him no more than 3 minutes to get there. He checked his watch, it was noon. Then he heard it. One of the things he found strange about Hamilton was that at high-noon each day, a fire siren, very much like an air-raid siren during the War, gave a single blast letting everyone know that it was lunchtime. *I guess there must be a shortage of watches in Bermuda,* he ironically thought.

He entered the bar, and after surveying the room, stepped up to the counter. "What's your pleasure, Mr. Carpenter?"

"Have we met before?"

"No sir. But I saw you get off Snapper's boat the other day and get into the big white car, so I figured out who you were. Snapper's a mate of mine. My name is Derrick."

"Nice to meet you, Derrick. Any friend of Snapper is a friend of mine. I'll have a scotch on the rocks."

"Coming right up."

"You the guy who told Snapper about the men who met Jack Bessemer?"

Derrick looked a little sheepish. "Yessir, I did."

Carpenter noticed his reaction. "No problem, it's alright. I think I might have met these guys somewhere before. Was this guy one of them?" He took the photo from his pocket and slid it on the bar. Derrick's eyes widened.

"Yessir. That was one of them alright. You know this guy, sir?

"Not really, but I have a friend who is trying to locate him. There's been a death in his family, you know."

"Well, Mr. Carpenter, I haven't seen him in a week or so, but if I do, I'll let him know."

"By the way, Dr. Bessemer's one of your regulars, isn't he?"

"Yessir."

"When is he usually here?"

"Oh, between 4:30 and 5 o'clock."

"OK, thanks Derrick, I'm gonna have my lunch now. See yuh." He took his drink and wandered into the dining room.

Carpenter returned to the Club at precisely 5:10. Derrick was still behind the bar. He glanced toward the back of the room. Carpenter followed his eyes and saw Bessemer in the corner. "Scotch Mr. Carpenter?" Carpenter nodded and walked directly to Jack's table.

When Jack saw him, he stood up, extended his hand and welcomed him warmly. "Good to see you again, Mr. Carpenter," Jack said. Derrick brought over the scotch.

"Jack, let's dispense with the formalities, just call me Bob. I just discovered that I have an automatic membership to this place. And it's so convenient from my office, just 3 minutes! Nice to be able to have an occasional taste, particularly after a hard day. You agree?"

"Sure do. You know, my wife Evelyn has really put down roots here. After having the baby she's become involved in several local charities and social groups, so she encouraged me to join up here so we can mix and mingle, you know what I mean."

"Yeah, sure Jack. So, do you have a boat here too?

"Yeah, just a little thing to putter around in, you know."

"Really, can I see it?"

"OK, it's right out there. Let's go." They got up from their table, taking their drinks with them and went outside to the dock. "There she is, over there, the little outboard. Just enough to get me and the misses and the baby out on the water occasionally. As beautiful as Bermuda is, it's most beautiful from the water."

"Yes, indeed. I saw that when I took that slow boat out to the Tower the other day." Bob pulled out a pack of Chesterfields, "Smoke?" Jack took one and they both lit up, slowly exhaling into the afternoon breeze with great satisfaction. Gently getting to his point, Bob said, "Jack, I have a friend of mine whose had a death in his family. I'm trying to find him. Do you know this guy?"

He reached into his pocket and slowly pulled out Ivan's photo and held it up for Jack to see. The colour drained completely from Jack's face, as he stared at the photo. His mouth, which a moment before, had a cigarette in it, gaped, dropping the fag to the concrete. Meanwhile, Bob fixed Jack's eyes with a steady, penetrating stare. Jack couldn't look at him, casting his eyes to the ground. Jack tried to speak but nothing could pass his lips. His voice, his tongue, his whole brain was locked down – completely inoperative.

"I repeat, Jack, do you know this man?" Bob said, hardening his tone, still fixing him with the stare. Jack still couldn't look at him. "Look, come with me." Bob grasped his arm, Jack following along like a 5-year-old boy. They sat down on a nearby bench in a place called, Barr's Bay Park. No one was around.

"Now Jack, you have to say something! I know that you know this guy. You do know him, don't you?" Jack nodded numbly. "Well, that's a start anyway. Seeing that you've lost your ability to speak, perhaps I should do the talking, huh?" No response. "This man, whom you know as Ivan Kairis is really named Ivan Bassler. He is one of the KGB's top assassins!"

Jack started to convulse, and he vomited on the grass next to the bench. He retched over and over again until there was nothing left to eject but bile. And still he heaved. Bob, having participated in scenarios like this several times before, realized that patience was essential for the encounter to be productive. Eventually, Jack exhausted himself and stopped puking, slumped down on the bench, breathing heavily. Bob reached into his pocket and gave Jack his handkerchief to clean himself up.

"Now, Jack, the good news is that clearly Ivan was not here to kill you, or you'd already be dead by now. How do you know Ivan Bassler?" Bob gripped Jack by the lapel and bellowed, "How the HELL do you know Ivan Bassler!"

"I don't know him," Jack sighed, somewhat regaining his power of speech, "I know the other guy, Dino. Dino showed up a week or so ago at the Club with Ivan in tow."

"Well, who the hell is this Dino, and what is he to you?"

Jack sighed and stared at the ground, "Dino's real name is Dimitri, and he is a KGB agent."

"WHAT THE HELL IS A MAN WITH YOUR RESPONSIBILITIES DOING HANGING OUT WITH TWO KGB AGENTS?" Bob roared; his face aflame. He paused. "From what I gather, they're not your friends." He paused again for a few moments, gathering his thoughts. Then it came to him. He refixed Jack with his x-ray stare. His voice almost a whisper now, "Do they have something on you?" He noticed a flicker in Jack's eyes. "Ah ha! What do they have on you, Jack? Are they blackmailing you?" Bob shoved his face right up into Jack's, wincing momentarily at his foul puke breath and roared, "ARE THEY GODDAMN-WELL BLACKMAILING YOU, JACK?"

Jack nodded dejectedly, still not able to meet Bob's stare.

"What is it, dirty money?" Bob demanded. Jack shook his head. "Then it's a woman. Is it a woman, Jack?" Jack nodded meekly. "Ah! The oldest trick in the book – the honey trap! So, they trapped you with a woman. Here?"

Jack shook his head, speaking almost inaudibly, "In London."

"So, what, they snagged you with some hooker in London and took your picture?"

"No, not a hooker, Anna, a girl I knew from my Caltech days. She turned out to be a KGB agent too!"

"That figures, Jack, don't feel so bad." Bob gave him a pat on the shoulder. "This sort of thing happens all the time. So much so, the Russians have a word for it, 'Kompromat,' that's what they call it."

"Not to me," Jack mumbled.

"What?"

"You said this sort of thing happens all the time. It's never happened to me before."

"You are not the first and you won't be the last. Trust me. Now, let's get to the serious part. You have access to highly sensitive information – top secret! Did you give them anything?" Bob once more fixed Jack with the stare, but Jack had already, long ago, surrendered. Jack nodded.

"I gave them a schematic drawing of a hydrophone, but it was the basic model. We've improved them 300-400 percent since then. We don't use those old ones out there at Argus anymore. Besides, the real secret is our ability to accurately interpret the sounds we hear."

"How'd you get it to them?"

"They said they never got it. I don't know why not. Anyway, I used Scaley DeSilva."

"You mean the same guy that was eaten by sharks at Challenger Bank? Jack, with Ivan on the boat, you can be sure it was no accident that he fell overboard in the middle of a shark feeding frenzy."

"Yeah, no shit."

"Why was Scaley involved?"

"There was this Cuban trawler, *La Pescadora Langosta*, hanging around the Tower, for months on end. Everybody assumed it was the Russians trying to figure out what we were doing out there."

"Yeah, I heard about it."

"Scaley was out there on Argus Bank almost every day, sport fishing. I used poor Scaley," Jack said with a sigh. "You see, I know this rich guy that was his business backer, and I encouraged this guy, after several rounds of black rum, to put his loans to Scaley as bets in a couple of gambling sessions. I conned the guy at cards and ended up pretty much owning Scaley. I forced him to do my bidding. One day, I took the schematic of the hydrophones put it in a bottle, sealed it, and gave it to Scaley. In a day or so, Scaley, pretended he was trolling and took it over close to *La Pescadora Langosta*, and made the drop. Even though I didn't see the final drop, *La Pescadora* disappeared from Bermuda waters that very same day – never to be seen again.

"But Dino said they never got it, so I guess the Cuban trawler never reached Havana. It was around the same time as hurricane Gracie was in the area. So, she may have sunk in that storm. Scaley's murder was clearly a warning to me!"

"Jack, you're in some serious shit! You've been colluding with enemy agents, giving them state secrets! That's Treason! You're caught between the assassin, Ivan the Terrible, on the one hand, and the wrath of Uncle Sam on the other. You're screwed, either way, Pal." Jack started to heave again, but there was nothing left to come up. Bob paused for what seemed like an eternity to Jack.

"But I've got a wife! I've got a kid!" He blurted out.

"You should have thought about that before you started banging Anna," Bob barked. There was another long pause. Then his tone moderated. "But there's one other possibility."

"Another possibility? What's that?" Jack's mind was desperately grasping for straws.

"You can work for me."

"What do you mean, work for you. You mean at the Consulate?"

"No, stupid!" Bob snapped harshly. "You PhDs have no damn sense!

"You will continue to cooperate with your Russian 'friends,' but you will answer to me!

"You will do exactly what I say, when I say it! You will give them the information that I allow you to give, in the form and in the place that I prescribe! You will report any and all contacts with your KGB 'friends' to me at once! You will tell no other living soul about our relationship! Otherwise, I will personally inform your dear wife that you've been banging a Russian agent." He paused.

"She probably knows this girl, doesn't she?"

Jack nodded.

"I will tell her about this KGB tryst of yours, then see to it that Uncle Sam puts you up in his luxury hotel at Leavenworth. Is that clear Doctor?"

Jack nodded.

"Say it! Is that clear?"

"Yes, sir. That is clear."

"Good. Now clean yourself up before you go home. Evelyn will smell you a mile off. I'll be in touch."

Bob Carpenter got up leaving Jack slumped on the bench. He strolled back to his office, whistling all the way. He thought, *Yesss! Again, we play the dangerous game! Haven't had this much fun in years!*

## Court Street

Carpenter was at his desk in the Consulate when Janice came in, "Sir, don't forget you have to write that report for the State Department. The deadline is this Friday."

"How am I supposed to write a report on the general, social and political situation in Bermuda when I've only been here for such a short time?"

"Well, Mr. Carpenter, we have loads of files here on events, people and institutions. Perhaps I can select a few to help you get a sense of what has gone on here."

"Excellent idea Janice. I'm most grateful." In five minutes, she reappeared with a stack of file folders which she plonked down in his "Inbox." Bob took it from the top. It was clear that Janice had been expecting this request, as the files were not randomly selected, nor in random order. As a former OSS case officer, he was a quick reader, but despite this ability, it took him well over 2 hours to plough through the information.

He gained a better understanding of how the white Establishment's control of the island's commercial and legislative sectors, was virtually complete. It also became clear, that, although Uncle Sam was welcomed here, the Establishment had a certain unease with the American presence, particularly as it related to the employment opportunities that the Yankee Dollar afforded the local black population. They were accustomed to being in complete control, and the large American presence was having the effect of loosening that grip.

During Carpenter's years of experience in the Caribbean and Latin America he encountered many small groups of ruling elites in the islands and the "Banana Republics," but none he had encountered had such a clear racial delineation as Bermuda's. Recalling his many long conversations with Maya, he was sure that there would be two sides to any national narrative. After he had read all the files Janice had provided, he felt they provided information only from a certain perspective, the white perspective. Having already met the likes of Snapper, Derrick and Milton, and considering the population of the island was about two thirds coloured, he was certain that there were major pieces of the puzzle missing.

He decided he would look through the files himself. He strode to the filing cabinets and randomly opened one of them. "Is there anything I can help you with?" Janice asked. She was clearly not pleased that he was rummaging through "her" files.

"I'm OK, thanks." She unsmilingly returned to her desk.

Randomly he opened the drawer labelled, "E-G." Under "G" there were thick files for names like "Gosling" and "Gibbons." He wasn't interested in these, as they were covered in the brief that Janice had provided him. He saw a file under the name of "Grant, Rodney Horatio." That name didn't sound familiar, so he plucked it from the drawer, along with a few others, and returned to his desk. Its contents were newspaper clippings plus a long memo from one of his predecessors. "My God – look at this! A Nazi spy, murdering his cook! A U-boat sunk by a Navy squadron, using a local fisherman as spotter! A British cover-up! Unbelievable! This is some juicy stuff!"

The 12:00 siren broke the spell. It was lunchtime and he decided to stroll to the Club for a drink and a bite. Stepping up to the bar, Derrick fetched him his scotch. "Derrick, do you remember that Captain Rodney Grant business?"

"Oh, sure, Mr. Carpenter! He was a regular here. He was a favourite among the members. Had everyone fooled, except for old Hooks, of course."

"Hooks, oh yeah, that was the fisherman guy. Whatever happened to him?"

"Went out one night, fishin', and never came back. Lost at sea. You know that Hooks was Snapper's Deddy, don't you?"

"You're kidding me!"

"Ya, Snapper's a chip off the old block. Got salt in his veins like his old man."

"Derrick, you're a walking encyclopaedia of things Bermudian."

"A lotta things happen in this-here Club bar. I keep my eyes and ears open."

Having wet his whistle, Carpenter went over to the lunchroom. After lunch he reread the file on Grant and decided that the sanitized perspective of Bermuda that his secretary and the Bermuda Establishment had given him was not the complete picture of a community that he had an obligation to understand, before he reported back to his superiors in the State Department. He pressed the button on his intercom. Within seconds Janice appeared in his doorway.

"Sir, something I can do for you?"

"Yes, Janice. I want you to get a Mr. A.B. Pace on the phone. He's the publisher of the local newspaper called the *Bermuda Recorder*."

"Of course, sir." A disapproving look overtook Janice's face.

In a few minutes Pace was on the line. Carpenter picked up. "Mr. Carpenter, this is an unexpected honour. I don't think this paper has ever received an unsolicited call from the top US official in Bermuda."

"Good day, Mr. Pace. As the new boy on the block, so to speak, I'm trying to get a feel for my new posting here, that is, through the prism of the entire spectrum of viewpoints. I have read through some of our files here in the Consulate and encountered a number of clippings from your newspaper. Some of it is very interesting stuff."

"Well, thank you, sir."

"I wonder if we could meet and have a chat?"

"Why, certainly! I can come …"

"No, no, Mr. Pace, pardon my interrupting," Carpenter interrupted, "I'd like to come over to your paper."

"You would?" Pace was incredulous.

"Yes. Is that a problem?"

"Ah … certainly not. We're running today's edition right now, so tomorrow morning would be a good time, say 10 o'clock?"

"Excellent, see you then." He hung up.

Carpenter knew that he was overstepping the normal parameters of diplomatic surveillance. Knowing the strategic importance of their listening posts on the island, and after the discovery of the activities of "Ivan the Terrible" in their midst, he felt he needed to assess all the risk factors affecting the successful continuation of Uncle Sam's listening activities on the island. He needed to know the probability of Bermuda exploding into race riots and putting the important functions of Tudor Hill and SOFAR at risk. He, therefore, was operating in that grey, overlapping area involving "diplomatic mode" and "spy mode."

The next day the big white car, with a fluttering Star-Spangled Banner on each fender, was waiting in Chelston's driveway. Just before he exited the vehicle in front of the Consulate office, Tony Fox said, "Mr. Carpenter, I'll be waiting here at 9:55 to take you to your meeting with the Recorder."

"That's OK Tony, it's a beautiful day, I think I'll walk."

"Walk? Are you sure sir? Do you know the way? I don't want you to get into any trouble."

"I'll be fine, and I promise you that you won't get into any trouble with Janice," he said with a chuckle.

He really didn't know the way, but thought, *How can I get lost in such a small place? I really need to see the other side of Town.*

After reading the most urgent missives on his desk from Washington, he set out to find the Recorder Building. First walking through Par-La-Ville Park, he turned left up Queen Street to Church Street. There, at the top of the hill, he found that Church Street was quite broad, by Bermuda standards, as it was the main public bus terminal, complete with British made, olive-green Seddon buses, roaring and spewing clouds of noxious diesel smoke. There was an empty lot behind the parked buses where Carpenter had read, once stood Bermuda's first hotel, the Hamilton Hotel. It had burned to the ground in 1955. Next to the empty lot was the spanking new Hamilton City Hall which had opened earlier in 1960. It was a large white building with what at first glance looked like a large clock tower. However, upon closer inspection, the clock face was, in fact, a compass rose with an arrow that indicated the wind direction instead of the time. Consistent with the nautical theme, instead of a rooster on the wind vane on the pinnacle of the tower, there was a square-rigged sailing ship. *Who needs a clock when you have a high noon siren?* Carpenter chuckled to himself.

Enjoying his freedom from his "Handlers" and following his instincts, he turned east along the part of Church Street in front of City Hall called "Nellie's Walk," until he reached Burnaby Street, just before the hill to the Anglican Cathedral, an edifice that totally dominated the city skyline. He turned left, walking north down Cedar Avenue. He knew from the files from the E-G drawer that it was somewhere around here that Professor Albert Einstein stayed while he was in Bermuda, eschewing the large luxurious hotels in town because they did not accept Jews.

Turning right at Dundonald Street he became aware that he was in a residential area of Hamilton and that this appeared to be the coloured part of Town. Somewhere along the way he had crossed an invisible boundary line. When he got to Court Street, he found several shops and restaurants. He had travelled widely throughout the Caribbean and he noticed this part of Hamilton's architecture and its people reminded him of that part of the world. He entered one store and purchased a pack of Chesterfields. He asked the coloured saleslady, "Ma'am, I wonder if you could tell me where the Recorder Building is, please?"

She smiled and said, "Sure, mate, it's two blocks up the road, that way."

Following her directions, he found the building next to a large church. It was a modest establishment, and when he entered there were all the familiar sounds and smells of printing. There was the clacking of a linotype machine, and the smell was that of molten lead. It was also noisy because they were still breaking down the press from yesterday's run. A short dark-skinned man appeared in front of him. He smiled and extended his hand, "Good morning, Mr. Carpenter, I'm A.B. Pace. Come in please, it's an honour to have you in my establishment."

"Hello, Mr. Pace. The sounds and smells of printing take me back to when I was a boy. My dad was the editor of a small-town newspaper in Pennsylvania."

"Really? So, I guess you are a journalist at heart, then."

"Yes, somewhere, lurking very deep inside," he replied with a wry smile.

"Would you like me to show you around?"

"Sure, Mr. Pace, a look 'round would be excellent."

"Everyone calls me A B."

"People call me Bob."

After the brief tour, they went into Pace's office which was small and cluttered with papers and other paraphernalia.

Carpenter started out, "A B, I'm trying to find out the lay of the land here in Bermuda. If I'm to be of any use to Uncle Sam, I need to know the facts about this place, not a narrative filtered by some wealthy member of the Yacht Club. You know what I mean?"

"Ya, I know exactly what you mean," Pace answered with his own wry smile.

"We have many clippings from your newspaper in our files, and I've read a few. It seems that you have your finger on the pulse of the coloured community here. What is the situation insofar as race relations are concerned?"

"You get right to the point, don't you?"

"Sometimes."

"Well, the pressure is on. Everybody in the coloured community wants the end of segregation, but the 40 Thieves are hanging on for dear life. They keep using you guys as an excuse!"

"Us? You mean Americans?"

"Ya. They say white American tourists won't stay in hotels that also allow coloured guests. They say white American tourists won't patronize restaurants that allow coloured customers. And tourists are our bread and butter! If we don't have tourists, nobody in Bermuda will have money, not the whites, nor the coloureds – nobody. They say that if we end segregation, it will be an economic disaster. We know it's segregated down in the Southern States, but it ain't like that in New York. I've been there! And most of our visitors come from the northeast."

"Go on."

"Well, there's tension among us coloured folks as well. There are some prominent voices that are so angry they want their complete freedom right now and they're willing to bust up the place to get it, if they have to. Then there are other prominent voices who are more like gradualists than revolutionaries, you know? They want change without the bust-up. There's a lot of tension between those two factions. Just like in the States."

"I noticed there are a lot of shops and restaurants around here where a lot of coloured people work. Who owns those businesses?"

"Most of the businesses around here are owned by us blacks. We call this neighbourhood, "Back a' Town."

"Back of Town, Why?"

"Well, you have Front Street and Back a' Town."

"OK, like in New York you have Downtown and Uptown."

"Right!"

"But, you see, here in Back a' Town, we're just getting the crumbs. Front Street is getting the whole loaf, plus the cake and icing too. When visitors come to Hamilton, hardly any of them venture as far back as Back a' Town, and it isn't because it's not safe around here. Back a' Town is safe. So, in order for us to get any part of that Yankee Dollar we have to work for the white man on Front and Reid Streets, in hotels and nightclubs, then spend our few dollars Back a' Town in our own businesses."

"So, would you say that Bermuda's a powder keg that's about to explode?"

"Well, I don't know. Sometimes I think so, other times not. What with all the civil rights protests going on in the States, people here are saying, 'why not us?' But I sure don't want any violence. Things are bad here, but violence would make things worse. We've made some progress, but tensions are still high."

"How does segregation work here in Bermuda? I don't see any 'whites only' signs in Hamilton."

"Well, in a small island like Bermuda you don't have to have signs. All of us know the places that turned us away, so we just didn't go there. There were no laws that explicitly enforced overt racial segregation in Bermuda. Our laws were silent on the subject of discrimination. So, if a hotelier or restauranteur wanted all white patrons, he could turn away coloured people and he would've offended no laws. According to our laws, the concept of racial discrimination just didn't exist. Same thing with Jews."

"I see. But I notice you're using the past tense." Even though Carpenter was appalled by this information, he felt he had to adopt an impartial façade as part of his diplomatic obligation not to get embroiled in local politics.

A.B. continued. "You know, everybody likes to go to the movies, right? Some of the theatres in Town were segregated."

"How'd they segregate movie theatres?"

"The whites could sit anywhere they wanted but the coloureds could only sit downstairs and on the sides. This allowed a whites-only balcony where they could throw spit balls or whatever down on us."

"Oh my!"

"Well, this shadowy group, called the 'Progressive Group,' got together and organized a boycott of the theatres."

"All of them?"

"Ya, all of them. They're all run by the same people anyway!"

"Oh, right."

"Not only did the coloureds boycott the theatres, they picketed them too! To add some muscle to the boycott. It went on for quite a while, but the company, Bermuda General Theatres, closed their theatres completely and after a while started to feel the pinch, and they eventually caved."

"Was there any violence?"

"No, none. It was beautifully executed."

"Who were the Progressive Group?"

"Nobody knows. Remains secret to this day. I guess they're scared of retribution by the 40 Thieves. The anonymity made them more powerful. But you could tell the tide was starting to turn."

"Uh huh. What happened next?"

"The next big thing was the in-your-face racism in restaurants, bars and hotels. Of all things, this was the most humiliating. There was this law, the "Innkeepers' Act," which allowed managers of such businesses the discretion to racially discriminate, or not. Again, it was silent on the concept of racial discrimination. That law had to be amended to recognize reality and prohibit racial discrimination. Well, they had been talking about improved race relations in Parliament for about 10 years. They had two Select Committees studying the issue in Parliament – studying it and studying it, but doing nothing. You see, the Front Street boys control Parliament, because you have to own land to vote."

"Really! You have to own land to vote?"

"Ya. This was another way the rich whites controlled Parliament. Elections had to be held on two consecutive days because if a rich white guy had land in all nine parishes, he would need the time, traveling in his carriage, to visit each of the nine polling stations to cast his vote."

"You mean to say, he could vote nine times?"

"Exactly! Most coloured people in Bermuda are tenants and don't own land and therefore can't vote. That's why Parliament is dominated by rich white guys."

"I mean, this is an incredibly archaic system."

"Ya, it is. It's like England and the States were some 200 years ago. But there are rumblings of change. I hear rumours of the formation of a political party. A black party! Now that would shake things up."

"Yeah, I guess so!"

"But I think the success of the Theatre Boycott got some of the 40 Thieves thinking that if they didn't give a little now, the pressure would cause an explosion later on and they might lose everything. And brother, they have a lot to lose! So, after many years of trying, the minority of coloured members of parliament were able to convince enough of these scared white members to amend the Innkeepers' Act to outlaw discrimination based on race in bars, restaurants and hotels. That was a big victory!"

"So, it's all over now?"

"Hell no! We've still got a long way to go. Schools are still segregated – some schools sit on land given to them specifically for the education of white children only. As I said, the voting system is rigged in favour of whites. There's segregation in the workplace because there're no anti-discrimination laws relating to employment. They even have whites only residential districts, even though there's no sign that says so. On top of that, the whites own 90% of the economy. And there are all kinds of hidden rules and regulations to keep us out, even if we had the money. And, by the way, we can't get the credit we need because these same old boys control the banks. So no, we've still got a long way to go."

"A.B., I've travelled throughout the islands and as bad as you say things are here for your people, they still look a lot better off than your counterparts in the West Indies. I don't see any shanty towns in Bermuda."

"We do a fantastic job of concealing it, but believe me, we have poverty. If you've got the time, I'll show it to you."

"OK. But how about our GI's. How's the US military treating your people?"

"That is the shaft of light in the darkness, my friend."

"Really, how so?"

"A lot of our guys, and gals too, have found work on the American bases. There're a lot of civilian jobs that Bermudians are doing on the bases. For instance, there's a company down there called the Maytag Company and they hire a lot of us to refuel airplanes. And there's a lot of refuelling to be done down there because Kindley Field is a major refuelling station for transatlantic military transports. And there are a lot of other civilian jobs down there too. And they pay US union wages, which are a lot higher than Bermudian wages. The Front Street boys hate this and have tried time and again to stop it, but none of it has worked. They hate it because it lessens their control. The base work has been a way for coloured people to get around their strangle hold and to earn a better living."

"Nice to be appreciated," Carpenter said, half sarcastically. "So, what about independence? A lot of the islands in the Caribbean are talking about independence from Britain. What about here?"

"Well, in spite of all the prejudice and injustices here, Bermudians are still a conservative bunch – coloureds too! Some are for it, of course, but I don't think we're going to rush into it. A lot of us just want to break down this colour barrier and get a fair share of that loaf and cake. You talk about our cousins in the Caribbean, they are dominated by British absentee plantation owners and landlords. Bermuda's white domination is local. Independence won't remove them. They are as intrinsically part of Bermuda as the blacks are."

"Well, A.B. I very much appreciate your candour. I'd better be getting back to the Consulate now. One more thing. You know Snapper Jones, right?"

"Yes, of course!"

"What do you think of him?"

"May I ask why you've asked me that?"

"Well, I've got something I want him to do for me and wanted to know what you think of him, seeing that you've known him longer than me."

"Well, I've known him longer than he's known himself. He comes from a fine upright family. I knew his father, Hooks Jones, well, and he was an exceptionally fine man. Same goes for his mother, Edith."

"Yes, I read about him in one of your articles."

"Snapper's a chip off the old block. Has a strong sense of right and wrong and is very responsible. Despite what those Front Street boys said about him in Parliament, he was a real hero in that *Wilhelmina* disaster – saved a lot of lives. You can rely on Snapper."

Carpenter rose from his chair and extended his hand. "Thanks for the background information. Really appreciate it."

Pace looked outside, "Where's yuh car?"

"I walked over. Made a wrong turn up there, but a nice lady gave me the right directions."

"You were walking around on Court Street? I'll bet you'll hear about it at the Yacht Club. In Bermuda, there are no secrets – there're eyes everywhere! Thanks for your interest and for coming by."

Carpenter laughed and ambled back to the Consulate.

Pace picked up his phone and placed a call to SOFAR. Eventually Snapper came to the phone, "Hello?"

"Snapper, this is A.B."

"Hey, Mr. Pace. This is an unexpected pleasure. What can I do for you?"

"Look, Snapper, just to give you a heads-up. The new Consul General was over here at the Press, on a tour. He asked me about you. Don't know what for, but something good might be coming your way. So, don't screw it up!" He hung up.

*Wonder what that's all about?*

# Drinks

Bob Carpenter didn't sleep that night as his mind wouldn't switch off. The next morning, he dashed up the stairs of the Vallis Building, having grown impatient with waiting for the sole elevator. On his way through the outer office, he made sure that he said, "Good morning," to all the staff as he passed by, Janice having previously taken him aside and informing him that failing to do so was akin to a "capital" societal offence in Bermuda. As she brought him his morning coffee he said, "Thanks. Janice, I want you to contact Dr. Jack Bessemer at Tudor Hill and invite him to drinks, at Chelston at 5:30 this evening."

"Sir, isn't this short notice, and is Mrs. Bessemer included?"

"Oh, I think he'll be able to make it. And no wives, we'll be talking shop."

Later on, that evening, at Chelston, Jack Bessemer drove into the driveway and was met by Milton Lawrence. "Good evening, Dr. Bessemer. The Consul General is expecting you. Right this way." Retrospectively, Jack was quite embarrassed at his own behaviour at his last encounter with Bob Carpenter. *I've got to conduct myself with more self-control and dignity than the last time. Who is this guy, Carpenter, anyway? Much more than meets the eye! Doesn't matter, he's got me by the balls.* So, he steeled himself.

He was led through a large vestibule, through a wood panelled passageway into a large study. The room was lined with bookshelves, almost up to the ceiling. The shelves were made of Bermuda cedar that had been exquisitely finished into a warm reddish-brown glow. The floor was covered with a magnificent Persian carpet. In one corner was a large custom built, antique Bermuda cedar roll-top desk, lovingly restored, complete with drawers on each side and slots and cubbyholes for mail and correspondence. As there was nothing on it, Jack presumed that it was more for show than everyday use. There were two windows in the room, featuring heavy drapes on the sides and gossamer sheers in the middle to allow in natural light. There were four heavy upholstered chairs, one of which seated the Consul General.

He rose, extended his hand warmly and said, "Welcome Jack. How do you like my new digs?"

"Pretty impressive."

Nestled between his third and index fingers of his left hand was a large glass of red wine. "Wine? Cote du Rhone blend. Quite spectacular, actually. This place has an amazing wine cellar."

"No thanks, just water, please." It was obvious that Jack was very nervous.

There was a decanter of water already set up in one of the corners and Milton poured it, brought it over and shut the door behind him as he departed.

Carpenter continued, "Jack, I'd like to think we should be able to conduct our business with cordiality and civility. Don't you agree?"

"Yes, I do."

"There are a few gaps that I need filled in. First of all, how did this Anna make contact with you in London? Did you already have her number or something? I mean did you already have a thing on the side with her?"

"No, I hadn't seen nor heard from her since our graduation."

"So, you two were an item at Caltech?"

"No. It was not for my lack of trying. I had a thing for her, and she knew it, but she always had her head in the books."

"So how did you make contact in London?"

"She works in the British Ministry of Defence as a scientific analyst."

"What! The British Ministry of Defence! She's a KGB agent in a NATO member's Defence Ministry?"

"Yes. Dino Sokratis was posing as her brother.

"After they revealed they had Kompromat on you, what did they tell you?"

"They said they wanted to know about project Artemis."

"That figures."

"No, not really."

"What do you mean?"

"Project Artemis is soon to be cancelled. It doesn't work!"

"Doesn't work? Well, then, what the hell are you guys doing up there in Tudor Hill, the Tower and SOFAR?"

"Well, Artemis was based on the same concept as active sonar on a ship or submarine. You ping something, you get a reflected sound, you measure the time lag of that echo, and thus you can tell the distance to the object. For a variety of technical reasons this hasn't proven to be successful on a much larger scale, like Artemis was supposed to be. So, it has no future. But we have developed the actual listening devices so much since we started, and we've hugely increased our ability to analyse and interpret what we hear. This has enabled us to track submerged objects passively."

"What do you mean passively?"

"If you drop a hydrophone down into the ocean, it's not silent. There are lots of natural sounds down there, made by the living inhabitants of the sea: fish and mammals, like whales, porpoises and dolphins. Then there're also sounds from seismic activity in the ocean floor. Many of these sounds are below our audible range but our hydrophones can pick all this stuff up. With that electronic gear you saw up there in Tudor Hill and the Tower, we can filter out all that extraneous stuff and focus in on the man-made sounds, like those from submarines. The big advantage of passive tracking versus active tracking is that if you're using active tracking, when you ping a submarine, it can hear the ping, so it knows it's being tracked. With passive tracking the target has no idea it's being detected and tracked.

"The low frequency sounds emitted by Soviet submarines carry a long, long way, in the SOFAR channel, and each boat type is characterized by its unique signature."

"So, you're telling me that the KGB are killing people in Bermuda for information on a technology they don't even know is defunct?"

"That's right. So, if we gave them the specs for the hydrophone like the one that I gave Scaley DeSilva, the same specs that got lost somewhere in the Bermuda Triangle, they would be happy."

"Wrong! They would be happy for a while, at least until such time as they discover that what you're giving them is useless. When they find out they're going to send in Ivan for you." Jack went pale again. "Are you willing to take that risk?"

After a long pause Jack replied, "I guess I don't have much choice, do I, sir."

"Well, I guess you don't. So, when they make contact again, we'll give them that useless schematic." Jack nodded. "How will they make contact?"

"Well, they've set up an offshore company here, a shipping company and a bogus shipping research NGO in London. We'll use them as a cover."

"So, Jack, what have you done with the deeds for Scaley's house and the note on his boat?" Bob asked, abruptly changing the subject.

"What? What deeds?" Jack was thrown off by the sudden shift in the conversation.

"Oh, oh! Why, nothing, sir."

"Well, they're ill-gotten gains. You will sign them over to me – right now. Here, take this pen and paper."

Jack went over to the roll-top desk and wrote what Bob dictated to him. Then he signed it.

"Good! Have the note and those deeds sent over to me tomorrow morning. That poor woman!" Carpenter muttered.

"What woman?"

"Scaley's widow, what's her name?"

"Maria, sir"

"These shenanigans you've been up to have taken that woman's husband and livelihood away from her and her son. We're going to fix that."

"How?"

"Leave that to me. Remember, let the Russians make contact with you first. Don't try to contact them. Now, I think it's time you got back to your family."

Realizing he had been dismissed, Jack Bessemer rose from his chair, nodded and said, "Good evening, Mr. Carpenter.

"Good night, Jack."

The next morning at the Consulate, a package arrived containing the title deeds to Scaley's home and the promissory note for the boat. Carpenter picked up the phone and dialed the SOFAR station in St. David's and asked for Snapper Jones. After a long wait he came on the line.

"Snapper, this is Bob Carpenter."

"Hi, Mr. Carpenter, um… um, Bob. Lookin' for another slow boat to the Tower?"

"Not exactly, Snapper. I don't think my heart can take trying to get on that ladder again."

Snapper laughed out loud.

"You going to be in Town any time soon?"

"Sure! *T-Boat's* dry docked for a couple of days – getting her bottom cleaned, so I've got some spare time. I could come up this afternoon if you like."

"Excellent. Why don't you come up to Chelston for a drink, say 5:30?"

"Chelston. Well, sir, I'm not really dressed for someplace like that."

"Don't worry about that, it's all very casual. In any case, it'll just be you and me."

"OK, I'll be there." The line went dead.

At 5:30 Snapper Jones turned into the gate of Chelston and parked his Zundapp on the side of the driveway. Milton came out to meet him, immaculately dressed as always, and he was shown into the study.

"Snapper, thanks for coming," said Carpenter.

"Wow, this place is amazing!"

"Yes, it is, isn't it? What'll you have?"

"Dark and Stormy please." Milton quickly produced the beverage.

"Snapper, you'll have to bear with me because I can't tell you everything you need to know for this all to make sense. As you know I'm responsible for US citizens on the island." Snapper nodded. "Well, I'm concerned that a US citizen has come into possession of something that is Bermudian, by dishonourable means, and in doing so, he has caused great distress to a Bermudian. You follow?"

"I'm not sure I do."

"Well, with Scaley DeSilva gone, poor Maria is home with the baby without any income whatsoever, isn't that what you said?"

"Ya, that's true."

"And it was a US citizen that caused that."

"Are you saying that a US citizen was responsible for Scaley's death, sir?"

"No, I'm definitely not saying that. What I'm saying is that a US citizen dishonourably obtained a note on the charter boat, the *Captain Crunch* and now that boat is just sitting there not earning any money for Scaley's family."

"Oh, I see. What's this got to do with me?"

"I have a proposition for you." He paused dramatically and Snapper leaned forward in his seat in anticipation. "How would you like to take over the *Captain Crunch*? On the condition that you share a specific portion of the earnings with Scaley's widow, Maria."

"You mean leave SOFAR and become skipper on the *Crunch*. You can make that happen?"

"Yes, I can make that happen."

"That would be fantastic!" After a few seconds Snapper became serious once again. "Ain't no white man ever done anything for me before.

"What's the catch here, sir?"

"No catch. I read the file on your father, Hooks Jones. He was quite a guy, and Uncle Sam owes him a great debt of gratitude for his heroism, a debt that was never repaid. This is the least we can do. But there is something I want you to do for me. I want you to go to Mrs. Desilva and tell her that you've made arrangements with Scaley's backer and that you'll be taking over the *Crunch* and will be regularly giving her, her share of the profits going forward.

"Ya, no problem. It's the right thing to do. I'm sure Scaley would approve. I've met Maria, she's a nice girl," a quick smile flashed on his face as her image popped in his mind. "And I'm sure she'll be so relieved." Snapper drained the rest of his drink. "There's one more thing."

"What's that?"

"SOFAR rely on me for a variety of things. Getting one of the guys to take over *T-Boat* is no big deal. However, I'm fill-in skipper on the *Sir Horace Lamb* when the regular skipper is unavailable. Without me they're stuck."

"Maybe you can come to a more flexible arrangement."

"Ya, that might work. Is there anything else sir?"

"No Snapper, that's it. Come by the office tomorrow and I'll have the paperwork ready for you to pick up at the front desk."

"Thanks again Mr. Carpenter, um... um, Bob." Snapper left Chelston with a spring in his step, jumped on his Zundapp and roared off in a cloud of smoke.

When Snapper told Carl Cardigan that he was quitting, the Director said, "What? You can't do that to us! You're one of the few local pilots that can drive anything, the work boat, the schooner, the *T-Boat* or the *Sir Horace*. Snapper, we can't replace you! What's brought this on?"

"Well, I've got a chance to have a charter fishing boat of my own. A really good boat: the *Captain Crunch*!"

"Gee, I know her, she's a nice boat. Look, what about working for SOFAR part time. I'm sure there are going to be times when we'll need somebody with your skills to supplement those of the skipper on those long voyages. We'll make it worth your while. What do you say, Snapper?"

"OK Carl, you got a deal, when you need another good wheel man on the *Sir Horace*, I'll be your guy."

The two men shook hands to cement the agreement.

Snapper had seen Maria DeSilva many times, in the past, mostly in the company of her late husband, Scaley DeSilva. Since Scaley had been his mate from childhood, he had always banished any untoward thoughts about Maria, but he couldn't help noticing the obvious, that she was a very beautiful woman. Since she was a little girl, she was known as Ria. His mate Scaley had been a lucky man – right up until he became the main course for a school of feeding sharks. He'd also met Scaley's son who was now 2 years old.

He rode his Zundapp into the yard of their modest two-bedroom cottage. The lady of the house was hanging out the washing to dry in the warm Bermuda sunshine. The little boy, Nelson, was running around the dusty yard, barefooted, trying in vain to catch the chickens, but having a joyful time in the process. When Maria saw who it was, she greeted him with a smile, but even though it was only nine a.m., she looked very tired, with dark circles underneath her eyes. Her hair was askew, and her clothes were damp from having just finished the washing.

"Hey, Snapper. How you doin' bye? Oh, please forgive how I look. If I'd known you were coming over, I would have cleaned myself up to look decent."

"Don't worry about that Ria. Sorry to barge in on you without warning. It's good to see you. Can I have a word with you, if you don't mind?"

"Come into the kitchen. I ain't got much, since Scaley died, but um got some lemonade." She poured some sweet lemonade for her guest. Snapper downed the beverage.

He fixed her with a concerned stare. "So, how are things, really, I mean, since Scaley passed?"

"Honestly? Bye, things have been rough. Scaley left us a few pounds that he had hidden away in a drawer, but that's almost gone. Um goin' to have to move back home with my parents pretty soon when it runs out. Scaley didn't tell me much about his business with the boat. I know he owed some money on it and we have a mortgage on the house too, but I dun know who to or how much we owe. Um worried one day somebody's going to come through that door telling me that I ain't paid the interest on the mortgage and that they're throwing me out of my house." Her lip quivered momentarily, then pausing to collect her thoughts, she said, "Um sorry, Snapper, I've been babbling on so much about my problems, I haven't even asked you what yuh doin' here. What are yuh doin' here?"

"Well, Ria, I'm here to bring you good news."

"Good news! I could use some of that."

"I'm here to tell you that you won't have to move out of this house, and you won't have to scratch around to feed young Nelson either. Look, Ria, Scaley owed a rich white guy a lotta money on the *Captain Crunch* and the mortgage on this here house too. His name was Bayard Smith. Here's the note he signed."

"Oh yeah, Scaley's mother used to work for him."

"Right, but Smith lost his stake in the boat and the house to another guy in a card game."

"A card game? I thought only poor drunks did that nonsense."

"Well, he may have been drunk, but he ain't poor. Anyway, I have acquired Scaley's interest in the boat and I've also taken over the note. So,

I'm the new owner of the *Crunch*. But I reckon, part of this boat is rightfully yours, so I have a proposal for you."

Maria looked stunned. Then she managed to say, "Proposal, what proposal?"

"I propose to share 40% of the money earned from the *Captain Crunch* with you. As you know, the *Crunch* is a great boat, and she earns a lotta money during the season. Should be plenty enough for you and the boy to live on. The mortgage has been transferred back to Bayard Smith, so your money from the *Crunch* will easily enable you to pay the interest. So, you don't have to worry about that neither. What do you say?"

"Is this for real, Snapper? What's the catch? Is this on the level? Don't play with me, bye! How'd you manage to swing this, Snapper? I know you're a good guy, but where'd you get this kind of money? Is this even legal?"

"Ria, Ria, take it easy, take it easy! This is for real! There's no catch. There's this guy, a really powerful guy, that my Deddy, Hooks, helped out many years ago, his name is Sam. He felt obliged to help me out because Hooks helped him out during the War. He helped me get the *Crunch*. So, this is all above board. So now you can get your share of the profits from the boat."

Maria's eyes welled up and tears began flooding down her face and she began to sob, looking up to the sky crying, "Thank you, Lord." Little Nelson heard her and came in the room with a concerned look on his face. She grabbed him and hugged him tightly and reassured him, "Mummy's alright, son, Mummy's alright."

Collecting herself, and through her tears, she looked straight at Snapper and said, "I've always been a good judge of character. Snapper Jones, you're a good man. There ain't many men who would share their good luck with a woman they hardly know. I accept your proposal." She extended her hand, and the deal was sealed.

After spending several days cleaning the *Captain Crunch*, both topsides and bottom, and servicing the engines, Snapper Jones was open for charter fishing business. She was still the fastest, best equipped charter boat on the island and commanded premium rates from sport-fishermen.

# The Governor

Bob Carpenter was sipping his coffee at the Consulate, brooding over what his next move should be. He was very concerned with the revelation that Anna Sokratis, Jack Bessemer's Kompromat date in London, was also a mole in the British Ministry of Defence. After consuming three cups of coffee, he made a decision.

"Janice, can you make an appointment to see the Governor. Tell them it's urgent."

"Right away, sir."

After about five minutes Janice appeared in the doorway, "Mr. Carpenter, His Excellency's secretary says you may come right over. I've already alerted Tony Fox and he's downstairs waiting." Carpenter picked up his jacket and headed for the elevator.

He didn't know Bermuda's governor very well, having only met him a few times at large social gatherings since coming to the island. So, he would have to play his hand carefully. His Excellency Sir Julian Hood KCMG, KCVO, CB, DSO, DL, perfectly suited Government House – straight out of a Rudyard Kipling British Empire storybook. Sir Julian was British Army – all the way. He was a monocle wearing patrician, an imposing figure of over six foot four, with his military bearing making him look even taller. He was a retired Major General, having served with distinction during World War II in Africa as well as Italy. Carpenter surmised he was well connected, not only in London, but in Washington, having been Deputy Commander of the British Mission in Washington, D.C. He had also recently hosted a summit conference between President Kennedy and Prime Minister MacMillan in Bermuda. "You can't get any better connected than that." With his military background and his excellent connections, Carpenter concluded that he was the right person to speak to about the Sokratis matter.

He was shown into the office and the Governor was there to greet him, towering over him. "Ah, Mr. Consul General. A pleasure to see you."

"Your Excellency, thank you so much for seeing me at such short notice."

After they were seated, the Governor inquired, "Tea or coffee?"

"Coffee, please." The secretary, Miss Cooper, scuttled away to perform her assignment. After she returned and the two men were alone, Hood inquired, quite directly, "So. Mr. Carpenter, to what do I owe this honour?"

"Your Excellency, I have come into possession of some information that is highly sensitive, but at the same time is vitally important to Her Majesty's Government and to NATO."

Sir Julian was looking at him intently, one eye directly, the other through his monocle. "To what information are you referring?"

"Well, sir, it's very sensitive and I must stress is a matter of national security, and therefore must be handled with great care."

"Come, come, Mr. Carpenter, as you know I'm a military man, I'm accustomed to being direct, so please speak plainly."

"Thank you for that, Your Excellency. I have uncovered and identified a Russian mole in the British Ministry of Defence."

"What! A mole in the British Ministry of Defence!" The Governor's monocle dropped from his face, swinging back and forth from a cord connected to his jacket. "How do you know that?"

"Well, sir, I'm unable to give details, but I thought it imperative that your government be made aware of this fact."

"Mr. Carpenter, we have our files too, and I am well aware of your career background. But this is very shocking."

"Thank you, your Excellency. The mole in question's cover name is Anna Sokratis, also named Anna Petrova, and she is an analyst at the Ministry. The thing is, she's part of a broader spy ring in London whose size and tentacles are unknown. Therefore, your officials may want to handle this with great discretion in order to discover the others in the ring. There is another agent who is posing as her brother that is part of the ring, Dino Sokratis, also known as Dimitri Tovovich."

The Governor replaced his monocle in its place and scribbled the names down on a scratch pad. "How is it that you have found this out? Are they operating here in Bermuda?"

"No, Your Excellency, they are not. There was an approach, but I've taken care of it. Might I suggest that you have MI5 monitor these two in order to identify the other members of their spy ring, and perhaps, in the meantime, feed Miss Sokratis either false or useless information.

"Excellent idea!"

"Well, Your Excellency, that's all I have. Thanks for seeing me at such short notice, good day, sir." He rose from his chair, shook hands with the Governor and showed himself out.

Sir Julian opened a drawer in his desk and pulled out a small red book. He flicked through the pages and then he found it. The notation stated, "Sir Dick Goldsmith White, KCMG, KBE., Chief of Secret Intelligence Service (MI6)," formerly at MI5. "Ah, right – Dick! ... Miss Cooper! I'd like you to put in a call to this gentleman please, right away."

# Longtails

Snapper had been successfully chartering for over three months and thought he should show his appreciation by offering Carpenter a free fishing charter on the *Captain Crunch*. They agreed on the day and set out. Instead of trolling, Snapper decided to try some tuna fishing. They anchored near Southwest Breaker and dropped their lines over the side. It was just the two of them, each man relaxing with a beer in his hand. They spotted a lone longtail, hunting for prey. "Look at that longtail! Beautiful creature, init." Snapper observed.

"Yeah," Carpenter said. "Did you know the proper name for them is the 'White-Tailed Tropicbird?'" He had recently seen that in research about Bermuda.

"Actually, the ornithological name is Phaethon lepturus." Snapper casually replied. Carpenter dropped his beer on the deck his mouth agape.

"Man, you're full of surprises!"

Snapper continued with a wry smile, "You'd be surprised what you can learn by hanging out with the geniuses at SOFAR. 'They nest in the coral cliffs of the island, starting early each spring, only to fly away, back out to sea, in the fall. They swoop, swirl and chirp in complex mating flight formations over the near shore ocean. Their prey is fry and other similar sized fish.' That's the spiel that I have for my charter customers. Charter boat skippers have to double as tour guides, you know. You've got to be prepared for all kinds of questions about Bermuda."

"I guess so," Carpenter said, retrieving what was left of his beer.

"But, for we-byes, you know, Bermudian men, there's another meaning to the word longtail."

"Oh?"

"Ya! A 'longtail' is a beautiful female visitor, whose numbers swell in the spring and shrink in the fall, just like their feathered counterparts. As tourism has grown since the War, longtail watching, longtail hunting and longtail dating has become a very popular pastime for we-byes. It's a fun game. I know because I'm a player."

"Do tell!" This really caught Carpenter's interest.

"Starting with the college student's spring break, local longtail hunters find the island's beaches, bars, hotels and nightclubs rich hunting grounds. During the days of segregation, we-byes couldn't go into some of them bars and hotels as customers, but a lot of us used to work at them bars and hotels, and that's how we got that part of that longtail action. The longtails didn't care if we worked there or not. Also, in those days, there were the coloured-owned hotels like the Sunset Lodge, Archlyn Villa, and Imperial Hotel. That's where you got the coloured longtails. Today, now that the colour bar has been lifted, longtail hunting is much easier. A lot of these longtails have lots of money to spend and are looking for companionship and excitement with, not only members of the opposite sex, but often of the other race. For some of my mates it's an obsession! But there are other longtails that don't have much money and take these guys to the cleaners.

"You married?"

"Why, no. Why do you ask?"

"Unfortunately, many of my married mates continue to ply the longtail circuit, it being an addiction, or at the very least, a preoccupation, to many of them. This sparks untold difficulties for these guys at home; but many continue regardless. With me, there's little pretence as to what these longtail adventures are all about. When their vacation is over, there are no strings attached. As with charter fishing, 'longtailin' is all part of the Bermuda 'Tourism Product'," he said with a wink.

"Yeah, right!" Carpenter replied with a chuckle.

"You know, back when I was driving the *Wilhelmina*, I had a deck hand named Bully Simons. Bully was built like a tank – the strongest man I've ever known, but he got hooked on longtails. They used to come to see him on the ferry and everything. The thing was, he was married, wife named Sheila, and had three kids too. But in spite of those responsibilities, Bully couldn't get enough of those longtails, the kind that you had to spend money on. So, he used to spend most of his pay on these chicks and come home broke. When Sheila complained he would smack her around. And believe me, getting hit by Bully would be a serious blow.

"One Sunday evening he came home, full-hot, having been out all weekend and spent all his Friday pay on the longtails."

"Full-hot? What's that?"

"You know, completely drunk."

"Oh, right!"

"Well, when he swayed into the kitchen, Sheila lit into him, screaming at the top of her voice. He exploded with fury and started knockin' her across the room. He pinned her in a corner and started to choke her. She couldn't get him off her. Hearing the ruckus, the children came into the kitchen and tried to pull their father off their mother – to no avail. She thought she was going to die. Sheila's hand happened upon a carving knife lying on the counter and she plunged it into Bully's chest. She stabbed him three times before the big man released her throat and fell to the floor.

"The autopsy said the last stab cut his aorta."

"Wow!"

"The police charged her with murder. Can you believe that? But she was acquitted by the jury. So, longtail hunting can be a dangerous past time."

"But not for you, I suppose." Carpenter raised one eyebrow.

"For a single man like me, it's a lotta fun. But you know what the biggest difference between those birds and the human longtails?"

"No. What?"

"With the birds it's clear who's the hunter and who's the prey. Among we humans, it's hard to know who's the predator and who's the prey."

"Yeah, we men chase and hunt them, until we get caught!"

Ya, it's like yuh mate, the Major."

"The Major?"

"Ya, he got caught by one of the girls from the Grenadian Hotel."

"What?"

"Ya, after he got a taste of, you know, that-there, he was no more good. She took him to the cleaners. He even bought her a house – in her name, no less – for cash."

"Wow! You'd never think of him as a sucker. We all have our weaknesses, I guess."

"Ya, his weakness cost him a lot of money. As for longtails, sometimes, we would get one onboard the *Crunch*, but charter fishing is usually a male thing. The women on my charters are almost always with their husbands or boyfriends. You know, spoken for. My routine would be, after a day on the water, I'd go to a beachside bar and longtails will just come up to me and start a conversation. You know me, not too shy, and have many interesting sea stories to tell."

"Uh huh."

"I've become pretty successful at this game. Quite frankly, the girls love it. And when I come across a longtail that's lookin' to spend my money, I just move on to the next one. When a longtail's trip is over and she returns to the States, I'll merely pick up another one who's visiting the island."

"I should quit my job in the State Department and become a charter boat skipper." Carpenter quipped, getting up to fetch himself another beer from the cooler, chuckling all the way.

When he returned to his seat, Snapper was gazing out over the blue horizon, his voice trailing off, caught up in a reverie. He mumbled, "Ya, there was this one time …." After falling silent for a moment, lost in a memory, he continued.

"There was this New York, Wall Street guy named Joel Boone who chartered us for a day of deep-sea fishing, a party of two. We picked them up at the Evan's Bay public dock, as they had rented a nearby Southampton house. Me and first mate, "Boo" Brimmer, arrived early, 'cause high paying clientele like to find their charters waiting for them. The taxi dropped them off at the dock and I saw that this party of two consisted of an interracial couple: Joel and Betty Boone.

"Joel looked like your typical wealthy Wall Street executive, mid-sixties, his thinning grey hair combed over in a hopeless attempt to hide the bare crown of his head. His belly showed too many years of sitting at his Wall Street desk. By his side was his trophy wife, Betty. She was a showstopper! She was a middle-aged woman, maybe 45, but she looked like she stepped directly out of Ebony Magazine's fashion section. She had on colourful short shorts – not Bermuda shorts – short shorts, and a halter top. Her legs were long and shapely – an overall figure of a twenty-five-year-old. Her Hollywood style sunshades, underneath a broad Panama hat with a band-with-a-flowing-tail on it, matching the shorts. She was wearing high, high-heels but was thoughtful enough to have a pair of sneakers stowed in a tote bag that also matched her shorts and hat. Her eye liner, eye shadow and makeup drew attention to her large brown eyes. Her colour coordinated lip-gloss magnified the impact of a most alluring smile. The overall effect was of smouldering sex appeal. Like having Eartha Kit onboard the boat.

"Eartha Kit, huh?"

"Ya! Betty said she'd been coming here each year for years, and she knew many Bermudians and they all said that the *Crunch* was the best boat on the island for deep sea fishing.

"We cruised through the Little Sound, around the US Naval Operating Base with its many patrol seaplanes pulled up on ramps. It was still early morning, so Boo offered the guests sodas and juices. The harder stuff would come later. After clearing the NOB point, we headed straight for Watford Bridge at full throttle. They looked thrilled by the *Crunch's* speed, the high rooster tail and her frothy wake. Betty appeared to be interested in receiving a running commentary on places of interest we passed by, so she climbed the stairs up to the flybridge, next to me. I obliged her by giving her descriptions of places we passed, plus stories that I had accumulated over the years. It was hard to remain professional with such an alluring creature so close.

"After passing a few competing boats on the way to the Tripod Marker at full throttle, we slowed so that Boo could prepare the boat for trolling. We decided to troll just off the edge along the South Shore. Betty went back down to be with her husband. Then I heard Boo shout, 'Whales! Whales!' He was pointing off the starboard quarter. I slowed the boat to idle then shifted her to neutral, not wanting to unduly disturb the gentle giants. There were two of them, spouting plumes of spray high into the air.

"Joel asked excitedly, 'Wow! What kind are they?'

"Boo said, 'Humpbacks. You guys are really lucky, they're usually all gone by now. These two are stragglers. Looks like a mother and calf. They stop here each year on their way north from the Caribbean to their Arctic Feeding grounds. They generally spend about 3 to 4 months in Bermuda waters before continuing north. Nobody knows why they stop here.'

"After lolling around on the surface for several minutes, the humpbacks dove deep, and we brought the *Crunch* back to trolling speed. After trolling for an hour with not even a nibble, a fish struck one of the lures. The reel whined loudly as the fish dashed away with the hook in its mouth. Boo and I, after shifting the *Crunch* into neutral, busied ourselves, bringing in the other lines and setting Joel up in one of the fighting chairs.

"'What is it?' Betty asked excitedly.

"'Not sure yet, ma'am, but it moves like a dolphin.' Boo said.

"'A dolphin!' she exclaimed in horror. 'You can't possibly mean you're going to catch one of those lovable creatures!'

"I said, 'No, no, Mrs. Boone! Not the mammal, the fish! They call them Mahi-Mahi in Hawaii.'

"She said, 'Oh,' somewhat embarrassed. But then, not missing a beat, she added with a flirtatious bat of those lashes, 'You can call me Betty.' Just then a flash of colour erupted from behind the boat, about 50 yards out. 'What's that?' she asked excitedly.

"'That's your dolphin, or should I say, your husband's dolphin, one of the most beautiful fish in the ocean. So, Joel, you got her?' I asked.

"'Yeah, yeah, I got her! I got her!'

"Boo was coaching Joel Boone, telling him when to crank the reel and when and how to pull back on the rod. The dolphin kept jumping out of the water, but eventually he tired, and they got him right up to the boat. The visiting anglers couldn't stop exclaiming, 'Look at all those colours – iridescent colours of the rainbow! The most beautiful fish I've ever seen!'

"Betty said, 'Do we really have to bring him into the boat? It would be a shame to kill such a beautiful creature.' She looked at Joel beseechingly.

"I interjected, 'You should know, dolphins are an extremely good eating fish.'

"Joel said, 'That settles it then. Bring it aboard.' I gave Boo the high sign and he grabbed the gaff and hauled the dolphin aboard. It was a good-sized catch, about 5 feet long. It flapped about on the deck for a while until Boo took a club and wacked it on the head. But, instead of it being a moment of triumph for the two Yankee anglers, instead they watched in sadness when the spectacular colours faded to grey as the creature's life force ebbed away."

"Really?" Carpenter asked. "Their colours disappear when they die?"

"Ya, it's true. Maybe we'll catch one today, then you'll see.

"Anyway, Boo reset the outriggers, the lures and bait and we started to troll again. We had no further action before lunch. We provided the usual lunch for our clients – sandwiches and beer. After lunch we resumed trolling, slowly zig-zagging back and forth off Bermuda's southern coast.

"It wasn't long before there was another strike. This time the reel screamed the alarm. 'It's something big and fast!' I told them. Boo helped Joel set himself in the fighting chair as the reel kept on playing out line. 'If we don't do something soon, we're going to run out of line.' I went forward and shifted both engines in reverse to reduce the rate of retreat of the hooked fish. While this helped, it was still taking line. 'OK, Joel, we're going to hit the brakes on this-here reel – it's called the drag. Be ready because you're going to take the full force of this beast.'

"He said, 'OK. I'm ready.'

"I tightened the drag as tight as it would go and, suddenly, the rod bent over sharply and Joel who was already strapped in exclaimed, 'Whoa!' He was again under the tutelage of Boo Brimmer, telling him what to do and when to do it. Despite the drag being at its maximum, the fish was still taking line. We increased the reverse speed of the *Crunch*. Driving in reverse, with her ass-end ploughing into the sea, every time the stern dipped into the waves, sea water would wash over the transom onto the deck. Betty started to look frightened.

"'Not to worry, Betty, this often happens with big fish.'

"Just then our prey broke the surface in an attempt to throw the hook. 'There!' Boo shouted. 'It's a big blue! A blue marlin!' He cast his eye on Joel Boone, labouring in the fighting chair. 'How you doing, bye?' Joel was sweating bullets.

"'Hey Boo! Get Mr. Boone some water. Keep workin' it, Joel. You're not as strong as he is – none of us is – so you have to outlast him, tire him out. That's the only way to catch these big byes," I said.

"After an hour Joel was totally fagged out – running only on fumes. He said, 'Skipper, I can't go on. I'm finished. Really, I'm done!'

"I released Joel from his fighting harness and took his place. The marlin still had plenty of fight left in him. I told Boo, 'Faster astern!' As he increased the speed astern, larger quantities of seawater began washing over the transom with each wave. Betty retreated forward. Joel was too tired to move. The drag finally started to hold, and we began to reel in the great fish. 'He's getting tired now, you-byes. Slow her down Boo.' After another hour we finally got our quarry close to the boat.

"Joel exclaimed, 'That fish is huge!'

"'Ya, a granddaddy, looks like a 1,000 pounder!' Boo replied. 'He's worn himself out.'

"Joel wanted to bring him aboard and that it might be a record.

"I told him, dejectedly, 'No, we're going to let him go.'

"Joel was shocked, 'Let him go!'

"'Ya, Joel we've got to let him go. He might be a record, but because it took two of us to bring him in, it won't count. And since no one's going to eat that marlin, we're going to try to undo that hook and let him go.' I gripped the dangerous pointed beak with a pair of heavy-duty gloves, and Boo reached over and freed the great fish from its torment. It sank motionless for a moment then slowly swam back to the deep, no doubt, highly traumatized.

"It was mid-afternoon by then and we started to head back to port. Boo hauled the dolphin out of the fish box and started the unpleasant process of gutting, scaling and cutting up their catch into steaks for human consumption. Joel found a comfortable seat and fell asleep – totally spent. Betty returned to the flybridge with me and engaged me in pleasant light conversation but occasionally threw flirtatious gestures my way, with those big hypnotic eyes. Ordinarily, I would have gladly taken this bait, as a frequent longtail hunter. But, with her husband asleep mere feet below us, I was on my guard. As we approached Evans Bay dock, Betty said, 'Snapper, we're having a small party at the house this evening, why don't you come along?'

"'A party? This evening? Are you sure the two of you will be up to that? After a day of fishing, most times people are ready to turn in early.'

"'Oh yes, I'm sure,' she said 'Why don't you come around about 10 o'clock? Here's the address.' She descended the stairs, woke up Joel and collected their things. Joel turned out to be a very handsome tipper.

"I gave them a couple of packages of fresh dolphin steaks, saying, 'You should eat these tonight or tomorrow. There's nothing better than freshly caught Bermuda fish. And make sure you don't overcook 'em.'

"'Thanks again,' she said brightly, looking just as glamorous as she did when she embarked that morning. 'See you later.'

"I took the *Captain Crunch* back to her mooring near Somerset Bridge, and along with Boo Brimmer, cleaned her and buttoned her up for the night. I went home to my apartment, cooked a few steaks of fresh dolphin and cleaned myself up for the evening's social engagement. When I arrived at the address, I found myself in the driveway of an impressive mansion, complete with butler and cook. I was shown into a spacious living room and waited for my hosts to appear. There was no sign of other guests.

"After a half hour wait, Betty finally appeared. As I stood up to greet her, she exclaimed, extending me her hand, 'Oh, Snapper, darling; my, you do clean up very well!' I was decked out in a single-breasted navy-blue blazer over a well pressed and starched white shirt with a thin, deep red tie. I was sporting maroon Bermuda shorts with long navy-blue socks.

"'My, my, Betty, I must say, you look absolutely stunning! Pardon my ignorance of such things, but you look like an Ebony Magazine fashion model. How do you think Ebony would describe your outfit?'

"Delighted with my comments, she played along. 'Well, if it was a fashion show the commentator would say, 'She is hot in a colourful, long sleeved Pucci shift. The shoes are stilettos by Roger Vivier, from the House of Dior. Her timepiece is a black leather strapped Cartier tank watch.' Then she held out her perfectly manicured right hand, her wrist glinting and jingling with gold bangle bracelets and said, 'The clutch Bermuda cedar handled handbag is from H.A.& E. Smiths.' And don't forget the earrings," as she gently threw her head about and twirled around, causing her gold hoops and the short, swirlishly-styled hairdo to toss from side to side. I couldn't help but marvel that, although the dress was loose fitting, it revealed the contours of her body as she moved, producing an effect that was simply hypnotic.

"'Wow!' I exclaimed.

"She smiled graciously, saying, 'Thank you, darling.'

"'But am I early? Where are your other guests? Are they not here yet?'

"'There are no other guests, darling – just you,' she said,

"'What? Just me? But where's Joel?'

"She said, 'Oh, gosh, he's gone to bed. After all that fish fighting, he'll sleep right through the night.' She smiled at me slyly.

"'Now, hold on Betty. I dun' want no trouble. Joel had a good day today and has treated Boo and me very generously. I dun' want to get into any trouble with him.'

"'Relax, big boy,' she said. 'My husband and I have an arrangement. He is fully aware that I occasionally enjoy the company of other men. We have what is called an open marriage.'

"'An open marriage, huh! So, he knows I'm taking you out tonight? We are going out, aren't we?'

"'But of course, darling! Where shall we go?'

"'Well, Betty, you've caught me off guard, but I do know that the Talbot Brothers are performing at the Angel's Grotto tonight. They have a great dance floor there too, where we can dance under the stars. Why don't we try there?'

"'Sounds divine, darling. Let's go!'

"After she started for the door, I said, 'Hold on, hold on, with you looking so gorgeous and all, we can't very well have you on the back of my Zundapp, can we. As a single man I have no need for a car.'

"'No problem, darling,' she laughed. 'The owner of this little shack has his car parked in the garage. We can use his.' And off we went.

"When we arrived at Angel's Grotto, heads turned as we entered the room. While Betty was probably over 15 years older than me, I was sure that every man in that room would have given his eye teeth to have Betty Boone on his arm. Shortly after we arrived, the show started and the Talbot Brothers were terrific, as expected. After the show, we slow-danced under the stars on the patio. Then, as I was driving back to the Southampton mansion, I was wondering what would come next. Usually at this point with a longtail, I would be headed to her hotel room, but this was quite different. Then I smiled and thought, *Not to worry, mate, Betty's already got the next move figured out. Just go with the flow.*

"When we pulled into the mansion driveway, Betty asked, 'Would you like a nightcap, darling?'

"'Sure.' We went into the kitchen and found a bottle of champagne in the fridge along with two glasses.

"That sly look crept over her face again and she said, 'You know, we rent this place every year. One of the nice things about it is that it has its very own separate guest cottage. Want to see it?'

"I couldn't hold back my own sly smirk. 'Ya, let's check it out. Lead the way!' We walked out through a set of French doors, across a patio that looked like a spoked wheel, with a small fountain as its hub. One of the spokes was a gravel pathway, at the end of which was a small three roomed Bermuda cottage containing a lounge, a bedroom and a bathroom. We entered and shut the door behind us. I turned and pulled the window curtain shut. 'Don't want no Webbers, do we?'

"'Webbers, what Webbers?' She asked, quite confused.

"'That's what we Bermudians call Peeping Toms.'

"'Oh,' she said with a laugh, "Webbers huh – Charming! We definitely don't want any of those.'

"I opened the champagne bottle and poured two glasses of bubbly. Raising my glass, I said, 'Here's to a lovely evening with a lovely lady.'

"Betty smiled broadly, 'The evening's just starting, darling.' She slipped off the Pucci shift, letting it drop to the floor, and unhooked her bra, dramatically tossing it across the room, giving me an opportunity to have a good look at her exquisite topless form. Her big brown eyes locked onto mine as she approached me. My pulse quickened. Then she gave me a deep delicious kiss and I carried her into the bedroom.

"Dun know if I was the hunter or the prey, but if that is the fate of the prey, you can hunt me anytime!"

Carpenter laughed and said, "I'm definitely in the wrong line of work!"

## Dinner At Chelston

Bob Carpenter was continuously receiving invitations from local matronly hostesses and while some of them were quite charming, as a bachelor, there was never anybody of the female persuasion that was remotely interesting. He decided to reciprocate with a dinner party at Chelston.

"Janice, I want you to organize a formal, white tie dinner party at Chelston."

"Oh, certainly sir." This was right up her alley. "Do you have a guest list in mind?"

"Well, yes. I have scribbled down a few names: H.E. Sir Julian Hood and Lady Katherine Hood, Sir James Foxworthy and Lady Jennifer Foxworthy, Sir James being a pillar of the establishment and Speaker of the House of Assembly; Commissioner Peter Radcliff and Mrs. Christine Radcliff; Mr. Frank Copperfield, a prominent Hamilton businessman and Mrs. Mary Copperfield; Mr. Philip Oldham, an established hotelier, and Mrs. Abigail Oldham, Dr. Jack Bessemer and his wife Evelyn. And you, Janice, will act as hostess. You will be my date for the evening. Your husband won't mind, will he?"

"Oh no. He won't mind at all," she said. Carpenter had never seen her so excited. "Just leave everything to me."

After many telephone calls to arrange a convenient date for all guests, in three weeks, the appointed evening arrived, and the guests' cars started to arrive at Chelston's grand entrance.

Seated in the back of the official, chauffeur-driven, Commissioner's car were Peter and Christine Radcliff; destination – Chelston. Christine said, "Got a letter from Willy today."

"Really?" the Commissioner asked. "What's he saying?"

"He's received his first posting out of Dartmouth. He's been posted to a destroyer, as 2nd Lieutenant. This letter was written the night after he reported for duty. He apparently loves it already."

"Well, that lad's living his dream. All he ever wanted to be, was a Royal Navy officer. Not like me. I've always enjoyed ships, but from a respectful distance, not onboard," the Commissioner said with a chuckle. "Willy loved boats from the first time he laid eyes on them, and now he's a Naval officer. How about that? Proud of him!"

Christine fell silent. Her mind flashed back twenty odd years when she was a censor for the Imperial Censorship Department at the Princess Hotel, during the War, reading through mountains of transatlantic correspondence in search of messages from enemy agents and Nazi sympathizers. "I was so immature and impressionable in those days. Impressed by all the old rich fools, like the ones we're going to see tonight, and most of all, impressed by that mysterious, handsome gentleman, Captain Rodney Grant. He swept me right off my feet. Literally! It was so hard to accept that he was actually a Nazi spy and that he had made a complete fool of me.

And then I found out I was pregnant! Thank God I'd been playing Peter along all that time, or else my reputation would have been permanently shattered. The poor bugger still doesn't know that he's not Willy's real father. It's ironic though, genes don't lie. Willy's like his father, a man who loves the sea."

The car pulled up to the entrance of Chelston. Milton opened the door and said, "Good evening, Commissioner, good evening, Mrs. Radcliff. Welcome to Chelston." The Commissioner took his wife's arm and escorted her to the receiving line.

Janice had arranged the time for the other guests to arrive at 6:45 so that they could already be there when the guest of honour, H.E. the Governor, arrived at 7:00. At precisely 7:00pm the governor's Rolls Royce limousine turned into the driveway and gently stopped. The black, uniformed chauffer opened the door and Sir Julian and Lady Hood alighted the vehicle. His Excellency was dressed in a tuxedo with tails, formal shirt with wing tips and white bowtie. His jacket was cut away at the waist in the usual formal style, revealing a white vest with mother of pearl buttons. He had a row of medals and miniature ribbons pinned to his chest just above the left breast pocket, signifying his long, distinguished career in the British Army.

Lady Hood elegantly wore a long sleeved, powder blue, Norman Hartnell gown featuring gold brocade, along with white gloves. The ensemble included satin shoes dyed to match, and a matching satin clutch handbag. It was finished off by a string of large natural pearls.

Carpenter, also resplendent in a black tuxedo and white tie, but without tails, greeted the Governor and Lady Hood at the door and introduced them to Janice. She was dressed to the nines and flitted around the room like a hybrid between a hummingbird and a worker bee. He then worked the room and made sure all the guests spoke to the Governor. When Bob came to Jack and Evelyn he couldn't help but notice how smashing Evelyn looked. Her close fitting, full length royal blue evening gown that accentuated her long willowy lines was cut low in the front, showing off the necklace with those large diamonds, the same one she wore the night she and Jack met. Jack, in his own penguin suit, felt out of place in this elegant setting and decided to say as little as possible. Evelyn, on the other hand, was in her element and floated gracefully around the room.

After about half an hour of cocktails, Janice invited everyone to the dining room for dinner. Chelston's dining room easily eclipsed that of Government House. After the guests had taken their assigned seats, Carpenter rose and raised his champaign glass and intoned, "Ladies and Gentlemen, Her Majesty the Queen." Everyone rose and replied, "The Queen."

Janice had carefully arranged the seating arrangement so that spouses weren't seated next to each other but were seated next to someone with whom there was the promise of "interesting conversation." After everyone had retaken their seats, the Governor rose, raised his glass and intoned, "The President of the United States." They all rose again and ritually responded, "The President of the United States." With the formalities out of the way, the staff started to bring in the first course under Milton's watchful eye.

It was a table of fourteen, seven on each side with no one at the ends. Carpenter, as host, was seated at number four. Almost directly opposite him was the Governor. He took the liberty, as the host, to seat the two most beautiful women at the table on either side of him: Evelyn Bessemer to his right and Christine Radcliff to his left. Their respective husbands were seated at either wing of the large dining room table. Seated on the other side of the table slightly to his right was Sir James Foxworthy. Carpenter started the conversation, "Mr. Speaker, how are things going in the local Parliament these days? I hear through the grapevine that there may be a move to do away with all members being independents and establishing political parties in the House. Have you heard that?"

"Well, Mr. Carpenter, I've heard it, but I don't see any reason to change the system that we have now. Bermuda society has had the current structure for a very long time, and it seems to work well for everybody."

"Everybody? Really?" Christine countered. In the almost twenty years she had lived in Bermuda, Christine Radcliff had not lost any of her zeal for ideals she held dear, neither had she lost any of her penchant for outspokenness. She was appalled at how undemocratic the Bermuda political system was, although her opinions had been stifled because of the non-political position of her husband, the Commissioner of Police. However, the urge to tweak this insufferable old buffoon across the table was irresistible.

*Ah, I knew she wasn't just a pretty face,* Carpenter thought.

"I don't understand what you mean." The Speaker replied.

"Well, wouldn't political parties empower likeminded people to come together and present a cogent set of policies for the voters to consider and vote on, like in the British Parliament."

"Well, I don't know about that. The system we have right now allows voters to judge each candidate on his own merit and character, as opposed to some party-political platform. I think character and merit far outweigh a political platform, don't you, Mrs. Radcliff?"

"Well, we've had party politics in Britain for over 200 years, don't you think Bermuda's a bit out of date? And what about having to own land to vote? We did away with that in Britain years ago. A landowner being able to vote multiple times because he owns property in multiple constituencies can't possibly be fair in this modern day and age, can it?"

*Nice, bait and switch, Christine!* Carpenter thought.

"Well, in our system, the people who have the most to lose have the most influence at the ballot box, and that seems only right, isn't that right Frank." Sir James replied, looking across the table to his right for support.

"Quite right, Jim. Quite right!" Frank Copperfield chimed in, on queue.

Christine resumed, "Well, Mr. Speaker, my dear old Dad taught me, a long time ago, that the most dangerous man in the world is he who has nothing to lose. If you have people with nothing to lose here in Bermuda, then my Dad's rule applies. They can read the newspapers; they can hear the news on the radio from the States. They know about the civil rights movement over there. They've already forced the desegregation of hotels and cinemas – peacefully, thank God. But change is coming to Bermuda, Mr. Speaker, one way or the other. It seems to me that it's up to you whether you embrace change willingly or fight it, kicking and screaming, and lose."

"Oh, you think all that mess will come here, do you? I don't think so. Sure, we have a few troublemakers here, but overall, our coloured people aren't like that. We take care of our coloured people on this island so they're content with their place. So, don't worry your pretty little head about such things, it'll be alright." He smiled condescendingly.

"Oh, the main course!" Carpenter interjected. *This conversation was starting to get out of hand. I'm sure the Speaker's patronizing tone has infuriated Christine.*

Milton, taking his cue, announced with great precision and aplomb, "Your Excellency, Mr. Consul General, ladies and gentlemen, your main course consists of a Surf & Turf Delight – from the sea, we have broiled Bermuda Rock Fish with garlic butter and chardonnay sauce, and from the grill we have the finest cuts of filet mignon, with foie gras sauce and truffle oil, accompanied by fresh market vegetables and baby potatoes."

"Thank you, Milton, bon appetite everyone," Carpenter said. He turned to the Governor and queried, "What do you say about that, Your Excellency?"

"About what?"

"About what Sir James was saying."

"The policy of the Crown and Her Majesty's Government is to allow the locally elected representative assemblies to decide such matters. If they want to change then we can assist, if not, we won't interfere."

"I understand completely, Your Excellency." Carpenter answered.

Carpenter could sense, as she was sitting right next to him, that steam was about to erupt from Christine's ears, and that she was about to utter a rejoinder on this issue, but he intercepted her, "Christine, what was it like here hunting for spies during the War?"

"Pardon me?" She was momentarily flummoxed by the question.

He nudged her with his left foot, looked straight into her eyes, then smiled a kind, understanding smile. After a moment she understood, then she relaxed and smiled back, "Yes, of course, I was a spy hunter during the War." Then she launched into one of her adventures while she was working for the Imperial Department of Censorship. No mention was made about a certain Captain Rodney Grant, of course.

Meanwhile, on Carpenter's right, Evelyn was in conversation with Philip Oldham, sitting immediately to her right, owner and manager of a resort hotel on the Island. Oldham couldn't help but notice Evelyn's grace and charm as well as the huge diamonds draped around her neck. "So, Evelyn, where're you from?"

"California, the Napa Valley, near San Francisco."

"Napa Valley, eh, your folks in the wine business, by any chance?"

"Why yes, my family owns Benadetti Wines. Do you know our wines?"

"Benadetti Wines, yes of course!" He lied. California wines had not yet become common in Bermuda. "Our clientele tend to be very discerning and upscale guests. You know, from Greenwich, Newport or the Hamptons, that sort of thing."

"Oh yes! Jack and I have a house in Greenwich. We rented it out when we moved here. I love it here so much we might as well sell it. I've made so many wonderful friends here. Actually, the girls and I have afternoon tea at your establishment every Thursday. The local, coloured staff are so nice and attentive. You should be immensely proud of them!" she gushed.

"I'm always glad to hear positive feedback from satisfied customers. You know, Bermudians, especially coloured Bermudians, are very friendly people, and love to serve visitors. They're our secret weapon. But you should never put them in charge. They're just not able to handle the demands, complexities and the nuances of management. Just in their nature, I suppose."

"Really, I didn't know that." She paused thoughtfully, "You know, that's what they used to say about Italians too. Too lazy, too loud, too crooked, too dumb! My parents blew up that myth." Oldham's complexion turned bright red with embarrassment. Evelyn continued, "But maybe that doesn't apply here in Bermuda. I just know they are very, very nice people."

"Yes, thanks very much. I'll pass it on." He dove back into his main course.

After a few minutes and taking a few gulps of the claret from Chelston's well stocked wine cellar, Philip had an afterthought. "You know, the tourists just love their jungle stuff, too."

"Jungle stuff, what's that?" Evelyn inquired.

"Coloured people call it Gombeys."

"Gombeys! Never heard of it. What's it like?"

"Well, a few times a year, some of the local, coloured folk dress up in highly colourful outfits with tall, feathered head gear and masks. They dance round and round, like a kind of cannibal ritual, all to the rhythm of loud drums. They're quite scary looking, actually. I remember the first time I saw them as a boy, I was terrified. They come around to the hotel and dance for the tourists and they love them. Give them lots of money."

"Is it kind of like Mardi Gras in New Orleans?"

"No, not really. It's got nothing to do with Fat Tuesday or Lent. As far as I know, it's unique to Bermuda. They tell me it's been passed down from the days of slavery – a kind of African thing."

"Oh, I see."

"I don't get it. On the one hand these people want to hang on to their savage ancestry, yet on the other hand, they want us to treat them as equals. It's ridiculous, really."

Evelyn couldn't resist winding him up. "Are you sure you don't have any savages in your own ancestry, Philip?"

"My dear lady, the Oldham family has been in Bermuda for centuries and before that, straight from England."

"They say most establishment Bermudians, like yourself, were pirates and cutthroats in centuries past. Wouldn't you consider such people savages today?"

"Privateers, Evelyn. Not pirates."

She didn't like this sanctimonious old fool. "I've read the only difference was in the Letters of Marque and the name. The stealing and killing were about the same. Am I not correct, Philip?"

"I see you have done some research Mrs. Bessemer."

"So, Philip, if I were you, I wouldn't be so quick to call other people's ancestors savages. Quite frankly, after what we Europeans, and Americans, did to our fellow human beings during the War, over there in Poland and Hiroshima, I don't think we need go back as far as our distant ancestors for savagery, don't you think, Philip?"

"Ah, Milton! Dessert time! What's for dessert?" Carpenter exclaimed, breaking up everyone's repartee. Milton gave an eloquent description of the final course which was aflame when it was brought in.

After dinner, the Governor didn't seem to be interested in partaking in the usual unisex practice of "Cigars." So, that part of the evening sublimated into thin air.

As he was preparing to depart, he took Carpenter aside, "I say, Carpenter, I wanted to tell you that my friends in London were happy for the introduction you gave them. They'll soon have met all the members of the club."

"That's excellent Your Excellency. Glad to be of help."

After thanking his host, the Governor adjusted his monocle, collected Lady Hood and bade everyone else a good night. Some of the remaining guests took that as a cue to head for home as well. Others lingered for after dinner drinks.

The two beauties on either side of Carpenter had, independent of each other, landed jabs squarely on the jaws of some of the insufferable members of the 40 Thieves in their midst. One of them, Christine Radcliff, along with her husband, was part of the group that stayed for drinks. The Radcliffs were conversing with the Oldhams when she peeled off and approached Carpenter, saying in a semi-whisper, "Excusez moi, Monsieur." While she taught French in a local secondary school, she didn't get much of an opportunity to converse in French.

"Oui, Madame." Carpenter replied.

Continuing en français, she said, "Thanks for restraining me at dinner. I was about to knock that supercilious old nitwit clear across the room." Carpenter laughed out loud. She continued, "Peter would have been so embarrassed. You know, he's gotten to where he is by sucking up to the old establishment guys. I think most of them are antiques of a bygone age, an age I'd just as soon forget."

Carpenter replied, "I don't get much of an opportunity to speak French around here either. Uh … so, you two don't exactly see eye to eye politically, then?"

"We don't see eye to eye on virtually anything, really. We stayed together because of our son, William, but now he's overseas: in the Royal Navy. To tell you the truth, we have very little in common. He spends most of his time at the Police Club and I busy myself with a few charities and, of course, teaching. We're only together for appearances sake."

Carpenter smiled his best smile and, continuing in French, he said, "I hope you don't mind me saying, Christine, if I were the Commissioner, I would be attending to you very closely indeed."

She smiled and looked him straight in the eye replied, "Thanks, Bob, I don't get many compliments these days."

Continuing in French, Bob said, "Perhaps we can continue the conversation about global current affairs another time?"

Switching back to English, she replied, "Why, yes. Another time," still smiling. *He's so very charming! And ruggedly good looking!* "Shall we join the others, Monsieur Consul General?"

"By all means, Madame Radcliff."

After they had all left, Janice, still excited, declared the evening's proceedings a splendid success.

Carpenter was pleased with the news from the Governor and the verbal exchange with Christine.

# Celebrity Fishing

The charter fishing boat *Captain Crunch* had established itself as the first choice of celebrity visitors to the Island. One such celebrity was US Representative Adam Clayton Sewell, one of only four black members of the US House of Representatives. Although he was on a private visit for rest and recreation, he paid his respects to the US Consul General's office. While Carpenter would have always extended the usual courtesies to any visiting congressman, Rep. Sewell was a member of the Armed Services Committee and therefore warranted special courtesy. After the usual pleasantries Carpenter queried, "Well, Congressman, what are your plans while on island?"

"Nothing in particular; lie on the beach, see some sights and of course my wife wants to do some shopping."

"Ever do any fishing?"

"Fishing?"

"Yeah, deep sea, sport fishing."

"Actually, even though I'm a city boy, I've always loved boats. That sounds like it would be fun."

"I know the skipper of the best boat on the island. I can arrange a day trip for you, if you like. I'll contact you at the hotel when the charter is available."

"That'll be great. I'm sure Karen will love it too."

Three days later Rep. Sewell and his wife Karen were on *Captain Crunch* approaching Argus Bank. They had tried Challenger Bank earlier in the morning but hadn't had much luck, so Snapper decided to head out another eleven miles to Argus.

Sewell said, "Skipper, what's that oil platform thing doing all the way out here in the middle of the ocean?"

"That's not an oil platform, Mr. Sewell, that's the Argus Tower."

"Please call me AC. Everybody else does. Anyway, what's an Argus Tower?"

"It's a US Navy installation, set up out here to conduct Oceanographic Research."

"Oceanographic Research eh, I didn't know we were doing oceanographic research out here in Bermuda. I'm on the House Armed Services Committee but I know there's a lot of stuff the admirals and generals don't tell us. I do know we spend a hell-of-a-lot of money here in Bermuda for both the air force and the navy."

Snapper wasn't very familiar with the inner workings of the US Government, but his instincts told him he needed to be guarded as to what to say to this congressman, even if he was on the Armed Services Committee. He decided on a course of action that strongly relied on deflection.

"Well, AC, I used to skipper a supply boat for this tower, and I can tell you I wouldn't want to be stuck out here on that thing. It only has two levels, one for the research gear and the other for living facilities for the crew. It can really get rough out here and the ocean swells can get almost as high as the top of those big, piped legs. One hit from a monster wave and that thing would be history. See those twisted steel steps under there? They were damaged by ocean swells."

They trolled over Argus Bank and their luck changed. The Wahoo were biting and they caught a half a dozen of them. However, Sewell was still fixated on what the purpose of the Tower was. "I wonder what kind of ocean research they're doing out here?" AC asked rhetorically.

"Well, AC, as the saying goes, if you don't know, nobody does." Sewell just chuckled, somewhat ironically.

They had broken off fishing to have lunch when Sewell said, "Skipper, you ever been inside that thing?" pointing to the Tower.

"Ya, plenty of times. Why do you ask?"

"What's inside?"

Snapper chose his words carefully – he didn't want to lie. "Well, just a whole lot of electronic equipment. I'm not exactly sure what each one of those gizmos does."

"I guess you wouldn't, would you," Sewell mumbled.

"I think it might be something like the navy version of Jacques Cousteau. I've met Cousteau a few times. He is a frequent visitor to the island. Incredible guy! Never stays at a hotel when he's here, always stays aboard the *Calypso*."

"*Calypso?* Oh yeah, his research boat."

"Speaking of hotels, how's yours?"

"Oh, it's great. Great room and incredible view," Karen chimed in.

"Just so you know, AC, a few years ago, you and Karen would not have been allowed to stay at that nice hotel you're at, even though you're a member of the US Congress. They've even turned away sitting black Prime Ministers in the bad old days." Snapper drained the rest of his beer.

"Skipper, what's the racial situation like here these days? You know, Bermuda has had a pretty bad reputation in the New York area for the treatment of us coloured folk."

"Ya, I know. Things were pretty bad here during the fifties, but there has been some improvement."

"Oh, how's that?"

"Well, up till 1959 there was a colour bar on everything: hotels, restaurants and bars, schools, jobs and movie theatres; not to mention housing and the voting system."

"What happened in '59 to change all that?"

Snapper opened the ice chest and flipped open a fresh bottle of beer. "Well, first off, ALL hasn't changed, but some things have. It started with the movies. One of Bermuda's favourite pastimes, excluding cricket and football, of course, is the movies. Bermudians love the movies! Personally, I love movies about the sea, The Old Man and the Sea, Run Silent Run Deep, a great submarine movie, maybe the best ever, A Night to Remember, the story of the sinking of the "unsinkable" ocean liner Titanic and The Vikings, the story about how a slave won the favours of a beautiful princess over a Viking prince."

"Yeah, but that slave didn't look like us," AC interjected.

"Ya, that's true. 'Member The Defiant Ones, with Sidney Poitier and Tony Curtis; the story of a black man and a white man who, despite hating each other, had to cooperate to stay alive?"

"Uh huh."

"Bermuda General Theatres, the company that has a monopoly on the movies, is owned by local 40 Thieves."

"40 Thieves!"

"Ya, that's what we-byes call the white establishment."

Both AC and Karen laughed heartily.

"They decided to show The Defiant Ones only at the segregated 'Island Theatre.' That Island Theatre is so elegant, you know, with the smoked glass entrance doors that had inlaid, shiny, kidney shaped, brass push-plates. And inside, past the box office, you have the dark blue carpet that's plush and deep, as are the seats – even downstairs in the coloured section."

Snapper continued, "Even though it was a rule in our family not to attend the segregated theatres, I decided to be defiant myself and secretly defy my mum's rules, I just had to see that show. I wasn't disappointed either. I'd never before seen a black man in a movie portrayed as strong, independent and courageous. It was intoxicating. I left the show walking on air."

"Yes, a lot of us felt that way," AC said.

"Ya! But on my way home it hit me. I thought, why had the theatre company decided to show this particular movie only in the segregated theatre? My mood changed from elation to deep rage. I thought, they're sending us a message, *'Don't get any ideas from this movie, we're still in control here!'*

"It was bad enough that the 40 Thieves controlled all the money, the big business, the parliament and the government jobs. If the theatres were not segregated none of that would change. But this theatre thing was meant to publicly humiliate us, to drive home a message that black people were inferior, lest we forget. It was an ever-present reminder that they're on top and we're on the bottom, like gum under their shoes that they can scrape on the sidewalk whenever they want."

Snapper paused to catch his breath. He really had the Americans spellbound now.

"I tune into those Stateside radio stations at night, you know, when the reception is clear. I hear about the Civil Rights demonstrations, sit-ins, freedom riders and efforts by coloured Americans to dismantle the Jim Crow system and segregation over there. Read about it in the local *Bermuda Recorder* too. AC, I know the battle you're fighting over there. Your efforts give us hope and a hunger to help make things happen here, at home." Sewell smiled and nodded.

"One evening in '59 I had just left the Opera House, one of the theatres that was not segregated, having enjoyed Operation Petticoat when I stepped on a piece of paper with writing on it. I picked it up. It was a flier encouraging everyone to boycott all the movie theatres because of segregation, all theatres, even the ones that weren't segregated. It was signed by some people called the Progressive Group. I was walking towards my parked moped when I saw my mate, Derrick.

I said, 'Hey Derrick, you seen this-here?' He said that they were all over Town.

AC asked, "Who was this Progressive Group?"

"Nobody knew, but they had fliers, not just all over Town, they were out in the country, stuck on electric light poles, on walls – all over the place. Whoever they were, they were serious."

"Derrick told me, he heard that people were gonna start gathering outside the Island Theatre the next evening and picket the place. He said they couldn't stop us from doing that and we wouldn't be breakin' any laws or nuttn' like that.

"I said to him, 'Bye you sound like yuh one of the organizers.' But he said he wasn't. But he did say, 'Look mate, there's only one thing them Front Street byes like more than keeping their knees on our necks, and that's their money. I bet if we picket those theatres no white folks will have enough guts to break a picket line to see a show. They'll be too scared. As for the coloured folks who want to see a show, we can talk to 'em and explain what we're trying to do, and I bet they'll go home too. They might even join the protest. Pretty soon Bermuda General Theatres will be losing their shirts. And that's when we'll know we got em.'

"I waited one day, then on the evening of June 16th '59, on the second night of the boycott, when I arrived at the Island Theatre, I noticed a crowd of people. There was a man I vaguely recognized fussing over a large black box with electronics in it. After feedback squeal momentarily split everyone's ears, I realized it was an amplifier. People started to use it to make speeches, encouraging the demonstrators as to the justness of the cause and the injustice of segregation in Bermuda. One of the most dynamic speakers was a man named Kingsley Tweed and another man known as "Comrade" Lynch."

"Comrade Lynch! Was he a communist?"

"I dunno. I don't think so. We-byes in Bermuda have all kinds of nicknames. Anyway, some demonstrators were also outside the other segregated theatre, the Playhouse, which was diagonally across the street.

"I spied my mate, Derrick who said, 'Hey mate, I thought I might see you here.'

"I asked him, 'Them byes doin' all the talking, they the Progressive Group?'

"He said, 'No, bye. They're just making speeches. You know, the thing is, it's not that Bermuda General Theatres thinks that if whites and blacks sit together, whites won't go to the movies and they will lose business. They already know that's not true because none of their theatres in the countryside, like in Somerset or St. George's are segregated, and whites still attend, sitting alongside blacks. This segregation in Town is strictly to send an evil message to us.'

"I said, 'Ya, right! One of the Company's directors is a member of parliament, Mr. J. E. Spearmint. He said we won't last more than three days. He dunno how serious we-byes are! He told the *Bermuda Recorder* it's a 'Tempest in a Teacup.' It's a tempest alright, but it ain't no teacup.'

"Each evening, crowds gathered outside the theatres as the boycott continued. Messages from the shadowy Progressive Group were communicated to the public through letters published by the *Recorder*. Their message was:

1. Don't use violence.
2. Don't block traffic.
3. Don't get excited.
4. Don't give up.

"Despite being called "hoodlums" by the same MCP, J.E. Spearmint, the crowd carefully heeded their shadowy leaders' guidance. In an effort to de-escalate the situation, Parliament authorized the Attorney General, a white civil servant from England, along with W.L. Tucker, one of the black members of Parliament, to form a committee to negotiate with the Progressive Group to end the standoff. Instead of entering negotiations, they organized a motorcade, which grew to 150 cars long, to drive from Hamilton to St. George's, paralyzing traffic.

"The Progressive Group placed an article in the *Bermuda Recorder* saying there would be no negotiations, just end the segregation and they would end the boycott.

"Derrick said that was a smart move 'cause if they agree to negotiate, them 40 Thieves would discover who they were and then they'd put the squeeze on them – get them fired from their jobs, call their loans at the bank, or ruin their businesses in some way. That's how they operated.

"The boycott continued. On June 23rd, 1959, due to lack of business, all the theatres operated by Bermuda General Theatres, meaning all Bermuda's theatres, closed, "Until further notice." However, the crowds continued to gather, each night, outside the empty theatres. Eight days after the theatres closed their doors an announcement was made that on July 2nd the theatres would reopen on a desegregated basis. In addition, restaurants would be desegregated as well.

"Derrick, who is about 15 years older than me, and having faithfully tended the bar at the Royal Bermuda Yacht Club, the headquarters of Bermuda's white establishment, for over 20 years, just stood there, silently, with tears running down his cheeks, but with a smile on his face.

"I said, 'You ok, Derrick?'

"You know what he said? 'Bye, you know, I never thought I'd live to see the day that we-byes could force them-byes to blink.' He turned and locked me with an intense stare, and said, 'You youngsters now have a future in this-here island. You'd better grab that future with both hands and don't let go. We-byes, the older generation, have made a lotta sacrifices to move the ball down the field for you-younger byes. Don't let us down.'"

Snapper said, "I'll never forget that night."

AC said, "So who were this Progressive Group?"

"The Progressive Group? They remain anonymous to this day.

"Well, that's quite a story!" AC sat back in his chair in contemplation.

 "Ready to catch some more fish?"

"Sure thing!" AC replied, as Snapper brought *Captain Crunch* back up to trolling speed.

The wahoo were still biting and the excitement of hauling aboard another half a dozen of them, plus his boycott story, appeared to successfully deflect the congressman's curiosity about the Argus Tower. Snapper Jones didn't want to lie about what he knew about the activities at the Tower and was relieved he didn't have to answer any more questions from a US Government official about it.

# K137

Spring 1962 was the coldest in living memory in the Arctic. The scene in Polyarny Inlet, close to Murmansk, was still stark – black water, white snow-covered mountains with few trees. The only difference was that dawn was coming earlier. Kapitan 1st Class, Arkady Nimirov slowly examined, with pride, the multitude of gauges, dials, oscilloscopes, pipes, levers, buttons and switches that surrounded him in his Control Room. The most prominent features, in the middle of the compartment, were two large vertical cylindrical objects, that went from floor to ceiling – the boat's two periscopes. This was the Soviet Union's latest creation, the first of a new class of missile boat, one that would surely tip the balance of power in his country's favour. Nimirov knew what each one of these gadgets was for, and in what circumstance each was to be used. *This will give those damn American capitalists something to think about.*

*K137* was the first of, what NATO would call, the "Yankee" Class SSBN; SS designating her as a "submerged ship," B meaning that she was a "ballistic missile" boat, and N meaning she was "nuclear" powered. And she packed one hell-of-a-punch. She carried 16 SS-N-6 missiles, that (for the first time) could be fired while they were submerged, just like the American Polaris missiles. She also had 6 torpedo tubes, carrying 17, Type 53, torpedoes.

Within her compliment of missiles, 8 had high explosive warheads and 8 were "special" – thermonuclear! Each had a range of 1,500 nautical miles. Her 18th torpedo was also a "special" – nuclear tipped.

He had recently returned from sea trials in the Arctic testing the boat's capabilities, with an Alpha class attack sub. Nimirov was pleased with his boat's performance. He expected her to have a long list of problems, as was normal with any new class of sub. But *K137* ran like a Swiss watch. She manoeuvred easily, dove to her design depth with ease and without leaks, and, above all, was the quietest boat ever to come out of Mother Russia's shipyards. Their Alpha hunter couldn't find her in the icefields of the Arctic.

Missile drills were carried out in a satisfactory manner, although he was sure that, with constant practice, his crew would be able to spin up those missiles 20% faster than they were doing now.

The Executive Officer, Kapitan Lieutenant Alexander Fedorov approached him, "Kapitan, all the supplies are aboard, the ship is cleared for sea." Fedorov was senior enough to command his own attack sub, but he was happy to be involved in the maiden patrol of *K137*, the most potent vessel in the Soviet navy. They both climbed the stairs to the small cockpit at the top of the sail, the only place to see outside while the boat was under way.

"Mr. Fedorov, give the order to depart."

"Aye, Kapitan." He picked up the intercom and gave the appropriate orders. The well-trained crew slipped the lines and, with a little help from the grubby harbour tug, *K137* was under way. They proceeded through the long channel on the surface, but when they exited into the Barents Sea, Nimirov gave the order, "Mr. Fedorov, submerge the ship, I'll be in my quarters."

"Aye, sir. Submerge the ship." Then he gave the orders.

Nimirov descended to his quarters where he found Commissar Yevgeny Popov waiting for him. Popov was the sub's "Political Officer," a position that was obligatory onboard every submarine in the Soviet Navy. His job was to ensure that, while on patrol, the captain and his crew conducted themselves in a manner that was consistent, with the tenets of Soviet communist doctrine. "Good morning Kapitan, shall we open our orders?" It was essential that the political officer have joint custody of the orders for missile boats. They needed both the captain's key and the Commissar's key to open the safe containing their orders. They were, as expected, to proceed to the Atlantic and take up station in an area between the Azores and Bermuda, doing their utmost to remain undetected.

After posting the orders, Nimirov returned to the Control Room and said to Fedorov, "Number One, the orders have directed us to proceed to a patrol area in the mid-Atlantic, but they don't specify how we get there. Let's take the scenic route, shall we?" Fedorov looked at him quizzically. "I want you to plot a course to take us into the Arctic, under the ice, and then swing south through the Denmark Strait into the Atlantic."

"The Denmark Strait! With all due respect, sir, parts of the Denmark Strait are too shallow! Remember that subsea waterfall? It's a navigational hazard."

"Exactly, Sasha! The Americans will expect us to come out through the gap, between Britain and Iceland. That gap is riddled with NATO hydrophones. They won't expect us to take the Denmark Strait. This is supposed to be a stealth patrol, is it not?"

"Of course, sir. But what about that shallow section?"

Nimirov walked over to the plot, "Look here," he said, "We can hide underneath this thermocline here, which will really distort any acoustic signals we might emit. We'll also proceed as close to, or under the Greenland ice fields as much as possible. The grinding noise from the ice should further obscure our tonals." He moved his finger along the map. "When we get to the precipice of the underwater cliff, we won't have the cover of the thermocline, because we'll have to come shallow, but we can stay under the ice to give us cover. Then when we clear that submerged precipice, we take her as deep as she will go and then slip away."

"Excellent plan Kapitan! I will see to the details," Fedorov said with genuine enthusiasm.

As he turned toward his quarters, Nimirov said, "And Mr. Fedorov, make sure to come about frequently, to ensure our American 'friends' are not trailing us from Murmansk."

"Aye, aye, Sir."

After a few minutes there was a knock on the captain's door. It was Fedorov. He had a large rolled up chart in his hand and he set it down on the captain's table. "Kapitan, I wanted you to see this course plan. If they're out there, we're going to make any unwanted observer think we're on an Arctic patrol, so we're to take a North-Northwest course, 350 degrees, at the outset. Then we'll swing around Svalbard Islands, then turn south close to Greenland, then pass west of Jan Mayen Island, here. Then we approach the Straits, as you have instructed, underneath the Greenland icepack. With silent running we will lose them in the ice, assuming they're out there."

"They're out there, alright, Sasha. That looks good. You may execute the plan. Notify me as we approach Jan Mayen."

"Aye, aye, Sir."

Nimirov had great confidence in Fedorov and knew he didn't have to baby sit him as it related to routine procedures.

*K137* proceeded at 18 knots on a North-Northwest course, clearing her baffles several times. As they approached the barren Svalbard Islands, they slowed down to five knots for silent running. Hearing the slowing of the turbines, Nimirov picked up the intercom and punched the code for the Control Room. "Any contacts, Mr. Fedorov?"

"Nyet, Kapitan, the sonar is clear."

"Any evidence of a trailer?"

"Nyet sir. We've cleared our baffles several times and have detected nothing."

"That is good. How long before we make our turn South?"

"At silent speed, several hours yet, sir."

"Contact me before you make your turn."

"Aye, sir."

In three and one-half hours Nimirov's intercom beeped, and he returned to the Control Room.

"Time, Mr. Fedorov?"

"Time, sir."

"You may make your turn."

"Aye, sir. Helmsman, make your course 190 degrees."

"Aye, sir, making my course 190 degrees."

*K137* crept toward the Greenland coast underneath the icepack as well as the thermocline, as silent as a shadow. They could hear the ice above them, grinding against itself, in constant frictional slow-motion. The Arctic, as one of the world's most nutrient rich oceans, was alive with a multitude of creatures, both great and small, collectively emitting a cacophony of sound, thereby adding cover to the transit of its most lethal predator – the Yankee Class sub, *K137*.

After several hours Fedorov reported, "Kapitan we are due west of Jan Mayen Island."

"Very well, Number One, make your course 180 degrees." There was tension etched on the pallid faces of the crew in the Control Room, as all the officers knew the sub, at 200 meters depth, was heading on a collision course with a wall of solid bedrock, if she did not come shallow in time. But still they crept on. While their missiles and torpedoes gave them the confidence of being an irresistible force, they knew they were headed for what certainly was an immovable object.

After what seemed like an eternity, and after a final check with the navigator, the captain ordered, "Number One, take her up to 50 meters."

"Aye, sir. Planesman, take her up to 50 meters, ten degree up-bubble." There were two planesmen, one operating the hydroplanes attached to the sail, the other responsible for the planes at the stern. In this respect *K137* operated just like an aircraft. The sub gently glided up from the depths to a 50-meter depth. Their instruments were telling them their rise was none too soon, as the ocean floor seemed to be following them upward as they approached the precipice of the submarine waterfall.

The captain addressed the men in the Control Room, "Comrades, we're approaching an area where the northward flowing warm ocean current, a remnant of the Gulf Stream, which floats on the top, is being squeezed against the southward flowing, cold water current, from the Arctic Ocean, which Is flowing at the bottom. But as you can see from our instruments, the bottom is rising dramatically. At the precipice, the cold current spills over its lip and plunges over the other side to return to the depths, while the warmer current stays on top.

"At this point, where the two currents are squeezed together by the rising ocean floor, there is a great deal of turbulence below and rough seas on the surface. We will feel it momentarily. We have to be sure that we are shallow enough to avoid the precipice but not strike the swirling ice above."

As they approached the choke point, the boat started to roll, yaw and pitch, even though she weighed over 9,000 tons and was over 400 feet long. "Steady, comrades," reassured the Skipper. "Number One, take her to 40 meters."

"Aye, sir. Planesman, 5 degrees on planes, take her to 40 meters." The sailors on the hydro-planes repeated the order and *K137* rose to 40 meters.

"Comrades, it won't be long now. You'll know when we go over the top," Nimirov said. The sub continued to be buffeted by the colliding ocean currents. Everyone's face, except for the captain's, was taught with strain. The tense, rough ride dragged on and on. Then suddenly the buffeting stopped. It actually felt like the sub had come to a halt, but their instruments told them they were holding steady at 5 knots at 40 meters depth.

"Comrades, we're over the lip," the captain declared with a one-sided smile. "Mr. Fedorov, take her down to 450 meters, set course to 175 degrees. Continue silent running, we want to avoid that listening post in Argentia, Newfoundland. Regular clearing of baffles as before."

"Aye, aye sir."

Having successfully eluded the NATO hydrophones at the GIUK gap, *K137* returned to the depths, seeking the relative cover of yet another oceanic thermocline. She headed for her patrol area between Bermuda and the Azores, an area where the US East Coast was within range of her new SS-N6 missiles.

Nimirov cast his eyes on the officers in the Control Room, "Comrades, I have patrolled this area before, in our older boats, and it seemed that the Americans always knew where we were. Their listening devices have such acute hearing! The nearest brain connected to those ears is in Bermuda. That's why that island is always one of the first in our Target Packages of those "Special" missiles onboard." He allowed an evil smirk to creep over his face. "But I'm confident that this new, elusive and silent sub our Motherland has made for us, can be a game changer.

"That'll be all for now, comrades."

After two weeks, *K137* arrived in her patrol area between Bermuda and the Azores. After a few days in the area, it was clear to Nimirov that they had indeed eluded NATO forces. The captain addressed the offices in the Control Room, "Comrades, we have heard no sonar buoys, no low overflights by US Navy Marlins, no active pinging from NATO surface vessels and no sign of trailing by US attack subs. Comrades, we've made it! We're on station, undetected! Let's keep it that way."

# Ria

On the evening of the last day of the first month of their agreement, Snapper Jones rode his Zundapp into the yard and found Nelson engaged in his favourite sport with the family chickens. Maria was inside. He knocked, but before he could enter the house, a wafting aroma enticed his nostrils. "Ria! Are you home? What's that amazing smell?"

"What's that smell?" she called out. "It's dinner, of course. Go into the bathroom and wash yuh hands and sit down."

"Who, me? I'm invited to dinner? I'm just here to, you know…"

"We can do that after. Now go wash yuh hands, bye."

After washing his hands, he noticed that the little cedar table was set for two, plus the baby's chair. She called Nelson in, cleaned up his grubby hands and face and sat him at the table.

"What's for dinner?" Snapper inquired.

"Bacalhau," she replied.

"Bacalhau! What the heck is that?"

"You'll see", she said, as she brought the meal to the table. "This is Bacalhau," she said, as she shared out portions between the three of them. "It's a Portuguese dish that's got cod fish with potatoes, garlic, onions, olives and olive oil. Also, this here's Massa Sovada, Portuguese sweet bread. Some people call it Portuguese egg bread. That's what you were smelling. And that's Queijo Fresco cheese to go with yuh bread." She got up and went to the cupboard and retrieved two small glasses and a bottle of Vinho Verde, pouring some for Snapper and herself. After saying grace, they dove into the delicious repast. After they were finished, she brought out dessert – Arroz Doce, rice pudding. Snapper loved dessert and polished off two helpings.

"Ria, that was delicious!"

After dinner was over, Snapper helped with the dishes, and it was only after that was done, did he have a chance to sit down, take out a sheet of paper with columns of numbers on it and explain what had been earned that month from charter fishing, what the expenses were and what was left over for the two of them to share. She said, "You know, Snapper,

Scaley never once explained all this to me, over the years we were married. Thanks for taking the time. Maybe he thought I couldn't understand it."

"I know you can, Ria." He counted out her share of the net for the month, tucked it in an envelope and placed it in her hand.

"Now, Ria, be careful to save some of this-here. We can't charter 12 months of the year, you know. Even if there are tourists here in December, we'll get cut back a lot between December and March because of the weather. You need to hold some back for then."

"Ya, I know." She replied with a big smile. Snapper had noticed that she was looking more like her old self – beautiful and vivacious. The darkness below the eyes, the sad, worried expression and the unkempt hair had given way to this captivating creature – one who could cook!

"I'd better be going now. Thanks for dinner. See you next month.

"Yuh gone so soon? OK then, see yuh." She gave him a peck on the cheek, and he roared off on the Zundapp, in the usual cloud of smoke. And so, it began. On the last day of each month Snapper would enjoy a wonderful meal, describe the prior month's business, play with little Nelson and spend time with Maria. This was all rather new and strange for Snapper because he was a confirmed bachelor in his early thirties.

Both his mother, Edith, and his sister, Becky, had tried jointly, and separately, various strategies to find Snapper a suitable wife: either by inviting him to dinner at their homes coincident with another unattached female guest, or making thinly veiled suggestions about some other girl that they thought was acceptable, or some variation of those approaches. All attempts had failed, mainly because he was quite happy with his marital status and enjoyed his involvement in the Longtail circuit.

Edith strongly disapproved of it, on moral grounds, of course, and she made her feelings on the subject repeatedly and volubly known. "You know, Jesus said, 'For out of the heart proceed evil thoughts, murders, adulteries, fornications, thefts, false witness, blasphemies.' Yuh see, fornication is put on par with murder, stealing and lying. My son, are you a murderer or a thief or a liar?"

Snapper would merely look at the floor in response to this rhetorical question.

"Joshua, every Sunday I go to church and get down on my knees and pray, 'Lord Jesus, please send my only son a good woman so he can stop this sinful fornication.'"

In fact, these lectures were part of the motivation to move out of the family home in Somerset bridge, to his own digs. She was hurt by his decision to move out. But Becky weighed in on Snapper's behalf, "Mummy, a man, especially a young man, needs his own space. He needs to leave the nest and try his own wings. Mummy, you have to change with the times." Edith, nevertheless, continued to disapprove.

Of course, Edith didn't approve of Snapper becoming a pilot and a fisherman, like his father, either. This disapproval was based on fear of losing him at sea, like his father, rather than on moral grounds. But, of course, he became a pilot and fisherman anyway. These difficulties did not diminish her love for her only son, and she made sure she prepared him all his favourite dishes when he came over to see her at the homestead.

Becky, his older sister, merely rolled her eyes each time the subject of longtails came up. She just wanted her brother to be happy and knew he wasn't going to get happiness from longtail hunting. She hoped that he would eventually outgrow them. But, as he didn't live at home anymore, Snapper only had to endure this disapproval when he visited his mother.

Notwithstanding the longtails, Snapper Jones religiously continued his month end visits to the DeSilvas. Each time he went, his visit would get longer and longer. But something strange was happening, instead of merely becoming more blasé with Maria, there had developed an inexplicable tension between them, but it was a tension he looked forward to in the days preceding the meetings. In fact, he found himself dropping by just for social visits when there was no business to discuss. He was confused by this tension, having never experienced it before.

On the ninth month-end meeting, they had the usual delicious meal, cleaned up the kitchen and Snapper read Nelson a story before putting him to bed. It was his favourite, the story of Jonah and the whale. Snapper would always embellish the story with his encounters with whales off Bermuda. Afterwards, he and Maria were talking about Nelson's future and what school to place him in when he reached 5 years old. In the middle of the discussion, she turned toward him, and their eyes met. It was as though a veil covering his eyes had been raised, and he could now see clearly. He suddenly realized what had been bothering him was a conflict within him. His head told him that the relationship with his friend's widow must be strictly respectful and platonic. His heart suddenly realized that, in addition to a strong sexual attraction to Maria, he was now in love with her.

He looked away from her eyes, ashamed of his feelings, but she gently pulled his chin back towards her and said, "Snapper, don't turn away, look at me, please!"

"Ria, I … I don't want you to think that when I came here ten months ago, I was angling to take Scaley's wife for myself. I wasn't, you know. But when you look at me like that, I... I…"

"Like what? Like this?" Her big, liquid, dark eyes bored into him, to his very soul. "Like a woman who wants you more than anything else in the world?"

"Ya. Like that."

They were drawn, inexorably, into a long deep kiss. Their pent-up passions were suddenly unleashed, like a dam bursting from within. He squeezed her so tight she was lifted off the ground, whereupon she wrapped her legs around his waist. He carried her over to the little cedar dining room table and swept aside the few items on it containing salt and pepper. They landed on the floor, smashed to smithereens. He kissed her fiercely, on her lips then all over her face and neck. She could hear nothing but the deafening pounding of her racing heart. As he proceeded lower, he ripped off the bodice of her dress, unleashing her ample, bare breasts. So tender to the touch! He cradled each one in his hands, in turn, giving each one tender loving attention. Maria uttered a low groan of delight, her face distorted in a voiceless scream. Snapper's exploring hands found their way to Maria's most private area. Her panties were soaked through with desire. He eased them off. Then he took her, right there on the dining room table.

When it was over, they both were breathless, and suddenly, Ria gasped, "Nelson!" In a panic they both visually swept the room for the little witness. They saw no one. After breathing a collective sigh of relief, Ria got up and peered into the bedroom and there he was, fast asleep.

"Thank goodness that boy's a sound sleeper," Snapper said, giving her butt a long squeeze as she poured them some cool lemonade.

"Ya, let's hope that he not only sleeps sound, but long," she said giving him a mischievous look and leading him by the hand into her bedroom for round two.

Snapper grinned and thought, *Goodbye longtails*!

He put another long tender kiss on her lips, saying, "Ria, I love you."

She said, "I know. I saw it in your eyes when you first realized it and looked away. Snapper Jones, I've loved you for many months." They gently closed the door behind them.

Several months later, one summer evening, Snapper decided to take Ria and little Nelson for a slow sunset cruise around the islands of the Great Sound. It was the sort of thing that visitors to the Island would pay handsomely for, but this was a cruise of a different sort. Ria and Nelson didn't get to be on *Captain Crunch* very often, so for them, it was a treat. The sun had dipped below the hills of Somerset, and they were enjoying the long twilight that the Island offered this time of year. The air was warm and still, and the Great Sound became a mirror reflecting the pale blue sky, the scattered billowy orange, pink and white cumulous clouds, and the tiny islets surrounding Paradise Lake. The islets, silhouetted against the sunset, were accompanied by reflected images on the briny mirror, as though they were a double image on a giant pastel painting, folded at the waterline, creating a naturally surreal effect. The *Crunch* murmured a low, subdued hum as her bow cut the only disturbance on the glassy sea: a smooth, long, expanding "V." Snapper and Ria sat on the bench on the flybridge silently transfixed by the magical beauty of their island home, the greatest show on earth, absolutely free. Little Nelson was on the main deck with a small fishing rod in his hands, trying to see if he could hook Jonah's whale.

Snapper sensed that the moment was perfect. He opened a compartment next to the helm, retrieving a small box. Opening it, he turned to Ria and said, "Ria, I love you. Will you marry me?"

She was jolted from the reverie created by the magical surroundings and was surprised at the timing of the proposal. "Oh, yes, yes, yes!" was all she could say, before they sealed their engagement with a kiss.

It was autumn of that year that Joshua (Snapper) Jones wed Maria Theresa Almeida DeSilva at the newly consecrated St. Michael's Roman Catholic Church in Paget. The bride's best friend, Maura, was the matron of honour and little Nelson was the ring bearer. It wasn't a huge or high society wedding, but because it was the union of a well-known black man, the folk hero of the *Wilhelmina* disaster, and a Portuguese woman, the wedding attracted wide attention, including that of the redoubtable A.B. Pace who gave the event a prominent write up in the *Bermuda Recorder's* community events section. Pace noted the attendance of an unusual mix of guests, in a Bermudian society still divided by race. Guests included Dr. Carl Cardigan, Director of SOFAR, Dr. Jack and Evelyn Bessemer, Major Eugene Vindham and Captain James Smith, from Tudor Hill and Robert Carpenter, US Consul General.

Edith, who had no idea who these Americans were, other than that they were Josh's friends from work, was at the same time beaming and tearful. Looking up to the heavens, she whispered, "Thank you Jesus."

# Ocean Research

It was a Monday evening that Snapper got the call from Carl Cardigan, SOFAR's Director, "Snapper, we need you to skipper *SHL* next weekend. Clem McCann has been called back to the States due to a death in the family. There's a test on Sunday and we have to go out there and check it out. Can you come?"

Snapper knew that Carl couldn't be more specific on the phone, for security reasons, but he knew exactly what Carl meant. The US Navy was conducting another test firing of its Polaris missile and they needed SOFAR to take the *Sir Horace Lamb (SHL)* out into the ocean and listen for the impact of the dummy warhead hitting the water, and obtain an acoustic vector of that impact, thus helping the Navy obtain their best estimate of the exact location and how close it was to its intended target. *We just have to make sure we're not too close to something hitting the water at over 11,000 miles per hour. That's the risk built into these missions*, Snapper thought.

"Sure, Carl. When are you shoving off?"

"Friday morning."

"I'll be there Thursday evening to check things out."

"Great. See you then." The line went dead.

"Ria! Oh, Ria! Where are you, honey?"

"I'm here." She appeared from inside Nelson's bedroom.

"I've got to take the *SHL* offshore to do some deep ocean research. Clem can't go, so I'm filling in as skipper. I'll be back by next week Wednesday."

Ria had become accustomed to these occasional extended cruises on the *SHL* and she scowled fearfully, but knew not to ask many questions.

On Thursday evening Snapper said goodbye to Ria. She simply said, "Be careful, darling, we'll miss you." He kissed Ria goodbye and rode his moped to the top of St. David's Island and reported to SOFAR, striding straight through into Cardigan's office. Things were always very informal at SOFAR. Carl liked Bermuda shorts and wore them almost every day, regardless of weather. Also, he always had a plastic pen liner in his breast pocket to protect his shirts from the multiple pens he always carried there – a classic engineer's trait. They leaned over an old metal desk and Carl spread out a map of the Atlantic Ocean with their course and area of interest already laid out. "Here's the plan," he said simply.

Snapper studied it for several moments. "When are we to arrive on station?"

"Sunday morning. We'll update you when the firing takes place."

"Ya, OK. If we leave tomorrow morning that'll give us plenty of time to get there without stressing the engine too much." He carefully gathered up the papers then said, "I'm going down to the ship now and make sure everything is ship-shape. All going well, we can slip our lines at 07:30."

"Great, Frank will be with you on this trip."

"Oh great! See yuh." Frank Watlington was one of the veterans of SOFAR, having distinguished himself as the first person ever to have recorded humpback whale songs and identified them as actual songs and not merely random whale noises. No one was better than Frank when it came to listening to ocean sounds.

Snapper took his Zundapp down the hill, around Mullet Bay, to the dock and boarded the *SHL*. Most of the crew were already there readying the ship for its voyage. They all greeted Snapper warmly. He then inspected her from stem to stern, taking particular time to discuss issues with the engine with engineer Ed Stovell. He was satisfied that the *SHL* was in ship shape. He decided he would sleep on board and be ready for an early start the next morning.

After loading some last-minute testing equipment early Friday morning, they slipped their mooring exactly at 07:30. The *SHL* was a sturdy vessel but a relatively poor sailor, her round bottom causing her to roll heavily, even when the weather was relatively placid. In fact, her nickname was, "The Vomit Comet." You had to have a cast iron stomach to ride the Comet.

They were to proceed to a specified grid reference, on a course of 110 degrees to an area about 650 miles east southeast of Bermuda, drop their listening devices over the side and listen for and record the sound of the dummy warhead splash down. These warheads, dummy or not, hit the water with such tremendous force, they could easily be identified. At a speed of 15 knots, they would get there in plenty of time.

The transit to their reference point was totally uneventful. Early Sunday morning, before the break of dawn, Snapper knew he was nearing their destination and he slowed the *SHL* down to 5 knots. Out here in the mid-Atlantic, the only true reference points were astronomical and there had been occasional cloud cover reducing the frequency of opportunities to take star shots to ensure he was on course. He wanted to be sure he was exactly where he was supposed to be when the missile was fired. Fortunately, he was able to get a clear star shot shortly before the first evidence of dawn started to appear in the eastern sky. Even though the Atlantic was in a docile mood that evening, taking star shots with a sextant onboard any vessel was an art form, particularly, from the rolling deck of the *SHL*, "The Vomit Comet." Nevertheless, he was well practiced in this art form and was satisfied with the accuracy of his readings.

As the eastern sky grew lighter, more purple-grey and mauve clouds gathered in the eastern heavens. As the fiery orb peeked from under the edge of the blue horizon, its direct rays were obscured by cloud cover, but that did not reduce the dramatic splendour of dawn over the ocean. Rays of sunlight radiated from behind the low clouds like a crown of golden swords around the head of some colossal celestial creature. Snapper gazed at the eastern sky, muttering to himself, "Dawn at sea never gets old."

After dawn broke on Sunday morning and after checking, verifying and re-verifying his sextant readings, his charts, his chronometer and his tables, Snapper Jones was sure they were on station. He cut the engine. The plan was to lay down a number of sonar buoys in a large circle – diameter seven miles – the centre of which was the missile's target. The sonar buoys, arranged in this manner, would be able to pinpoint the splashdown point of the dummy warhead. The test, "dummy," warhead was actually not that dumb because it contained a SOFAR bomb in it, not a nuclear weapon. The impact of the warhead on the ocean's surface would release the SOFAR bomb which would sink down into the SOFAR channel and then explode. This sound would be picked up, not only by the hydrophones aboard the SHL, but at SOFAR in Bermuda, and other listening posts in the Azores and around the Atlantic Basin. All these datapoints would enable the US Navy to have a best estimate of the accuracy of their missile.

The crew assembled the various devices and arrays of hydrophones and rigged them onto the ship's winches ready to be lowered over the side to the prescribed depth. The next step would be to drop the sonar buoys overboard in the prescribed circle then retreat, lower the hydrophones, listen and wait. Then they would be not only on station, but also ready.

The hydrophones were connected to receiving electronic gear, located in the main cabin and the engineers were seated around it with headsets strapped on. There was also a loudspeaker hooked up so the rest of the crew could hear what was going on. The reel-to-reel tape recorder was operational.

There was a crackle on the radio. Snapper picked it up. The message was simple, "Tee time is 17:30."

"Roger that. On station." Snapper replied. Then he announced to the crew, "Launch time is 17:30." There were nods all round. The time was then 06:30.

Snapper said, "Right you guys, there's plenty of time before the launch, so let's drop our hydrophones over the side to test them out." With the main engine off, the only sound to be heard was the low hum of *SHL's* electric generator and the lapping of little waves against the vessel's hull.

With the hydrophone arrays dangling at various depths, at about 07:00 they started to pick up an unusual sound. Frank said, "Whoa, what's this?" He flicked a switch and put it on speaker.

Snapper said, "Don't know what it is, …. but it definitely sounds man made."

The sound gradually grew louder and louder: a rhythmic combination of whirring, pulsating and rumbling.

"That, gentlemen, is the sound of a submarine, passing either directly beneath us or close by. Are we getting this on tape?" Frank demanded. Snapper shot a glance at one of the other technicians in the cabin. The man gave a thumbs up. After a long while, the sound eventually started to fade and was audible to the human ear for about an hour, but for much longer for their equipment.

Snapper asked rhetorically, "I wonder if we have any boats in this area." Of course, nobody knew the answer to that question.

After that bit of excitement, the men went back to waiting and listening. One thing was certain, their hydrophones were definitely working.

At around 13:00, long after the mystery sound had faded, they started the engine, dropped their array of sonar buoys in a circular pattern around the intended target point, motored away to a safe distance, then tested them. The sonar buoys were wirelessly synced to equipment onboard and were working properly. "Tee time" came at 17:30 and everyone was on alert.

Many minutes later, in the gathering gloom over the placid mid-Atlantic, a loud sonic boom startled everyone onboard, then a huge geyser erupted in the area circumscribed by the sonar buoys. Their gear clearly picked up the violent impact on the ocean's surface. A few minutes later they picked up another explosion as the SOFAR bomb exploded. They recorded it, ascertained its distance and direction, documented it, hauled up their gear, collected the sonar buoys and headed back to Bermuda – mission accomplished.

When they were about 12 hours out, Snapper contacted the SOFAR station on the radio, "Carl, operation successful, plus we have a present for you, over."

"A present? What kind of present? Over."

"A real big fish, over and out."

When they returned to St. David's, Frank and Snapper walked into Carl's office, each with a reel of audio tape in his hand. They loaded one of them on Carl's player in his office and pressed play.

"Look who dropped by," Snapper said. Carl listened with rapt attention. "Do we have any subs in the neighbourhood?"

"How would I know? But if we don't, this is a big deal. I don't think we have picked up anything here. Let me check." He picked up his intercom. "Miles, have you picked up any submarine traffic east of us in the last 72 hours?"

"No Carl. Nothing."

"Do you guys know exactly where you were when you heard this?"

"Sure," Snapper said, "We were on station here," he pointed to the map, "And had been drifting for about an hour. There was no wind so we couldn't have drifted far."

Carl said, "Thanks guys, I need to run this by Jack Bessemer and those other 'brainiacs' up there at the NAVFAC." He picked up his phone and called Jack.

"Jack, I've got something I think might be important. I'm coming up to Tudor Hill right now. And get one of the head-honchos at the NAVFAC to your place for a conference. I'll be there in an hour." Carl picked up the tapes and the charts and rushed off to his Morris Minor parked outside on the curb.

When he got to Tudor Hill, Jack was waiting for him with Captain James Smith from the NAVFAC, along with the ever present Major Vindham. Carl said, "Listen to this." He gave Vindham the tape to load up on the player, then he laid out the chart on the table. "Gentlemen, this tape was recorded at 07:00 three days ago out here." He pointed out the place on the map. Then he looked directly at Captain Smith. "Do we have any subs in that area."

"Well, Carl, you know I can't say exactly – national security."

"Cut the national security bullshit, Jim. We're all working for the same team here! Yes or no?"

"Well, I don't know of any."

"I'll take that as a no."

"Are we tracking any Soviet subs in that area? No more bullshit, Jim!"

"I don't know for sure but I'm not aware of any right now."

Carl's normally jovial expression was one of suppressed fury. "Well, if you don't know, then nobody knows! So, I'll take that as a 'no' too. In that case gentlemen I'd say we've got a new Russian boat out there, roaming around the Atlantic, full of nukes aimed at us, a boat that WE DON'T KNOW ABOUT, and that lack of knowledge is making me shit my drawers! And you should be too!"

Everyone was stone silent.

Finally, Bessemer said, "Carl, how long did your guys record this mystery boat?"

"Well," Carl replied, "The tape was running a half an hour before they heard it but I'm sure the phones were picking it up before they actually heard it, and the recording after it passed them by goes on for over an hour, so I guess they've got about 3 hours of acoustics for you geniuses to play with."

Jack said, "Jim, why don't you confirm that you don't have anything in your portfolio of Russian subs that matches this, and I can work on that new IBM 1620 to tweak the algorithm to get a rough profile for you to load on your LOFAR machines over there in NAVFAC. Of course, we won't get a complete profile until one of our subs trails that thing."

"Roger that! Scuttlebutt says that the Russians have developed a new class of boat. Maybe this is it," Captain Jim Smith mused. "And I'm going to contact the commandant at the Naval Operating Base to send a couple of Marlins out there to drop some sonar buoys on that Russian to see if we can get a fix on him. He's probably long gone by now, but we've got to try even if it's a long shot. I've got to report this to the brass stateside right away. Jack, how long will it take to get a copy of this tape to me."

"Ah, here you go." Cardigan dug in his bag and produced the other tape. "The guys on board the *Sir Horace* dubbed the tape 'cause they thought it was important." Cardigan was satisfied that he had been successful in raising the alarm and his work up there was done — at least for now.

# New Assignment

"Kapitan, our sensors are picking up the sounds of a low flying multi-engine aircraft, probably our 'friends,' seaplane patrols out of Bermuda." A few minutes later they heard the gentle pings from sonar buoys.

Nimirov snapped, "Mr. Fedorov, take her down to 400 meters. Smartly!" Fedorov immediately repeated the order to the planesmen. *K137* plummeted further into the depths. Again, tension showed on the crews faces. "We're going to hide underneath this thermocline. Their sonar will not be able to penetrate it," the Captain explained. While Nimirov was calm, the rest of the crew knew that 450 meters was close to the sub's crush depth, where the boat would be crushed by the deep ocean's pressure. He looked at the strained faces around the control room and said in a reassuring tone, "Don't worry, Comrades, she can take it." He wasn't sure if his reassurance was working but after a while the tactic seemed to work insofar as the Americans were concerned, as they didn't hear the pings of the sonar buoys any longer.

This process repeated itself several times during their patrol. The only exception was one evening while patrolling at silent speed they detected a colossal explosion. They couldn't tell whether it was nearby or not. They didn't detect any other vessels in the area, so they didn't know what to make of it. Then they returned to the routines of the patrol. Nimirov made note of the sound in his captain's log.

*K137* had been on station for six months and was preparing to return home. She had been mostly successful in eluding her pursuers: the American Navy.

"Mr. Fedorov, the Americans seem to have an inkling that we might be out here, but they can't lock on to our location. So, we have this cat and mouse game going on, except, this time, the mouse appears to be doing better than normal in eluding the cat. And this mouse has huge, sharp teeth." A sinister one-sided smirk crept over his face.

Fedorov said, "Kapitan, it is time to come shallow to check on any last-minute orders before we head back to port. We've been out here for a very long time and the men need some shore leave."

"Very well, it is a few minutes after midnight, bring her up slowly and check for any flash messages." The executive officer gave the appropriate orders and *K137* rose slowly to periscope depth, raising her antenna to check for any messages from Fleet Command. The radio officer busied himself, as there were indeed messages for them. After a few minutes he approached the captain.

"Kapitan, I have a message from Red Banner Northern Fleet Command, for 'your eyes only.'" Nimirov took the message.

"I'll be in my quarters. Mr. Fedorov, take her down to 400 meters and continue silent running. And tell Mr. Popov to meet me in my quarters."

In his quarters he took out the "eyes only" code book and manually decoded the message. Popov knocked and took a seat at the table. After what seemed like forever, he was finished. He said to the political officer, "Comrade we have new orders. We are to proceed to make a rendezvous with the freighters the *Indigirka* and *Berdyansk*, at this grid reference. We are ordered to escort them to Havana and 'under no circumstances allow them to be boarded by any agents of a foreign power.'" He slid over his handwritten, decoded version and the code book for Popov to check his accuracy.

After he completed his check, he nodded to confirm the message. "Comrade Kapitan, what is the meaning of this message? What ships are these, and what cargo do they carry that is so important?"

"I don't know, comrade, I don't know. We've been down here dodging the Americans for five months. I have no idea what's happened in the world since we've been submerged. Obviously, something very bad has happened and it involves Cuba." Then he paused and scowled at Popov. "But here's what I do know. I know that Red Banner Northern Fleet Command knows the capability and weapons onboard this boat – that we have "special" missiles and a "special" torpedo aboard. If we have to use that special torpedo to prevent the Americans from boarding either the *Indigirka* or the *Berdyansk* then we might be starting World War III. Perhaps it's already started, but I think not, because our orders would be specifically about launching our missiles." Then he punched the intercom.

"Mr. Fedorov, come to my quarters at once." He appeared in barely a minute. "Sit down Sasha, we have new orders." He slid the handwritten paper to the Executive Officer.

After reading it he turned to his captain saying, "What ships are these and what is their cargo?" Nimirov shrugged his shoulders. Fedorov read the orders again, then his jaw slackened, and blood drained from his face, as the implications of the orders hit him.

Before he could say anything else, Nimirov flatly ordered, "Mr. Fedorov, plot and execute an intercepting course to these coordinates immediately. It will take us south of Bermuda, but I fear that to get there in time we're going to have to proceed faster than silent speed. It is a risk we have to take."

"Aye sir." Fedorov stood up and exited the compartment. When he reached the Control Room, and after a brief consultation with the navigator, he ordered, "Helmsman, come to course 225 degrees, increase speed to 15 knots. Gentlemen, we have new orders. We'll rendezvous with the *Indigirka* and *Berdyansk* about 1,500 kilometres from Havana and escort them in."

---------------

Dr. Carl Cardigan arrived at the SOFAR station at about 07:30 and was sipping black coffee when one of his technicians, Miles Masters, and Snapper Jones came into the room with a printout. It was a bunch of squiggly lines, like one would find from a seismometer measuring earthquakes. "Carl, look at this from overnight," Snapper said. Carl examined it.

"What am I looking at here?"

"Compare it to this." Miles laid another sheet just above it.

"The patterns look very similar. What is the second sheet from?"

"It's from that mystery sub that we recorded when we were on that Polaris run, and you were sure there was a new sub out there. But look, the peaks appear to be coming more often on last night's print out."

"Yeah, it's louder too. She's going somewhere in a hurry." Carl picked up the phone and dialled, "Hello, Jack? Have you seen the overnight hydro readings? No? I think our 'friend,' the mystery sub, is back, and in a hurry this time, not in stealth mode. Check with NAVFAC and call me back." He hung up.

About an hour later Jack Bessemer returned Carl's call. "Carl? Yeah, it's Jack. NAVFAC have it too. They still don't have enough data on this guy to form a signature for him, but the consensus is that it's the same sub

Snapper and Frank heard a couple of months ago, and who has been slipping through our fingers ever since. One thing I can't figure out, though."

"Yeah, what's that?"

"This guy has been so clever, so slick, up till now. Now, he's thundering through the sea like a rank amateur. What's with that?"

"Dunno. But what's NAVFAC going to do about it?"

"They're sortieing three P5M Martin Marlins from the NOB to go out there and look for him. We've got a triangulated location for him from our station in the Azores. They should be taking off momentarily."

"Those old slow birds are so noisy I can hear them through your phone!" Carl wisecracked.

"You're so right. Anyway, they're faster than the sub, that's all that counts. We'll see what they come back with."

Back on *K137*, several hours had passed since their orders to divert to escort the two Russian freighters and things were proceeding without any excitement. Then one of the sonar operators exclaimed, "Kapitan, I'm detecting that we are being overflown by a low flying multi-engine aircraft."

"Our American 'friends' are back. Mr. Fedorov, what a coincidence! They have the whole Atlantic Ocean to fly over and they just happen upon us here. Their ears are exceptionally acute. Mr. Fedorov reduce speed to 5 knots and make your depth 500 meters. Rig ship for silent running."

"500 meters! Kapitan that's too near crush depth!"

"Not to worry, she'll take it!"

"Aye, sir, planesman, take her down to 500 meters. Silent running."

After a few minutes, the sonar operator reported, "Kapitan, aircraft returning. I hear splashes, small objects."

"Sonar-buoys." Nimirov muttered. Moments later the gentle pinging of sonar-buoys could be heard throughout the sub. "Number one. Take her down to 550 meters." Everyone in the Control Room became very tense, but no one dared say a word.

After about an hour of pinging from sonar-buoys, and changing course many times, *K137* appeared to lose her American pursuers. They increased speed to 10 knots and proceeded on a course to intercept the freighters. They were going to be late, but they would get there. But after quiescence for about 6 hours they were picked up by another array of sonar-buoys. This pattern repeated itself three more times. Finally, Nimirov sighed and said, "Gentlemen, this mad dash to rendezvous with these freighters has blown our cover. The Americans know exactly where we are and what direction we are headed. We may as well surface, pop the hatch and blow kisses at that patrol plane up there."

In Tudor Hill, Vindham was in the NAVFAC office when Captain Smith said, "The Naval flyboys have the P5M Mariners out there taking turns in dropping sonar-buoys on that sub, from time to time, to keep close tabs on her. We don't know what kind of sub is down there, but we think it's some new Russian sub that is very quiet, so they need to frequently ping her to confirm her location."

"With all this Cuba missile stuff going on, this quiet sub could be very significant," the Major muttered.

"Yeah, no shit."

------------

Back aboard *K137*, when the time drew near for the rendezvous, the sonar man reported, "Kapitan, I detect a surface contact – twin screw." After a few minutes of listening he declared, "No, correction, sir, there are two separate contacts, each single screw. Revolutions are slow, consistent with cargo vessels."

"Mr. Fedorov, that is our quarry. Bring us to periscope depth between the two ships, then raise the antenna and notify them we are here on station to escort them to Havana."

Fedorov gave the orders and Nimirov returned to his quarters deep in thought. He made a note in his Captain's log: "Have followed orders, having been detected by the American Navy in the process." Then he thought, *Northern Fleet Command must've known that we couldn't make this rendezvous in time without being detected. What the hell could be so important about the cargoes of these two ships that is worth exposing the most potent ship in the Soviet Navy to our adversary? Something is very wrong up there in the world and I'm afraid we've sailed unwittingly right into the middle of it!*

## SSN 591

The attack sub, *USS Shark* – *SSN 591*, had been assigned to the Western Atlantic sector, an area covering Bermuda and the Caribbean. Senior officer, Commander Glen Rogers, was studying the plot when the radio officer brought him a message. "Captain, flash message from CINCLANT, sir." Rogers read it then referred to the plot again, locating an unmarked point on the map.

"Navigator! Plot a course to these coordinates, we have intel of an unidentified Soviet submarine in the area. We are to find it and trail it and await further orders."

"Aye, sir."

The Executive Officer, Sam Mason, arrived in the control room; the captain informing him of their new orders. "XO, everything's getting pretty tense up top. The Russians have placed nuclear missiles in Cuba and President Kennedy has blockaded the island, demanding that they be withdrawn. If they're not, we could be in World War III. This unidentified Russian sub poses a real threat. We don't know if it's a missile boat or an attack boat. From the course we've been given, it's approaching the US coast. Our job is to give her skipper a moment of pause before he does anything rash. If it's a missile boat, it could be closing the range for a missile strike on our East Coast cities. If it is an attack boat, it could be setting up to escort one or more of those Russian freighters headed for Cuba. The same ships the Navy has been ordered to stop. These are the coordinates to rendezvous with that sub." He handed over the written coordinates. "But make sure you bring us up on his tail very quietly. We don't want him to know we're there yet. I'll be in my quarters, if you need me. Mr. Mason has the conn!"

"Aye, aye Captain. We'll charge ahead for a while, to get closer quickly, then we'll come to silent speed and come up in her baffles."

"Very Well, Mr. Mason."

"All ahead flank!" *SSN 591* thundered off into the depths. After a few hours at flank speed, *USS Shark* slowed to 5 knots to listen.

"Conn, Sonar. XO, I'm picking up a faint contact, probably submerged, off our port bow."

"Incredible! Right where they said he would be. Navigator, let him pass by to starboard then bring us up on his tail, quietly."

"Aye, sir."

After about 2 hours, Captain Rogers re-entered the Control Room.

"XO, status report," he demanded.

"Captain, we are 200 yards astern of the Russian sub, 50 feet below him. There's no sign that he knows that we're here. Strange thing though, he hasn't cleared his baffles since we've been here. It's like he doesn't care if somebody is behind him or not."

"Well, let's not tell him."

"Yes sir," Mason said with a smile. "Sir, in the vastness of the Atlantic, this Russian is exactly where CINCLANT said it would be. Our intel is improving."

"Yeah, scuttlebutt says we've now got some 'Big Ears' in Bermuda."

Just then, over the PA system, "Conn, Sonar."

"Go ahead Sonar," the Captain said.

"Sir, I detect two surface contacts, both single screw, and the Russian sub is slowing."

"XO, Looks like he's on escort duty. Sonar, what's the course of the surface contacts?"

"Sir, 225 degrees."

"These must be Russian vessels headed for Cuba. XO, come to periscope depth and send a message to CINCLANT, updating them on the situation and asking for further orders."

"Aye, sir." He repeated the orders.

*USS Shark* backed off from her Russian quarry and rose to periscope depth. They sent a flash message to Fleet Headquarters. Then they returned to trail the Russian sub, the small flotilla heading south at 10 knots.

# Close Call

*K137* rose to inform the surface vessels that they were on station and to receive a situation report. After several minutes the radio operator handed him a message from the *Indigirka*. It read:

"We carry a "special" cargo for our comrades in Havana. Our orders are not to stop if confronted by the American Navy in respect to their illegal "Quarantine." In the event of an attempted boarding, we are ordered to scuttle our ships. The situation is extremely tense up here and the Americans have threatened to either board us or sink us if we attempt to breach their blockade line. We are very reassured by your presence. At this speed we should reach the blockade in 18 hours."

Nimirov's face went pale. He had no idea that the geopolitical situation had deteriorated so much since he put to sea almost 6 months ago.

"Kapitan, do you have a reply for the *Indigirka*?"

Collecting his thoughts, he replied, "Yes, yes I do. Tell both *Indigirka* and *Berdyansk* that, as we might be heading for an armed confrontation with the American Navy, I am assuming tactical command for the conduct of the three ships, *K137*, *Indigirka* and *Berdyansk*. And so long as I am escorting them, they must obey my orders. Send that right away and require them to acknowledge."

"Aye, sir."

In 12 hours the Sonar reported, "Kapitan, we have two new contacts, one off the port bow and the other off the starboard. Each are twin screw, consistent with being warships. Probably destroyers. Range 10 kilometres and closing."

"Battle stations, torpedo, Mr. Fedorov!"

"Aye, aye, sir, Battle stations torpedo!"

"Mr. Fedorov, instruct the officer in charge of the 'special' torpedo to load it in tube number one."

"Sir?"

"You have your orders, Mr. Fedorov!"

"Aye, sir."

One hour later *K137* came to periscope depth to receive a message from the freighters. The message read:

"We have been hailed by 2 American warships. They demand that we stop or turn around, or else we will be fired upon."

"Instruct the freighters to hold their course!"

Another hour passed. *K137* came to periscope depth for another update.

"The US destroyers have fired star-shells over our bows and have gone to battle stations."

"Mr. Fedorov, initiate special torpedo firing sequence. Find Mr. Popov and have him report to my quarters." Within a minute, Commissar Popov, the political officer, appeared, along with Fedorov. The firing of nuclear weapons required the permission of three officers, the captain, the first officer and the political officer. The safe required all three of their keys for it to be opened. Inside were the launch codes for the weapon.

"Gentlemen, it is apparent that in order to fulfil our orders, which are, 'under no circumstances can it be allowed to have agents of a foreign power board and inspect either of these ships,' we must use the special weapon we have on board. My decision is to launch the weapon."

"I concur, Kapitan. We must not allow ourselves to be bullied by these warmongering Americans," said Popov, taking his key from around his neck and giving it to the captain.

Fedorov stared at his captain in disbelief and horror. "Kapitan, the destroyers are too close. If you launch that weapon, it will not only destroy the two American destroyers but our two freighters as well, not to mention ourselves. Better to order them to scuttle themselves than launch the nuke. Sinking American naval ships is one thing, but with a NUCLEAR WEAPON! It would precipitate a nuclear cataclysm! The world as we know it would surely end. Even if we were not destroyed in the blast, we would have no home to return to, as the whole North Cape region would, no doubt, be obliterated by either US ICBM's or Polaris missiles from US subs. No sir, I do NOT concur with launching the 'special' torpedo!"

Nimirov turned crimson with fury. He leapt to his feet, roaring, saliva becoming airborne, "What? You DON'T concur? Give me your key Mr. Fedorov – that's an order!"

"Kapitan, this is the one thing you cannot order me to do. My key stays around my neck. It is my decision to use it, and mine alone, and I do not agree to launch that weapon."

"Mr. Fedorov, I will see to it that you NEVER command one of our motherland's ships. You clearly don't have the stomach nor the character to be a submarine captain. You are relieved of duty!"

"As you wish Kapitan, but my launch key stays with me. At least we will have a home to return to, so that you can have me properly Court Marshalled, Sir. Meanwhile, you may want to take some time to reconsider your intended course of action. Sir!" Fedorov, saluted, turned on his heels, and retired to his quarters.

Meanwhile, on *USS Shark*, the sonar operator reported, "Conn, Sonar."

"Captain here."

"Captain, sonar has picked up sounds that the sub has flooded his torpedo tubes and opened his outer doors. He is preparing to fire, sir."

"Good God! XO, ping him! Ping him now!"

A loud "Ping" was emitted from *USS Shark*, then another, then another. It could be heard all over both submarines.

"XO, Firing Point Procedures! Target that sub!"

"Aye, Captain. Fire Control Officer, Firing Point Procedures, flood tubes one and two, open outer doors and plot a firing solution!"

------------

Back on *K137*, the loud ping startled everyone. Nimirov punched the intercom and demanded, "Control Room, where'd that come from?"

The Sonarman, who had had to snatch off his headphones after the first ping rung bells in his head, answered, "Kapitan, it came from directly behind us!"

"All stop! I'm coming up."

Nimirov stomped into the Control Room, "What do you have?"

The second lieutenant reported, "Kapitan, since we stopped engines, we have detected an American sub some 200 meters directly behind us, he has flooded his tubes and opened his outer doors. He is ready to fire, sir."

All eyes were on Nimirov. They pierced through him like lasers. He had never ordered a retreat before, and he hated the taste of it now. Everyone in the Control Room held their breath. They knew their skipper was a warrior, a leader who feared nothing, someone who would never blink first in a show down, someone they could follow into hell if they had to. But they all knew it was checkmate! They didn't want to die. After they were turning blue from holding their breath, slowly he said, "Number 2, come to periscope depth and send this message to both *Indigirka* and *Berdyansk*. Tell them to come left to new course 360, speed 10 knots. Number 2, also close outer doors to all torpedo tubes. Navigator, plot course to Murmansk, we're going home." Everyone aboard exhaled.

----------

The Sonarman aboard the *USS Shark* reported, "Captain, the Russian sub is coming shallow."

"XO, stay with him."

"Aye, sir."

After several minutes the PA system came alive again.

"Conn, Sonar. Captain they're turning, sir."

"What about the doors?"

"I hear the doors closing sir."

"That's good. Let's escort him out of the area, shall we? In his baffles, as before, please." Sweat was running down his nose.

Mason said, "That was close, sir."

"Yeah, too close. Thank God for those 'Big Ears' in Bermuda," Rogers muttered.

# December 1962

– London

Anna sat alone at a table in the Spartac Arms pub, staring into her drink. Her mind wondered back to her childhood in a village just outside Leningrad. Her parents were peasants on a farm owned by a wealthy aristocratic family that were part of the Romanoff court in Petrograd. She remembered hearing stories of how, before the revolution, they were desperately poor, often not having enough food to eat. She was born after the sweeping changes precipitated by the Bolshevik revolution, but one thing remained – the family remained poor.

Her father, Sergei Petrov, had been a volunteer in Lenin's revolutionary army, and he was very proud of having played his part in permanently overthrowing the corrupt and tyrannical rule of the Romanoff Tsars. He would frequently regale the family with stories of his and his comrade's exploits, exploits leading to a new type of government, a government for and by the proletariat, not the elite.

As an only child, she had the daily routine of a lonely, five mile walk to school, sometimes in the harshest of conditions, and sometimes on an empty stomach. It was during these long, solitary treks that she developed determination, tenacity, fortitude and self-reliance. She was also a very diligent student, attaining a high level of proficiency at school. Her teachers observed once on her report card, "Anna is the sort of girl that will excel in anything she turns her mind to." She adored science and math. Her dream was to study physics at Moscow State University and become a scientist, making important scientific discoveries for Mother Russia.

But fate had a different plan for Anna. One day when Anna was 17, one of her father's old comrades-at-arms visited them. He had stayed in the army and had risen to the rank of colonel. After she told the Colonel what her ambition was, he promised to help her. A few months passed and the family received a letter from the Colonel saying that she was to report to Red Army headquarters in Moscow in seven days, for a series of evaluations. Anna, Sergei and Olga were thrilled, and happily said their goodbyes at the train station, their mood buoyant with pride and hope.

That was the last time Anna saw her parents. Soon after she arrived in Moscow, Hitler's Wehrmacht unleashed Operation Barbarossa – the invasion of Russia. Her father promptly reenlisted in the Red Army and was killed in the early phase of the conflict. The Wehrmacht marched on to Leningrad and laid siege to the city. Her mother, trapped in Leningrad, died during the long and deadly siege.

Meanwhile, now on her own in Moscow, Anna's scores on her evaluations were virtually off the charts. The army, air force, diplomatic corps and intelligence services all wanted her. After several more rounds of interviews, it was mutually agreed that she would join the intelligence service – the KGB. She was plunged into a period of paramilitary training, including weapons training and hand to hand combat, followed by a series of intensive course studies, which included learning English, French and German. Her supervisors were amazed with her performance, particularly her mastery of the English language, without a trace of a Russian accent.

She was first assigned to London to get familiarized with the culture. It was then she assumed the persona of Anna Sokratis. The insertion of Anna into Britain was relatively easy, as the Russians and the British were Allies against the Nazis. She was part of an extensive team the KGB had in the UK. While they were on the same side as the Brits, it didn't mean they fully trusted them. The capitalist "Tommies" had to be closely and surreptitiously observed.

As a teenaged girl, Anna was universally known as a bookworm – having no interest in boys. After insertion into the UK, she discovered that men found her exceptionally attractive, giving her amazing power over them. It was an ability she would later be taught to hone into a weapon. The UK assignment ended when she was recruited to a team of KGB agents deployed to the US to find out what their American allies were up to at Los Alamos. As a relatively inexperienced agent, Anna's assignment was a low-level one. Her mission was to see if there was any nuclear related activity in the West Coast's top scientific university: Caltech.

Posing as a physics undergraduate student, she discovered that Caltech was indeed involved in quite a lot of top-secret work, for virtually all branches of the US military. As Jack Bessemer had said, the side with the best technology would win the war. She discovered that there were different levels of secrets: secret, top secret and ultra-top-secret. The ultra-top-secret projects at Caltech were impossible to penetrate. She was pretty sure there were no uranium related testing or fabricating facilities at

Caltech, as there was no evidence of any yellow "Danger Radiation Hazard," signs with the black dot surrounded by three radiating black fans. But she suspected that the ultra-top-secret projects might have some connection in some way to Los Alamos – merely because of the incredible level of security. She dutifully passed on to her handlers the few crumbs of information she gleaned during her four years there, but she never thought any of it was earth shattering. To her surprise, she liked Jack-the-nerd, finding him charming and intellectually interesting, and she knew he really liked her. But the voice in her head warned her to keep him at bay, for risk of blowing her cover. She had learned from experience to heed the warnings of that voice. The most important thing was not to blow her cover.

While Anna loved the Western lifestyle, in her heart, she was a committed communist, having been steeped in the ideology by Sergei, her beloved father. She would do whatever she was ordered on behalf of Mother Russia.

As she was finishing her degree at Caltech, the world became aware of what the Americans "were up to" in Los Alamos when two atomic bombs were dropped on Japan, effectively concluding the War, changing the world forever. It was timely for Anna to be recalled to Russia for debriefing. The War's end radically altered the relationship between the two remaining, triumphant superpowers – allies in war but now adversaries in peace – warily eying each other across the plains of central Europe and the vastness of two oceans.

Mikhail Petrosian, KGB chief, was reviewing Anna's file with her supervisor. He said, "Viktor, with Anna's strong scientific background, coupled with her mastery of the English language and culture, she could be a very valuable covert asset in the West."

"Yes, Comrade Director, I agree."

"But she just needs one more arrow in her quiver to become a super-agent."

"What's that, Comrade Director?"

"Mastery of the art of seduction – to become a Sparrow," holding up the photo. "Look at her!"

"I agree, Comrade Director."

"See to it at once!" Petrosian scribbled something in the file, closed it and handed it to Viktor who promptly stood and took his leave.

When Viktor met with Anna, he explained what was next for her. As with all aspects of the spy game, the KGB had an academy for this also. "Anna, I have met with the Director, and he has agreed that your performance has been exemplary and that the next step for you is to attend Sparrow School."

Anna was taken aback, "Sparrow School! I thought he said my performance was exemplary! Why am I being punished?"

"Look, Anna, you're not being punished. You should think of this as a promotion. With all your tremendous attributes, your technical knowledge, your mastery of English, French and German, you have the potential to penetrate right to the heart of NATO, like no other agent we have. Remember NATO is an organization whose sole purpose is the destruction of the nation that has been built from the spilled blood of patriots, like your Sergei and Olga. We've got to use any means necessary and whatever tools we have at our disposal to prevent that from happening."

Anna sat there in silence, for several minutes, staring at the wall, inwardly communing with the voice in her head. Viktor was worried she might say no, he'd given it his best shot. Then she looked directly at him and nodded, "Alright, it is my duty to do my part for Mother-Russia. I will do as you ask."

As with everything she turned her mind to, Anna excelled in all aspects of this skillset: theoretical, psychological, and physical. Subsequently, she returned to London in the service of Mother-Russia.

Anna's reverie was broken as Dino pulled up a chair and sat down. He was in a foul mood. "Your 'boyfriend' has been playing us for fools!"

She scowled and jabbed her forefinger in his face. "Dimitri, I am goddamned sick and tired of you accusing me of having a soft spot for Jack Bessemer. What I did with him was strictly for Mother-Russia. Is that clear?"

"Ok, Ok. Don't be so sensitive! But me thinks thou doth protest too much." She gave him an icy glare. "No matter, he has indeed played us for fools. The technical data he has been feeding us on the capabilities of their listening post in Bermuda has been pure shit."

"How do you know that?"

"I got the word from Moscow. Murmansk's newest, most advanced and quietest submarine ever, was detected and tracked over 1,000 kilometres out at sea by Bermuda. They sortied patrol aircraft out to find her and they did. Then they sortied an attack sub to trail her and it did. She was part of that humiliating Cuban misadventure. There's no way the technology that he's told us about could have done that. He's been jerking us around!"

"My God! I didn't think he had that kind of spunk in him. I've misjudged Jack." Anna paused for a moment, then she looked darkly straight at Dino. "Or maybe … maybe he's been turned."

Dino's face changed from anger to fear. "Hmmm… maybe. Maybe you're right. In that case he may have blown our covers too! All the more reason to cut the head off this snake and tie it off. Now!" He said decisively.

"Agreed."

"I'll contact Ivan.

Anna sighed, "Yes, I thought you would say that."

"I'll see if we can get a seat on BOAC in the next 3 days." Dino downed the rest of his drink and started to get up.

The little voice in her head was saying, beware! Anna gestured for him to sit back down.

"I have a bad feeling about this, Dimitri. People in Bermuda have seen you and Ivan before. You need to be very careful. You must send me a telex to the Imperial Institute of Oceanographic Research as soon as your business is done. Simply say, 'ship sold for scrap.' OK?" Dino nodded and left Anna Sokratis staring very disconsolately into her half empty glass. She did indeed have a soft spot for Jack Bessemer, but it had to be done. Business was business.

– Bermuda

The next day in the Vallis Building, Janice poked her head into Carpenter's office, "His Excellency the Governor on line one for you, sir."

He immediately picked up. "Your Excellency, nice to hear from you. To what do I owe this honour?"

"Mr. Consul General, we've been keeping an eye on your club on the other side. We think we have tabs on all the members now."

"Excellent!"

"In any case, a little birdy tells me that your two shipping friends are booked on the Speedbird from Heathrow the day after tomorrow. Thought you'd like to know."

"Right! I'll take it from here, sir. Thanks very much, sir. Goodbye." After Carpenter hung up, he sat there, silent, for several minutes, the only sound to be heard was the strumming of his fingers on the desktop. Then he made a decision and made five phone calls: to his old friend, Stan Ross, to Jack Bessemer, to Snapper Jones, to Major Vindham and Derrick, the Yacht Club bartender.

He thumbed through his little black book then instructed Janice to make the overseas call. After the connection was made, he picked up, "Stan, I'm glad they haven't fired your ass yet, man."

"Me too," Stan replied with a chuckle.

"I have a big favour to ask."

"Man, every favour you ask is big."

"You got any friends left at CINCLANT, or have you burned them all by now?"

"Well, I may have one or two. You remember this is not a secure line, don't you."

"Yeah, but this can't wait."

"OK, then."

Bob told him what he wanted. "That is a big ask, Bob. But I'll see what I can do."

"Thanks."

He dialed the SOFAR station and asked for Snapper Jones. After a long wait, Jones picked up, "Hello?"

"Snapper, this is Bob Carpenter. Are you busy tonight?"

"No sir, I'm not."

"What about coming over to Chelston for a drink tonight. Say, 6:00?"

"Sure, that's fine. I'll be there."

He made similar calls to Jack Bessemer and Major Vindham, all for 6:00 that evening. They all arrived on time and were shown into the study. Carpenter was already there and waved them to a seat. Milton took and delivered their drink preferences. "Gentlemen, you obviously all know one another, but I'm sure you're wondering what this is all about. Major, did you bring that thing with you?" Vindham nodded. "Let me see it." Vindham fished an object out of his briefcase and gave it to Carpenter. It looked like an oversized hockey puck.

Jack explained, "In order to get it this small, I took off the receiver, the transmitter and related components. That's only the pinger and a battery right there. The battery in there is small, so there's a limited time that this gadget will work."

"How long?" Carpenter asked.

"Probably about three hours, max."

"That'll be good."

"What's this for, anyway?"

"Well, gentlemen, our friend, Jack, here, has a problem and he doesn't even know it yet." He paused for effect. "There are two men coming to Bermuda to kill him." He paused again, just to let that sink in. They all looked horrified and turned to look at Jack who was turning green with nausea. "And we're going to stop them."

"The two men are killers, Soviet agents. They've already killed Snapper's friend, Scaley DeSilva, and his mate, Rusty Roberts." Everybody's eyes were now locked on Carpenter, albeit Jack's face was a picture of terror. "Now, here's the plan…"

He explained the plan in detail. After he was finished, he declared, "Major, as chief of security you are in charge of this operation. But, for God's sake, please don't shave for the next week, you look too clean to be a mate on a fishing boat. Snapper, you're the boat's captain, and therefore in charge of all things nautical. These guys got away clean the last time, and I'm counting on them trying the same gambit again. But just in case they don't, Major, put 24/7 guards on Jack and his family. Is that clear? Can they do that without standing out like sore thumbs?"

"Yes, sir. I'll see to it. But begging your pardon Mr. Carpenter, there's a hundred things that can go wrong with this plan. Why don't we just pick them up as soon as they land at the airport? And deal with them as enemy agents."

Carpenter replied with feigned bemusement, "We? Who's we? You mean we, the US of A? You do remember that this is not American soil, don't you? We just can't go around arresting people. Or perhaps you mean we, the British. These guys carry British passports and can demand all the legal rights against improper arrest, evidence and trial in a British court. Besides, there's no evidence of them having committed a crime is there? The local authorities will just make fools of themselves. In any case I'm not going to rely on that imbecile Police Commissioner for anything."

The Major looked embarrassed, but Carpenter didn't care.

"Snapper, let me know the moment you hear from them."

"OK."

"Well, gents that's all for now. Have a good evening. Jack, can you hang on for a moment?" The rest filed out into the cool evening breeze.

"Jack, you think I'm using you for bait, right? And you'd be 100% right," he declared unapologetically. "Look, it's not easy being the bait, but I've told the Major he must be armed and ready for any unforeseen development. You'll be OK."

"How in God's name did I get myself into this situation?" Jack asked rhetorically. Carpenter looked directly at Jack, knowingly raising one eyebrow. "Yeah, I know, it's my own fault. But with all due respect to the Major's military qualifications, Ivan still scares the shit out of me." He turned with his head hung low and took his leave, like a man condemned to the gallows.

## Speedbird

Dino and Ivan stepped aboard the large, sleek, silver plane with the proud BOAC, "Speedbird," logo resplendent on her tail, and almost everything else onboard. Dino said to Ivan, "They called her, 'The Whispering Giant.' She's the Bristol Britannia, a marvel of British aviation engineering," he said sarcastically. "This sleek beauty will enable us to fly directly from Heathrow, non-stop, to Bermuda, without having to refuel in Shannon and that dreadful place in Canada, err…. Gander." Ivan didn't reply. He was totally uninterested in aviation technology. He was only interested in technology that were weapons. The two agents therefore arrived in the island feeling relatively refreshed. After checking in at the Princess Hotel, they thought they would check the Yacht Club bar, in case Bessemer was around. There they saw a familiar face, Derrick, behind the bar.

"Good afternoon gentlemen. Haven't seen you for a long time, welcome back. Now let me see, scotch for you, sir," pouring it for Dino, "And vodka martini for the gentleman," mixing it for Ivan.

Dino exclaimed, "You remember us and our drinks from so long ago? Incredible and impressive." He gave Derrick a big tip.

"Thank you, sir," beamed the bar tender. They went to a corner table and waited for Bessemer. After a while they surmised that Jack wasn't going to show, and they signed for their drinks and returned to the hotel.

After they left, Derrick picked up the telephone and called Chelston. Milton answered and Derrick said, "Hey mate, it's me, Derrick, tell Mr. Carpenter Speedbird has landed. They're staying at the Princess."

"OK, got it."

When Carpenter got the message, he immediately contacted the other members of the team, Vindham, Jack and Snapper, conveying the simple message, "Speedbird has landed."

After dinner, Dino and Ivan were in Dino's hotel room engaged in a heated argument. "Nein, nein, nein!" Ivan hissed. You cannot use the same m/o twice in a row. You increase the risk of getting caught. We must do it another way."

"Look, Ivan, the last time we were here the thing went so smoothly. None of these dumb, inbred islanders had a goddamned clue what we did. And that Police Commissioner, what a dunce! They have a saying in America, 'If it ain't broke, don't fix it.' And, comrade, it ain't broke!"

"Look how that bartender remembered who we were. He might suspect something."

"That guy's as dumb as a post. In any case, you think anybody will believe him?" Dino retorted dismissively, "He's black, for Christ's sake! The only thing he knows is drinks. That's it. Otherwise, he'd be doing something more important than tending bar.

"Look, Ivan, just like the last time, I remind you that this is my mission, I'm in command here, and I say how we do it. We do it my way! Besides, we have a better plan this time, I have a marine map of the island and after we take care of Bessemer and the skipper, we can figure out how to get back to the island on our own. We can find some secluded harbour where we can ditch the boat. Also, unlike the last time, we have our little friends with us." He walked over to his duffle bag and withdrew an eight shot, 9mm Makarov pistol – standard KGB issue. He cocked it with a loud double-click, then put it on safety. Ivan gave up. Dino was senior to him in the KGB, and he had to take his orders. Frustrated, he stomped back to his adjacent room and slammed the door.

The next day they booked the *Captain Crunch* for the following morning. Since they had their Makarovs, they didn't care if the skipper had a mate or not. They had lunch at the Club, ambled around Hamilton for an hour or so, then returned to the Club bar and waited for Bessemer to show up at his usual time. At 5:15 Jack entered the bar and saw the two KGB agents at a corner table. Dino noticed he looked more afraid than shocked. *No matter, fear works just as well as shock.* Derrick prepared Jack's usual libation and he glumly and fearfully sat down at their table.

"Hello Jack. You don't look so happy to see us. Is there some reason for that? Eh? You remember Ivan, don't you, our chief of breaking and disposing of useless ships." Ivan gave Jack a leering, reptilian smile. "In any case, this is just a social visit. We're here to sort out some shipping business and we wanted to check on our friends on the island. Speaking of which, we're going deep sea fishing tomorrow morning. You will join us?" Dino fixed Jack with a stare. "You **will** join us, won't you Jack?" Jack nodded weakly. "It will be fun, and we can talk more about our business, more privately. We'll meet you at the Princess dock at 5:30. Nice to see you again, Jack." They rose and left Jack to his own thoughts.

Meanwhile, Carpenter had received a call from Snapper that the boat trip was on for tomorrow. He immediately called Stan Ross. "Is everything arranged? Good. They are leaving the dock at 0530 and will be above Challenger Bank in about an hour or so after that."

"OK, I'll pass it on. Everything is a go."

It was one of those "out-of-body experiences," where Jack was looking down on himself, sitting bolt upright on the seat in the main cockpit of the *Captain Crunch* – petrified. He knew that he was the real bait, not those objects at the end of the fishing lines. He knew that the sharks were not overboard, but onboard, a mere 10 feet away. He knew that it was his own fault for allowing himself to be trapped in this suicidal situation. *If I'd only kept my zipper up and left Anna's flat that night, I would not now be marked for death at the hands of Ivan the Terrible.* Ivan was relaxing in the *Crunch's* fighting chair. Overwhelmed by a sense of foreboding, something inside Jack was convinced that his life was over.

While the two assassins were absorbed searching over the side for the arrival of sharks, he saw Vindham nonchalantly amble over and take out his pistol and slide it inside his belt at the back. He gently patted their duffle bags, trying to find their guns, but couldn't find them.

Then he heard Ivan say, "Looking for this?"

Vindham and Jack turned towards Ivan's voice and there, to their horror, was the assassin holding his 9mm Makarov in his hand. The Major, stupidly, made a move to draw his Colt .45, by quickly reaching behind his back. Ivan coolly shot Vindham straight between the eyes. He was dead before he hit the deck.

Detecting movement in the corner of his eye, Ivan swung around to Snapper who had started to move toward him. The Makarov barked twice, in quick succession, the force of the bullets knocking the skipper backwards. Losing his balance, his momentum threw him against the gunwale, and he fell backward over the side.

Dino casually walked over and picked up the Major's Colt .45 and motioned to Jack to move toward the transom where Ivan stood. "Now, you clever little man, you're not clever enough to realize that you can never double-cross the KGB, without paying the ultimate price." He put the muzzle of the weapon right against the back of Jack's head.

Jack pleaded, "No, wait, wait, don't do this. PLEASE……" A single shot rang out!

Then, sitting bolt upright in bed, body trembling, heart pounding and sweat pouring, Jack awoke. He heard a distant voice, barely penetrating through the pounding in his ears from his racing heart, "Jack! Jack! Wake up, honey! It's only a nightmare. Everything's alright." Evelyn enveloped him in her comforting arms. "Honey, you were yelling, 'Don't do this. Please!' What was this dream that had you so terrified?"

Eventually, collecting himself Jack mumbled, "I … I can't remember. Probably something I ate." He lied.

"Here, let me get you something." She padded off to the kitchen and brought him back some soothing hot chocolate. She turned off the light, but Jack never got back to sleep. He saw, out of his bedroom window, the early signs of the dawn of the dreaded new day.

At 05:00 Snapper Jones slipped *Captain Crunch's* moorings at the little harbour next to Somerset Bridge. It was still dark. He had a new mate aboard: Major Eugene Vindham who had done his best to look like a grubby mate on a fishing boat, which was not easy after a lifetime of USMC spit and polish. The five-day facial growth helped tremendously. "Snapper, you can't exactly call me Major on this trip, now, can you. You have to call me Gene."

"OK Maj .. Um, um .. Gene," Snapper said. They glided quietly into the channel off Wreck Hill, then he gunned it taking the *Crunch* to her full speed of 35 knots. It wasn't long before they were approaching the dock outside the Princess. Shortly after securing their lines, their clients for the day appeared, each carrying a small duffle bag. "Welcome gentlemen, I'm Snapper Jones, your skipper for today."

"Oh yes, I recognize you! You're the guy who rescued us out at Challenger Bank!" Dino exclaimed.

"Yes, that's right," Snapper replied.

"Well then, we are in excellent hands today!"

"Thank you. Um… um, Gene, help these gentlemen aboard with their stuff, won't you. This is Gene Mallory, my first mate." Vindham dutifully helped the two agents settle themselves aboard. The Major closely examined each assassin. They were dressed in light weight cotton shirts tucked into summer shorts. They wore docksiders with no socks. *There's no way they can have guns underneath those clothes without it showing. They must be in their bags.* Jack Bessemer appeared in the hotel doorway and approached them. His eyes were red with dark circles around them, not having slept very much the night before. Vindham held his arm firmly as he boarded, silently trying to reassure him.

"Gene, loose those lines, if you please. Let's get under way," Snapper ordered. He maneuvered the *Crunch* away from the dock and they roared off towards Two Rock Passage. They transited Watford Bridge with the outriggers splayed to get under the bridge, and once they cleared the Pompano Tripod Beacon, Snapper slowed to about 8 knots and set about, with the help of his first mate, rigging out some lines for trolling. They set two rods secured in holes in the transom that were made especially for this purpose. The lines were set with the traditional steel leaders and trolling lures and hooks. They did the same with the rig for the portside outrigger. On the starboard outrigger, the line was attached to an object that looked like a large hockey puck. The fishing lure and hooks were attached to the bottom of the object, and the line was played out beside and behind the boat. The hockey puck, a sonar buoy pinger, had no buoyancy and sank, even though it was being dragged through the sea. Neither of their client anglers noticed the difference with this rigging. No one on the surface could hear the pinging it was emitting. It was an entirely different matter for anyone under water.

"What are we doing?" Dino asked.

"To catch the fast swimmers, like wahoo, sailfish or marlin, you have to have lures and bait that are moving through the water, imitating the behaviour of their prey."

Dino said, "Can we catch sharks like this? We want to fish for sharks."

"No problem," the skipper replied, "When we get to Challenger Bank, we can drop anchor and throw some chum over the side to see if we can attract them. Do you eat shark?"

"Oh, actually, I've never eaten shark. Is it tasty?"

"Why yes, if prepared properly. My wife makes a great shark hash."

"Well, we just like to see them, we're not interested in eating them. They're such magnificent predators."

"Well, they're great scavengers too. Eat damn near anything. There's plenty of them out on the banks. You won't be disappointed."

"OK then." Dino sat in one of the fighting chairs, reached into his pocket and pulled out a Cuban cigar and lit up. Ivan, not a smoker, simply sat in the other fighting chair looking at the fiery golden orb slowly rising from beneath the horizon. A spectacular view, even this human, shark-eyed, predator was dazzled by it.

The drone of the engines in trolling mode was hypnotic and had the two KGB agents in somewhat of a trance. However, Jack, sitting bolt upright, a little further forward, was watching every move the agents made. Eventually Snapper noticed the ocean getting shallower; they had reached Challenger. When his depth sounder showed a depth of around 200 feet, he cut the engines and released the anchor chain.

Snapper brought out the chum to attract the sharks. But first he brought in the trolling lines and replaced the trolling hooks and lures with those appropriate for shark fishing, all except for the starboard outrigger. That line was left hanging over the side. Using a knife, Vindham cut up small fish they had on board and baited the new hooks and threw them overboard. Snapper took the large ladle and started to chum the water. Vindham, in his role as mate, Gene Mallory, rigged out other gear, including a large gaff which was used to grapple large game fish. On this occasion they would use it to pierce and drag onboard hooked sharks. He also had a smaller bucket with chum in it. Then he went into the cabin ostensibly searching for something to ladle out the chum from the small bucket. The anglers were focused on the chum already in the sea and the sighting of sharks. Jack stayed in his chair, not getting too close to the transom, or the two assassins.

While the others were focused on sighting sharks, Major Vindham took his Colt .45 automatic from his duffle bag and slipped it inside his belt behind his back with his shirt covering it; it was already cocked with the safety on. Then he nonchalantly patted the duffle bags of the two agents, feeling the outlines of pistols. He carefully and silently unzipped their bags, removed their pistols and placed them in the secondary pail containing chum, and rezipped the bags. Then he approached the stern where Snapper and the two assassins were looking for sharks.

"Skipper! Any sharks yet?"

"No, not yet."

"Maybe they need some more chummin'. Here I got some more in this-here bucket." He swirled the chum around in the bucket then dumped it over the side. It hit the water with a loud plop.

After a short while, Dino spotted some disturbance on the surface about 100 meters off the aft, starboard quarter. "Look over there, here they come!" He pointed enthusiastically. All eyes were riveted to the spot, even Jack's.

There was bubbling. "That ain't no shark!" Snapper exclaimed. "Must be whales!"

"Whales! Whales are attracted by chum?" Dino asked in astonishment.

"No, they're not."

"But what else could it be?"

"Dunno."

The bubbles were growing in ferocity and volume. Then the creature causing them emerged from the deep. It was black, alright, but much bigger than the biggest whale, and much more terrifying. First the sail, then the long cigar shaped hull, as the beast showed itself. The *USS Shark* surfaced just 100 meters off the starboard beam of the *Captain Crunch*. Everybody on board was transfixed. Two officers appeared at the top of the sub's sail; one had a bull horn.

"*Captain Crunch*, this is *USS Shark*, stand by to be boarded." Men appeared on the deck starting to rig out an inflatable raft.

It was only then that the KGB agents realized what was going on. They simultaneously started towards their duffle bags. Then they froze. There was Major Vindham standing with his automatic drawn and pointing at them.

"Not the kind of shark you were expecting, gentlemen? By the way, forget about your guns, I dumped them overboard with the chum." Vindham's calm self-assurance made Dino realize this was no ordinary fisherman's mate.

"Who in the hell are you anyway?"

"Eugene Vindham, Major Vindham, US Marine Corps, head of security of the US Naval facilities in Bermuda. Put your hands up where I can see them gentlemen, now!"

Both agents obeyed. Snapper moved away from the two agents, and away from the arc of fire of the Major's weapon.

However, Ivan's face didn't reveal that he was willing himself into a greatly heightened state of mental awareness of everything around him. All his sensory organs: perceiving every detail of every image around him, detecting even the subtlest audible sounds, sniffing all the complex bouquet of scents in his immediate environment, were sending all this data to his brain and processing them at light speed, like a predator on the hunt, even though it was the other guy that had the weapon pointed at him. He had practiced this mental technique countless times and used it to great effect in times of high stress or danger.

The inflatable raft with a little electric motor was on its way to the *Crunch*. There were two seamen aboard, one seated at the stern operating the motor, with a pistol strapped to his waist, the other with a submachine gun slung over his shoulder. Ivan carefully noted the proximity, or expected proximity, of each of his potential adversaries and prioritized them in terms of their immediate threat. Mentally, he studied the Major, the weapon in his hand, the way he held it, measuring the range between himself and the target, assessing his reaction time, in view of Vindham's advancing years. Looking at the approaching dinghy, he performed a detailed mental analysis of the two armed threats on board. A plan was crystalizing in his mind.

The rubber raft came alongside close to where the two agents were standing with their hands raised. As the first seaman was clambering aboard, Ivan's decades of training, experience and evil intentions were instantly unleashed, like the sudden release of a powerful coiled spring. He swung his left arm, so fast it was a blur, and delivered his trademark move, a karate chop to the first seaman's larynx, crushing it instantly. The seaman fell back toward the sea clutching his throat. Ivan whisked the submachine gun over his head before he hit the water. He dropped to one knee, released the safety and fired a burst at Major Vindham. Three rounds hit the Major, one in the leg, another in the arm and the third in the chest. Vindham got off one wayward shot before flying backwards and falling to the deck in a heap, dropping his pistol. Ivan's third target was the other armed seaman on the inflatable. He whipped the submachine gun around and unleashed another burst at him. He was dead before he could get his gun out of its holster.

Ivan felt better now, knowing that he had neutralized the three armed threats. He relaxed, releasing his brain from its hyper-sensory processing state. As he turned to face the remaining defenceless ones, he felt a searing pain between his shoulder blades, as though he had been stabbed in the back. The only thing he saw was Snapper standing there with a pole in his hands with a murderous look on his face. The hook on the end of that pole was in Ivan's back. Snapper yanked the gaff viciously and Ivan cried out in pain. He lost feeling in his legs and started to stumble to the deck. Snapper yanked the gaff again. This time a reflex action to try to remove the painful object in his back caused him to drop the submachine gun which clattered on the deck. He fell face down, bellowing in agony, like a wounded beast.

As Snapper placed his foot on Ivan shoulder to pull the gaff out of his back, he saw movement out of the corner of his left eye. Dino was lunging for the submachine gun. Snapper whipped the gaff around at Dino's head. Dino blocked the attack with his left forearm and gripped the wooden handle with his right. The two men violently wrestled each other for possession of the gaff, pushing and pulling each other with all their strength. Dino was a trained killer but the adrenaline coursing through Snapper's bloodstream magnified his strength and aggression. In the ensuing struggle they toppled against the boat's gunwale with such force that their momentum carried them over the port side.

By this time, the sharks had arrived and were swirling around in the red water, feasting on the bodies of the two seamen that Ivan had killed. Just as Dino surfaced to gasp some air, he felt a searing pain in his foot. He looked down and saw a six-foot shark attached to it. Screaming in pain, he was terrified, having witnessed what the sharks had done to Scaley Desilva some time back. Impulsively, he kicked at the fish with his other foot and the attacker instinctively released his grip and rapidly sheered away. Dino tried to collect himself. Peering around in the water, he could see there were sharks swirling about everywhere. It was only his KGB training that prevented him from succumbing to total panic. Ducking under water, he spied the Navy rubber dinghy, still tethered to the *Crunch's* starboard side. Remaining submerged and kicking his feet, one of them streaming blood, he headed under the *Crunch* for it. He came up for air right beside it, desperately reaching up for something to grab onto. Fortunately, there was a grapple-rope that ran around the top edge of the dinghy, exactly for this purpose, as the little craft was designed for rescue purposes. Glancing over his shoulder he saw a dorsal fin break the surface, headed towards him. Another shark had picked up his blood trail. A fresh flood of adrenalin and panic penetrated his KGB armour of composure. With all his might he hauled himself aboard the dinghy and collapsed in its belly, furiously panting for breath and glad to be alive.

Meanwhile, Snapper had managed to wrest the gaff from Dino's grip but at the cost of falling overboard among feeding sharks. After coming up for air, he dove down to assess the situation. He saw Dino heading for the dinghy, his foot trailing blood. He didn't want to go there, so he had to think of another option. Nothing else came to his buzzing mind, so he decided to hide underneath the *Crunch* between the propellers for as long as his breath would last. He hoped the sharks would not be able to distinguish between him and these unappetizing, inanimate steel objects. The gambit appeared to be working as the predators swirled about devouring the remains of the two dead seamen.

His lungs felt like they would burst. He intended to return to his hiding place between the props after he had gasped some air. When he surfaced, he noted that Dino was still on the dinghy, as he could see one of his feet resting on its gunwale. *I wonder what kind of shape Dino's in?* he thought. He took a deep breath and ducked down beneath the boat again. Unfortunately, his movement had caught the attention of one of God's most efficient killing machines, the Tiger. Out of the blue haze, he saw it heading straight for him. He was bug-eyed with fear at the sight of certain death. Snapper tried to fight panic with his lifetime of experience as a seafaring man. He had thought that he had seen everything there was to see out here on Challenger Bank, but he'd never seen this before.

Fighting desperately to block his fear, something registered in the back of his mind, his logical mind, "My God, that thing's huge – a 16-footer. With that massive girth, must be a female." Snapper, still holding his breath and the gaff, placed the boat's prop and a rudder between himself and the predator. It opened its huge jaws to devour him, but its blunt nose struck the underside of the *Crunch* and its jaws clamped on one of the blades of the propeller. The Tiger thrashed its head from side to side, violently rocking the 54-foot vessel. Snapper took the handle of the gaff and jabbed the massive fish in the eye. It released the propeller, now badly bent, and wheeled away.

*I've got to get the hell out of here!*

He resurfaced, gasping for air, noticing Dino was still in the dinghy. Snapper hoisted himself up to peep over the dinghy's rubber gunwale.

Dino was lying in its belly, his chest heaving up and down – hyperventilating. Pulling himself on board, he saw that Dino was offering no resistance. He had been totally traumatized by the sharks. Snapper stood up and said, "Don't you move a muscle, you son-of-a-bitch, or I'll give you the same as Ivan," pointing the hook of the gaff at the spy's throat.

Meanwhile, Jack had sat there in a trance, like a tree in a petrified forest. After the boat had started to rock violently from the Tiger shark attack below, he snapped out of it and realized that, amazingly, the Major was still alive. Ivan was lying, face-down, on the deck in a pool of blood, moaning in pain, unable to move. No one else was aboard. He stood up and ventured a glance over the side, only to see the skipper emerge from the water, gaff still in hand. "Snapper! Thank God you're OK!" Jack exclaimed. "The Major's still alive!"

Snapper barked, "Doc, there's a first aid kit in that drawer over there. Get it out and help the Major." Jack complied with instructions. Then Snapper reboarded the *Captain Crunch*. He examined Ivan. He was paralyzed from the waist down as the gaff had damaged his spinal column. He leaned over to Ivan, holding his face close to the killer's ear, and hissed, "I know it was you who fed Scaley to the sharks and you shall now enjoy the same fate." Then from underneath the boat the massive grey striped shape glided past. "Aha, time for the Tiger's breakfast!" Calling out, rhetorically to the great fish, he shouted, "I guarantee, girl, this-here will taste a lot better than that prop!" Once again, Snapper grasped the gaff and fiercely penetrated Ivan's back with its point and heaved him up, over the gunwale and overboard. He struck the water flailing and screaming. The big fish circled Ivan once then came in for the kill, gripping him with its mighty jaws, maniacally thrashing its head back and forth, banging Ivan against the hull several times, cutting the assassin's torso in two.

Snapper looked up at Jack and said, "You don't have to worry about that one," pointing to Dino, "The shark experience has messed him right up." The sub was sending another inflatable over. Commander Glen Rogers, having witnessed the whole incident from on top of the sub's sail, realized that he only had one spy to pick up and that the fight was over. Unfortunately, there was nothing left of the two seamen that had the bad luck of a confrontation with Ivan the Terrible. "How's the Major?" Snapper asked.

"The bullet in his chest looks like it missed his heart but may have collapsed his lung, but he's a tough old bird, I think he'll make it," Jack said. After a few minutes, they looked over at the USS Shark. Dino had been secured aboard and she was under way. In a few more minutes she disappeared beneath the waves.

As the adrenalin ebbed away, and even though it was still early morning, Snapper suddenly felt very weary. He pressed the button to weigh the anchor and as that was taking place, he brought in and stowed the hooks and gear they would have used for a normal day of fishing. After using the medical supplies in the boat's first aid kit to help the Major as best he could, Jack helped clean the deck that had become sticky with chum and human blood. They had slowed down the bleeding, but Vindham desperately needed proper medical attention.

Jack said, "Hey Snapper, we've got a problem: we can't exactly return back to the Princess dock with a man with three bullet wounds in him, can we."

"Ya right Doc." Then Snapper had an idea. He shifted the ship-to-shore radio channel from the normal Channel 16, that fishermen used, to a lesser used one that SOFAR often used.

"SOFAR station, this is *Captain Crunch*, come in please." After a few seconds, a voice replied.

"*Captain Crunch*, this is SOFAR station. How can we help you?"

"This is Snapper. There's been an incident on board that I can't divulge over the air. I'm coming back to dock at the NOB pier. I have an injured passenger aboard who needs urgent medical attention. Please have medical personnel standing by for us when we arrive."

"Understood, Snapper. Will pass on your message to NOB."

The *Captain Crunch* limped back around the Tripod Marker at the entrance to the Pompano Channel. She was going as fast as she could without shaking herself to bits, due to the bent propeller. As they eventually approached the NOB pier, they noticed that a navy ambulance was waiting for them, with lights flashing. After securing the boat's lines, two navy EMT's hopped aboard the *Crunch* with a gurney. One turned to Jack and inquired, "Ahoy there, skipper!"

"Are you crazy? This is the skipper, Snapper Jones," Jack replied, with a hand gesture.

"It's OK, Doc," Snapper said with a wry smile. "As the only white guy on deck, he just assumed you were in charge."

"What is the nature of this guy's injuries?" the EMT inquired, as they hoisted the Major on the gurney.

"Gunshot wounds," Snapper replied, in a matter-of-fact tone.

"Gunshot wounds! What the hell?" No civilians had guns in Bermuda. In fact, they were illegal.

"Got anybody with experience treating gunshot wounds in that navy hospital of yours?"

"Well, I dunno. How the hell did he get gunshot wounds?"

"Stop asking questions sailor and get this man a doctor. I'll personally make a full report to your CO. Now get crackin!"

Even though Snapper was not a US Naval officer, his tone was so authoritative and commanding from years of giving orders aboard vessels, the navy EMT instinctively did what he was told, loaded up the ambulance with the wounded Major and sped off with the siren screaming.

"Doc, let go them-there lines, if you please, I'll drop you off at Albuoy's Point." The *Captain Crunch*, wounded from her encounter with the big Tiger shark, limped onward to her next stop.

As Jack was stepping onto the dock, he looked back at the skipper and said solemnly, "Snapper, thanks for everything, especially for saving my life. I will always be in your debt."

"Sure, Doc. It has been kinda rough, init?" he said nonchalantly. He manoeuvred the *Crunch* away from the dock and headed for Somerset.

# The Aftermath

Jack walked directly from Albuoy's Point over to the Consulate Office.

"Mr. Carpenter, Dr. Bessemer's out here to see you. He looks like he's been in a fight!" Janice announced.

Jack came in.

"Jack! Man, you look like hell! But at least you're still alive. Janice, get Dr. Bessemer a cup of coffee, will you? What happened out there?" Jack related the morning's proceedings in graphic detail. His hands were still shaking.

"My, God!" Carpenter exclaimed.

"What do I do now?" Jack asked.

"I'll tell you what to do. Go home to that beautiful wife of yours and tell her two Soviet agents tried to intimidate you into spying for them, and when they failed, they tried to kill you. You needn't tell her about Anna, and I certainly won't. Then you can get on with your life. Having met Evelyn, if I were you, I'd hold on to her for dear life. You're a lucky man, but don't push your luck any further." Jack finished his coffee and Janice had Tony Fox drive him back to Fairylands.

Carpenter called in Janice. "I need to talk to the Governor, ASAP."

A few minutes later she buzzed him, "He says to come right over. Tony Fox is taking Dr. Bessemer home, but he'll be right back."

In half an hour Carpenter was sitting in Sir Julian Hood's office. He gave the Governor an update on the latest developments. "Sir Julian, I think the time has come to pick up the rest of this London spy ring, before they discover what has happened here. The fact that their agents came here with the intent of killing Dr. Bessemer, instead of threatening to expose him, means that they figured out that the data we were feeding them was bogus. In any case, they're going to wonder why their two guys haven't been heard from in a day or so."

"Right you are. I will call my friend who used to run MI5 right now and have them rounded up before they simply melt away. They've identified a dozen of them, you know! Congratulations, Mr. Carpenter, splendid job, you've dismantled a major Russian spy ring in London from all the way out here in Bermuda."

"All in a day's work for Uncle Sam, Your Excellency," Carpenter said with a wry smile as he took his leave.

Later that morning, as Snapper was returning home on his Zundapp after securing the Crunch in Somerset, a feeling of acute guilt began to weigh on him, like a steamship's anchor. When she heard his footsteps outside the front door, Ria exclaimed, "Snap, is that you? Yuh home so early! Was the charter cancelled?" She looked up from her chores, observed her husband in the doorway, and was stunned. "Snap, what in God's name has happened?" She rushed to where he was standing. "You feel sick? You look awful! Here, come sit down." He sat down in a chair at their little cedar dinner table. "What's the matter, darling? Do I need to call Dr. Canfield?"

"No, Ria. I'm OK," he replied glumly.

"OK? You sure as hell ain't OK. So, you mean there's nothing physically wrong with you?" Snapper shook his head. "Well, let's get you a cup-a-tea. The water's already hot." She went to the gas stove and lit it. Within a minute the water boiled, and she brought him a mug along with a large slice of Portuguese egg bread. Normally his eyes would have lit up when this was put in front of him, but on this occasion, he just stared gloomily at the floor. "Come on now, bye, take a sip and tell me what's got you messed up like this."

He reached for the mug of tea, but his hand started to tremble. He raised his eyes and beheld his trembling hand. *These are the hands of a killer!* he thought. When his eyes rose to meet those of his wife, tears welled up, then streamed down his face.

"Oh my God! Oh my God! Oh my God!" she cried, wrapping her husband in her arms and holding him for what seemed like an eternity – well, at least long enough for him to draw sufficient strength from her to collect himself. Sensing his despair was receding, she finally released him, saying, "Ok, now, what happened?"

"Ria," he hesitated, reluctant to let the words pass his lips. "I...I killed a man today," his voice trembling with emotion.

"What? You KILLED a man? What man?"

"The man who killed Scaley."

"What! Killed Scaley? How you sound, bye! Scaley's death was an accident!"

"No, it wasn't. He was murdered!"

"Murdered?"

"Ya, murdered, by Russian spies – professional killers!"

"Uh?"

"Didn't you find it weird for Scaley, of all people, to slip on chum and fall overboard – in the midst of feeding sharks, no less. Scaley was far too good a seaman to do a stupid thing like that. And that deck, full of chum and blood, you know Scaley would never tolerate that kind of mess on his beloved *Crunch*. I always had my doubts about that story, knowing Scaley as I did. And that guy, Ivan, looked so evil."

"Ivan! Who's Ivan?"

"One of the killers. I really, never talked to you about my suspicions before because I knew it would upset you. The same guys that were on Scaley's boat that day he died were on my boat this morning."

"What!"

"Ya. They killed Scaley as a warning to Jack Bessemer of what would happen to him if he didn't cooperate with them. And they were here to kill him today because he had been giving them bogus information. They were planning to kill me and Major Vindham too, you know, loose ends to be tied off."

"My God!"

"The whole thing was set up by Bob Carpenter, the US Consul General. You remember him, he helped us get the *Captain Crunch* back." She nodded. He told her the rest of the story in detail. Ria had been on the edge of her seat, but now she sat back, deep in thought.

*Hmm, I can't believe a thing like that could happen here in little Bermuda. But I'm going to have to change my opinion of Mr. Carpenter. He put my husband's life at risk on his little spy caper, but conveniently kept his own ass safely in his office.*

"I went along with his plan, confident that the Major had everything in hand, him being a US marine veteran of two wars and all that. But Ivan moved at lightning speed."

He paused, hung his head, then looked at his wife with liquid eyes. "Yuh know, the Good Book says, 'Thou shalt not kill.' And I have broken that commandment. I'm going to hell for sure, now." He hung his head again, gazing at the floor.

"No, no, no, baby." She reached out, gently placed her two hands under his chin and forced him to look at her. "Remember, the Good Book also tells us that David killed Goliath in battle. They were in a battle of good against evil, like you were today. You're a good man, Snapper Jones. The best man I've ever known. Today you were God's instrument in a fight of good against evil." Then she gently took his hand and again gazed in his eyes. "If you hadn't fed that guy, the guy with the shark eyes, to the sharks, he would have killed you and you would have been shark food yourself. It was self-defence, pure and simple. You mustn't blame yourself. You also saved Jack Bessemer's life and the Major's too. The fact that you're so torn up about it testifies to what a good man you are. Anyway," she said with a half-smile, "The Lord couldn't have wanted me to lose two husbands to that same evil killer."

Snapper, heartened by his wife's words, tried to pull himself together. He then fixed her with a stare, "Ria, you cannot tell a living soul about this. Nobody. Not family, not girlfriends. Nobody! This incident never happened. OK?"

"Ya, OK honey. It definitely never happened." She said solemnly, squeezing his hand. Then, still holding his hand, she placed it on her belly and broke out into a broad smile, "But one thing that definitely is happening is that you're going to be a father."

"Really?"

"Ya, really!"

For the first time since he had come home, Snapper Jones smiled.

# The Voice

Anna waited impatiently in the office of the Imperial Institute of Oceanographic Research for confirmation from Dino of the kill. She found herself consuming copious volumes of black coffee and pacing back and forth in the Institute's one room office in the dark. The office contained one telephone and a telex machine. Both remained silent. She waited 4 hours, 6 hours, 12 hours! Nothing. It was 4:00am in London.

Something was terribly wrong! She had specifically told Dino to immediately confirm to her that his business had been concluded successfully. The voice in her head, the one that had always been her guiding light, at first started whispering, then murmuring, now it was screaming, "Run!! Run!!"

She momentarily questioned herself, *Anna, stop it! You're panicking!* But the voice kept on screaming. "Run!! Run!!"

She always carried her British passport in the name of Anna Sokratis, in her handbag, but, hidden in a secret compartment, she also kept a West German passport in the name of Anna Langer, for emergencies. She also had a small tote bag containing toiletries and miscellaneous items, in a drawer in the office, just for a situation like this.

She couldn't go back to her apartment to collect any of her things, that was too risky. If her cover had been blown, they would surely be waiting for her there.

*They could be waiting for me on the high street outside the office too*, she thought. Using a service entrance that led to an alleyway behind the building, she ventured out into the dark. The alley led out into another backstreet which eventually led to an adjacent high street, not the one her office was located on. She carefully scanned the area. It was deserted. She stood in a dark alleyway, waiting for the Tube to start for the day. At 5:00am she walked to the Tube station and caught the train to Waterloo Station, then took the first train to Dover. There she boarded the Channel Ferry to Calais, using her West German passport. Then she boarded a train for Paris, transferring to another, bound for Frankfurt. There she transferred to the special train that travelled along the narrow corridor non-stop through East Germany to Friedrichstrasse Station in Berlin.

There she proceeded to the checkpoint known as the "Palace of Tears," the gateway to East Berlin. Over and over again one of the East German guards looked at her papers, indicating she had a business appointment in the East,. He eyed her suspiciously. But Anna flashed her megawatt smile and all suspicions melted away. She was allowed to proceed. She breathed a long sigh of relief as she walked through to East Berlin, safe at last.

# The Bankers

Carpenter scowled at his morning correspondence from the State Department. The Russian spies were being rounded up in London, Dino had been taken away by submarine for interrogation Stateside and Ivan the Terrible was dead. He should have felt pleased, but something didn't quite add up. Once again, he had an itch where he couldn't scratch. His mind continued to play and replay, in a continuous loop, the events that had taken place. Then his own words came back to him, "Spies spy for three reasons, ideology, kompromat, or money." Then he realized, *I haven't followed the money, if there is any.*

"Janice!" He called out. She appeared in a few seconds.

"I want to meet Mr. Jackson, of Bank of Bermuda and Mr. Fields at the Bank of Butterfield. Both today if possible."

In ten minutes, she reappeared saying, "You have an appointment to see Mr. Jackson at 11 o' clock and Mr. Fields this afternoon at 3. Is that alright, sir?"

"Perfect."

He took the short walk to the Bank. He was shown right into the Chief General Manager, Mr. Henry Jackson's office. Carpenter knew that Jackson was an extremely powerful man in Bermuda, probably the most powerful of all the 40 Thieves. He was a big man, with a pot belly and a hearty laugh, a manner which belied his often-forceful personality and overarching influence. Carpenter had met him before at the Governor's party a short while ago and had been impressed with this titan of the local establishment.

"Come in, Mr. Carpenter, it's good to see you again. Have a seat. Can I interest you in a cup of coffee or tea?"

"You're so kind, but no thank you. I don't think I'll be taking up much of your time today. Wow! I must say, the view from your office is the most spectacular I've ever seen – right across the Harbour and up past Two Rock Passage!"

"Well, the view helps me clear my mind."

After a few more minutes of small talk, the banker said, "So, Mr. Consul General, how may I be of service?"

Carpenter reached into his inside jacket pocket and fished out a piece of paper with handwriting on it. He leaned across the large walnut desk and placed it in front of the banker. "What's this?" Jackson asked.

"I would like to know if either of these two people have accounts with your bank, and if so, what the balances are in all of them, and the sources of any large deposits."

Jackson turned red with thinly suppressed fury, "Mr. Carpenter, I know you haven't been here very long, but such a request is not only impossible, it is also highly improper and, quite frankly, most offensive. We hold our clients' banking information in the highest confidence and cannot, and will not, reveal it to anybody, including foreign Governments. Perhaps I should emphasize, especially foreign governments!"

"Sir, I know, understand and respect your rules and practices, but as a representative of the US State Department, I must tell you, confidentially, that this is not a tax matter, it is a matter of national security. In view of the current precarious state of world geopolitics, national security should be everyone's top priority. I'm sure I don't have to remind you that we narrowly avoided a thermonuclear war just a few weeks ago! This request is totally confidential, that is why it is in my personal handwriting. No one in the Consulate has any knowledge of this matter."

The banker's fury had not diminished one iota. He leaned forward over his desk and fixed Carpenter with a stare. A thought flashed across Carpenter's mind, *Ah ha! This is now the powerful boss issuing a command!*

"Mr. Consul General, I'm afraid there is NO circumstance under which the bank can comply with this request." And he slid the paper back across the desk toward Carpenter, sat back and folded his arms.

Carpenter sat in his chair, unmoved and expressionless, appearing nonplussed. Then, fixing the banker with his own steady stare, he said, in an even tone, "Mr. Jackson, with the greatest respect, I'm afraid there definitely **is** a circumstance under which the bank can comply with my request." The banker looked shocked; he certainly was not accustomed to being contradicted. Carpenter continued, "Sir, the circumstance is that, after I leave your office here today, you personally will be placed on a Stop List. This means you will find that the next time you land in any port of entry into the United States, you will be immediately detained and placed into custody. After interrogation by border officials, which could last for an unspecified period, you will be placed on a return flight to Bermuda. Even if you travel to the US from a third country, I assure you, you will be detained at whatever port of entry you land in and deported back to Bermuda, after interrogation by US officials, of course. I hope I've made myself unmistakably clear."

The banker exploded in total apoplexy, his ruddy countenance turning purple, his eyes almost popping out of his head. "Who the hell are you to threaten me!" He roared. "You're nothing more than a junior functionary, a glorified clerk! I'll go over your head! That's what I'll do. I know people in Washington too! You'll regret this! Just who the hell do you think you are anyway?"

Carpenter rose from his chair and nodded to Jackson, making sure to leave the piece of paper on the banker's desk, and just before he opened the door exiting the office, he turned and said, "You should calm down sir: this is not good for your health. I'll expect to hear from you by Friday. You know how to reach me, and sir, please don't try to leave the Island before then. Good day sir." He turned and left the banker to rage on in the privacy of his own office.

*Well, that went pretty much as expected.*

The meeting with Mr. Fields at Butterfields went the same as the morning meeting – with explosive fury and invective. The bankers had four days to give him what he wanted. He was confident that he would get it. On Friday, afternoon, at 4:00, Janice pressed the intercom, "Sir, there's a messenger at my desk with an envelope under instructions to personally place it in your hands." He came out and signed for it, and before he could return to his office another messenger appeared with the same instructions. Carpenter smiled, *I've bluffed those guys right out of their Bermuda shorts!*

# Question Time

Jack took Carpenter's advice and privately consigned his tryst with Anna Sokratis to the dustbin of history. However, in London, the matter had not been similarly consigned. Investigative reporter for the Manchester Guardian, Simon Banks, was following a whiff of scandal at the Ministry of Defence. His source had indicated that there may have been a Russian mole discovered by MI5, embedded in the Ministry of Defence. As the Guardian was renowned for its left leaning editorials, it was not going to pass on the opportunity to have a go at those arrogant Tories. Officially, of course, the Ministry's answer was predictable, "We do not publicly comment on speculation, particularly on matters relating to national security."

Banks kept pressing his confidential source for more information. His source was well aware that he was breaching the Official Secrets Act by talking to a reporter and was paranoid about being discovered. The most he was going to give was that the mole was a woman and was part of a larger ring that had been rounded up by MI5. Beyond that, he had reached a stone wall. He conferred with his editor, Maxwell Hereford, "Max, my source is scared shitless, but I'm sure he's telling the truth, and the spooks are covering their asses. I'm telling you where there's smoke there's fire."

"Have you checked all your sources on this?"

"Yeah, I've kicked over every rock that I know of. Some even twice."

"OK, Simon, we're going to have to take this to another level." He flicked through his rolodex, found a number and dialled. "Hello, Courtney. Yeah, it's Max, how're you doing? Yeah, yeah, great thanks." Courtney Hollister was an Opposition, Labour Party Member of Parliament. "Look, I'd like a favour. When are the next Minister's Questions coming up for MOD? A week Wednesday? Splendid! Would you mind asking a question for us? Brilliant! I'll send it over this afternoon." He hung up the phone.

"Well?"

"He said he would add our question to the Opposition's questions during the Question Time. We'll shake the tree and see what falls out. The downside is this will cause our competitors to start digging as well. It may preclude your exclusive, but it may increase our chances at getting to the truth. Anyway, you'd better get started on that question."

"Righto, Max," and he picked up his notes and left. In about thirty minutes Banks returned to the editor's office and placed his draft of the proposed parliamentary question. After reading it, Max took the paper crushed it with his right hand and threw it into the rubbish bin. Banks was shocked.

"Look Simon, you've got to learn how to play the game. You can't officially blind-side a Minister with a question. MOD has to have received your question in advance. The minions there will prepare a bland answer, nicely wrapped up in an equally bland bow. It will signify virtually nothing. However, Courtney Hollister will be entitled to ask a supplementary, or follow up, question. That is when he can lower the boom on the Minister because he will not have had the luxury of carefully crafted and prepared civil servants' answers. And if he is clever enough to avoid answering Hollister's follow up question, his Opposition colleagues can try to trap the Minister into giving a more meaningful answer with their own follow up questions. Why don't you give Courtney Hollister a call and work something out. Here's the number."

"Oh, OK! I get it. I'll give him a call." Simon beetled off on his assignment.

In ten days, it was the Minister of Defence's turn to face his parliamentary colleagues in Question Time, which was to last an hour. Simon wanted to witness the occasion and found a seat in the gallery. The first two questions put to the Secretary of State for Defence concerned the current state of readiness of Britain's attack submarines at its base at Faslane in Scotland and the size and role of the Royal Navy surface fleet. The third question was posed by the Labour Member, Mr. Courtney Hollister who rose from his green Opposition bench.

"Mr. Speaker, will the Right Honourable Secretary of State for Defence inform this Honourable House as to the measures taken by MOD to ensure that sensitive information pertaining to national security is safe from our country's international adversaries?"

"Minister?" the Speaker said.

"Thank you, Mr. Speaker." The Secretary of State for Defence, The Right Honourable Sir Thomas Montague, intoned, "The Ministry of Defence is acutely aware of this country's critical role, along with our role in NATO, in defence of democracy and freedom against socialist, totalitarian states represented by the Warsaw Pact. We are steadfast in our state of readiness and are assiduous in carrying out procedures that ensure that state secrets are kept absolutely secure from leaks or infiltration by elements sent by or representing the adversaries of the United Kingdom or NATO." The Defence Minister droned on for another five minutes extoling the lengths to which his ministry went to ensure the security of state secrets. He then took his seat.

"Supplementary questions?" asked the Speaker.

Hollister rose again and sprung the trap. "Yes. Mr. Speaker, I have a supplementary question. Will the Right Honourable Minister please inform this Honourable House the name of the KGB agent who was recently identified and removed from her position at the Ministry of Defence by MI5?" The Chamber erupted into uproar. The Minister was crimson with apoplexy.

"Order! Order!" The Speaker said, banging his gavel. "Minister?"

"Mr. Speaker, the question posed by the member breaches rules for questions pertaining to national security and is out of order!" The uproar in the Chamber exploded once more. The Speaker banged his gavel again.

Hollister rose again and was recognized by the Speaker. "Mr. Speaker, the breach that is in question here is not the rules, it is whether the Ministry of Defence has had a security breach that it is trying to cover up from the British people. Mr. Speaker, I would ask again, has a KGB mole been discovered by MI5 in the Ministry of Defence?"

"Mr. Speaker," the Minister replied, "I cannot confirm or deny that such a person exists or has ever existed." Further uproar!

Another Opposition member rose from his seat and was recognized by the Speaker. "Mr. Speaker, can the Right Honourable Minister confirm that the KGB mole in the Ministry of Defence was a woman?" More uproar!

"Mr. Speaker, I cannot confirm or deny that such a person exists, neither can I comment on such a person's gender."

The Opposition had a field day at the expense of the Right Honourable Secretary of State for Defence, Sir Thomas Montague, who, when it was all over, almost had to be carried out of the Chamber, having perspired almost a quart of sweat. While he revealed nothing specific, his failure to "deny" the allegations in question was fresh blood to the bloodhounds. Every newshound in Fleet Street began hammering away at his or her sources within government and elsewhere about a possible mole in the MOD. The Guardian, having been the first to pick up the trail, was better prepared than the others and emblazoned the verbal exchanges during Parliamentary Question Time across the front page, accompanied by purely speculative editorial analyses about the consequences of such a breach. The assault by Fleet Street was such that it was inevitable that more information would leak out.

Back at the Guardian, Simon was in his editor's office planning strategy. "You know, Max, I always thought proceedings in the Commons were just empty, schoolyard bickering, but this was quite riveting drama. It was amazing how worked-up old Montague became. I thought he was going to burst a blood vessel in his head. In addition to turning crimson, there was this large vein in his forehead that looked as though it was going to pop!"

"Really?" Max rhetorically asked, staring into space in thought. "I know Montague, covered him years ago. He's a veteran politician. He's had several portfolios prior to this and has always handled himself very calmly. He has a reputation as a very cool customer. I wonder why this thing has him so exercised. It's not like him at all."

"Just old age, perhaps? Can't handle the pressure anymore?" Simon suggested.

"Perhaps, but the body language you describe suggests this is personal. I'll bet this mole was someone close to him."

"Maybe he was having an affair with her." Simon ventured. He reached in his pocket and pulled out his briar pipe and tobacco pouch. He stuffed a wad of tobacco in the bowl with a gadget that doubled as a pipe stuffer and a knife to ream the bowl clean when required. Then he took out his lighter and, after many short puffs, lit up, filling the room with aromatic smoke.

"Simon, I don't know why you just don't smoke cigarettes. They're much simpler. And you don't need all that paraphernalia."

"The paraphernalia is half the fun!"

"Right! Err … an affair, yeah, maybe. But not necessarily. Montague's an old fashioned, man of honour – a man of principle. That's why he was given this very important portfolio, not because he's ex-military or a geopolitical scholar. If it was someone who was there because of him or he was doing someone a personal favour or for some other personal reason, a man like Montague would feel particularly aggrieved if that someone betrayed him."

"But the MOD is a huge sprawling bureaucracy, we would never be able to narrow down the numbers!"

"It's not that bad." Max said. "First of all, you're looking for a woman. That narrows down the numbers a lot. Then, you're looking for a woman who probably works close to him. That would likely exclude women directly in the RAF, Army or Navy. It's someone at the Ministry headquarters! Now get to work!" Max declared with a broad grin.

"Hey, that narrows it down to a few thousand! This should be easy!" Simon said, as he left the room, with more than a little sarcasm. He and his assistant, Amy, began combing through public records. "Even though Max has dismissed the 'affair' theory, I'm not so sure. Let's restrict our search to MOD offices in London. If an affair was involved, she would definitely live in London."

Amy said, "Still, with the Cold War so tense, the staff of MOD in London is huge, and that does not include the staff of GCHQ – the comms centre – but that comes under the Foreign and Commonwealth Office, doesn't it."

"Yes, you're right. Look, it says here that the Defence Minister has at his disposal a multitude of advisors on a variety of subjects like geopolitics, Cold War military strategy, economics, science, telecommunications. It's still like finding a needle in a haystack."

Simon said, "Let's try to compare the previous year's list with the latest list and zoom in on positions that have either been abolished or positions that had been filled but are now vacant."

This was soul destroying work and he and Amy had been going through names for two weeks without any positive leads. After pursuing a large number of dead-ends, they compiled a short list of possible candidates and tried to find them to determine why they had left the Ministry. Most of the ones they contacted had legitimate reasons: pregnancy, finding a better paying job, emigration to another country, etc. Amy said, "Simon what about this one? She was a science advisor to the Minister named

Anna Sokratis. Nobody seems to know where she's gone, but I've got the address on file." Simon smelled blood.

"Let's check it out."

It was in the Greek neighbourhood of London. They buzzed on the door of the apartment building without success. Then they eventually found the building manager who told them, "Anna Sokratis used to live in one of the flats but left suddenly, with no forwarding address, I'm afraid."

"Has the flat been let to anybody else?" Simon asked.

"Why, no, not yet. I've had a few inquiries, but no one's taken it yet."

"Do you mind if we look around the place? Simon asked.

"Well. I don't know. You say you're from the Guardian?" Simon nodded. "Well, then, you might be interested in renting the place, eh?" She gave him a wink.

"Yeah, sure, we might."

"Well then," the manager said, smiling, "I can show it to you." She walked them up the two flights of stairs to Anna's flat. She unlocked the door. "Here, yuh go. There's nothing in here. Some big blokes came and cleared out all of Anna's stuff, but you can take as long as you like, just make sure you lock the door when you leave."

"Will do. Thanks ever so much," Simon said. The apartment was small and had been completely stripped of furnishings. They entered what must have been the bedroom. It was small. On one wall there was an outline on the wallpaper of where a mirror and a vanity must have been. Simon noticed that in the middle of where that outline was, there was a patch of wallpaper that, while matching the same pattern as the rest of the wall, was clearly of a newer vintage. "Amy, look at that patch."

"Yeah, I noticed it too," she said. Simon took his right middle finger and knocked against the wall, moving around until he came to the area that was patched. The tone over that area was noticeably different.

"I wonder what's behind there," he said. He reached into his pocket and retrieved his pipe packing/reaming gadget. Pressing the wallpaper with his left hand, he could feel the outline of a plug, or drawer or door or something underneath the paper. He took the reamer part of the pipe gadget and cut around the edge of whatever it was behind there and peeled the wallpaper off. There before them was a clear glass door. It was spring loaded so that when you pushed it, it sprung open. Inside the cavity was empty except there was an electric receptacle neatly nestled into the base of what was essentially a small hidden cupboard.

"What's this?" Amy inquired.

"I dunno," Simon mumbled, gazing around the room. In doing so he noticed a patch on another wall in the room. "Look over here! Another one. Look, there was a painting or mirror on this wall too." He repeated the process and found exactly the same thing – a hidden cupboard with an electrical receptacle in it.

"Simon, what does this all mean?" Amy asked again.

Simon paced back and forth in the little bedroom, trying to figure it all out. He reached for his pipe, lit up and filled the room with the intoxicating aroma of his tobacco. Then it finally came to him, and he started to smile. Amy watched him in total bewilderment. Then he spoke, "This place is a sparrow's nest."

"A sparrow's nest? What the hell are you talking about. I believe that sweet smoke has gone to your head."

"The KGB have these specially trained female agents – all very beautiful, very sexy and masters of the seductive and sexual arts. They're known as sparrows. They seduce their prey and usually get the action on film and blackmail the victim to perform whatever treasonous errand they require of him. The Russians call it Kompromat. These hidden cupboards are where the cameras were – both behind mirrors. The occupant of this flat, Anna Sokratis, must be our KGB mole in the Ministry of Defence. You've got a camera with you?"

"Yes"

"Well, start taking pictures. We've got the biggest story of the Cold War right here." She took out her Pentax from her tote bag, attached the flash and started snapping away.

"Where is Anna now, I wonder?" She thought out loud.

"She's either in jail, skipped the country, in the Russian embassy or dead, not necessarily in that order of probability." Simon said. "If MI5 got her before she could take off, then she's in jail. They'll probably keep her and try to swap her for one of our guys that the Russians have. On the other hand, the Russians might consider her a liability if they think she'll get caught and spill the beans, so they might have just liquidated her before MI5 could get there, to tie the whole affair off."

"Who do you think her victim or victims were? Montague, perhaps?"

"Maybe, but regardless of whether he was or wasn't, he's finished! Let's go, I've got an article to write."

The next day's edition of the Guardian created a national sensation, the headline reading: RUSSIAN MOLE REVEALED. Simon had managed to obtain a photo of Anna from one of his government sources and it was splashed across the front page. The studious girl at Caltech had become the talk of the town.

Upon seeing the Guardian exposé, 10, Downing Street urgently tried to reach the Minister of Defence by telephone without success. They eventually sent police to find him. When they did, they discovered that he had taken a massive overdose of insulin and had no pulse.

## 'Fess-Up

A few days after the Guardian's explosive exposé about the mole in the MOD, the newspaper reached Bermuda and was read by His Excellency the Governor who called Carpenter. "I say, Carpenter, I think you should see the Guardian. I'm sending it over." Carpenter read the articles and pondered the possible consequences of the revelations and further leaks.

"Janice!" he called out. When she appeared, he said, "Can you see that Dr. Bessemer gets this, if you please?"

"Certainly sir."

The next day at Tudor Hill, Jack received a package containing the Guardian newspaper with a "Compliments of the US Consul General," slip clipped to it. He opened the paper and there, looking back at him was the girl with the megawatt smile. He was so startled he almost spilled the hot coffee on his desk. As he quickly read the exposé, he realized he had a decision to make: either hope that Evelyn doesn't see or hear about this scandal or 'fess-up and throw himself on the mercy of the court. He was sure that the story would, at some point, be the main chatter on the cocktail circuit into which his wife had become closely connected. Once they mentioned the British Ministry of Defence, she would start quizzing him and he would be busted.

He decided to 'fess-up. He sat at his desk long after everybody had gone, trying to find the courage to leave for home. Eventually he stashed the newspaper in his briefcase and took the long, slow drive to Fairylands from Tudor Hill in the rattletrap Morris Minor. Despite the positive outcome with the murderous KGB agents in Bermuda, it seemed like he was still going to be the loser in this spy game. He felt that his whole life was about to be over. He parked the car in the driveway and entered the house. A voice from within called out, "Honey, is that you?"

"Yeah, it's me."

Evelyn emerged from the kitchen with a concerned look on her face. "What's the matter, honey? You sound desperately depressed. What's happened?"

"Where's Dwight?"

"It's past his bedtime, I put him to bed. Come darling, it's late, you must be famished, come and get your dinner."

"Evelyn, I'm not hungry. I've got something to tell you."

"Well, tell me. Come on, it can't be that bad."

"Honey, sit down, please."

"Jack, you're scaring me, now."

He reached into his case and fished out the Guardian and gave it to her. She opened it to the front page and was taken aback. "Anna!" she said. "Is she dead?"

"No, it says she's a Russian spy planted in the British Ministry of Defence."

"A spy! Incredible. That's what's got you so upset?"

"Read the article, darling, please." She scanned the main article."

The wheels in her mind started to turn, then she looked at her husband with suspicion. "Was she at the conference that you went to in London?"

Jack looked at the floor, "Yes. I had no idea she worked for the Ministry of Defence. She just appeared."

"That's it? She just appeared? What else? You're not this upset because Anna just appeared at your conference. What happened, Jack? Spit it out!" Her voice had risen in pitch and taken on an edge.

Jack's voice, however, had dropped to not much more than a whisper. "I slept with her. She filmed it and was blackmailing me."

"What!" She sprung to her feet, screaming. "What? You two timing piece of shit! Blackmail? She extorted you for money. You gave her money?"

"No, worse than that."

"Worse than that? What the hell could be worse than that?"

"They wanted me to give them secrets about Project Artemis."

"Oh my God!" She went from being furious to frightened, putting her hands to her face. "What have you done, Jack. You've betrayed your country on top of being a shit-heel?"

"No, I've been working with Bob Carpenter to foil their plans."

"He knows what you've done?"

"Yes, he knows everything." He then filled in some sketchy details. Between the waves of fury when she verbally erupted, she just sat back down and sobbed uncontrollably.

"How could you, Jack, how could you? You've betrayed me, your son and almost your country. I knew from the moment I laid eyes on her, that bitch was trouble, and that you had the hots for her. Now you've let her ruin our marriage."

"Honey, I'm so sorry."

"Sorry? Go to hell!" She got up and paced back and forth across the room. Then she glared at Jack and hissed, "I can't stand it here! I'm taking Dwight and moving back to California!" She stalked out of the room, into the bedroom and slammed the door behind her.

Jack didn't know what to do. He dejectedly walked to the couch, took off his shoes and lay down, knowing that was his fate for the foreseeable future.

The next morning Evelyn continued to give Jack the glaring, silent treatment. Instead of driving all the way to Tudor Hill, he decided to drop in at the US Consulate. He was shown into Carpenter's office. Carpenter immediately noticed the glum look on Jack's face. "What's wrong Jack?"

"I decided to tell Evelyn everything and she's leaving me, going back to California."

"Oh God no. Jack, I'm so sorry!"

"She's taking Dwight with her!"

"Oh, man! Look, let me talk to her."

"Would you?"

"Now, hold on. I'm not making any promises. But I will talk to her. You go on to work."

After a long pause, he replied, "OK."

Carpenter sat quietly in his office for about an hour then he asked Janice to call his car around. When they reached Jack's house, he told Tony to wait. Carpenter knocked and Evelyn soon opened the door.

"Bob! What a surprise."

"Hi Evelyn. May I come in?"

"By all means. Can I get you something? Coffee? Come in the kitchen."

"Thanks."

As she was putting the percolator on, she said, "Is this about Jack?"

Carpenter nodded.

"Did he send you here to beg for him?" The pitch of her voice started to rise.

"No, Evelyn, I volunteered." They sat at the little table in the kitchen. Evelyn was quite composed and polite, with her hands in her lap but there was a flicker of anger in her eyes. "I'm not here to justify or make excuses for Jack's infidelity. That's a matter between husband and wife." He noticed her body relax, somewhat. "He may not have told you all of the circumstances and the type of people he unwittingly became involved with."

"Well, I met that bitch Anna out at Caltech!" she blurted out.

"With the greatest respect, Evelyn, Anna wasn't a bitch, she was a sparrow."

"Whatever!" She replied dismissively.

"Do you know what a sparrow is?"

"What, a female spy?" she sneered.

"No, Evelyn, not just a female spy. The KGB carefully select the most beautiful girls and then thoroughly indoctrinate them for their mission. Then they are comprehensively and rigorously trained in the art of psychological and sexual seduction. Every move they make is for the purpose of completing their mission. They are like ballerinas: everything looks so graceful and effortless, but every move is meticulously planned and carefully executed. For example, you knew Jack was attracted to her during the time they were at Caltech. What guy wouldn't be?"

She didn't respond to that obvious rhetorical question.

"That was before he met you, of course." That only elicited a flicker in her eye. "Jack repeatedly tried to date Anna, but she gave him nothing. Nothing at all. She was a bookworm. Why was that? Because Jack Bessemer wasn't her mission, that's why. She was there to see what she could glean about what was going on in Los Alamos – the place where they were building the atomic bomb. Jack didn't know anything about it, so she ignored him. She was very disciplined. The Soviets became concerned about project Artemis, something Jack was intimately involved with, so, at that NATO conference the KGB happened to have an asset perfectly placed to get Kompromat on Jack."

"Kompromat?"

"Yeah, the Russians even have a word for what Anna was doing. It's the word for blackmail for political purposes. Seeing that she already knew Jack had liked her, with her being highly skilled in seduction, poor Jack really didn't stand much of a chance."

"You expect me to feel sorry for him? Her eyes flashed. You men are so weak!"

"Weak for women? Yeah, we are. Hard wired that way, I guess. Did he tell you about Ivan, the assassin?"

"Yes, a little."

"They called him 'Ivan the Terrible.' Well, two KGB agents came here to put the fear of God into Jack. To that end, they murdered the charter skipper Scaley DeSilva and his mate – fed Scaley to sharks. Jack was deadly afraid for you and Dwight. He was a terrible spy. He confessed to me that they were blackmailing him, and I forced him to become a double agent, and, despite the risks, he kept feeding them out of date, useless information. So, it was I who put him, and, by extension, you and the boy, at further risk. I hatched the plan to deal with these assassins. When the Russians found out he had been playing them, Ivan and Dino came back here to kill Jack."

"They came here to kill Jack?"

"Yes. For my plan to work Jack had to pose as the bait, on a fishing boat 14 miles off Bermuda, no less."

"No wonder he was so terrified. He had a horrific nightmare the night before he went out on the boat."

"Fortunately, everything worked out all right. Evelyn, those are not the actions of a weak man. Having stumbled into a hornet's nest of sparrows, spies and assassins, with absolutely no training for it, your husband is a patriot. Quite frankly, he's lucky to be alive."

"Really?"

"Yeah, really. Out on the *Captain Crunch* I had counted on Major Vindham to steal the guns from the two KGB agents and get the drop on them. But Ivan was so quick he shot the Major before he could get a shot off. As the bait, your husband would have been next. If it hadn't been for Snapper Jones' quick action, you'd be a widow for sure."

Evelyn noticeably blanched, "My God!"

"Anyway, I thought you should have the facts at your disposal before you make a decision about what to do about your husband's indiscretions. He was trapped by a trained agent and marked for death by trained killers.

"I know you all didn't sign up for this when you agreed to be posted in Bermuda. He's a scientist, not a spy, and you didn't sign up to be a spy's wife. But we've rounded up the whole spy ring both here and in London, except Anna. She's disappeared. So, there is no more threat.

By the way, none of what I have told you can be discussed with anyone, except your husband, of course. National Security. Well, thanks for your time and the coffee. I'll show myself out. Have a nice day."

As he touched the front doorknob to leave, he heard quick, approaching footsteps, then, "What kind of man are you?" He turned and saw her advancing toward him – eyes on fire – fists clenched – face flush with rage. "You use people as pawns in your little chess match. You used my husband as bait for human sharks. Didn't you? You're not much better than those killers yourself, are you? What if Snapper Jones hadn't defeated those assassins? I'll tell you what, my husband would be dead – dead! Dwight would've been without a father. And you, the creator and director of this horror show, didn't even have the balls to go out there on that boat yourself to face down your own enemies. Instead, you sent poor Jack out there, a scientist, not a killer, not a CIA agent, to do your dirty work. My husband may not be perfect, but you, Mr. Carpenter, are a manipulating, piece of shit. Now get out of my house and don't you dare darken my doorstep ever again. Get out!"

He headed through the door, remaining silent. There was nothing left to say. He knew she was right. After departing, in the back seat of the white consulate car, Carpenter was reflective. *I guess I had that coming. Well, I've done my best to patch up things for Jack, I owe him at least that, a man I deliberately put in harm's way, as a pawn in this dangerous chess game with the Soviets. I'm not really proud of what I did to him, but all's well that ends well. Now I can relax a bit. Perhaps I'll give Madame Radcliff a call and invite her to tea.*

# Celebration

Major Vindham was very lucky. The wound to his chest not only missed his heart but miraculously missed all major blood vessels, the bullet exiting through his back, thereby obviating the necessity to remove the bullet. His right lung had indeed collapsed but was repaired at the Naval Operating Base hospital. The round that struck his right arm had snapped the radius, and his arm, complete with cast and sling, was mending. The one in his leg passed right through the quadricep without breaking any bones. Although the hospital staff had virtually no experience tending to gunshot wounds, Vindham was released after only one week in surprisingly good shape. He was glad to be alive despite being temporarily consigned to a wheelchair.

Carpenter convened what he called, "Celebratory Drinks," at his favourite venue, his study at Chelston. The guests were Snapper Jones, Major Vindham – now walking with a cane, Captain James Smith, NAVFAC C.O., and Jack Bessemer. All arrived on time and were shown into the study. Milton furnished them with the libations of their choice.

"Welcome gentlemen. This meeting is a mini celebration of sorts, albeit belated. You all have been instrumental in serving the cause of freedom in NATO's confrontation with the Soviet Union. These little victories in the Cold War are important to celebrate because there will be no medals or citations, and there won't be any celebrations anywhere else, just here. So, please lift your glasses."

"First of all, here's to Snapper Jones. Without you, my friend, this whole operation would surely have turned out to be an unmitigated disaster. Your improvisation and bravery, under extremely dangerous circumstances, both man-made and natural, saved the day and the lives of Jack and the Major. Like your father, Hooks, Uncle Sam owes you a great debt of gratitude. Cheers!"

They all rose, even the hobbled Major, and in unison, raising their glasses and shouted "Cheers!"

"Thanks guys." Snapper grinned,

"Now gentlemen raise your glasses again, 'To a successful operation!'" They all repeated the toast, raising their glasses then gulped down their preferred choice of alcohol.

Carpenter continued, "Now Jack, now that the bad guys are either dead or captured, there is a niggling detail that keeps bothering me."

"What's that?"

"Well, how did the Russians arrange that honey trap for you so quickly?" Jack looked embarrassed and uncomfortable. "Relax, Jack, I'm not trying to embarrass you in front of friends, they know what happened to you. You were a victim, although it probably didn't feel like that at the time." A smirk crept over Carpenter's face and Jack looked more embarrassed. "But, seriously, was it just coincidence that Anna Sokratis happened to be at that conference?"

"Yeah, a coincidence, I guess," said Jack, collecting himself.

"If it was, how did they set up that honey trap so quickly for you at her place? I mean you only bumped into her after the first meeting was over, you went straight to the pub for a drink, then you went straight to her place. Right?"

"Uh huh."

"There wasn't much time to set things up, you know, cameras, film etc., if they weren't expecting you to be there. Perhaps Dino set up the film after he left the two of you at the pub."

"I guess so." Jack said. "But maybe trapping men at her apartment was her primary job – hence the see-through mirrors, cameras and film were always ready."

"I suppose so, but Dino would have had to have known you and she had a history beforehand to anticipate that you would come to her place and that she would seduce you." Carpenter reasoned. "In fact, you weren't even supposed to be there. You were a last-minute substitution for Hank, right?"

"Yeah, right. But Hank had to have told them a week in advance that I was coming. But I don't understand where you're going with this Bob?"

"Ok, ok. Bear with me for a moment, please, Jack. Who exactly did Hank tell?"

"He told the head of the American delegation. He knew I was making the presentation, but I don't think any of the other member countries knew, because on that first day Hank's name was still on the agenda when I presented my credentials. I was the one that made them put my name on the agenda when I arrived that day."

"So, what you're saying is, that none of the other NATO officials likely had advanced knowledge of your being there."

"Yeah, that's right."

"Not even the UK government?"

"No, not even the UK."

"Anna took you straight from the conference to the pub where you met Dino for the first time. She really didn't have time to tell him before hand."

"Well, I guess not," Jack murmured.

"Well then, how did Dino know to go and set up the cameras beforehand?"

"But it all seemed so spontaneous!"

"A belch is spontaneous, Jack. You walked into that honey trap just as if it were a beehive hung right over a dead-drop bear trap. There had to have been malice aforethought at play here. It was planned. Somebody told them you were coming, either from here or in New York."

"Nobody in New York knows the importance of what is done here, only Hank!"

"Au contraire! People at CINCLANT know!" Captain Smith interjected.

"As do some at Langley. But let's ignore them for the moment. The person that knew that you were being substituted also had to have known of the history you had with Anna. Or else any tryst between you and her would have been a very long shot. I mean, no doubt she was good but not that good." Bob said, taking another sip of his cocktail.

"Who the hell here would know that?" Jack asked rhetorically.

Captain Smith countered, "It was not necessary for somebody here to know the details of that connection, all they had to do was to tell their agents in London you were coming, and Anna and Dino then set the trap for you on their own."

Carpenter was unconvinced, "That's true, but it could also have been someone who had access to your personnel and security clearance file, Jack."

"Why?" Jack mused.

"Your security files would have had the dates you attended university etc. Someone who had that information, and was a Russian spy, might have known when you and Anna attended Caltech, and that you were both scientists. As that person already knew Anna was a KGB agent, he or she could have guessed that there was an opportunity to trap you."

Bob stroked his chin, then poured himself another drink. "There's only one person who could have had that information at hand." He turned in his seat, looking straight at Vindham. "You, Major. You were the only one who would have had access to such information."

"Is this some kind of a sick joke? Me, a Soviet spy? I've served and bled for my goddamn country for over 30 years. Mr. Carpenter you insult me with an accusation like that. How dare you sir! How goddamn dare you! While I was dodging Japanese bullets in the South Pacific, what would a paper pushing, politically connected opportunist like you know about serving America? You're here because you 'know somebody' in Washington or raised some money for some politician," he sneered. "What would you know about serving your country?"

Every man in the room was in shocked silence, waiting for the next man to speak.

Bob replied, in measured tones. "Good question Major. What was I doing during the War? Well, I'll tell you, I was working for the OSS, now known as the CIA."

The Major's face morphed from angry disdain to a combination of shock and fear.

"You see, Major, Langley was acutely aware of the importance of the anti-submarine mission here in Bermuda and felt that the Soviets would do anything to penetrate our secret operations here. They didn't want to leave the security of our facilities solely up to the military. While they didn't know there was a Russian mole here in Bermuda, they wanted someone to investigate, someone with a more multi-dimensional approach, than the military; someone, well, like me. Upon arrival, and after touring US facilities here, and making acquaintances with all the possible players, I eventually judged that, if a mole really existed, my suspects could be narrowed down to just a few people. The first person I eliminated was you, Snapper. You just didn't fit the profile.

"Then I stumbled onto you, Jack. The problem with you was that you were a godawful spy. And after I confronted you, and you caved, I figured that this was just too easy. There had to be something or someone else. One thing our friends in the Kremlin are not, is stupid. The Russians couldn't have been so stupid as to rely solely on you, Jack, a rank amateur, for such an important mission. The survival of their first strike nuclear capability depends on knowing exactly what we are doing on this island and what our capabilities are. With that knowledge they could work out some way to defeat this listening post. Prudence would dictate they would use a layered approach to find out what they wanted to know in Bermuda.

"The thing is, people spy for the Russians for one of three reasons: for ideological reasons, blackmail, or money. Jack you were being blackmailed. In terms of people that really knew what was happening here it came down to you, Captain, or you, Major. I just couldn't get my head around either of you two spying for ideological reasons. I didn't know if either of you were being blackmailed. I would first have to eliminate the possibility of either of you spying for money. So, I decided to follow the money. Then I remembered that story about how you, Major, purchased a house for your little lady friend, err.... Jenny, with cash – no mortgage involved! Tongues wagged at that, Major, wagged enough to reach me. That's pretty impressive on a marine's pay. This gave me a further desire to follow the money.

"As an emerging offshore financial centre, Bermuda would be a perfect and convenient place to hide any dirty money. So, I paid courtesy calls on Mr. Fields at Butterfield's Bank and Mr. Jackson at Bank of Bermuda and inquired about the money movements in accounts in both of your names. Of course, they both refused, point blank, citing confidentiality of client business. So, I told them that if they didn't cooperate, the next time they set foot on American soil I would have them arrested and held in federal custody on unspecified charges, and then deported.

That didn't garner their affection, but it definitely got their attention. As it turns out, you, Captain, were clean, but you, Major, have an account with large unexplained periodic deposits originating from a bank in Istanbul, the, ...um, First Anatolian National Bank – a bank we already know the KGB uses to funnel money to their overseas 'assets.'"

"You're full of shit. You're bluffing! If I were a Russian spy, why would I allow myself to get shot by an actual Russian spy?"

"Good point Major, but you were in so deep, your London spy ring didn't know who you were. They knew they had an asset here, the one that told them Jack was coming to London, but they didn't know who the asset was. From the moment that I told you my plan to have these two agents transported back to the States by submarine out there on Challenger Bank, you knew it would be better for you to kill them than allow them to be sweated for information back in the States. So, your plan was to kill the two of them aboard the *Captain Crunch*. The problem you had, Major, was that you didn't know enough about the actual science and technology that was being developed at SOFAR, Tudor Hill and NAVFAC to get the right information to your Russian handlers. Even if you had a rudimentary knowledge of science, what they're doing up there is so leading edge it could never be found in any textbook. You were not able to discern what was critical and what was not. So, the opportunity to trap Jack into becoming an informant was golden. Jack knew everything about the technology! The problem was, Jack was a lousy spy, and after I turned him, and when the Londoners found out he was playing them for fools, they came here to terminate him."

"But the Major took a bullet for me!" Jack protested.

"He took a bullet alright, three in fact, but not for you. He knew about Ivan Bassler. He was a well-known killer in espionage circles. Langley identified him for me. He knew that there was no way Ivan was going to meekly surrender to the US Navy. He was ready for Ivan to put up a fight, it's just that Ivan was too quick for the Major. Old age is a bitch, isn't it Major."

Vindham's face was now a florid mask of fury. He pointed his cane at Carpenter. "I should have goddamn well let you fall into the drink out there on Argus Bank!"

"No doubt! Nobody could have anticipated that Snapper would neutralize Ivan with a gaff and Dino would be neutralized by sharks. A gaff no less! Hell-of-a move, mate," Carpenter said, trying to sound Bermudian. Jones simply acknowledged with a nod. Well, that's it, gentlemen.

"You can't make any of this stick. Nobody's going to believe this cockamamie story of yours! I've served my country with distinction. Got the medals to prove it," the Major growled.

"You may have the medals, Major, but unless you can explain that rich uncle you've got in Istanbul, you're screwed."

"Go to hell!" Vindham snarled.

"After you, Major. To help you on your journey, the Base Military Police are waiting for you in the vestibule to escort you to the brig. Let's invite them in, shall we?" He pressed a button and in a few seconds three burley, uniformed men with MP armbands entered the study and escorted the Major away.

Carpenter then rose from his chair and said to Snapper. "I'd like to go deep sea fishing with you again some time, but this time no sharks, OK? You can come too, Jack."

"Oh, hell no! I wouldn't be caught dead out there, ever again! I came too close the last time."

"OK. Are the spy games all over now?" Snapper inquired.

"Well, yes, although, maybe, we could keep it going with some longtails aboard."

"No way, man! I'm a married man now, soon to be a father. Longtails are history. Just let me know when you want to go and I'll be there. The *Captain Crunch* is still the fastest, best equipped boat in Bermuda. And now, the luckiest!"

# Fact & Fiction

Fiction

- Triangle of Blood, is a work of fiction built around a series of factual events and situations. All the main characters are completely fictional. There are many minor characters who represent real people but whose names have been changed. There are two minor staff members of SOFAR whose names have been retained.

Fact

- The events and subsequent inquiry of the fire aboard the ferryboat *Wilhelmina* are true to the coverage of the event. The subsequent Parliamentary debate as described by the *Royal Gazette* has been paraphrased using fictional names for Members of Parliament. Some of the conclusions drawn are those of the author. *Wilhelmina's* actual skipper was Raymond Charles Reginald Dill.

- The descriptions, functions and importance of the SOFAR Station, the Tudor Hill Lab, the US Navy NAVFAC and the Argus Tower (AKA Argus Island) relating to tracking of USSR nuclear missile submarines are all factual.

- The names and functions of the SOFAR vessels are factual.

- *La Pescadora Langosta* is fictional, but Soviet spy ships often prowled around the Tower and the Island.

- The description, functions and importance of the Kindley Field Air Force Base are factual.

- The 59th USAF Weather Reconnaissance Squadron, the "Hurricane Hunters" were stationed in Bermuda for several years.

- The segregation in Bermuda and the structures ensuring the continued dominance of the 40 Thieves are accurately portrayed.

- The "Theatre Boycott" is described as it actually happened.

- The popularity of "Longtail" hunting among Bermudian males was a fact, although the anecdotes involving longtails are totally fictional.

- The scenario involving a submarine in the Cuban Missile Crisis is a well-known fact, but it was not a Yankee Class sub and its discovery by SOFAR in Bermuda is speculative.

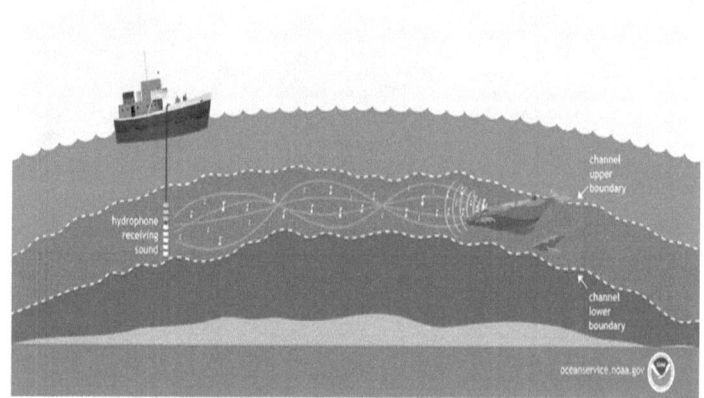

Ferry Wilhelmina

Wilhelmina Burnt-out Hulk

Surrey-with-the-fringe-on-top taxi.

Argus Tower

## SOFAR Station St. David's

T-Boat

Sir Horace Lamb

264 Triangle Of Blood

Marlins overflying Southampton, Bermuda.

How an underwater explosion near Perth, Australia was heard at the SOFAR Station in Bermuda.
(The Perth/Bermuda Experiment.)

Hurricane Hunter at Kindley Air Force Base

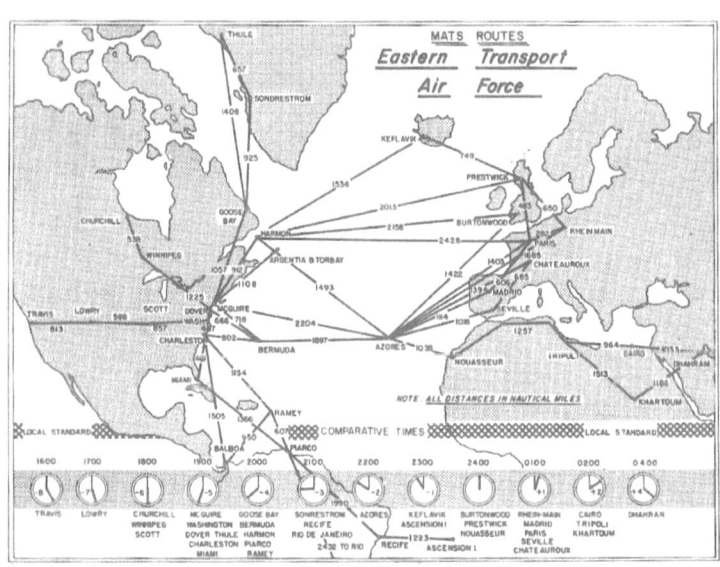

Naval Facility Bermuda (large building at left) and Tudor Hill Laboratory (upper right).

BOAC Strato-Cruiser

BOAC Bristol Britannia in Bermuda

Zundapp moped

MATS Globe Master cargo transport.

www.ingramcontent.com/pod-product-compliance
Lightning Source LLC
LaVergne TN
LVHW091533070526
838199LV00001B/38